PRAISE FOR THE GRIPPING SNIPER ELITE SERIES FROM THE COAUTHOR OF THE #1 NEW YORK TIMES BESTSELLER *AMERICAN SNIPER*

GHOST SNIPER

"Action-packed and suspenseful."

—*Washington Times*

"The rousing plot and bloodstained action are strictly on-target. . . . The authors keep the suspense high right through to the surprise ending."

—*Publishers Weekly*

"*Ghost Sniper* is a pulse-pounding military thriller . . . extremely intense, and the action is almost nonstop. Reading the book, it feels like you're in the middle of it all."

—*San Francisco Book Review*

THE SNIPER AND THE WOLF

" [A] military series that just keeps getting better."

—*Booklist*

"[A] white-knuckle realistic military thriller. . . . Gil Shannon is a man to be reckoned with, delivering non-stop energy, vivid imagery, and intense scenes of combat making [the novel] simply impossible to put down."

—*Military Press*

TARGET AMERICA

"Gil Shannon is the most addictive thriller character alive today. Pick up *Target America* and you will see why—rapid-fire action, unforgettable characters, and explosive scenes."

—Richard Miniter, author of *Losing Bin Laden*,
Shadow War, and *Leading from Behind*

"*Target America* delivers the goods. The harsh reality is that McEwen's fiction isn't far from the truth. Few writers I know would have the guts to go there. McEwen does, and so should you."

—Brandon Webb, former Navy SEAL, editor of
SOFREP.com, and author of *The Red Circle*

"As good as any fictional battle scene in recent memory. Readers will want to see a lot more of SEAL Team Black."
—*Publishers Weekly* (starred review)

ONE-WAY TRIP

"An unfiltered portrayal of modern warfare backed by complex yet compelling storytelling, this one hits the target."

—*Publishers Weekly*

"*Sniper Elite* is a gripping, fast paced adventure. Packed with action, it takes the reader into the shadow world of real military operations. A great read—don't miss it!"

—Dan Hampton, author of *Viper Pilot*
and *The Mercenary*

GHOST SNIPER

SCOTT McEWEN

WITH THOMAS KOLONIAR

GH⊕ST SNIPER

A SNIPER ELITE NOVEL

Pocket Books

New York London Toronto Sydney New Delhi

Pocket Books
An Imprint of Simon & Schuster, Inc.
1230 Avenue of the Americas
New York, NY 10020

Copyright © 2016 by Scott McEwen with Thomas Koloniar

First Pocket Books paperback edition June 2017

POCKET and colophon are registered trademarks of Simon & Schuster, Inc.

For information about special discounts for bulk purchases, please contact Simon & Schuster Special Sales at 1-866-506-1949 or business@simonandschuster.com.

The Simon & Schuster Speakers Bureau can bring authors to your live event. For more information or to book an event contact the Simon & Schuster Speakers Bureau at 1-866-248-3049 or visit our website at www.simonspeakers.com.

Manufactured in the United States of America

10   9   8   7   6   5   4   3   2   1

ISBN 978-1-5011-2614-7
ISBN 978-1-5011-2615-4 (pbk)
ISBN 978-1-5011-2616-1 (ebook)

This book is dedicated to the memory of the thirty Americans who lost their lives in Afghanistan on the mission Extortion 17, including seventeen members of SEAL Team VI. It was the most devastating loss of life in the history of the United States Navy SEAL teams. Some of these men were personal friends of mine. All of them were warriors and patriots of this nation. *Respect*.

PROLOGUE

PARIS, FRANCE

Gil looked over at his best and often-reckless friend.

"So tell me about this girl."

Crosswhite took a drag from a cigarette. "Not much to tell."

"I know better than that. You moved to a communist country to be with her, for Christ sake."

"It's actually not all that communist anymore—just dirt poor."

They were crossing a storage lot on the outskirts of Paris, not far from the rail yard where Gil had had his first run-in with Chechen sniper Sasha Kovalenko.

"So you're not gonna tell me about her?"

"Well, she's a little younger than me."

"How young?"

"Twenty-one."

Gil whistled. "Twenty-one's a good age."

"She wants to get married soon—have a baby."

"You should do it," Gil said, lighting a cigarette of his own. "Be good for you."

"The idea of havin' a kid freaks me out. And what happens when *you* get yourself in another jam? Who's gonna save your ass?"

"Don't use me to try and wriggle out of it," Gil said. "Besides, I was just in another jam. You were nowhere around."

"Yeah, and you damn near died, from what I hear."

"I damn near died the other two times."

Crosswhite stopped and turned to face him. "Fuck is that supposed to mean?"

"Means I think you should get married and have a baby, dumb-ass."

"Yeah," Crosswhite said with a sigh. "Sure." They set off walking again. "She's Catholic. I gotta start goin' to church on Sundays. I hate fuckin' church."

"It ain't gonna kill ya. You'll have to stop with the drugs too."

"Already did. You talk to Marie lately?"

Gil became immediately sad at the mention of his wife. "She doesn't want me back until I'm out for good. And I just ain't ready to quit."

"You know these young guys comin' up," Crosswhite said. "They're faster, stronger, more dangerous than we are."

"I know it, partner, but I ain't ready."

They arrived at an orange overhead garage door with a big white number *9* stenciled on the front of it.

"So what the fuck do you suppose is gonna be in there?" Crosswhite wondered aloud. "A booby trap?"

Gil tossed the cigarette to the ground and stepped on it. "I doubt it."

"You're absolutely positive you don't wanna tell Pope about this first?"

"Yeah." Gil stepped forward, inserted the key in the lock, and gave it a turn. The door went up automatically, and both men stood staring.

"You gotta be shittin' me," Crosswhite said.

The phone in Gil's pocket rang.

"Hello?"

"So what's behind door number nine?" Pope asked.

Gil glanced up at the sky, not at all surprised. "I think you'd better get on a plane and come have a look for yourself."

ROBERT POPE, DIRECTOR of the CIA, arrived in Paris the next day, returning with Gil and Crosswhite to the storage unit.

Gil inserted the key into the electric lock, and the door rose slowly, revealing numerous ammo and weapons crates stacked at the back. What caught Pope's attention, however, was the wooden workbench against the wall with a large lump sitting on top of it covered with a green canvas tarp.

"The crates are full," Gil remarked.

"What's under the tarp?" Pope asked.

Grinning, Crosswhite stepped in and pulled it back, revealing two hundred neatly stacked bars of shiny gold bullion. Each bar was stamped "1000g/999.9 Gold." He watched Pope's eyes for any hint of shock or surprise, but there was none.

"How many bars?" Pope asked.

"Two hundred," Gil replied.

Pope did the math in his head. "That's almost nine million dollars. Close the door and give me the key."

Crosswhite shot a startled glance at Gil and then back

at Pope. "What the hell are you talking about—*give you the key*?"

Pope didn't reply.

"Come on out," Gil said quietly.

"Hey, this puts us on easy street!" Crosswhite said. "Mission complete. Game over. Winner takes all!"

"This puts us *in business*," Pope said, his blue eyes piercing. "Now close the door and give me the key."

"Gil, what the fuck?"

Gil turned the key.

The door began to close, and Crosswhite stepped out quickly, incredulous. "Don't tell me you're down with this. You're gonna let him take all of it for himself?"

Gil took the key from the wall and handed it to Pope. "Let's go. We got a plane to catch."

1

**DISTRITO FEDERAL,
MEXICO CITY, MEXICO
08:45 HOURS**

Chance Vaught stood in the back hall of the US Embassy in Mexico City, talking with Bill Louis, US ambassador to Mexico. A former Green Beret with eight years of combat experience in Iraq and Afghanistan, Vaught was now working as a special agent with the US Diplomatic Security Service (DSS). Currently, he was the special agent in charge of security for Alice B. Downly, the director of the Office of National Drug Control Policy. The "drug czar."

"So you're telling me we have to run the gauntlet between here and the Mexican senate building?" asked Vaught, thirty years old, with green eyes and a black goatee set in a Latin visage. "I thought the entire week was scheduled for here in the embassy. What the hell happened?"

"Between you and me?" Louis lowered his voice. "Downly offended the Mexican delegation yesterday—namely, Lazaro Serrano. First by suggesting they allow US Special Forces teams into Mexico to act as advisors in their war against the cartels, and then by implying the teams would operate independently—the same way our operatives did down in Colombia back in Pablo Escobar's day."

Vaught rolled his eyes in disbelief. "Comparing Mexico to Colombia—very diplomatic." He took a can of Copenhagen tobacco from the cargo pocket of his trousers and put a dip into his lower lip. He was sure that the security at the Mexican senate building—known in Mexico as La Casona de Xicoténcatl—would be tight, but he would have zero control there. Meetings held off US Embassy grounds were always cause for heightened anxiety, and it was a growing problem for the DSS all over the globe. After the Osama bin Laden–orchestrated terrorist attacks of September 11, 2001, billions of American dollars were spent fortifying US embassies, making them look more like supermax prisons than houses of diplomacy, and many foreign diplomats simply refused to meet in the blocky, fortresslike structures. This forced American diplomats to take meetings in less secure locations—like this morning, for example.

"It's only two miles." Louis, a round man in his forties, bald, with pale blue eyes. He was fluent in Spanish and understood Mexican culture very well. "They're sending the usual federal escort—two trucks, four motorcycles—and with our three vehicles, that'll be plenty. It's only an eight-minute ride."

Vaught had seen the world go to shit in eight minutes.

"I'll brief my people and get them ready to roll," Vaught replied. His mother was from the state of Jalisco, so he had family in Mexico and grew up speaking the languages of both countries interchangeably. This had enabled him to form an immediate rapport with the ambassador. "I wonder what she plans on asking for today—our own air base right here in DF?"

Louis chuckled as he turned away. "Avenida Reforma is the most direct route. I'll make sure the proper arrangements are made over at the senate building. Let me know if you need anything else."

Vaught assembled the other nine agents of his security team in the motor pool behind the embassy. They were all handpicked, each one a former operator with Special Forces. All of them had seen extended tours of combat. "Here's the deal, guys. Downly managed to piss off the Mexican delegation yesterday, so today they want to meet at the Xicoténcatl a couple miles from here." The name was pronounced "shēko-*ten*-katl." "That's the building where the Mexican senate meets, for those of you who don't *habla*." The others laughed. "They're sending the usual escort, so the run shouldn't take us more than eight minutes, but I want you guys max-attentive the entire way. Are we clear?"

There were a number of "Rogers!" and "Aye-ayes!" in response, depending on the agent's former branch of service, and they broke up to prep the transports: three black Chevy SUVs with bulletproof glass and doors.

Vaught took aside his number two man, an African American named Uriah Heen, also a former Green Beret. "I'm putting Sellers in the lead vehicle with the trio. Jackson and I'll be in the middle with Downly, her two aides, and Ambassador Louis. You'll bring up the rear with the other three, but make sure Bogart's behind the wheel. I want somebody who can drive covering our tail. Clear?"

Uriah gave him a nod. "Clear. How'd Downly screw up?"

Vaught spit tobacco juice onto the concrete, tired of swallowing it. "She suggested setting American A-Teams loose down here to fight the cartels. I guess it went over like a fart at a baptism."

Uriah chuckled, rubbing the back of his shaved head. "Who'd she do to get this appointment?" Alice Downly was a highly educated, forty-year-old brunette with a photogenic face and an infectious smile, but she wasn't exactly known for her political acumen around the DC social scene. Her appointment to the office had surprised more than a few people in the know.

Vaught's face tightened. "Secure that shit while we're in-country."

"Roger that." Uriah got serious. "I'll get everybody dialed in."

AN HOUR LATER, the American delegation loaded into the vehicles, and they were off. A Mexican Federal Police four-door pickup truck with four officers led the column, another truck brought up the rear, and two pairs of motorcycles leapfrogged from stoplight to stoplight, preventing civilian traffic from cutting through the caravan. The DSS men were dressed in khaki cargo pants, black North Face jackets, ball caps, tactical boots, and Oakley sunglasses. Each carried a concealed Phase-5 Tactical CQC pistol on a single-point bungee sling and a Glock 21 for backup. The CQC (close-quarters-combat) pistol was essentially a snubbed-down M4 carbine with a 7.5-inch barrel in .223 caliber. The buttstock had been removed, leaving only the buffer tube, which looked something like a padded broom handle that could be braced against the shoulder for greater control. Each weapon held a thirty-round magazine, and each DSS agent concealed an additional four magazines on his person by Velcroing them to his body armor—armor bolstered by 12-inch ceramic rifle plates front and back.

The column turned right, leaving the embassy grounds. They traveled southwest, briefly entering a large rotunda before turning right again to roll west. After making another right at the end of the block, they drove on a northerly heading for a quarter mile before making yet another right and driving two more blocks. Finally, they bore left around another large rotunda northward and onto the main avenue through Mexico City. The motorcycle cops were skilled at their job, herding the traffic away from the caravan much the way that horses could be used to herd cattle, and there was never a pause in the column's progress.

Vaught rode shotgun in the center vehicle, with Jackson, a former Navy SEAL, in the driver's seat and the four diplomats in the back. "Shit," he muttered, watching the motorcycles bear to the right down a single narrow lane, "they're taking us down the lateral." The lateral lane ran parallel to the main avenue, separated by a raised median divider lined with trees, park benches, bus stops, and various concrete stanchions. The purpose of the lateral lane was to allow for traffic not traveling the entire distance of the avenue to turn off without hindering the flow of traffic along the main drag. Vaught didn't like to use the lateral on diplomatic runs because it left the column tightly hemmed in between the median divider on the left and the buildings on the right, with virtually no route of escape.

He activated his throat mike, talking over the radio net. "Look sharp, people. It's gonna be a little tight for the next half mile." He glanced left at a city bus passing the column on the opposite side of the median divider, and the terrified eyes of the passengers alerted him that something was wrong. The hair raised on the back of his neck as he caught a glimpse of a figure in a black ski mask. Vaught swung his arm over the back of the seat. "Everybody down!" he shouted. "We're gonna be hit!"

Ambassador Louis grabbed Director Downly, pulling her toward the floor. Downly's aides, a man and a woman seated behind them, ducked down, with the woman muttering, "Oh my God!"

Vaught was in the midst of barking a warning over the radio when the big green-and-yellow bus swerved over the median divider, bashing aside a bench full of people, and slammed into the Federal Police truck at the head of the column, driving it through the front of an Oxxo convenient store. A rocket-powered grenade streaked out of nowhere to strike the lead DSS vehicle in the driver's door, detonating with a horrible explosion that killed all four DSS agents instantly.

"Everybody dismount!"

Vaught jumped out even before Jackson had stopped the vehicle. He jerked open the back door and yanked Louis out by the collar, reaching back inside to grab Downly by the arm and hauling her out so abruptly that she didn't even have time to get her feet beneath her. She fell out onto the pavement as another RPG slammed into the driver's door and exploded. Vaught was thrown off his feet by the blast and landed on his back. The SUV burst into flames. Downly's male aide managed to scrabble out with his clothes burning and face covered in blood, but the woman remained inside, already consumed by fire. There was virtually nothing left of Jackson but a set of mangled legs on the floorboard.

Vaught was on his feet in a second, his mind processing the scene with computerlike speed, seeing almost in slow motion the four DSS agents to the rear rapidly dismounting the passenger side of the third vehicle. Another RPG struck the unarmored Federal Police truck at the tail of the column, exploding the fuel tank and tearing apart the truck as the men inside were bailing out, killing them all.

Vaught instinctively traced the contrail of the rocket back along its trajectory. He swung up the CQC pistol and took a knee beside the burning Chevy, firing on three men taking cover near a white van parked on the far side of the avenue across seven lanes of traffic. The rocketeer went down, stitched from the groin up, and his two compatriots opened up with AK-47s.

Vaught rolled behind the burning vehicle as Uriah and the other three agents arrived to provide covering fire. Another fusillade erupted farther up the lane where the bus had slammed into the lead truck. Five masked gunmen were piling out of the back of the bus, and people were screaming everywhere, running for cover in all directions as the gunners fired wildly from the hip. Vaught was struck on his body armor and the upper left arm. He knew he had to get his diplomatic charges off the street, but there wasn't any time, and there wasn't anywhere to run if there had been. This was a point-blank shoot-out to the death.

Ears ringing, Uriah knelt beside him, and they poured on the fire, knocking two of the gunmen off their feet.

"Reloading!" Vaught dumped the empty magazine, pulling a fresh one from inside his jacket. Uriah dropped his own empty weapon to draw his Glock 21, firing into the remaining three gunners. Another went down, but not before Uriah took an AK-47 round to the chest plate and fell over backward.

Vaught brought the CQC pistol back up and cut down the remaining two men as they fumbled to reload. Uriah rolled to his feet and helped the other DSS men cover their diplomatic charges. With the storefronts along this block locked up behind metal gates, there was no place to seek shelter. The burning vehicles provided some cover, but there was the danger of further explosions.

Three masked motorcyclists zipped past, spraying them with 9 mm fire from Uzi automatic pistols. A DSS agent fell dead with a bullet through the brain. Another was struck in the legs. Downly's male aide crashed to the sidewalk, hit through the liver and spleen. He would bleed out in seconds.

Downly screamed and dropped to her knees beside the aide, covering her head with her hands. The bikes whipped back around in the now-empty street and made a second high-speed pass, spraying the scene again while the DSS men returned fire. Ambassador Louis and another DSS agent went down. Vaught ran out into the street to draw a careful bead on the last rider as they raced away, squeezing the trigger and knocking him off the bike with the last round in the magazine.

The four motorcycle cops suddenly reappeared, speeding past him in hot pursuit of the other two fleeing motorbikes.

"Where the fuck are the cops going?" Uriah screamed. "We need 'em here!"

"It's a goat fuck!" Vaught switched out the magazine as he came back from the street. "The whole thing's a goddamn setup! Help Bogart get Downly off the ground while I check on Clay. We gotta move!"

"To where?"

"Anywhere's better than here!"

Bogart's real name was Stevens, but he looked a lot

like Humphrey Bogart, and he was having trouble getting Downly up with one arm, needing to keep the other arm free to shoot. The drug czar was completely petrified, refusing to carry her own weight and screaming hysterically with her hands pressed over her ears. Uriah grabbed her other arm, and they hauled her to her feet.

Vaught crouched beside Agent Clay, the DSS man hit in the legs. "Can you move under your own power?"

Clay shook his head, gripping his weapon, eyes searching everywhere, bleeding from both thighs and a knee. "The knee won't support my weight. We're in deep shit here, Chance. Why are all these fucking storefronts locked on a Tuesday?"

Vaught stated the obvious. "To keep us out here on the street." He stood and pulled Clay up onto his better leg. By now, the remaining Chevy was also fully engulfed in flames, having been too close to the other burning vehicles. "Let's skirt around the bus and keep moving up the street until we find an open building. We should be hearing sirens any time now."

"Why aren't we hearing them already?"

"They'll wait until they've gathered a large enough force to handle whatever the hell they think is going on down here."

Just then Clay's body exploded, spattering Vaught with the soldier's blood and viscera. He staggered back as the cannon shot echoed up the avenue from down the block.

"Holy fuck! It's a Barrett! Everybody down!"

Hesitating a fraction of a second too long, Bogart was struck in the back by a .50 caliber sniper round weighing 45 grams and traveling at 2,800 feet per second. The bullet blasted off his left arm and shoulder, sending the appendage twirling up into the air. He fell on the concrete, locking eyes with Vaught as the life ran out of him. The arm and shoulder landed beside Downly. She shrieked in horror, scrabbling back to her feet and running frantically out into Avenida Reforma.

Vaught and Uriah looked at each other from across the walk, knowing that to go after her was suicide. "Stay down!" Vaught sprang up and gave chase. He was almost halfway across the avenue when Downly exploded at the waist, her entrails whirling off in what seemed like all directions as the two severed halves of her hit the pavement in a twisted mess, with nothing but her spinal cord holding them together.

Vaught had completely failed in his mission to protect his charges, and he'd lost nearly his entire team in the process. It might not have been through any error of his own, but he was still responsible, and he knew it.

With the image of the bullet's vapor trail—cutting through the morning air faster than the microscopic water molecules could get out of its way—seared into his brain, he knew now where the sniper was. Without pause, he spotted an abandoned taxi and sprinted past Downly knowing that to turn back would give the shooter a clear shot at a motionless target, even if only for a fraction of an instant.

Vaught took cover beside the taxi and got on the radio to Uriah. "I know where the fucker's at. He's firing from the rooftop of the glass building on my side of the street at the end of the block. He doesn't have an angle on you, so stay put. I'm going after him."

Uriah's reply was immediate: "If he's shooting from the glass building, he doesn't have an angle on you either. Just stay outta sight and let the local heat handle this!"

They could hear sirens now far up the avenue.

"I'm going after him!" Vaught said. "You stay alive and make sure our people know what happened. Don't let the Mexicans debrief you without somebody from our embassy being there." He doubled-checked his weapon and jumped into the taxi, speeding off as a dozen federal squad cars and trucks came screaming down the avenue behind him.

2

Vaught sped around the corner in the procured taxi, tires squealing, gunning the motor halfway down the block. Abruptly, he slammed on the brakes and bailed out of the taxi, shedding his jacket and making sure his DSS badge was still hanging around his neck. A half dozen curious bystanders stood huddled in a group at the end of the block. When he asked them in Spanish whether anyone had come out of the glass building, they backed away around the corner.

A bored-looking old man sitting on a stoop and smoking a cigarette pointed up and said, *"Francotirador."* Sniper.

Vaught saw for the first time that the building was still under construction and that the lower floors were wrapped around with heavy plastic to discourage the general public from entering. He found a way inside and vaulted up a staircase, knowing he had twelve floors to climb. As he arrived at the tenth floor, a door clanged open up on the twelfth; he heard hurried voices descending, weapons clanking against the steel railing. He peered up between the stairs and saw four shadowy figures circling quickly downward.

Two masked men arrived on the landing directly in front of him, and he blasted them from ten feet, splattering the freshly painted white wall with bullets and dark crimson. Someone above fired down and missed, but he felt the spall from the ricochets cut into his shins and danced back out of sight, spraying a burst of fire upward. Sirens howled outside the building, and booted men were quickly mounting the stairs below. The men above retreated back toward the roof, and Vaught gave chase.

He kicked open the door to the roof and stood aside, waiting for a hail of bullets that did not come. Stealing a quick look around the jam, he saw two figures opening another door on the far side of the roof a hundred feet away. One of them disappeared behind it, toting a Barrett sniper rifle. Vaught shot down the second man before he could slip inside; then he ran across. But before he could make it all the way, the Federales came pouring onto the roof behind him, screaming, *"Alto! Alto!"* Halt!

Knowing they would not hesitate to shoot him, Vaught pulled up short, thrusting his hands into the air and turning around with his weapon dangling from the sling, his DSS badge glinting in the sun. *"El francotirador se escapa!"* he shouted. *"Por ahí, amigos! Por las escaleras!"* The sniper's getting away! Over there! By the stairs!

Seven hard-eyed Federales surrounded him, covering him with M4 carbines and shouting for him to get down on his knees. They didn't seem to hear what he'd said. Vaught repeated it, and someone kicked him behind his knee to drop him. They shoved him onto his face and shackled his hands behind his back.

"Are you deaf?" he shouted in Spanish. "The sniper's getting away!"

One of the Federales pressed down on his neck with a lug-soled boot, saying in a sonorous voice, *"Cállate."* Shut up.

Vaught was stripped of his weapons and radio, and then brought to his feet. He spit out what was left of the tobacco in his lip and looked at the captain who'd stood on his neck. The patch over the man's breast pocket read "Espinosa." He was tall and muscular, with a black mustache and heavy-lidded, obsidian eyes.

"Tell me you've got men covering the stairs, Captain. Tell me you're not just letting that son of a bitch get away."

The captain jerked his head toward the exit, ordering his men to take Vaught below.

"What the fuck is going on?" Vaught demanded. "Those are our people down there dead in the street! You're letting the bastard escape!"

Below, Vaught was stuffed into the back of an unmarked car with black-tinted windows. He lowered his wrists and stepped through the cuffs to get his hands back in front of him, and sat watching as the captain spoke with two detectives in plain clothes. At length, they nodded and got into the car.

Vaught asked in Spanish if the sniper had been caught.

The man in the passenger seat said, "Everything is under control. Don't worry."

"I need to be debriefed by my people immediately."

"First, you go to see our people."

"No, that's not how this works! I've got diplomatic immunity. You have to take me directly to my embassy. Are you federal cops or municipal?"

"La inmunidad diplomática," the passenger echoed to the driver, and both men laughed.

Vaught sat back with a sigh, muttering in English, "Fuck you both."

Within a few blocks, it was apparent they were not circling back toward the Federal District but were continuing on a course carrying them ever farther away from el Distrito Federal.

"Where are we going?"

When they ignored him, Vaught lunged over the seat for the steering wheel, hoping to wreck the car. The man in the passenger seat was ready, jamming a high-powered stun gun into Vaught's neck, shocking him over and over until finally he lay crumpled on the floor behind the seat, virtually paralyzed.

"Cabrón!" the passenger cursed, throwing the stun gun onto the dash and straightening his tie. Asshole!

Ten minutes later, Vaught was dragged from the back of the car by two different men and taken into a building at the end of an alley. There was no doubt that he was now in the hands of the cartels and that he likely didn't have long to live. He made up his mind to take out one of the bastards the very first chance he got, but with his hands cuffed together, that wasn't going to be the easiest stunt to pull.

He was thrown onto a musty couch that smelled of cat piss. A different guy with the same stun gun appeared and jammed the weapon into Vaught's gut, giving him another five jolts. Vaught screamed involuntarily, his muscles contracting uncontrollably until his bladder let loose.

A number of men stood laughing.

"Knock it the fuck off!" someone ordered in English, and the room fell into an abrupt silence.

Vaught opened his eyes to slits, catching a glimpse of a

white male dressed in jeans and an olive drab T-shirt. He stood in the doorway holding a Barrett sniper rifle by the carrying handle. His sandy blond hair was cut high and tight above a pair of merciless blue eyes, and there was an Airborne Rangers tattoo on his bulging left bicep. He grunted out orders in heavily accented Spanish and then disappeared down a hall, carrying the weapon that had blown Alice Downly in half.

Someone took away Vaught's badge, body armor, and boots, leaving him in his stocking feet. He felt like an idiot for having let them take him alive, but what was he supposed to have done? Gun down a bunch of cops on a rooftop in Mexico City? The sad reality was that he'd put himself in this rat-fucked situation by going off the reservation, so he wasn't about to blame anyone else. He'd just have to get himself out of it—or take the damn bullet without complaint.

Out of nowhere, he was given another jolt from the stun gun and shoved off the couch, onto the floor. One of the handcuffs was released long enough to roll him onto his belly and recuff his hands behind him. This gang wasn't taking any chances, and Vaught saw his hopes of going down fighting quickly slip away.

A stun gun took a lot out of a man, the electricity forcing the muscles to do a tremendous amount of work in an extremely short period of time, converting the blood sugar into lactic acid and leaving the victim completely exhausted in a matter of seconds. Vaught already felt as though he'd gone ten rounds with a heavyweight fighter, and he was pretty damn sure he hadn't experienced the last of that fucking stun gun.

There weren't all that many people to say good-bye to, really. He'd grown up in a Marine Corps family, raised in numerous locations around the world, so he didn't have what most people would call regular friends. He was the youngest of three brothers (the two eldest both being marines), and his father, a gunnery sergeant, had named him for the Chance Vought F4-U Corsair flown by his paternal grandfather—yet another marine—in the Korean War.

Determined to escape the shadows of his older siblings, Vaught had decided to break with the family's USMC tradition and enlist in the US Army—one month after the Bin Laden attacks—boldly stating his intention to become a Green Beret.

He'd discovered early that he was a natural leader. Within a month of his first hour in combat, he was promoted to a Special Forces weapons sergeant with the Fifth Special Forces Group out of Fort Campbell, Kentucky. Vaught then went on to serve multiple tours over the next eight years with an ODA (Operational Detachment–A, or A-Team) in both Iraq and Afghanistan.

Now as he lay drooling on the floor with his face pressed against the filthy concrete, a commotion flared up down the hall, and there was a heated discussion over the unbelievable stupidity of bringing an American DSS agent to that location.

"Hey, I'm happy to leave," he mumbled in English, and couldn't help a sardonic chuckle.

One of the men standing over him kicked him in the ass. *"Cállate, cabrón."*

Vaught didn't say anything more, fearing that another electrical jolt might sap the last of whatever strength he had left. As it was, he wasn't sure if he could even get to his feet without help, much less put up a fight.

Then a glowering Senator Lazaro Serrano—the head of the Mexican delegation to fight drug trafficking—stepped into the room, and that was the icing on the cake of Vaught's day. He was hard-pressed to stifle an ironic laugh.

"Buenos días, Señor Serrano. Gusto en verle." Good morning, Mr. Serrano. It's good to see you.

Serrano didn't reply. He turned and began haranguing the apparent leader of the crew, a skinny fellow with an AK-47 over his shoulder. "You didn't even put a fucking bag over his head, cabrón? Now he's seen my fucking face, and we *have* to kill him! You stupid fucking cabrónes—all of you!" He slapped the man upside the head and stormed out of the room, hissing angrily over his shoulder, "Get rid of him!"

He shouted for someone to follow him on his way out of the building, and a heavy door slammed shut.

Vaught lay waiting for the sniper to reappear, but he did not. The men milled around the room for a minute or two, talking among themselves as they discussed who would kill the American. Suddenly there was a horrendous burst of automatic fire. As the bodies dropped around him, Vaught closed his eyes, waiting for the lights to go out.

An empty magazine clattered against the concrete, and he looked up to see one of the cartel members smiling crookedly down at him as he slipped another thirty-round banana clip into the AK-47 and pulled back the charging lever.

"Can you sit up?" the fellow asked in Spanish.

"I can try." Vaught rolled to his back, and with some effort did manage to sit up on his own.

The skinny gang leader, now sprawled out on the far side of the room, riddled with bullets, began to choke on his own blood, and the gunner put a single round into him, silencing him for good.

The gunner then crouched behind Vaught and slipped a key into the handcuffs.

"I'm Mendoza," he said. "An undercover agent with

the PFM." This was the Policía Federal Ministerial, or Federal Ministerial Police, an agency formed in 2009 to fight corruption and organized crime throughout Mexico, modeled loosely after the FBI.

Vaught sat rubbing his wrists where the steel had bruised him. "Where were you earlier, when my people were getting slaughtered in the street?"

Mendoza shrugged. "I learned of the planned attack only a few minutes before it happened. By then, there was no way for me to send warning without getting myself killed. I'm afraid my saving your life is going to cause the PFM a lot of trouble. I'll probably get reprimanded for not letting these people kill you. It's taken eighteen months to work my way this deep into the cartels. Now all that time is entirely wasted. After what I've done here, I can't risk going back to them as the lone survivor. They'd kill me whether they believed me or not—just to be absolutely sure."

"Well, I'm really sorry about that," Vaught said.

"You should be, cabrón." Mendoza helped him to his feet. "What you did was stupid. You don't have the authority to pursue criminals in Mexico. Your job was to protect your people, nothing more."

Vaught swayed slightly, and Mendoza guided him to a chair, taking a phone from his pocket. "I have to call my superiors now to find out what to do with you."

"I need to get back to my embassy. You can help me do that."

Mendoza waved a finger. "Your embassy is already surrounded by Mexican security. Right now Lazaro Serrano thinks you are dead. It might be best to keep it that way."

"Hey, look," Vaught said. "My people need to know about that sniper as soon as possible. He's an American, trained by our special forces. What do you know about him?"

"Almost nothing. He's someone the cartels brought in special for this assassination. We didn't know anything about him before today, but I did hear someone say he's been contracting for the cartels for some time."

"Who said that?"

Mendoza gestured at the dead man he'd just shot. "He said it."

After a tense telephone conversation with his commander, Mendoza slipped the phone back in his pocket. "As I expected, my superiors are angry I didn't let these people kill you. They say you asked for it. Now, because of you, my deep-cover operation is blown, and other agents might be at risk. My commander made it clear that under no circumstances are you to go back to your embassy. The PFM will now use you to build a case against Serrano. That will keep me out of the picture and protect my identity—which will also help to protect our other deep-cover agents within the cartels."

"I'm sorry," Vaught said, leveling his gaze, "but I don't work for the PFM. I work for the DSS. I have diplomatic immunity, and I'm getting back to my fucking embassy."

Mendoza took the stun gun from inside his jacket and set it on the table. "I don't want to use this again, but I will."

"Again?"

Mendoza smiled his crooked smile once more.

"You made me piss myself!"

"I had to make sure you didn't do anything else stupid before I could figure out how to save your worthless life."

"So what the fuck do we do now? I've got a bullet in my arm, and it's going to need attention soon."

"Right now the PFM is asking the CIA for permission to use you."

"I don't work for the C-I-*fucking*-A either!" Vaught flared in English.

Mendoza had a hatchet face, bushy eyebrows, and a protruding Adam's apple. "We'll soon see who you work for, my friend."

"Fuck this!" Vaught said, again in English, getting up weakly from the table. Mendoza took up the stun gun and zapped him in the thigh to send him toppling to the floor.

Vaught grabbed his leg. "Oh, you fuckin' cocksucker!"

Mendoza sat laughing in the chair. "You owe me a life, my friend. So now we're going to wait until my superiors talk to the CIA."

"You motherfuckin' cocksucker," Vaught muttered, digging the can of Copenhagen from his pocket and putting a dip into his lip. "You just wait!"

3

Wearing a camouflage snow parka, Gil Shannon lay well
ensconced within a copse of tall pines halfway down one
of the most challenging ski runs in the mountains above
the village of Malbun, a .308 Remington modular sniper
rifle pulled into his shoulder as he eyed his target: a man
dressed in a yellow ski jacket and green pants. He and
his blond fiancée were flanked by five security men, all
of whom had pulled to the side of the run for a breather.
A heavy snow had begun to fall over the past few minutes, and with the coming of late afternoon, Gil knew this
would be the group's last run of the day. If he didn't take
the shot now, it would mean spending a fourth night in
the Malbun ski lodge.

Landlocked between Switzerland and Austria, the
small country of Liechtenstein covered only sixty-two
square miles and was the only nation located entirely

in the Alps. Traveling on a Canadian passport, Gil had spent the last three days stalking Sabastian Blickensderfer, a forty-year-old Swiss banker on holiday with his wife-to-be.

CIA Director Robert Pope had targeted Blickensderfer for termination because of his financial ties to the Islamic terrorist organization Al Qaeda in the Arabian Peninsula (AQAP). Blickensderfer's money-laundering operations were well known to the CIA. However, the US and British governments considered him untouchable due to his close financial and familial ties within the Swiss government, which viewed Blickensderfer's illicit business affairs as inconsequential: if Blickensderfer didn't launder AQAP money, someone else would, and at least the millionaire businessman was able to provide useful intelligence on the movements of certain Islamic clerics. This was enough to keep Western intelligence agencies such as the CIA and MI6 from filing serious grievances.

There were more and more profiteers like Blickensderfer operating in and around Europe, and Pope understood the important role they played. He also understood that if they began turning up dead, others would take notice and be forced to think twice about doing business with Islamic fundamentalists. As the world stood at present, there was one rubric for the ruling elite and another for the bottom 99 percent. Pope regarded these hypocrisies and double standards as anathema, and his aim was to change the dangerous paradigm from within.

Gil's aim was to destroy whomever Pope put in front of him. At present, that person was Sabastian Blickensderfer. He'd read the corrupt banker's dossier and agreed the man was in need of removal. For Gil, the mathematics were simple enough: Blickensderfer was making it easier for AQAP to carry out terrorist operations. AQAP was responsible for the 2012 attack on the American mission in Benghazi, Libya. Former Navy SEALs had been killed in Benghazi. And if Sabastian Blickensderfer didn't mind helping to kill Navy SEALs, Gil Shannon sure as hell didn't mind killing Sebastian Blickensderfer.

Of course, Gil knew that Pope's future targets might not always be quite so easily sorted out, but the Swiss banker was a good place to start. If Pope ever targeted anyone Gil didn't agree needed to be removed, he would simply take a pass.

As he eyed Blickensderfer through the scope at a hundred yards, he watched the man laughing and handing a flask to one of his security men whom Gil knew—from seeing around the lodge over the past few nights—to be carrying a Beretta pistol beneath his jacket.

At last, after three long days of stalking his prey on the snowy mountain, the moment came right. The air was still, and the snow fell straight down all across the slope. Gil placed the reticule on Blickensderfer's sternum over his heart and began to squeeze the trigger.

Inexplicably, Blickensderfer's fiancée lunged forward into the sight picture just as the trigger was passing the point of no return. Gil twitched as the rifle went off, and the .308 Lapua magnum blasted almost silently from the end of the suppresser at more than 2,500 feet per second. His heart stopped as he watched, waiting for the woman's head to explode. It did not. He saw her blond hair kick up at the nape of her neck as the round passed through it, soundlessly impacting the white powder thirty feet beyond.

The woman brushed absentmindedly at the back of her neck and pulled her ski poles from the snow with a laugh. Apparently she had lost her balance and nearly toppled off her skis.

Gil rolled behind the trunk of a pine and pulled the white watch cap from his close-cropped head, breathing a deep sigh of relief. He had very nearly murdered an innocent woman.

He lay there with large snowflakes landing silently on his face in the quiet surroundings. He stroked his stubbled chin and tried to recall his estranged wife's face. Montana seemed very far away as he dug the cigarettes from his parka and lit one with a Zippo lighter. He knew that Pope could not have been watching via satellite due to the cloud cover, but that was a moot point. Gil was on his own for these off-the-books missions, which meant no overwatch.

Still, he told himself, you never knew what Pope was up to.

As the Blickensderfer party skied off down the mountain, Gil finished the cigarette, knowing he'd see them around the lodge again that night. "Fare thee well," he muttered, thinking of the pretty woman who had no idea that a hot .308 had passed within two inches of her spine at the base of her skull. "And enjoy yourself tonight, Sabastian. I won't make the same mistake tomorrow."

Tucking the cigarette butt into his pocket, he disassembled the rifle and packed it away before taking off his reversible parka and turning the red side out. Then he stripped the white pack cover from his red rucksack and skied off down the slope dressed as a begoggled member of the Malbun Ski Patrol.

4

Cletus Webb, deputy director of the CIA, stepped out of the restroom in the CIA building in Langley to find Mark Gurich, director of foreign operations, standing against the wall waiting for him. Webb glanced at the red file folder in the man's hand. "I take it that's for me?" he said, put off to be ambushed outside the john.

"I couldn't find you," Gurich said. "The proverbial shit just hit the fan down in Mexico. Alice Downly and Bill Louis were assassinated in what looks like a major cartel attack. Damn near her entire DSS team was wiped out. Our embassy's on full lockdown—marines, machine guns, all the frills—and Mike Ortega, Mexico chief of station, is asking me for an Operational Immediate I don't think I've got the authority to give him."

A crease formed in Webb's brow. "You're telling me Downly's dead?"

"That's been confirmed by Mexico station."

"What the hell happened?" Webb was tall, with a basketball player's build, thinning blond hair, and contemplative blue eyes.

"Mexico station says it looks like she was killed by a sniper, but that hasn't been confirmed."

"You're the director of foreign operations." Webb grabbed the file. "What do you mean you don't have the authority to give an Operational Immediate? What the hell is Ortega asking for, a drone strike?"

"Not exactly." Gurich, a foot shorter than Webb, had darker features, brown eyes, and a prep school haircut.

Webb spent the next couple of minutes standing there in the hall outside the restroom, reading.

"As far as I know," Gurich remarked, "nobody's done anything like this since the Cold War, and I didn't think I'd better give it the green light without first getting your approval."

Webb did not look up from the file. "Have you spoken with DSS?"

"Not yet."

"So Agent Vaught's people don't know whether he's alive or dead?"

"Correct."

Webb finished reading the five-page affidavit and handed the folder back to Gurich. "Give it to Fields."

Gurich's eyebrows went up. "Isn't this a little public for him?"

"Give it to Fields," Webb repeated. "This Vaught character went off the reservation when he damn well knew better. He's lucky he's alive, especially since virtually everyone he was responsible for is dead. Give it to Fields. I'll clear it with Director Pope."

"What do I tell Mexico station? The DSS?"

"You tell Ortega to remain poised to assist whatever assets Fields puts into play, and you tell DSS that Agent Vaught is now under the aegis of the CIA in accordance with recent amendments to the Foreign Service Act. I'll brief them personally after I've spoken with Pope. As long as we're keeping DSS in the loop, they're not going to raise any hell over it. Vaught's little cowboy stunt in the face of his failure to protect Alice Downly isn't exactly going to endear him to the director general of the US Foreign Service."

Like most agents with the Diplomatic Security Service, Agent Vaught was also a member of the Foreign Service, which in turn fell under the protective wing of the US State Department. This meant that Vaught was both a federal law enforcement agent and an arbiter of US Foreign Policy, and for an arbiter of US Foreign Policy to go chasing bad guys through the streets of a foreign capital—beyond the legal scope of his diplomatic duties—was a real good way to embarrass both the US Foreign Service and the US State Department.

"So I take it to Fields, and then what?"

"Tell him I said the ball's in his court. He'll handle it from there."

THREE MINUTES LATER, Gurich stepped into the office of Clemson Fields. There was no name or title on the door.

Nancy Proust, Fields's secretary, looked up from her desk. "Hello, Mr. Gurich. How can I help you?" She was a matronly woman in her forties. Her dark hair was cut in an angled bob. She never wore makeup, and Gurich had never seen her dressed in any color other than black.

"Is he in?"

She picked up the phone. "Mr. Fields, Mr. Gurich is

here to see you." She put the phone back down. "He said to go right in, Mr. Gurich."

Gurich thanked her and crossed into Fields's inner sanctum to find the mysterious CIA analyst (his official job description) sitting at his desk, reading the *Washington Post*.

Clemson Fields was a medium-size man in his early sixties, dressed in chino slacks, a button-up short-sleeve shirt, and a subdued tie. He was balding from front to back and wore a pair of round wire-rimmed glasses. He folded away the paper and stood up to shake Gurich's hand. "I assume this has to do with Mexico City?"

"You've heard?"

"Just." Fields put out his hand for the red file folder.

"Did the DDO already call you?"

Fields shook his head and smiled. "Red is the only color anyone ever brings me."

Gurich gave him the folder. "Webb said to tell you the ball's in your court."

"Of course." Fields took it and sat down to read, saying, "Thank you, Mr. Gurich," in what was obviously a dismissal.

Gurich eyed him for a moment and then left the office.

Two minutes later, Fields finished reading the affidavit and set it aside to reach for the phone. He dialed a number and waited for someone to answer.

"This is Clemson," he said. "I assume you've heard the news by now?"

"About what?" asked the man at the other end.

"Alice Downly was assassinated right there in Mexico City—less than two hours ago."

"Who the fuck is Alice Downly?"

5

Daniel Crosswhite hung up the phone after talking to Fields and went back into the bedroom, where his twenty-one-year-old wife, Paolina, lay in bed. They had finished making love only a couple of minutes before the phone rang.

"Who was it?" she asked in Spanish. She spoke no English.

"The devil's little brother." He rolled his eyes and took a soft pack of Camels from the edge of the dresser. "Don't look at me like that. We knew one of Pope's men would call sooner or later. Today's the day, that's all."

Crosswhite was a former Delta Force operator and Medal of Honor winner. He had returned to the US after multiple tours in Afghanistan to take up a life of crime as a vigilante but had gotten himself caught. Only the intervention of Robert Pope of the CIA and Navy SEAL Gil Shannon had saved him from life in prison.

Paolina lay on her side in the midday heat and caressed her growing belly, which was just beginning to show. She was a Cuban national, but CIA Director Pope had pulled some strings for her and Crosswhite, enabling them to move to Mexico City, along with Paolina's three-year-old daughter, who was taking a nap in the next room.

"Who is Pope sending you to kill?"

Crosswhite smiled. "Nobody."

She rolled onto her back and propped herself up on a couple of pillows. Paolina was five feet tall, slender, with dark skin, soft brown eyes, and long black hair full of tight curls. "I don't trust him. He helped us move here only to use you as an assassin against the cartels."

He sat down on the edge of the bed, running his fingers through her hair. "I made a deal, *corazón*." He caressed her breast and got to his feet. "I have to get dressed and go. You remember everything we've talked about, right?"

"Yes. I want to know what's going on before you leave."

"One of the cartels assassinated the US ambassador and some American woman a couple hours ago." Crosswhite snatched a pair of jeans from the back of a chair. "I have to bring in a wounded DSS agent who can't be seen at the embassy. He's shot in the arm, so make a spot in the kitchen. It sounds like I'll have to remove the bullet and sew him up."

"DSS?"

"Diplomatic Security Service." He crushed out the smoke in the ashtray on the dresser. "Hand me my socks, baby. Have you seen my boots?"

"Under the bed."

USING THE GPS in his Jeep Rubicon's console, Crosswhite found the building that Fields had given him the address for about seven miles from his house. He and Paolina lived in a nice neighborhood where there were a lot of Canadians, so he didn't stick out, and all of their neighbors knew that Paolina was Cuban, so no one suspected he was CIA. Most everyone was under the assumption he was a retired American GI living on a government pension.

He took out his phone and called the number Fields had given him.

"Bueno?" answered a Mexican voice.

"Soy Crosswhite. Estoy aqui." It's Crosswhite. I'm here.

A door opened, and Mendoza waved for him to come inside. Crosswhite did not generally move around armed because getting caught with a gun in Mexico meant many years in prison, so unless he was sure there was going to be big trouble, he chose to rely on his fists, much preferring death over incarceration.

He locked the Jeep and stole inside the building. The smell of death and burnt powder flashed him back to combat, and his internal systems came online. The hair raised up on the back of his neck. Mendoza smiled, turning to lead him down the hall to a room full of dead bodies and one very pissed off Chance Vaught, who sat in a chair, handcuffed to a steel doorknob.

"Why is he handcuffed?" Crosswhite asked in Spanish, glancing around at the dead cartel members. "Is this your work?"

Mendoza nodded.

"I'm handcuffed because he's a fuckin' bastard," Vaught said in English.

Mendoza explained that he'd needed to take a dump and couldn't trust Vaught not to leave. Afterward, it had been easier to leave the increasingly mouthy American handcuffed to the door.

Crosswhite looked at him. "You ready to go, champ?"

"Go where?"

"I got you a room at the fuckin' Hilton. You ready or not?"

Vaught looked sullenly at the floor. "Yeah, I'm ready."

NINETY MINUTES LATER, Vaught sat in a chair in Crosswhite's kitchen, flexing his wounded arm, examining the suture work. "It's not exactly straight."

"Well, this ain't exactly a triage unit." Crosswhite snapped off a pair of rubber gloves. "And I'm not exactly a medic."

Paolina sat staring at Vaught from across the table, her gaze flat and reproving. She wanted him out of her house but knew they were stuck with him unless and until Pope's man Fields found someplace else for him to hide out.

Vaught smiled, asking Paolina her name in Spanish. *"Como se llama?"*

"Paolina," she said, not overly friendly. She glanced at Crosswhite.

"Nice to meet you. I'm Chance. I appreciate you welcoming me into your home like this."

"If it were up to me," she said, getting up from the table, "you wouldn't be here." She caressed Crosswhite's arm where he carried a scar identical to the one Vaught would now carry in almost exactly the same spot. "I'm going to buy food," she told him. "I'll be back soon."

"Careful," Crosswhite said. "We're working now."

She nodded, kissing him. "Valencia is playing in her room." Paolina left the house.

Vaught stared after her, unable to deny his attraction. "She's Cuban, isn't she?"

Crosswhite went to the sink to wash his hands. "Yeah. If you touch her, I'll kill you."

Vaught nodded, reaching for his can of Copenhagen. "Roger that. So what's next?"

Crosswhite dried his hands and shook a cigarette loose from its pack. "We wait to hear from Ortega at Mexico station."

"Who's Ortega?"

Crosswhite lit the cigarette, tucking the lighter into his pocket. "CIA's chief of station here in DF."

"So you work for Ortega?"

Crosswhite stood leaning against the ceramic-tiled counter. "Never met him." He went to the fridge and took out a couple of Coronas, setting them down on the table. "Ortega has to wait on orders from Clemson Fields—who takes his orders directly from Bob Pope. It's my guess you'll be kept out of sight until the PFM needs you to testify against Serrano. So in effect you—"

"Building a case against Serrano could take months!"

Crosswhite popped the tops from the beers with a church key. "Welcome to the CIA, amigo."

"I don't work for the CIA." Vaught took a pull from his beer. "And I sure as hell don't work for the PFM. I'm a DSS agent. That means I—"

"You don't belong to DSS anymore. You belong to the CIA by executive order—at least, you will within the next few hours, or however long it takes to get the paperwork shuffled across the president's desk—and there isn't jack shit you can do about it."

"So who the fuck is Clemson Fields?"

Crosswhite took a drink. "Shit," he muttered to himself. "I hope she remembers limes. Fields is the last of the old guard—a right bastard."

"I don't follow."

"Okay, look." Crosswhite sat down. "During the Cold War, the CIA wasn't restricted to using personnel from special mission units like Delta Force and SEAL Team

Six the way they are today. We were fighting the big, bad Soviets, so they were allowed their own in-house contractors with no official ties. Fields was a recruiter and part-time assassin—an operational goon."

Vaught took another drink. "So you work for Fields?"

"No. I work for Pope. *Technically* Fields isn't even CIA anymore. He's attached to the ATRU."

"The ATRU? What the hell are you talking about?"

"The Anti-Terrorism Response Unit. Congratulations, champ. You're now privy to a newly formed SMU that the vice president of the United States doesn't even know about."

Vaught didn't like the sound of that one bit. "Who gave you clearance to bring me into the loop?"

Crosswhite grinned. "You're finally starting to ask the right questions, champ."

"The name's *Chance*."

"Whatever. You've been put on ice because you're a political embarrassment to both countries now. You went off the reservation when you chased that sniper, and you killed three Mexican cops."

Vaught put down his beer. "I didn't kill any fucking cops!"

"The guys in the stairwell and the guy on the roof were all Federales."

"They were wearing fucking ski masks and carrying AK-47s!"

"Well, they might've been *crooked* Federales, but they were still Federales, and that embarrasses—"

"We were taking sniper fire! My entire team was wiped out!"

"Hey, I get it," Crosswhite said easily. "Everybody gets it. And the PFM probably gets a secret kick out of it.

But it's political now, champ, and politics trumps everything. You've embarrassed the Mexican government, and you've made powerful people look bad on both sides of the border, which means nobody's in a hurry to see your face. They don't know how to spin this yet, so it's easier to let everyone think you're dead for the time being. Putting you with Fields is probably the best way of doing that. Pretty soon the PFM's going to release a statement saying the body of an American DSS agent was found with those of known cartel members. That will put Serrano at ease, and he'll drop his guard, thinking you're dead."

"In the meantime, my family gets to think I'm dead, too? No way."

"You come from a military family, champ."

"Chance!"

"They'll bear up well enough," Crosswhite assured him, "and think how happy they'll be when they eventually find out you're still alive."

"Who the fuck are you?"

"Dan Crosswhite."

Vaught stared at him for a long moment. *"Earnest Endeavor* Dan Crosswhite?"

Operation Earnest Endeavor had been an unsanctioned rescue operation led by Navy SEAL sniper Gil Shannon to liberate female Night Stalker pilot Sandra Brux, who was being tortured by Islamic extremists in the Panjshir Valley of Afghanistan. Crosswhite and Shannon had both received the Medal of Honor for their part in the operation, but both men were ultimately run out of the military by jealous and resentful superiors, costing Crosswhite the career he had loved.

Crosswhite frowned. "That's me."

"Last I heard, you were dead. You were supposed be

working down here undercover for the FBI or something."

Crosswhite smirked. "Look at me, champ."

"*Chance*, goddamn you!"

"Look at me, champ. How is a gringo gonna work undercover in Mexico? Grow a mustache and buy a fuckin' sombrero?"

"Well, I can tell you this," Vaught said. "I'm not sitting around here waiting for the PFM to build a case against Serrano while my family gets the news I'm dead. And another thing: there's a GI sniper running around down here doing contract work for the cartels. Somebody has to put that guy down, and since I seem to have a lot of extra time on my hands at the moment—"

"You wouldn't even know where to begin looking."

"Well, unlike you, I don't need a fuckin' sombrero. I already look the part, and I happen to know one or two people down here."

"I've been briefed on your Mexican family. I don't think letting the cartels get wind of them is a good idea."

Vaught got up from the chair. "You let me worry about that."

"I don't think you'd better go fucking around out there," Crosswhite said nonchalantly, setting down his beer on the counter. "You'll only make shit worse."

"I know what I'm doing." Vaught shouldered past. "Thanks for the beer and the shitty stitch job, hero."

Crosswhite let him pass. Then he slipped the stun gun that Mendoza had given him from beneath his jacket and zapped Vaught in the ass. The agent dropped to his knees with a shout, and Crosswhite stepped forward to zap him again between the shoulder blades, sending him flopping forward onto his face.

Paolina came through the door a few seconds later with

a plastic bag of groceries in each hand and stood in the threshold gaping. "Daniel, he's drooling on my kitchen floor."

Vaught lay paralyzed with his cheek mashed against the ceramic tile watching a tiny piss ant making its way past his face as it carried out its little piss ant business. "You fuckin' cocksuckers," he mumbled.

6

Later that evening, Vaught sat brooding on the floor in the corner of the living room, handcuffed to an eyebolt protruding from the concrete wall. Paolina sat on the leather sofa, reading a book to her young daughter, Valencia. Crosswhite had stepped out for more beer and limes.

Vaught cleared his throat, and Paolina looked up to see what he wanted. He tugged at the handcuff. "Can I have my can of tobacco?" he asked in Spanish.

"No," she said. "I don't want you spitting in my house."

"Can I have a cigarette?"

"We only smoke in the bedroom." She caressed the dark-skinned child's curly black hair. "And never around my daughter."

Vaught sat looking at her. She was heartbreakingly pretty, but there was a stark maturity about her that he had to admit was intimidating.

"What have you been through?" he asked.

"None of your business." She returned her attention to the storybook.

"You know, you don't have to put up with me," he said after a while. "Give me the key, and I'll be gone in ten seconds."

"I would love to. Now shut up and let me read to my daughter."

Ten minutes later, Crosswhite arrived with more beer. "Did you make the salsa, baby?"

"It's in the refrigerator," she answered. "There's guacamole also."

"How's our guest?"

"Annoying."

Crosswhite laughed from the kitchen. "Has he been giving you trouble?"

"He wants to spit in my house."

"I wasn't going to spit in the house," Vaught said in protest. "I'll swallow it, for God's sake."

Crosswhite came into the living room and offered Vaught a bottle of beer with a wedge of lime in it. "I don't set the rules of the house," he said in English. "I just live by them."

"I'm getting that," Vaught said gloomily.

Crosswhite took a pull from his beer. "It's been awhile since I've had another dogface to drink with. Too bad you're shackled—kinda feels like drinkin' with a fugitive."

"Then let me loose."

"Can't do it, not until I hear from Ortega." Crosswhite went and sat beside Paolina, taking the little girl into his arms. She nestled against him, hugging a stuffed turtle and sucking her thumb.

"Is there a woman waiting for you back in the States?" Crosswhite asked.

"Would you give a fuck if there were?"

"Watch your language around this little girl," Crosswhite warned. "And I'm not the reason you're here. You put yourself in this mess." A phone rang in the other room, and he went to answer it. He came back a few minutes later and offered a satellite phone to Vaught. "Doctor Doom wants to talk to you."

"Who?"

"Fields."

Vaught took the phone. "This is Special Agent in Charge Chance Vaught. To whom am I speaking?"

There was a chuckle at the other end of the line. "That sounded rather official coming from a man chained to a wall."

"Then who the fuck is this?" Vaught said, stealing a cautious glance at Crosswhite.

"Agent Vaught, I'm Clemson Fields, CIA. I'm your handler, and you're going to do exactly as you're told until this situation has been resolved to the president's satisfaction. Do you understand?"

"I'll tell you what I understand," Vaught said. "I understand that I haven't seen any credentials *what-so-ever* from Crosswhite here, and *you* could be anybody. So until I see some kind of documentation verifying this CIA bullshit, you're just a voice on the goddamn phone. You copy that, asshole?"

Crosswhite whispered to Paolina, who picked up the child and took her into the bedroom, eyeing Vaught coldly as she passed.

"Very good," Fields said. "The Mexico station chief will arrive tomorrow morning with the proper credentials, at which time you'll be made to understand exactly what is expected of you. I'll warn you in advance: you're not going to like it. You're going to be working with the

PFM—more specifically, with the PFM agent who saved your life, since he's the only one we're reasonably sure you can trust."

"Trust?" Vaught said. "Let me shove a stun gun up *your* ass, and we'll see how much fucking trust you feel."

"Agent Vaught, if you believe nothing else, you'd better believe this: the president, your commander in chief, is highly pissed about your leaving the reservation after allowing Alice Downly to run out into the street and get herself blown in half."

Vaught cringed. "That's not exactly how it happened."

"I've seen the video," Fields said. "So has the president—and that's exactly how it looks to him, I can assure you."

"What video?" Vaught croaked.

"There's always an eye in the sky, Agent Vaught. You should know that by now."

At that moment, Vaught realized Fields was talking about a surveillance drone with stealth technology, and most of the fight left him. "Well, video or not," he said quietly, "nobody who wasn't on the ground can know how it went down. We were taking fifty-caliber sniper fire. You can ask Agent Uriah Heen how bad it was."

"From what I understand, Agent Heen has been recalled to the US. I guess we'll see soon enough what he has to say. In the meantime, is it safe for Crosswhite to set you free, or should he leave you there in your little corner until Agent Ortega arrives in the morning to swear you in?"

Vaught drew a breath and let it back out with sigh. "I won't go anywhere."

"I understand you're interested in pursuing the sniper who killed Alice Downly," Fields went on. "We might be able to work with you on that, but not until you've shown yourself to be a team player. Understood?"

"I don't want my family thinking I'm dead," Vaught said. "You assure me they won't be told that, and I'll do my part down here. Can you agree to that much?"

"I don't see why not," Fields said. "You're from a military family. I'm sure your brothers and parents can be made to understand the importance of secrecy—especially since your life might depend on it. You can give me back to Crosswhite now."

Vaught offered up the phone. "He wants to talk to you."

Crosswhite took the phone. "I'm here."

"I think it's probably safe to set him loose," Fields said. "He sounds sufficiently cowed to me. Have you mentioned the ATRU?"

"It's come up."

"You'd better fill him in all the way. Pope's looked over his service record, and he wants him. The president's already given his approval."

"I'll fill him in."

"All right," Fields said. "I'll be in touch—and I heard the Doctor Doom remark."

"I don't expect to lose much sleep over that." Crosswhite pressed the disconnect button and tossed the phone onto the sofa.

He took the handcuff key from his pocket. "I won't try to stop you from leaving. I've done everything required of me, so if you take off now, it's between you and Bob Pope. He's a vindictive bastard who carries a grudge, and I have no doubt he'd find a way to convince the president to string you up by the balls." He tossed the key to Vaught and went back into the kitchen to start preparing dinner.

Vaught freed himself and stood up, looking at the stun gun on the sofa.

Paolina came back into the room with her daughter, eyeing him suspiciously as she sat back down.

Vaught looked at her, at her unbridled nipples pressing through her T-shirt, wishing he could see her naked just once. "How do you like Mexico compared with Cuba?"

She shrugged. "Probably less than you like looking at my nipples."

His face reddening, he averted his eyes and stood near the corner feeling stupid.

Crosswhite came back into the room chuckling. "Sit wherever you want, Chance." He kissed Paolina on the lips and whispered something in her ear. She looked up at him, and he kissed her again, whispering something else to her.

Paolina was less cold during dinner—not much, but a little.

After dinner, she bathed Valencia and put her down to sleep. Then she joined Crosswhite on the couch in the living room, where Vaught was protesting his circumstances.

". . . but I work for DSS. I'm not CIA, and I sure as hell don't work for the ATRU. I don't care what Pope says."

Crosswhite leaned forward, resting his elbows on his knees. "You don't get it. You've been disowned. You're an embarrassment. DSS doesn't want you anymore. Your career with them is over. Even if they keep you on, you'll never be in charge of another security detail. Hell, an incident like this can even follow you into the private sector. Your entire team was wiped out, man. Whether you want to accept it or not, Pope is doing you a favor."

"Oh, bullshit!"

Crosswhite chuckled. "I didn't say he was doing you a favor out of the kindness of his heart—he doesn't do those kinds of favors. He only does favors for people who are useful to him."

"If I'm such a fuckup, how am I useful?"

"Well, there's different kinds of fuckups," Crosswhite replied. "Some can be rehabilitated. Some can't. Pope's looked you over, and he's seen something he likes. He's asked the president to let him bring you aboard, and the old man's given his consent."

Vaught sat up straight. "Fields told you that?"

Crosswhite nodded. "So you can either get with the program or tell the government to stick it. If you do the latter, you'll never work security for anything more important than a football game. Pope will see to it."

Vaught smirked, seeing the picture. "He sounds like a real prick."

Crosswhite sat back and slid his arm around Paolina, pulling her close and kissing her hair. "I think of him more as a god—kinda like Zeus: indifferent if he has no real use for you, but generous if you excel at his favorite pastime."

"Which is?"

Crosswhite smiled. "War."

7

Gil was in the lodge lounge, drinking a beer and smoking a cigarette, when Blickensderfer's fiancée came striding into the room. She wore a black dinner dress, with her blond hair flowing to the small of her back and a pair of diamond pendant earrings. Her blue eyes piercing, she was tall and stunning and seemed to possess the room the moment she entered. Gil watched her as she crossed to the bar, noting her black heels and the slit of her dress that extended halfway up her thigh.

He knew from the mission dossier that her name was Lena Deiss, a Swiss national, age thirty, and that she came from a wealthy family. A member of the jet set, she valued a man who could accommodate her lavish lifestyle and keep her entertained. In addition to alpine skiing, she enjoyed other adrenaline sports such as skydiving and car racing.

The harshness of her gaze this evening was a change from what Gil had seen over the past few nights around the lodge. She was not her usual happy self. She looked pissed, and Gil guessed that she and Blickensderfer had argued. He didn't care. Blickensderfer wasn't going to be a problem for anyone a whole lot longer.

Lena accepted her cocktail and turned from the bar, making steam straight for his table. He glanced involuntarily over his shoulder, hoping he'd misjudged her heading, but there wasn't anyone seated behind him.

"Shit," he muttered, exhaling as he adjusted his posture to crush out the cigarette in an ashtray on the table.

Lena's look lost its severity as she approached the table and smiled. "I haven't seen you on the slopes all week," she said in perfect English. She sipped from the martini, the color of her crimson lipstick unmistakable at his range. "Yet I've seen you here in the lodge every night."

Clearing his throat, Gil recalled the .308 that had nearly severed her spinal column only hours before. "I keep to the easier runs. I'm more of a novice."

"May I sit down?"

"Sure," he said, feeling himself quicken. He'd been separated from his wife, Marie, for more than a year now and hadn't been with anyone else in all that time.

She reached for his pack of cigarettes, her eyes questioning.

He nodded and picked up the lighter as she poked a cigarette between her lips. He lit it for her with the Zippo, and she sat back, exhaling through tightly pursed lips.

"You're married," she said, a little sad suddenly. "I can tell."

He smiled in spite of himself. "Separated, actually."

"American?"

"Canadian," he said quickly.

She took a drag from the cigarette. "I don't blame you for lying. I imagine you're better received as a Canadian when you travel."

He chuckled. "What makes you think I'm lying?"

A hint of her sternness returned. "I spent a year with a man who served with the British SAS. You have his same restless look, so if you're really Canadian, you must be a soldier—and not just an ordinary one."

Gil realized that Marie would have this same kind of intuition about any Special Forces operative that she would meet, so he decided to meet Lena halfway, taking his Canadian passport from his back pocket and setting it on the table. "I'm retired from the CSOR."

She reached for the passport. "Which is?"

"Canadian Special Operations Regiment."

She opened the passport to read his name. "So I guess that's a point for me then, isn't it, Conner MacLoughlin?"

He took a moment to light a cigarette for himself, tossing the lighter onto the table. "Are we keeping score?"

She was looking him in the eyes. "Would you like to keep score?"

Fuck it, he thought to himself. "Yes, I would. What's your name?"

"I'm Lena." She offered her hand.

The spark of chemistry was instantaneous, and Gil knew he was in trouble. "Where are the men I've seen you with?"

"They're upstairs with their cigars, playing cards." Her annoyance was palpable. "One of them is my fiancé. Does that bother you?"

He took a drag. "Should it?"

She shrugged, tipping an ash into the ashtray. "He's a rich and powerful man—or so many people believe."

"Do you?"

She shrugged again. "Money is power—and he has more than most people can imagine."

Gil took a drink. "You're pissed he left you alone to-night."

She smiled wryly. "But I'm not alone."

"His men carry guns. I'm not lookin' to get shot."

Lena laughed. "Is that something you worry about?"

"Always," he said, shaping the ash against the rim of the ashtray.

Twenty minutes later, they stood naked before each other at the foot of Gil's bed, and Lena was touching the battle scars that covered his muscular torso. "My," she whispered, feeling a warmth between her legs. "The things you must have seen and done."

"You don't wanna know the things I've seen and done." He slid his left hand behind her neck, taking one of her full breasts in his right to give it a firm squeeze, softly thumbing the nipple. She sighed and put her head back as he laid her down on the bed, kissing her lustfully and allowing the animal within him to run free.

As he prepared to mount her, she placed her hands on his chest. "Stop."

He stopped. "Something wrong?"

"I should warn you." She swallowed, her ardor burning. "I should tell you that—that I think you're about to make a very dangerous enemy."

"How so?"

"What I mean is that I think you're about to give me reason to cancel a very expensive wedding."

He laughed and pushed gently inside of her, burying

his face in the golden storm of her hair. She gasped and dug her heels into the small of his back, clawing the flesh of his ass.

"What a fool," she moaned softly.

"Who?" he whispered.

"The one down the hall." She sank her fingers into his hair, nipping at his ear. "The one losing to me in a fucking card game."

8

Agent Mike Ortega of the CIA arrived at ten sharp the next morning. He was a big guy with broad shoulders, dark brown eyes, and a thin mustache. The Mexican American carried himself with an arrogance that annoyed Crosswhite the moment he opened the door. Agent Mendoza, the PFM agent who had saved Vaught's life, stood just behind him, dressed in regular clothes now, his face turned to watch the door to the enclosed carport, his oversize Adam's apple protruding.

"You're Crosswhite?" Ortega asked.

"Right."

Ortega offered his hand. He was one of those guys who felt it necessary to half crush the other guy's hand during a handshake, but he realized at once that Crosswhite's grip was at least as strong as his own. This surprised him, given that Crosswhite stood a head shorter and was built on a lighter frame. "I understand you've already met Agent Mendoza."

"I have." Crosswhite shook his hand as well. *"Bienvenido."* Welcome.

"Is Vaught still here?" Ortega asked.

"In the living room." Crosswhite motioned the two inside.

Vaught stood waiting in the center of the room and shook hands with both men. There was a moment of mild tension between him and Mendoza, but it seemed to pass quickly enough.

"Sorry I couldn't make it over here last night," Ortega said. "This is my first time at bat in this kind of operation, and it's taken some time to get the kinks ironed out. They're still not ironed out completely, but I'm afraid there's going to be a lot of OJT for everyone involved."

Paolina came out of the bedroom with Valencia in her arms, crossing the living room to take a seat on the sofa and set Valencia down beside her.

Ortega watched her for a moment, looking at Crosswhite. "Okay, look, we can't have indigenous personnel sitting in on this conversation, so she's going to have to step out for a while."

Paolina didn't understand what had been said, but she knew from her husband's face that she had been insulted in some way, and she prepared for him to lose his temper.

"First of all," Crosswhite said, "she's not *indigenous*. She's Cuban. And second of all, she's my wife. You got that, asshole?"

Ortega took offense immediately. "Hey, we're all on the same side here, fella."

Crosswhite stared back at him.

Vaught glanced at Paolina, who sat watching passively, almost as though she knew what was about to happen.

"Well, suit yourself," Ortega said, openly annoyed. "If you don't mind endangering her life, I don't see why I should."

Crosswhite struck him with a closed fist just above the right eye to send Ortega reeling backward across the room. The CIA agent stumbled over the recliner and crashed heavily to the floor against the wall.

Vaught and Mendoza looked at each other in shock, eyes wide as Crosswhite stepped between them to stand over the bigger man lying on the floor between the wall and the overturned chair. "Either you apologize right now, or I kill you."

Ortega's impulse was to get up and pound Crosswhite into the floor, but there was a fury in the smaller man's eyes that told him he'd better not even try it. "You're fucking crazy. Do you know that?"

"I'm not gonna tell you again," Crosswhite said. "And you'd better hurry, because Fields is about ten seconds away from needing to find another goddamn station chief."

"Okay, I apologize!" Ortega snapped, rubbing his forehead, where a slight goose egg was already beginning to form. "I meant no offense. I was only trying to protect her."

Vaught glanced again at Paolina, who hadn't taken her eyes off of Crosswhite the entire time.

Crosswhite pointed at the overturned recliner, saying to Ortega, "That's your chair." He turned to Mendoza, calming himself and indicating the far end of the sofa. *"Por favor, siéntese,"* he said easily. *"Nuestra casa es su casa."* Please sit down. Our house is your house.

Mendoza smiled at him, saying, *"Gracias"* and moved to take a seat.

Crosswhite sat down in the center of the sofa between Mendoza and Paolina as Vaught gave Ortega a hand, hauling the big man to his feet and helping to right the overturned recliner.

Vaught turned to Crosswhite. "Can I bring a chair from the kitchen?"

Crosswhite nodded, and Vaught went into the kitchen. Paolina followed him. Vaught returned with a chair made of leather and split tree branches called an *equipal*. Paolina returned a minute later with a plastic bag of ice, which she gave to the embarrassed Ortega.

"*Gracias,*" he said quietly, putting the bag against the swelling over his eye.

"You're welcome," she said in heavily accented English, sitting back down beside Crosswhite and pulling Valencia into her lap.

Crosswhite wasn't the slightest bit apologetic or uncomfortable. Fields had said to him the night before: "It's important that you impress upon Ortega from the start that this is not his operation. It is *my* operation, and nothing less than his one hundred percent cooperation will be acceptable."

Crosswhite felt he had done a fair job of establishing the hierarchy of who shit where in the woods, while at the same time making it clear to everyone present that Paolina wasn't to be regarded as anything less than the lady of the house.

"So where were we?" Ortega said timidly, understanding Crosswhite's utter lack of respect for him must have meant that he was well protected from on high—very probably by Pope himself. He switched to Spanish for Mendoza's benefit, addressing Vaught: "I'm the one who requested the Operational Immediate putting you under the aegis of the CIA."

"Oh, then fuck you very much!" Vaught retorted in English.

Mendoza chuckled, apparently knowing enough English to understand that much.

"I'm sorry," Ortega said, "but I believed then, as I do now, that it's extremely important. Lazaro Serrano is simply too high up in the Mexican government to let this opportunity pass—not to mention, he's very probably the one who ordered the assassination of Alice Downly. If he didn't order it, then he certainly made it possible. What I don't understand, however, is why Langley doesn't want this handled by Mexico station. My people are more than capable of handling the logistics of such an op and providing you a safe place to stay."

Vaught cleared his throat, glancing at Crosswhite. "Well, my new friend here has already explained the reasoning behind that—at least he has to me."

Ortega wasn't interested in making eye contact with Crosswhite. "Then Mr. Crosswhite is privy to information that hasn't been made available to me." Crosswhite offered no explanation because Ortega wasn't cleared to know about the ATRU. Ortega turned his gaze on Mendoza. "Agent Mendoza?"

Mendoza leaned forward, pressing his palms together. "The PFM agrees this is very, very important," he began in Spanish. "We've suspected Serrano for some time, but there's never been any evidence against him before now." He looked up at Vaught. "The PFM is pleased with what you've done. You've helped to shed light on the corruption inside the Federal Police, and you've given us our first real evidence against Lazaro Serrano."

Vaught always knew when his balls were being buttered. "Yesterday you were pissed I'd blown your cover. What's changed?"

Mendoza sat back. "My point of view. Yesterday I had just killed five men. I had never killed anyone before, and

I was very affected by it. The true purpose of a deep-cover operation is to obtain information, to obtain evidence, and had you not taken action yesterday, I never would have been in a position to witness Serrano order a murder with my own eyes. That action alone proves he is far more than complicit—he is an actual decision maker within the cartels. This is very significant information. Also, if not for you, I would not have been there to confirm the existence of the gringo sniper. Until now, this man has only been a ghost—always rumored, never seen. So today it is obvious to me and to my superiors that you have done Mexico a service.

"Now we must plan together how best to use this information to our mutual advantage. It is true we can arrest Serrano for ordering your murder, but he has powerful allies, and our word might not be enough to gain a conviction on this charge alone. Our court system does not work the same as in the US—there are no juries, for example—so it would be best to draw Serrano into a trap; to find a way for the PFM to catch him in the act of conspiring with known cartel members."

"And exactly how do you plan on doing that?" Vaught asked.

"Right now we have two distinct advantages," Mendoza went on. "One, he has no idea that we now know for certain what he is. Two, he thinks you're dead. Tomorrow the PFM will announce that your body was found in a building along with the bodies of five known cartel members. No one will be sure of exactly what happened because a grenade blast will have left the crime scene impossible to decipher. This will put you out of Serrano's mind. Then, when the time is right, after he has forgotten all about you, you can magically reappear—but only at a moment when he has begun to feel vulnerable in other ways. The idea is to scare him into making a mistake."

"So you're planning to apply pressure in the meantime," Crosswhite said.

Mendoza grinned. "Yes. Pressure creates stress, and men under stress are prone to making mistakes at crucial moments. Up until this point, Serrano has lived a stress-free existence, with little more to worry about than which woman to take to bed on a given night. With your help, Agent Vaught, we're going to change that."

"And the gringo sniper?" Vaught asked.

Mendoza turned to look at Crosswhite, saying in slightly accented English, "I understand you've had some experience in this area, Agent Crosswhite. Or is my information incorrect?"

Crosswhite looked around the room, chuckling under the collective gaze. "Well, hey, I'm just here to provide the beer on this one. I'm not going operational."

Paolina was staring hard at Mendoza, her eyes like brown bullets.

"Yes," Mendoza continued, switching back to Spanish, "I understand, but the PFM would very much appreciate your help in this operation. We feel it's time you gave something back to Mexico in exchange for the unfettered privacy you have enjoyed as a guest in our country."

Crosswhite glanced at Paolina, who now looked like she wanted to claw out Mendoza's eyeballs. Then he looked back at the PFM agent and laughed. "Yeah, okay, sure. I'd love a chance to give back."

"Excellent," Mendoza said, rubbing his palms on his knees. "Mexico is grateful for your generosity."

Vaught snickered, leaning across the coffee table to offer Crosswhite his hand. "Welcome to the team, *champ*."

Paolina jerked the stun gun from between the sofa

cushions and leaped over the table after him. Crosswhite grabbed her around the waist as Vaught shoved himself over backward in the *equipal*, only narrowly avoiding the outstretched weapon, its cruel blue arc of electricity snapping and crackling in the air as Crosswhite swung her around with a *"Whoa!"* and lifted her off the floor, setting her down safely on the far side of the room and blocking her path. "Easy, baby."

9

The next morning, Lazaro Serrano was eating breakfast on the patio behind his expansive home. A young woman in a green-and-red bikini swam in the pool, pushing around a Chihuahua on a small rubber raft. The little dog was barking at her and wagging its tail, and she was laughing and calling for Serrano to look. He smiled and waved and went on eating. He was fifty years old with a belly and thinning hair, bushy eyebrows, and a thick black mustache.

Oscar Martinez, his chief assistant and confidant, came onto the patio with the morning edition of *El Universal* and sat down across from Serrano; one of the servants had already set a place for him. He was a slender man in his midforties, with a head of thick, dark hair and a boyish face that easily shaved ten years off his age. "The body of the American DSS agent has been found," he said, sipping from a porcelain coffee cup.

Serrano looked up from his breakfast with a measure of surprise. "So soon? What did those fools do with it?"

Oscar rubbed his hands together before reaching to put a spoonful of sugar into the coffee. "Well, it seems they did not do anything with it. The body was found in the same building where you last saw him, along with the bodies of six of Ruvalcaba's people." Hector Ruvalcaba was a powerful narcotics trafficker—a *narcotraficante*, also referred to as a *narco*. The year before, with Serrano's help, Ruvalcaba had escaped from a maximum security prison via a three-quarter-mile-long tunnel dug from beyond the facility's walls to directly beneath his cell. Serrano had since helped him take over the southern narcotics trade, leaving Antonio Castañeda as his only competitor. Castañeda controlled the North. "They were all killed by a grenade blast. It seems to have been accidental."

Serrano went back to eating. "One of those idiots must have dropped it and blown them all up." He shook his head in disgust. "Why am I surrounded by fools, Oscar? Tell me that."

Oscar smiled and sipped his coffee. "I do not know."

"You're sure the American is dead?"

The younger man set the cup down on the saucer, wiping his mouth with a linen napkin. "Yes," he said, clearing his throat. "His name was Chance Vaught, a US Army veteran."

"Are you sure it's the same man? The agent I saw on the floor was Hispanic."

Oscar nodded confidently. "Yes, it's him. His father is a gringo, but his mother is Mexican. They're shipping the remains back to the United States this week."

"Good," Serrano said, taking a sip of freshly made orange-carrot juice. "We don't need him stinking up Mexican soil." He sat back with a smile and wiped his mouth. "Be sure to send my condolences to the Vaught family through the American Embassy. It's important to maintain good relations with our neighbors."

"I will," Oscar said. "I've already sent them to the embassy itself. Should we expect problems concerning the three federal policemen that Vaught killed?" He tapped the edition of *El Universal*. "They're on the front page today."

Serrano shrugged, picking up his knife and fork. "That's Captain Espinosa's problem." Espinosa was the Federale captain who had turned Vaught over to the detectives working for Ruvalcaba. "He's got people inside the city police. He's a true professional, that one, a man I can count on—like you."

A thin smile spread across Oscar's lips, and he wondered for perhaps the thousandth time what would happen if Serrano ever found out he was gay. *I'd probably disappear too*, he told himself, making a mental note to increase his vigilance.

"Will the project in Toluca still be going forward?" he asked. Serrano and Ruvalcaba had been trying to turn the town, located southwest of Mexico City, into a trafficking hub for the past six months.

"Yes, of course," Serrano said, cutting off a piece of steak. "Why wouldn't it be?"

"Well, I thought you might want to postpone it because of all that's happened here."

Serrano stabbed his fork into the piece of meat and pointed at Oscar with it. "I'll tell you this, Oscar. That chief of police in Toluca is a brave man; a true Mexican with very large *huevos*, but he is another fool. Why can't he see which way things are going in this country and go with them? Because I tell you this, my friend, sooner or later, those stupid gringos in the North are going to see there is no way to win this useless war. Then marijuana will become legal, and all of this"—he waved his free hand at the *estancia*—"all of this money, it goes away. This kind of business cannot last forever. So why doesn't this policeman in Toluca accept Ruvalcaba's offer now to secure himself a future? Why does he throw his life away so uselessly? I will tell you why: it is because he is a fool. A brave fool, but a fool."

He poked the meat into his mouth and chewed as he spoke. "We all want a stronger Mexico. Me more than anyone. I am a true patriot, a man of my country. But this strength cannot come without money. And am I not generous with my money? Do I not give back to the people? This idiot policeman could do the same"— Serrano stabbed a finger against the side of his head in frustration—"but he is too stubborn to listen! No, *this brave man*, he is going to rebuild the country all by himself, like Pancho Villa reborn. Well, Pancho Villa was gunned down in the dirt like a dog, my friend, and this Toluca man is no better than him."

"Lazaro!" the young woman called from the pool. "When are you coming to swim, my love?"

He smiled and held out his hands. "Later, *mi amor!*" He turned to look at Oscar. "Do you see? I am not even finished eating, and she wants me to go in swimming already. Like I have no other responsibilities besides swimming with a dog that pisses in my pool." He shook his head and went back to cutting his steak. "Fools, Oscar. I am surrounded by fools."

10

Gil was still asleep in bed when he heard a knock at the door. He sat up and took a Parkerized subcompact Springfield .45 pistol from the nightstand drawer, glancing at the clock. Lena hadn't left until well after six in the morning.

He slipped naked from the bed and went to have a look through the peephole. Seeing Lena, he unlocked the door. She came into the room with an orange backpack slung over one shoulder. The gun in his hand didn't seem to frighten her at all.

"Did you get some sleep?" she asked, kissing his cheek and crossing the room to toss the backpack onto a love seat.

"Yeah, look," he said, scratching his head. "I'm not exactly who you think—"

"Of course you're not," she interrupted. "If you were, I wouldn't have just canceled a wedding that was supposed to take place ten days from now."

He set the pistol down on the table. "Lena, I'm not sure—"

"You don't need to be. *I'm* sure."

"But I'm not lookin' to—"

"Neither am I," she said with a laugh. "You still love your wife. That's obvious. What I want is adventure. I'd almost forgotten what that was, being with Sabastian. You reminded me last night. I'm not really sure what I was thinking when I agreed to marry him."

He grabbed his pants and stepped into them. "First of all, I can't give you the kind of adventure you're looking for. I don't have that kind of money."

"I've got my own money, Conner."

"*Conner's* not my even my name," he said with a sigh.

She took his pack of cigarettes from the nightstand. "Then what is it?"

"I'm sorry," he said. "I can't tell you. I can't even tell you what I'm doing in Liechtenstein."

She lit the cigarette with a chuckle, dropping the lighter onto the nightstand. "And you say you can't give me adventure."

"Look, this isn't a game."

"All life is a game."

He shook his head, regretting his weakness the night before. "People get killed in the games I play."

She sat down on the bed. "People get killed jumping out of airplanes—yet that's my favorite sport." She gestured at the gun. "And I assume that's yours?"

He picked up his shirt from the floor. "Where's Sabastian?"

"Headed for the airport."

"He's pissed? Heartbroken?"

She looked thoughtful for a moment. "I'd say he's *offended*. Men like Sabastian don't get their hearts broken.

He'll have another woman like me by the end of the week—maybe not one as wealthy."

"Last night you said I'd make an enemy."

"And you have—but I gave you fair warning in that regard. Do you want to spend more time with me or not? Because now *I'm* beginning to get offended."

He grinned. "Well, we wouldn't want that."

They agreed to meet in the lounge after Gil had showered and made some calls. In the meantime, Lena would schedule a flight for the two of them to Switzerland.

Gil got Pope on the phone and told him the truth about what had happened between him and Lena.

"All right," Pope said. "These things happen. You can finish the job in Switzerland. I'll figure out a way for it to look like a Mossad hit. Blickensderfer is on their list too." The Mossad was Israel's version of the CIA.

"Bob, no. I've blown this op. I can't sleep with a guy's girl and then kill him."

There was a long silence at the other end of the phone.

"You there?"

"Yeah," Pope replied. "I'm trying to understand what you just said. You're telling me you can't kill a man if you've slept with his woman. What does one have to do with the other?"

"I guess it's personal now." Gil didn't know how else to explain it.

"I've got news for you," Pope replied somewhat coldly. "If Blickensderfer ever finds out who you are, this will become a great deal *more* personal."

"I've blown this one, Bob. I'm sorry. It won't ever happen again, but I can't move on Blickensderfer now. I've crossed a line. I've told you before I wasn't trained for this James Bond shit."

"Well, if you can't do it, you can't do it," Pope said,

warmer suddenly. "You're entitled to a mistake. You're also entitled to a vacation. You've been operational for almost two years without a break. We'll discuss things after you've had a couple months off. How's that?"

"Okay," Gil said. He'd known Pope long enough to understand that the director likely wasn't happy with this outcome, but hopefully he wouldn't hold it over his head for too long.

"Sounds good. Have you checked on Crosswhite and Paolina?"

Pope was silent again.

"Did I lose you?"

"No, I'm here," Pope said. "They're both fine, but Crosswhite's operational. A US diplomatic convoy was just ambushed in Mexico City. It was a cartel hit, and all of our diplomats were wiped out—most of the DSS team as well."

"You know Paolina's pregnant."

"I do, but I need him—and he owes me."

Gil didn't entirely agree with that, but this was not the time to argue the point. "How deep does he have to get involved?"

"That remains to be seen," Pope said. "There's an ex–US Army sniper doing hits for the cartels, and it looks like he's the one who pulled the trigger on our people. He used a fifty cal."

Gil was immediately pissed that one of his own had turned bad. "Do you have a name?"

"Not yet."

"Get me a name and a face to go with it. Then get me in-country so I can punch the fucker's ticket."

"We'll have to see how things develop," Pope said quietly. "I'm not sure Mexico is the place for you. You don't speak the language, and Crosswhite's a big boy."

"He's got vulnerabilities, Bob: a pregnant woman and a little girl to worry about."

"What did you expect, Gil? That I would pay him and not use him?"

Gil let out an impatient sigh. "All I'm asking is that you consider his circumstance."

"I have," Pope said. "It's the circumstance he's put himself into. Crosswhite doesn't use his head when it comes to women. He never has. Be careful you don't start falling prey to the same lack of judgment."

Gil was annoyed when they got off the phone, but he reminded himself that so far Pope had always played him straight and that he owed the man a lot.

He was coming from the shower when the door to his room burst open, and three burly men covered in tattoos bum-rushed him, tackling him onto the bed and raining down punches. The blows landed like sledgehammers against the side of his head, and he went unconscious.

When Gil came around, he was duct-taped naked to a chair, and his mouth was taped shut. Four ugly men sat around the room staring at him with vacant expressions. Blood was leaking into his left eye, and his head throbbed. At first he thought they were Blickensderfer's people—which would have been bad enough—but then he took a closer look at their tattoos.

They were Bratva—the Brotherhood. Russian Mafia.

This is it, he told himself. *And it's gonna be ugly.* He closed his eyes for a moment, just long enough to say good-bye to Marie and to promise himself that he'd go out with as much dignity as possible—but he didn't have much in the way of confidence. These men were professionals at taking away a man's humanity.

11

The gringo sniper's name was Rhett Hancock, and he was no longer the innocent, towheaded little boy his mother had taken to church on Sundays. He was now afflicted with a sickness—a brutal sickness that went well beyond the posttraumatic stress of war. Something inside of him had long snapped, and he knew it. He was addicted to riding the meteor of pure adrenaline, and he simply could not get enough of it.

Today he was in a cantina on the outskirts of Acapulco, a once-thriving vacation destination that had recently been all but eliminated from the world's tourism brochures due to ever-increasing drug violence in the region. Hancock was thirty-five, a former US Ranger and a veteran of both the Iraq and Afghan wars, with twenty enemy kills to his credit. Diagnosed with severe posttraumatic stress shortly after the end of his fifth tour, he was honorably discharged from the US Army against his wishes and offered a meager disability pension on his way out the door. With his army career in ruins and no other marketable skills, Hancock had immediately jetted off to Latin America in search of mercenary work.

First he had sought to offer his skills to the Autodefensas Unidas de Colombia through a Colombian national he had met in the army. The AUC, or, in English, the United Self-Defense Forces of Colombia, was a paramilitary organization formed in 1997 to fight left-wing insurgents seeking to take political control of various regions within the cocaine-producing country. By 2008, however, the AUC had been labeled a terrorist organization and was broken up by the Colombian government with the help of the US military. So Hancock had turned to the Mexican cartels.

An intermediary had introduced him to Hector Ruvalcaba, and the meeting had gone well. Hancock was impressed with the paramilitary infrastructure of the Ruvalcaba cartel, and Ruvalcaba offered him a lucrative one-year contract that same day. It wasn't until after he'd assassinated two different competing cartel bosses, however, that he finally learned of Lazaro Serrano's existence. And once he'd met with Serrano himself, Hancock understood that *this* was the man who actually pulled the strings of the Ruvalcaba cartel.

Hancock sat in the far back corner of the dimly lit cantina with a half empty bottle of Jose Cuervo tequila and a shot glass resting before him on the roughly hewn tabletop. He was dressed in jeans and combat boots, a black Under Armour compression T-shirt, and a black cowboy hat. Billy Jessup walked up to the table and sat down with a bottle of Estrella beer. Jessup was not a Latino, but his mother was 100 percent Lakota Sioux, so his features were similar to those of many Mexican people, and he did not stick out among them, being generally regarded as Mexican himself until he opened his mouth to demonstrate his terrible Spanish. He was Hancock's spotter and intelligence collator, keeping in contact with Serrano's number two man, Oscar Martinez. He and Hancock had met in the army during the war.

"I've got some troubling intel," he said, tossing a manila envelope onto the table and rocking back in his chair, with the beer resting on his Texas longhorn belt buckle.

The gringo sniper stared at him with his lifeless blue eyes, downing another shot of tequila. "Troubling how?"

Jessup took a drink. "Have a look."

Hancock opened the envelope and removed a photo of another gringo with dark hair. The man was standing on a street corner with one arm around a pretty little Latina with long black hair, and a small child under his other arm. Hancock put down the photo. "So who the fuck is he?"

"His name's Daniel Crosswhite, a Green Beret who served in Afghanistan. Oscar's contact inside CISEN says the PFM went to visit the dude three days ago in Mexico City. The contact doesn't know why they went to see him, but it was the day after your hit on Alice Downly." CISEN was Mexico's version of the CIA.

The half-drunk Hancock sat nodding his head. "I got an idea. Why don't you ask that faggot Oscar why Serrano doesn't have a guy inside the PFM? If he did, then maybe we'd *know* why they went to visit this motherfucker. Isn't a spy inside the Mexican CIA pretty much fucking useless unless you're fighting the fucking Russians or something?"

Jessup took another pull from his beer. "Serrano's been trying to get a guy inside the PFM for two years, but that agency's locked up tight. Hell, most PFM agents use false names, so there's no way anybody can even get at their families."

Hancock lifted the tequila bottle by the neck, thumping the bottom of it against the photo. "So why bring me this?" He poured himself another shot and set the bottle aside. "Who gives a fuck about some gringo and his Mexi-whore?"

"You don't think it's a heavy coincidence for the PFM to visit an ex–Green Beret living in Mexico City the day after you assassinate an American official?"

Hancock chuckled. "Maybe he's a suspect."

Jessup sat forward to put the legs of the chair back on the floor. "Would you still think it was funny if this Crosswhite was ex–Delta Force and a Medal of Honor winner?"

The gringo sniper sobered up very quickly. "How the fuck could the PFM know a gringo did the hit on Downly?"

Jessup shrugged. "Rumors about a gringo sniper are all over the place down here. Maybe somebody's finally started taking them seriously. Maybe this guy is some kind of a hunter. Who knows?" He tapped the photo with his index finger. "But I'm telling you: this shit right here ain't no goddamn coincidence. It's got something to do with you."

Hancock elbowed aside the tequila bottle and leaned into the table, a faint spark showing behind his eyes. "Then I'll go to DF and kill the fucker."

Jessup shook his head. "Don't be stupid. There's no way you can go anywhere near Mexico City now. Besides, we've got the Guerrero hit coming up in Toluca. Serrano is serious about making an example of him."

Hancock poured himself another shot. "I've got something special in mind for Guerrero—something fun." He downed the shot. "Why bring me the intel on this Delta pussy if you're not gonna let me hit him?"

"To show you things are getting dangerous for us down here."

Hancock looked at him. "You expect me to run?"

"No, Rhett. I don't expect you to do anything. That's why the Ruvalcabas are gonna make Crosswhite disappear for us."

12

Another man, well dressed in a black suit, came into Gil's hotel room carrying a black leather valise. He was blond with a merciless gaze and fewer tattoos than the other men. He dropped the valise onto the bed and sat down across from Gil with a mirthless smile.

"You are in some big trouble," he said in accented English.

Gil nodded, resigned to his fate.

"You killed many of my men in Istanbul," the Russian went on. "You stole my whores and took them back to Moscow. You made me look like a fool in front of very important people."

Gil stared back at him.

"You don't recognize me, do you?"

Gil shook his head.

The Russian held up his middle finger. "You made this

gesture to me at the airport in Istanbul. Do you remember me now?"

Gil did not remember the man's face, but he remembered giving a pair of Russians the finger at the airport the night that he and a Russian Spetsnaz operative had freed more than a dozen kidnapped Russian women who'd been forced into prostitution. He shrugged, and then he nodded.

"Good," the Russian said. "Because I want you to remember that it was *you* who made this personal—not me."

Oddly enough, Gil saw his point.

The Russian opened the valise and took out a pair of common pliers. "I will use these to crush your testicles." He set them aside and took out a pair of jagged pinking shears. "These I will use to remove your scrotum—which I will feed to you after I break out your teeth. Your penis I will tear off by hand."

Gil felt himself beginning to sweat. At least the Afghanis just chopped off your head and left it at that. But like the man said, Gil had made it personal.

Note to self, he thought, snorting in spite of his growing fear.

"Something is funny?" the Russian asked, vaguely amused.

Gil shrugged.

The Russian told a particularly heavily tattooed man in their own language to take the tape from Gil's mouth.

The man arched a dark eyebrow. "What if he screams?"

"Then I will crush his windpipe. Do as I say."

The tattooed man stepped over and ripped the tape from Gil's face.

Gil pursed his burning lips and sat looking at the men.

"You're not going to scream?" the Russian asked.

Gil was resolute. "Trust me. I'd scream like a little girl! if I thought it would do me any good."

The Russian nodded. "What was funny?"

"I just made a mental note not to let shit get personal in the future." He smirked. "It still sounds kinda funny."

The Russian grinned. "It won't sound funny for very long."

"Maybe we should get started then," Gil said grimly, sweat running down from his armpits. "I got someplace I gotta be."

The Russian gestured, and the heavily tattooed man pressed the tape back over Gil's mouth. A second later, there came a knock at the door. Gil jerked around in the chair, but one of the Russians was fast to put a knife to his throat.

Everyone sat still.

A few moments later, there was another knock.

Someone stole a peek through the peephole, and then came back and whispered to the Russian that it was the Swiss banker's woman.

The Russian looked shocked. "What the hell is *she* doing here?"

The other man shrugged.

Gil knew it had to be Lena.

"What do we do?" the heavily tattooed man asked.

"Shit," the Russian muttered, wiping his mouth. "Let her in."

The other man opened the door, and Lena came into the room. Her eyes grew wide when she saw Gil taped to the chair, naked and bleeding from a gash over his eye.

She wheeled on the Russian, hissing in English: "What the fuck are you doing?"

"This man is CIA," the Russian said. "He—"

"Of *course* he's CIA, you stupid fool! Where do you think Sabastian gets his intelligence? From barbarians like you? Let him loose from that chair—now!"

The Russian gestured lamely at Gil. "He—"

"He *what?*" she demanded, putting her hands on her hips.

The Russian was about to tell her that Gil had stolen thirteen of his sex slaves six months earlier, but he suddenly realized that Sabastian Blickensderfer—a billionaire weapons dealer—couldn't care less about such things. "I didn't know he was here with Blickensderfer."

"You'd better get your men out of here." She moved toward Gil's chair. "I have to get this man cleaned up before Sabastian finds out what you've done to him. He's supposed to be under Sabastian's protection! How do you think this makes my man look in front of the CIA?"

Browbeaten, the Russian gestured for his men to leave the room. "We had no idea."

"Fine. Just go." She began stripping the tape from one of Gil's wrists. "Get out!"

The Russians left, taking the black valise with them, and she quickly freed Gil's wrists and ankles.

He peeled the tape from his mouth and got to his feet. "What are you doing?"

"Saving your life, obviously." She grabbed his pants from the floor. "Hurry and get dressed. The second Sabastian finds out about this, they'll be back."

He began to get dressed. "They work for Sabastian?"

"They're regular customers." She handed him his shirt. "They buy guns. I didn't know they were here until I saw them down in the lobby, but I knew they weren't here to see Sabastian, so that left only you—*because they sure as hell don't ski.*"

He put on his shoes, grabbed the Springfield from the dresser, and slipped it beneath his jacket.

"So you're CIA," she said, looking at him, a half smile on her face.

"Kinda." He moved toward the door. "How soon before they talk to Sabastian?"

"About this? Hopefully never. But I guess that depends on what you did to make them mad."

Gil recalled that, in addition to flipping the Russian the bird at the airport, he had also mouthed the words *Fuck you*, making it even more personal. "I'm guessing it probably won't be too long."

13

Without telling anyone other than Paolina where he was going, Crosswhite hopped an early Volaris airline flight to the city of Guadalajara, northwest of Mexico City, to meet with a CIA/ATRU agent he trusted. Agent Mariana Mederos had agreed to meet him in the American retirement community of Ajijic near Lake Chapala, where Crosswhite wouldn't look out of place. Chapala was the largest freshwater lake in the country; dozens of launches were tied up along a concrete pier that tourists could hire to take them for rides along the shoreline.

Crosswhite had worked with Mariana in both Mexico and Cuba the previous spring, eliminating two key traitors to the US government who had attempted to assassinate both CIA Director Robert Pope and Crosswhite's best friend, Gil Shannon.

They met in a restaurant overlooking the lake. "Thanks for coming down," he said.

"It's no trouble." Mariana was a Mexican American in her early thirties, with dark hair that she usually wore in a ponytail. "Pope's got me based out of Austin now. He wanted me in position to help you if anything happened down here. I swear that man has a sixth sense. He told me last week that Downly coming down here was a bad idea."

Crosswhite signaled the waiter. "I joke about Pope having superpowers too but he's just a man—a man with a helluva lot of information at his disposal and a brain big enough to make sense of it."

She chuckled. "Sounds like a superpower to me."

"Touché."

They placed their orders with the waitress.

"How's Paolina?"

He smiled. "Three months pregnant."

She sat back, a little stunned, a little envious. Crosswhite was so much different from the last time she'd seen him. Calmer somehow. He had saved her life in Havana, and she'd kept a special place in her heart for him since then—which was odd, because she couldn't stand him when they'd first met. "Congratulations," she said quietly.

"Thank you," he said, knowing that Mariana had initially disapproved of him marrying a former prostitute.

"Aren't you afraid of starting a family, considering the work you do?"

He stared across the lake. "It's not something I think about. Life's too short."

"And it can turn on a dime," she warned. "We both know that."

He looked at her, recalling her rape in Havana; how

she'd nearly been killed and how he'd beaten both of her assailants to death. "How are you?"

"I'm okay," she said truthfully. "I have days that are tough, but the work helps, and I've got a good therapist."

"Are you seeing anyone?"

She nodded. "He's a nice guy—a lawyer. He has no idea what I really do for a living, so I'm not sure how long it will last. I don't make a very good liar."

Crosswhite took a pensive drag from a cigarette. "One day at a time."

She was squeezing a wedge of lime into her beer. "So exactly what the hell is going on down here?"

"I've been shanghaied by the PFM."

"Because of the Downly assassination?"

He nodded. "You heard they reported Chance Vaught dead this morning?"

"Yeah, Pope gave me the heads-up."

"Well, he's been shanghaied along with me as a witness against Serrano—which Pope must already know as well—but I'm not sure he knows there's an American GI running down here doing hits for the Ruvalcabas. A Ranger sniper. He's the one who blew Downly away."

The latter came as a surprise to Mariana. "Have you told Fields?"

"Fields knows, but I don't know how much intel he's kicking upstairs to Pope. He told me over the phone this was *his* operation. I don't like the sound of that, so I want you in the loop."

"That's fine with me, but Fields might not like it."

"Fuck Fields. He's a spook. I understand why Pope is using him, but I don't trust the guy."

"But if Pope trusts him, doesn't that sort of—"

"Sort of what?" He watched her eyes. "Do you assume we can trust Pope?"

She sat up straight. "Since when don't *you* trust him?"

He shrugged, his wary eyes scanning the passersby. "Let's say I've learned a few things about him. Nothing to doubt his patriotism, but it's still the last refuge of a scoundrel."

Her face twisted into a sardonic smile. "Remember what you told me last spring? You said this is the business that we're in, and if I couldn't live with it, to find something else to do."

"And I stand by that. All I'm saying is that Pope's trust in Clemson Fields shouldn't automatically translate into *our* trust in Clemson Fields."

"Fair enough," she conceded. "Should I mention your doubts about Fields to Pope or keep them to myself?"

"Pope's sharp enough to read between the lines. Besides, we're not going to change his mind about anything. He's already a dozen moves ahead of us, and he's going to do whatever the hell he wants."

"You do realize," she remarked, "that he's probably the single most powerful man in Washington now—after the president."

Crosswhite exhaled smoke through his nose. "And Congress loves him. After saving San Diego from the nuke last year and surviving two assassination attempts in the same week, they see him as the hero-protector."

She sat chewing her lip, lost in thought. "Damn, why do I feel like we're sitting here speaking treason against Caesar?"

He smiled. "Are we? Is Pope like Caesar now? I don't know."

"Well, the ATRU *is* slowly becoming his own private army, isn't it?"

"You don't know the half of it."

She stared. "What don't I know?"

After a moment's hesitation, he told her about the gold bullion and Pope's plan for the money. "He's hitting whoever the hell he wants—based on his own judgement—and he's hiring free agents off the books; pipe hitters from all over the world."

She sat back and took a sip of beer. "Men like you and Gil?"

He nodded. "And Chance Vaught has just been added to the list. Little by little, Pope is putting together a lethal team—a team of assassins; let's be honest. And I have no idea how many other cells there are. Or will be."

"Will the president stand for it?" Mariana wondered, but seeing Crosswhite's frown, she checked herself immediately. "Forget I asked that. The president's never going to know what the ATRU is really being used for or how many men are being recruited."

"Or women." He gave her a wink. "Don't forget, honey, you helped me remove two of Pope's enemies from the board. So *our* little cell already has four assassins—not three."

"My God," she muttered. "He really has become like Caesar. What does Gil think?"

Crosswhite shrugged, watching off across the lake again. "Therein lies the problem."

"Gil believes in him, doesn't he?"

"With every breath he breathes."

"So what's going on with the PFM?" she asked, changing the subject. "Why are the Mexicans so keen to use you?"

"Because of Lazaro Serrano," he said. "Serrano's probably going to be PRI's candidate for president next year, and if he is, he'll probably win because PRI wins ninety percent of the time down here. If that happens, the cartels are gonna take over this country, and the border war is gonna explode."

PRI stood for Partido Revolucionario Institucional—Institutional Revolutionary Party—and it had been Mexico's most powerful political party over the last thirty years. The PRI was purportedly the more liberal wing of the Mexican government, with PAN supposedly the more conservative, but the two were not as clearly defined as the political parties in the United States were, and, in reality, there was hardly any daylight between them. PAN stood for Partido Acción Nacional, or National Action Party.

"Is that what Serrano wants? More trouble on the border?"

"Serrano hates the US, so anything that makes trouble on the border is okay with him, but what he *wants* is money."

"Did the PFM tell you this?"

He shook his head. "No. There's something Pope doesn't know. I've been involved in the internal politics down here for a few months now—before this Downly shit kicked off."

That worried her. "What are you up to?" she asked quietly.

"I'm acting as a military advisor to a police chief down in Toluca who's been fighting his own private war against the Ruvalcaba cartel. It's what I was trained for."

She gaped at him. "Are you crazy? You've got a wife and baby to worry about."

"I know," he said. "I know, but I couldn't sit around with nothing to do, and the guy needed help, so I've been spending time down in Toluca training his cops to fight—with American tactics."

"You'd better hope Serrano never finds out about *that*."

Crosswhite flicked the ash from the end of his cigarette. "If that fat bastard can hire American mercenaries, why can't the people who actually give a shit about this country?"

She glanced around. "How much are you being paid?"

He laughed. *"Ni un peso."* Not a dime.

Her surprise was evident. "You're shitting me."

"Nope." He pulled from his beer and set the bottle down on the table. "I took the job for the love of the game."

"I think you took it for more than that," Mariana said, seeing through him.

14

Chief Juan Guerrero was thirty-six. He had been appointed chief of police in the city of Toluca after his predecessor was finally arrested for corruption the previous fall. Guerrero's first promise was to clean up the department and restore law and order to the city. He had fired and replaced half the police force by Christmas and succeeded in arresting dozens of members of the ruthless Ruvalcaba cartel, driving the *narcotraficantes* off the streets and back into the shadows where they belonged. By the beginning of the new year, crime in Toluca had been cut dramatically, and citizens were beginning to feel safe again walking the avenues after dark.

Guerrero did not delude himself about being a target. Men were out to kill him, and he accepted this with peaceful resignation, knowing that sooner or later an assassin would find a way through his security. He did have a slight advantage over most government officials who attempted to fight corruption: a distinct lack of familial vulnerabilities, with only his younger brother, Diego, to worry about. The two of them had grown up in the seminary, believing as boys that they would one day be ordained as priests. Their discovery of women during their teenage years had altered those intentions, but the Guerrero brothers remained close to the Church all of their lives, believing fully in the blood of Christ and that they had been placed on the earth to serve mankind.

They'd found their true calling as policemen, and had managed to serve throughout their careers without ever taking a single bribe, always watching each other's back whenever fellow police officers tried pressuring them into corruption. They had faith in Mexico and its future.

Juan Guerrero believed his life was in the hands of God, and that God alone would decide his fate. If he were to fall, it would happen through His will, and Guerrero's own example would leave a lasting impression on the youth of Mexico. He was not pride-filled in his faith, though he did believe that a man could aspire to a great deal less in the world before being called home to sit humbly in the shadow of the Holy Father.

Today was the first communion of his goddaughter, Nayeli, and he was seated in the front row of the church, dressed in his uniform and smiling proudly as the priest spoke over the precious eleven-year-old girl who sat before him in a chair, her back to the congregation. She looked simply resplendent in her white dress, with her raven hair coiled so carefully and beautifully about her head as she prepared to receive the body of Christ for the first time.

Nayeli was the closest Juan Guerrero would ever

come to having a daughter, and he was every bit as proud of her as her own father was. This was an important day in the life of a Mexican girl, as she prepared to enter the world of womanhood, and it was important to him that she be treated as the princess he believed her to be in his own private heart. This was why he had humbly petitioned her parents, who were relatively poor, to accept his financial gift and throw a big party for her and her many cousins.

With the ceremony drawing toward its conclusion, Juan Guerrero stood beside Nayeli as she received the sacrament, and his heart swelled with the knowledge that her life would be forever different from this moment on; that she was a woman now in the eyes of the Holy Father. He received the sacrament himself a few moments later and was unexpectedly struck by a vision of himself as the priest he had never become. For a brief instant in time, it was as though he stood outside of his own body to see himself wearing the vestments and offering the Holy Communion.

He had never believed in visions before, but the suddenness of this daydream—the very vividness of the moment, was undeniable, and he was overcome by the most fulfilling sense of peace he had ever known, like warm water poured from a holy chalice. He looked toward the great door of the church to see beyond it a bright and beautiful day bathed in the rays of the sun. And he knew with absolute certainly that his Calvary awaited him beyond the threshold.

He shook hands with the priest and Nayeli's parents, congratulating them on their daughter's achievement. Then he touched her hair and smiled, leaning to kiss her on the cheek and whispering into her ear that only God was greater than herself. She smiled bashfully and thanked him. His brother appeared at his side a few moments later with two other policemen, all of them dressed in their class-A uniforms for the occasion.

"The car is ready out back," said Diego Guerrero.

Juan Guerrero smiled at his brother. "Isn't she the most beautiful child on earth?"

His brother smiled back. "They're all beautiful, brother."

The chief of police shook his head. "Not like her. I wish I did not have to miss the party."

"We agreed it was safer for the family if you didn't go," Diego said. "You're not changing your mind, are you?"

Juan Guerrero shook his head. "No. No, of course not. I'm just going to miss her, is all."

Diego chuckled and patted his brother on the shoulder. "She's not growing up that fast, brother."

"No," said Juan Guerrero. "I know that. Let us go out the front with the family. It is such a beautiful day."

Diego looked at him, seeing a serenity in his brother's eyes that he had never seen there before. "What is it, Juan?"

"Do you remember when we were young?" Juan reflected. "When I first told you that I had decided not to become a priest? We were standing barefoot in the mud along the river where Señor Alvarado used to fish."

Diego remembered the day like it was yesterday. It had been his own day of personal deliverance. For if Juan had decided not to become a priest, then he too would be free to make that same decision. "Yes, I remember."

"You trusted me then," said Juan, his eyes bright. "And you've trusted me since."

"Ever since, brother. Yes. Why are you saying these things?"

"Because I want for you to trust me now," said Juan. "I want for you to trust that I know what I am doing."

Diego felt pressure begin to build behind his eyes. "I trust you, Juan. I will always trust you."

"Then promise me something very important."

"Yes, anything."

"Promise me that from this day forward, you will listen to what our gringo friend has to teach you—and to live by the true meaning of our name."

"I promise, Juan. Of course, I promise."

Guerrero was the Spanish word for warrior.

15

Gil and Lena were headed for the airport in a rented car. Lena was driving, and Gil had a hand inside his jacket as they sped along the snowy mountain road, his eye on the side-view mirror.

Lena kept a firm grip on the wheel. "Are you going to tell me why they wanted to castrate you?"

Gil shivered involuntarily, flashing back to the pinking shears. "Thank you for saving my ass."

"It wasn't your ass that I saved—and you're evading my question."

"I killed a bunch of their friends in Istanbul awhile back—freed some girls who'd been sold into prostitution."

She cut him a surprised glance. "The Russian rescue that was in the news? That was *you*?"

He still had his eye on the side-view mirror, a bad

feeling rising up in his gut. "Me and a grumpy Spetsnaz guy, yeah."

"No wonder," she said. "You've brought them international attention, and it's hurting their business. They won't rest until you're dead."

He shrugged. "It might not have been the smartest thing I ever did, but it needed doin'."

"The Russian mob is everywhere. Aren't you afraid they'll go after your wife in the US?"

He looked at her. "Somebody else already tried that. No. I'm not worried."

They were approaching a tight curve bearing to the left, and Lena downshifted to slow the car. "Sabastian will help them find you—because of me."

"Well, he hasn't wasted any time," Gil said, seeing a black sedan appear in the mirror. "This is them. Keep driving!"

He opened the door and bailed out as they went through the curve, rolling into a snowbank and springing to his feet. He pulled the Springfield .45 from his jacket and charged the approaching car.

Shocked to see the American suddenly coming at them, the driver braked hard, putting the vehicle into a slide on the snowy road as Gil planted his feet, thrusting the pistol forward.

"*Hoo-yah!*" he growled, emptying the pistol rapidly into the windshield of the oncoming car. The bodies danced around in their seats. One man bailed out the back door, and Gil shot him through the neck as he rolled to a stop. The sedan plowed into a snowbank and stalled.

The only one still alive was the guy in the passenger seat—the same guy who had intended to remove Gil's private parts. He was bleeding from two holes in his chest and one through his cheek. Most of his teeth were shot out, and it was obvious that he was paralyzed, probably due to a bullet nicking his spinal cord.

Gil opened the door, reaching inside to snatch the Russian's pistol from his lap. "Watch close now." He shot the Russian in the face and jerked his body from the car, dragging it to the guardrail and throwing it over the cliff. He did the same with the other three bodies. Then Gil got into the car and took off after Lena, who, to his surprise, had pulled to the side of the road to wait less than a mile beyond the curve.

He pulled up beside her, his adrenaline still pumping but glad she'd waited. "Thought I told you to keep driving."

She grinned, her blue eyes shining. "If this is going to work, you'll have to get used to me not doing what I'm told."

"Roger that. Can you hide me in Switzerland?"

"Absolutely."

He put the car in motion toward the cliff and stepped out, watching it drop over the edge and go careening downhill into the tall mountain pines. The sky was dark, threatening snow, and he knew that no one would likely spot the vehicle before spring.

The second he got back into Lena's car, she leaned across the seat and planted her mouth on his, pulling at his belt.

"Lena, we gotta go."

"Why?" she said, aggressively yanking at the buckle. "Didn't you get rid of the evidence?"

"What about Sabastian?"

"Halfway to Stuttgart by now." She was openly wanton, biting at his lips. "I'm not kidding, Gil. Take your pants down!"

16

Paolina practically threw Vaught's breakfast at him as she brought it from the stove, shoving the plate across the table to smack against his glass of orange juice. Crosswhite had left before sunrise without telling Vaught where he was going, and Paolina hadn't said more than two words since he'd gotten out of bed. He didn't bother to thank her for cooking, knowing she'd only spit his words back at him. He was afraid of her and didn't want to antagonize her, particularly when Crosswhite wasn't there to protect him. Her resentment was palpable now, and he felt it was probably best to leave as small a footprint in her world as possible.

If Crosswhite didn't return before he finished eating, he would wash his own dishes, and then go back to the guest room and shut the door. There was a television back there to pass the time. He was curious where Crosswhite had gone, believing it must have something to do with the operation, but he knew that Paolina was too loyal to tell him anything Crosswhite didn't want him to know. Oddly enough, this didn't really worry him. Crosswhite was so straightforward about everything that Vaught couldn't help trusting him. What you saw was what you got with Crosswhite.

He drew a breath and stood up from the chair, making his way to the sink.

"Leave them," she said without turning around.

"Thank you for breakfast." The words slipped out before he could pull them back, and, of course, she didn't answer.

He went back to his room and closed the door, switching on the television. The news came on shortly, and within fifteen minutes, Chance Vaught learned that he'd been reported dead to the entire world. He knew it was coming, but the report still hit him hard, and he panicked for a minute, feeling unexpectedly trapped and alone. The news ended a few minutes later, and he switched off the television, getting up from the bed and stepping out into the living room, where Paolina sat on the sofa reading to Valencia.

"I'm sorry," he said, putting his hands into his pockets. "I apologize for jeopardizing what you and Crosswhite have here."

She looked up at him, holding his gaze for a moment, and then went back to reading.

He shrugged and went back into the room, closing the door.

A HALF HOUR later, Paolina heard someone rap on the steel gate to the carport. Assuming that it was a neighbor, she set aside the book, telling Valencia to wait for her on the couch, and stepped outside into the carport, calling, *"Quién es?"* Who is it?

"I'm with the Institute of Health, señorita," a young man answered in Spanish. "There's been a case of dengue fever in the neighborhood, and we have to speak to everyone to make sure they know the symptoms and how to prevent mosquitoes from breeding in and around their homes."

This was common in Latin America. Dengue fever was caused by a virus spread by mosquitoes, and this was the government's usual response to an instance of the disease in any neighborhood. Paolina crossed the carport and peeked out the slot in the door to see a young man in his early twenties wearing the Institute of Health uniform and the proper ID tag around his neck. She knew that if she didn't open the gate to take his literature and listen to his little spiel about the disease, either he or someone else would keep coming back until someone had heard them out. She pulled the latch to unlock the gate, and it burst violently inward, hitting her in the face and knocking her backward.

The young man clamped his hand over her mouth and kicked the gate shut. He had a gooey wet cloth in his hand that stunk of something medicinal. She felt herself beginning to go unconscious and stopped trying to breathe, pulling a razor-sharp stiletto from the small of her back beneath her shirt and swiping viciously at his groin.

She got him pretty good, just missing his penis and cutting deep into the thigh muscle. He let go of her instantly, seizing his crotch in both hands and shouting for help. Paolina stumbled dizzily backward and fell to the concrete, the effect of the chloroform too strong to resist. Two more men rushed in as she struggled to get up. They fell on her and slapped her unconscious, taping her mouth, and quickly securing her hands and feet with duct tape.

"Get her into the van!"

Vaught was still watching television in his room. He heard the young man's shout and lowered the volume to listen for more. Hearing nothing else, he ran the volume back up.

Valencia slid off the couch and went to stand in the open doorway. Seeing two men in the process of kidnapping her mother, she immediately began to scream.

Hearing the scream, Vaught ripped open the bedroom door and was already moving at full speed by the time he vaulted over Valencia and into the carport. The two men lifting Paolina from the concrete watched in stunned confusion as he came at them, having had no idea there was anyone else in the house. Vaught drove his knee into the closest man's face, knocking him backward against the door with his nose smashed flat, blood jetting. Then he spun smoothly around with a high backward kick that caught the second man in the side of the head and sent him sprawling.

The counterfeit health worker was bleeding in the corner and didn't want any part of the fight, so Vaught ignored him, turning back to the first guy as he struggled to rise. He put him back down with a punch to the trachea and snatched Paolina's stiletto off the ground, using it to stab both men in the throat before finishing off the imposter from the health department with a brutal kick to the temple. Then he lifted Paolina up and swept her into the house past Valencia, who was still crying. He set the young woman on the sofa, pulled the tape away from her mouth, and began freeing her hands and feet as the chloroform wore off.

She came awake flailing, and he grabbed her wrists.

"You're okay!" he said in Spanish. "Look at me! You're okay!"

Paolina jumped unsteadily to her feet and tottered over to her daughter, sinking to her knees and taking the frightened little girl into her arms to settle her. "Mommy's okay. Mommy's okay . . ." She glanced at Vaught. "We have to leave—now."

He glanced around. "Where the hell are we gonna go?"

"Daniel said if anything ever happened while he was out of the city to go to Juan Guerrero."

"Who's Juan Guerrero?"

Still dizzy, she got to her feet and lifted Valencia into her arms. "The police chief in Toluca."

"Toluca's thirty miles south of here. Where the hell is Crosswhite?"

"Guadalajara."

"What the hell's he doing up in Guadalajara? That's a six-hour drive. Did he fly? When's he coming back?"

She moved toward the bedroom. "Stop complaining, Chance. Call for a taxi."

"Goddamnit," he muttered. "Right when you think things can't get any more fucked up."

17

TOLUCA, MEXICO

The gringo sniper's Barrett XM500 .50 caliber sniper rifle rested on the floor, propped on its bipod near the end of a long hallway in an abandoned elementary school. At the opposite end of the hall was a one-square-foot opening cut into the base of the concrete wall overlooking the street one story below. Almost a quarter mile away, at the far end of the avenue, was a church where a young lady's first communion ceremony was taking place. Taped to the wall, knee-high off the floor, was an eight-by-ten color photo of Police Chief Juan Guerrero.

Rhett Hancock sat against the steel door of an empty classroom, studying the gentle features of the face in the photograph. He would have time for only one shot, and it would have to be on the correct target. The chief had a gentlemanly look about him: dark eyebrows and soft brown eyes set in an oval face. His hair was cut short without style, and to Hancock he looked more like a gardener or a waiter than a defiant cop.

The Barrett XM500 was not a common model like the M82A1 or the M107. This rifle was of a bullpup design, with the action located behind the trigger, allowing for shorter overall weapon length. It was a variant of the old M82A2, which had never generated much interest on the weapons market. Another difference was that the XM500's barrel remained stationary when the weapon was fired, facilitating greater accuracy at long ranges.

Hancock's partner, Jessup, sat around the corner at the far end of the hallway. After Hancock's shot, he would quickly shove the concrete block they had cut from the wall back into place to prevent anyone from pinpointing their location. The rifle report would be muffled by the building and covered up further by the clanging church bell.

Hancock stared at the photo, visualizing the shot in his mind's eye. There was no greater feeling, no greater thrill in the world to him, than shooting another human being at long range. He had become addicted to the experience almost immediately during the Iraq War, and though the cartels were paying him extremely well, he would have gladly done the work for food money. He was willing to shoot anyone. Man or woman—it didn't matter.

He used his own modified ammunition, having paid a munitions expert in Nevada to design him a special soft-tipped round that would pancake to the size of a hubcap upon entering the human body. As it was, the standard .50 caliber sniper round did a devastating amount of damage—the hydrostatic shock of the impact being hundreds of times more powerful than the body could absorb—but Hancock sought maximum devastation with every shot now, like a junkie needing a larger and larger fix as his addiction progressed. He had used the special round to blow Alice Downly's guts all over the street, and it still made him snicker to think about the way she had exploded. One second a raving lunatic—the next, total obliteration.

The phone vibrated in his pocket with an incoming text message: *"listo,"* meaning "ready." This was the signal from their man inside the church letting him know that Guerrero would soon be coming out the front door, as they had hoped. There had been some initial concern when the informant reported that the police car had been pulled around behind the church, but apparently the chief was feeling lucky today.

Well, Hancock thought, putting on his protective earmuffs, *I'm gonna give the dude a stiff dose of a bad time.*

He felt his blood begin to thrum as he slid in behind the rifle to peer through the Leupold 4.5-14x50 Mark 4 scope. The church doors were open, and people were coming out slowly. The first person to really catch his eye was the young lady whose special day it was. She was dressed all in white and shone like a beautiful pearl in the bright sunlight. Next, there was the chief of police, standing perfectly in his crosshairs between two other policemen. The timing was sublime, the shot pristine, and there was no hesitation, no need to even think. Hancock squeezed the trigger, and the 600-grain projectile streaked down the hallway at 2,800 feet per second, blasting out through the hole near the floor and speeding its way down the street to strike Chief Juan Guerrero in the base of the throat, severing the spinal cord perfectly. Guerrero's neck disintegrated. His head went twirling up into the air like a pop foul, slinging blood on the little girl's dress in bright globs of crimson as his body dropped to the sidewalk. The head landed and bounced once before coming to rest near the feet of one of the other policemen.

No one in front of the church heard the faint report of the rifle over the clanging of the bronze bell above them, but many saw the chief's head ripped from his body, and no one needed to be told what had done it. Bedlam ensued as everyone began to scream, scrambling back inside the church for safety. One of the policemen grabbed up the little girl and swept her inside along with the rushing throng.

As Jessup slid the block into place, plugging the hole, Hancock stripped off his ear protection and rolled onto his back, laughing uproariously. The vision of the chief's twirling head was more comical to him than any cartoon had ever been in his youth.

Jessup ran up the hall, shouting for him get up and move, but Hancock rolled to his side, holding his belly as he continued to roar with delight.

Jessup grabbed the Barrett by its carrying handle and snatched up the spent shell casing. "Rhett! We gotta get the fuck outta here!"

Hancock did not seem to hear him, his laughter continuing in a maniacal craze.

"Rhett!" Jessup kicked him in the ass with the side of his boot. "Get the fuck up!"

But Hancock did not rise until he had finally laughed himself out, nearly two minutes later. He sat up against the wall. "Oh, fuck me!" he said, wiping the tears from his face. "Oh, Christ, it was beautiful—a once-in-a-lifetime shot!"

Jessup couldn't have cared less. "You're gonna get us fucking killed! We gotta go!"

Hancock chuckled one last time, exhausted from his fit. "Calm down, Cochise. There ain't nobody lookin' for us. They think we're long gone. Besides, they're all too busy piling out the back of that goddamn church."

"Ruvalcaba's people are waiting in the alley, but they're not gonna wait all day!"

Hancock stuck up his hand, and Jessup hauled him to his feet.

"Fuck, Rhett. Sometimes I wonder what the fuck is wrong with you."

TWO HOURS LATER, they sat in a cantina on the outskirts of Mexico City, safe in the heart of Ruvalcaba's territory. Hancock was drinking straight from a bottle of Jose Cuervo, and Jessup sat across from him, nursing a beer.

"Are you sober enough to comprehend some bad news?" Jessup asked harshly.

Hancock nodded slowly.

"I just got a call from Oscar, and it looks like the snatch-and-grab at Crosswhite's place must have gotten fucked up. All three of Ruvalcaba's people are MIA, and the place is crawling with cops. I told you we should have shot the bastard instead of fucking around with him. Now he knows we're after him, and he'll go to ground."

Hancock shook his head drunkenly from one side to the other. "Nope. No, he won't. He'll come after me. And that's okay. It's what I want."

"'He'll come after me!'" Jessup echoed sarcastically. He shook his head. "You're dreaming."

Hancock gripped the bottle by its neck and held it in his lap between his legs, inching closer to the table. His eyes lost their glassy appearance, and he seemed strangely sober all of a sudden. "I had a little talk with one of my own sources late last night."

"What source?"

"Never mind. What's important is what I found out."

A doubtful frown appeared on Jessup's face. "And what's that?"

Hancock tossed the tequila bottle into the corner and braced his elbows on the table top. "Crosswhite's a contender."

Jessup cocked an eyebrow. "A contender for what?"

Hancock turned to look over at the bartender. "Hey, cabrón! Where the fuck is my steak?"

The bartender disappeared into the back, and Jessup let out a weary sigh. "You never asked for a steak."

"I just did," Hancock said. "Didn't you hear?"

"Are you gonna tell me about Crosswhite?"

"Yeah." Hancock got up from the table and went to the bar, pulling out his penis and pissing into the drain at the base of the bar stool, which was not an uncommon sight in some of the older, rougher cantinas. "Turns out the guy was part of Operation Earnest Endeavor. He's a Medal of Honor winner. The leader of a special Ranger unit in Afghanistan. They were one of the first teams incountry, even before the bombs started to drop." He finished taking his leak and shook himself dry, zipping up his pants and coming back to the table.

"And that's why you think he'll come after you?" Jessup asked.

"Fuckin' A, he'll come after me." Hancock sat back and spread his arms. "This ain't the kinda dude to spend the rest of his life hiding from nobody. He'll look to end this shit, and that's gonna bring his ass right into my crosshairs, Cochise. Wait and see."

Jessup took a swig from his beer. "Cochise was an Apache, you stupid shit. How many times I gotta tell you I'm a Sioux?"

"Name me a famous Sioux."

"Sitting Bull, jag-off."

"Fuck that." Hancock glanced over his shoulder, looking for the bartender. "I ain't callin' you no goddamn Sitting Bull."

Jessup took another drink. "We need to talk about these last two missions, Rhett. Today was the second time you tried to get me killed. If I can't count on you to perform like a professional, I'm the fuck outta here." He'd been on the roof with Hancock in Mexico City on the day of Downly's assassination, acting as Hancock's spotter. Downly had been in the open from the time she had exited the vehicle, and Jessup had kept calling for Hancock to shoot her, but Hancock had chosen to shoot the ambassador and two of the DSS agents first, wasting valuable escape time. Jessup had ducked into the stairwell only seconds before Vaught had reached the roof and killed their security team of crooked policemen.

Hancock yawned and stretched. "I'm getting hungry."

"Or better yet," Jessup said, "why don't we split? We've got plenty of money now."

"No," Hancock said, shaking his head. "If you wanna split, split. I'll start taking things more seriously, if you want, but I ain't goin' nowhere. I don't give a fiddler's fuck about the money. Shit, you can have mine. This is the only the fucking thing I was ever any good at, and I'm gonna keep right on doing it until somebody better comes along and stops me."

But Jessup knew it went deeper than that, and he couldn't help but wonder if it might be better for everyone involved for him to put Hancock down himself. There was, after all, such a thing as taking shit too far.

18

CIA Director Robert Pope was talking with Clemson Fields in his office. Pope was tall, in his midsixties, with a head of thick white hair and boyish blue eyes peering out from behind his glasses. His professional relationship with Fields dated back to the Cold War. They weren't what most people would consider friends, but neither man was the type who valued friendship a great deal.

". . . and you have a soft spot for Shannon," Fields was saying. "That could be problematic for us. He does whatever the hell he wants—like this nonsense with Blickensderfer's fiancée. He wasn't trained by the CIA, and I think you're trying to teach an old dog too many new tricks."

"His unpredictability is what makes him effective," Pope said. "And his loyalty to me is unquestioned."

"For the moment. What about Crosswhite?"

"Crosswhite belongs to me lock, stock, and barrel. If need be, I can use the girl and the baby to control him."

Fields sat back in the chair. "And Shannon will stand for that?"

"Gil understands that Crosswhite is reckless and needs a firm hand."

"And now Shannon is getting reckless."

"He got horny," Pope said dismissively. "Not having your ashes hauled will do that to a man."

Fields was skeptical. "I think you'd better be careful not to ask too much of him. He's too principled. And he's not young anymore—he doesn't have anything left to prove. If he stops believing in what we're doing, you'll have to retire him."

A dark shadow fell over Pope.

"I don't mean *retire* him," Fields said. "I mean pension him out."

"Know this now," Pope said, pointing a finger at Fields. "No one ever touches Gil Shannon. Is that understood?"

"Completely," Fields replied easily. "That was a poor choice of words. But my point stands. He's too principled for what you have in mind for the ATRU. You're selecting targets that won't be defined well enough by his standards."

"Gil's a specialist," Pope said. "I have no intention of using him as a general-purpose operator. That's what men like Chance Vaught will be for, and the other men I'm recruiting. Speaking of which, I want you to activate one of our people in Europe—someone out of Berlin. I want Blickensderfer dead as soon as possible. If Gil ends up shagging Lena Deiss for more than a few days—and I have to assume that to be a strong possibility—Blickensderfer might move against him."

"I'll see to it," Fields said. "And what happens if Shannon disapproves?"

"Gil will have nothing to complain about. He's got the girl, and he doesn't have to pull the trigger. If he has any complaints after the fact, they won't be of any concern to me."

"If you say so," Fields remarked. "Now, what about Hancock?"

Pope rocked back in his chair, scratching at his neck. "That's a serious problem. We have to neutralize him before the Mexican government can make a positive ID. If they can prove one of our own people pulled the trigger on Downly, they'll throw this entire incident right back in our faces."

"Will the president clear the ATRU to handle this?"

Pope nodded. "He already has. I told him I want Vaught, so Vaught officially belongs to me."

"Then that takes care of that, but there's something else."

"Yes?"

"Mariana Mederos flew down to Guadalajara early this morning and then flew back to Texas a few hours later. I have no idea what she was doing down there. Did you send her?"

"She must have gone down to meet with Crosswhite."

"About what?"

Pope chortled. "Kids pass notes in class when the teacher's back is turned. A good teacher learns to tolerate a certain amount of it. They're both patriots. Crosswhite is probably just looking out for Paolina. I can't blame him."

"Do you want Ortega to look into it?"

"No," Pope said. "Don't use Ortega any more than necessary. Crosswhite already had to punch his lights out. Next time he might kill him, and I don't need the hassle of replacing the Mexico chief of station in the middle of this mess."

When Fields was gone, Pope's Japanese American assistant, Midori Kagawa, came into the room. She was in her early thirties, with shoulder-length black hair and a round face. Aside from being a genius in her own right, Midori was the single person in Pope's life that he trusted absolutely. "Should I have him watched?" she asked. "He obviously has doubts."

"Fields doubts everyone and everything," Pope said. "That's why he's still in the game. But, yes, you'd better begin your electronic intrusion. Be extremely careful. Fields is nobody's fool."

"What about Mariana Mederos?"

"I'm not sure yet." Pope was staring out the window. "Something happened between her and Crosswhite down in Cuba, something that brought them closer together. I have no idea what it was, but it's been intriguing me for a while now."

"Isn't it obvious?" Midori said.

He looked at her. "You mean sex?" He shook his head. "No, whatever happened, it was nothing as trivial as sex. We'll have to keep an eye on that relationship. Despite what I said to Fields, it could become a thorn in my side if I'm not careful. Mederos and Crosswhite are both too damn smart for my own good."

19

By seven o'clock that afternoon, Crosswhite was back on the ground in Mexico City. During the flight, he'd received a coded text message from Paolina letting him know that she was leaving for Toluca, but his phone had been turned off, so the message was already an hour old by the time he landed. He was able to exchange another coded message with her before leaving the airport, verifying that she was okay and that they would meet in Toluca.

He was sitting in his Jeep at a stoplight on the outskirts of Mexico City when the vehicle began to vibrate as though it had broken a motor mount. "What the hell is this now?" he wondered aloud.

A few seconds later, chunks of concrete began falling off the aging office building across the street, and the traffic light started bobbing up and down on its metal arm.

A man hawking bottled water in the street stood outside Crosswhite's open window.

"*Terremoto!*" he said. Earthquake!

Crosswhite got out of the Jeep to feel the earth trembling underfoot. He'd been in Los Angeles during the quake of '94, and he could already tell this one was shaping up to be somewhere along those lines. He had to get on his knees, as there was no way to keep standing with the vibrations. He knew that Mexico City was built on an ancient lake bed of mostly sand, and that soil liquefaction would exacerbate the quake's effects to the extreme. The shaking became more intense, and all at once, the ten-story office building collapsed as if in a controlled demolition.

Cracks appeared in the asphalt, and the power to the streetlights failed. Crosswhite's first reaction was wanting to hide under the Jeep until the shocks passed, but he forced himself to get back in the vehicle and got the windows up just as a billowing gray cloud of dust engulfed everything.

Within two minutes, the earth grew still, but Crosswhite knew there would be aftershocks, believing the quake to have easily been a 6 or 7 magnitude. The city's last major quake, in 1985, had registered 8.1 on the Richter scale. That one had killed at least twenty thousand people. This one wasn't as strong, but Crosswhite knew that it had been plenty powerful enough to bring the city to a halt. It would be months before everything would be back to normal.

He took out his phone to call Paolina, but there was no signal. "Shit!" He threw the phone down on the seat beside him.

By the time the dust began to clear enough for him

to see, sirens were wailing. A fire engine roared past with klaxons honking as the emergency services machine came to life.

Getting to Toluca in a hurry would now be easier said than done, but he had a four-wheel drive and a full tank of gas. Crosswhite shifted into drive and sped off down the road, knowing the police would be too busy to worry about enforcing traffic laws.

20

Vaught and Paolina were in a taxicab headed south for Toluca when the earthquake hit. The taxi was just entering a tunnel that ran beneath a circular intersection when a portion of the tunnel collapsed, blocking the exit with large chunks of concrete. The result was a thirty-car pileup at fifty miles an hour. The taxi was smashed, and Paolina's head hit the window, knocking her unconscious. Three-year-old Valencia was tossed into the front seat, where she bounced off the dashboard and bloodied her nose. Vaught slammed into the back of the driver's seat but took no damage. Meanwhile, the cabby was pinned behind the wheel with a pair of broken legs.

Vaught kicked open the door and got out, taking a look up and down the line of crashed traffic. A propane truck exploded ten cars ahead, and he ducked back inside, covering the unconscious Paolina with his body as the roiling black-orange cloud of fire swept across the ceiling of the tunnel. Valencia shrieked from the front seat, and injured motorists fled past the taxi, some of them in flames. Two more cars caught fire and exploded, threatening to engulf the entire tunnel.

Vaught reached forward to pull Valencia back between the seats.

"Ayúdame!" moaned the cabdriver. Help me!

"Women and children first," Vaught grunted in English, pulling Paolina from the backseat, with Valencia gripped in the opposite arm. "Good thing you're so tiny," he muttered, hefting the young woman over his shoulder.

Two more cars exploded as he ran toward the entrance to the tunnel, with the cabby shouting for him to come back.

Once clear of the tunnel, Vaught found a safe place to put down Paolina and Valencia, and then started back for the cab driver. Burn victims ran past him as the tunnel filled quickly with black smoke, obscuring his vision. He reached the cab to find the driver praying out loud for his life.

He jerked at the door but couldn't open it, so he slid across the crumpled green hood and climbed in on the passenger side, seeing the firewall jammed up against the driver's knees. "Goddamn," he said, choking on the smoke. "You're stuck!"

Burning gasoline on the pavement set the engine compartment on fire, and the driver began to scream, sweat pouring down his face.

"Keep calm," Vaught told him. "I gotta think!"

But the driver did not calm down: he began thrashing around like a wild man as the flames licked up around the hood.

"Santa Maria! Santa Maria!"

Vaught grabbed the cabby's shoulders and pulled, but his legs were caught fast, and the man howled. Smoke now filled the car, making it almost impossible to breathe, and Vaught knew he would have to let the man burn to death. Fleetingly, he considered knocking him cold and breaking his neck to save him the suffering, but he couldn't do it.

"I'm sorry! I can't get you out!"

"Please!" the man begged. "Please!"

The car in front them burst into flames, and the heat became intense.

"Don't let me die!"

Vaught got out, standing beside the open passenger door. "I'm sorry!"

"Don't leave me! For the love of God!"

That's when Vaught realized for the first time how close the seat was to the steering wheel. He ducked back inside and reached beneath the driver's legs, finding the release lever and pushing the seat back a full six inches. The driver gasped with relief, and Vaught yanked him free, heaving him over his shoulder and running for the entrance as the taxi burst into flames.

Paolina was holding Valencia in her lap when Vaught finally set down the driver beside them at the side of the road. As of yet, there were still no emergency personnel on the scene.

"I thought you left us," she said, cleaning the blood from Valencia's face with the little girl's shirt.

"Why the hell would I do that?" he asked irritably.

She shrugged. "It would be easier for you."

He glanced around at the injured and the people helping them to get clear of the acrid black smoke now billowing from the tunnel. "Well, you don't know me, Paolina. You don't know me at all."

21

When the emotionally shattered Diego Guerrero lifted his head to see Crosswhite standing in the threshold of what had been his brother's office, it was as though Saint Michael the Archangel had suddenly appeared before him with a pistol tucked into the belly of his jeans.

"I understand there's been some trouble," Crosswhite said in Spanish.

"Yes," croaked Diego, now the de facto chief of police. "My brother is dead."

Crosswhite shook a cigarette loose from its pack, pulled it out with his lips, and lit it. "It was the *francotirador* . . . the gringo sniper."

Diego rose from behind the desk, trying to look like the chief of police without feeling it. *"Estába espeluznante,"* he said despondently. It was horrifying.

"That's how it is the first time," Crosswhite said. "And this won't be the last."

"I know. I will be next."

Crosswhite nodded. "Possibly, but that's not what you think about. What you think about now is keeping your police force together—*your* police force. The Ruvalcabas will be moving to take over the town again."

Diego's voice was thin and reedy, his eyes filling with tears. "I am afraid."

Crosswhite drew from the cigarette. "Get angry," he advised. "After that, the rest takes care of itself."

Diego smirked despondently. "What good is anger against a man who kills from so far away—like a ghost?"

Crosswhite stepped into the room, dropping his ruck onto a chair. "Popular opinion holds that it takes a sniper to kill a sniper, but a sniper's no different from any other predator. He's got two eyes set in the center of his face. That means he doesn't see what's comin' up from behind him—so that's where we'll be."

"For that, we need to know in advance where *he* will be."

Crosswhite smiled, squinting against the smoke of the cigarette. "Nothing worth doing ever came easy."

Diego watched the American for the slightest hint of put-on bravado, but there was nothing phony in what he saw. "Why do you want to help this town? You are not even from this country."

The American glanced out the window with a sigh. "Maybe it's because I got debts no honest man can pay."

The Mexican watched him a moment longer and then said, "That makes no sense."

Crosswhite looked at him. "It means I cannot be redeemed, Diego."

"We are all redeemable in the eyes of God."

Crosswhite took another drag. "It's not the eyes of God I'm worried about." He moved the pistol around to the small of his back beneath his jacket. "Your brother was a brave man. His same blood runs in your veins. You remember that."

Diego looked at the floor. "I will try."

"You'll do better than try," Crosswhite said. "I guarantee it. Now let's see to your men. Unless I miss my guess, Serrano's gonna try to make an example of this town. That's why he had your brother killed."

Diego looked up. "*Lazaro* Serrano?"

"Right. He's the real power behind the Ruvalcaba cartel."

Diego dropped into the chair, sinking his fingers into his dark hair and pulling. "Oh, my God. Serrano is going to be the next president of Mexico."

Crosswhite turned for the hall. "Don't bet on it. Now get your butt outta that chair. We got work to do."

22

"I WANT TO know who this Gil Shannon is and what he was doing in Liechtenstein," Sabastian Blickensderfer said to his German attorney, seated across the table from him in a private dining room. He was a calm man, handsome, blond, with blue eyes and an unmistakable air of importance. "A man who takes the fight to the Russians in Turkey does not go skiing alone in Malbun."

"I've already had him checked out," said the well-dressed attorney, stirring sugar into his coffee. "It's not good. He is an American war hero, one of their navy's elite—and he was in Malbun to kill you."

Blickensderfer scoffed. "Nonsense. I'm protected by the CIA."

"You *were* protected," the attorney replied. "The CIA has a new director now, a man named Pope, and he fired nearly everyone at the executive level when he took over.

So the old guard is gone, and it's not likely any of their agreements will be honored."

"But if Shannon is with their navy—"

"Shannon is CIA. I can't find anything to link him directly, but he's one of theirs. He was killing Russian mobsters in Turkey five months ago. And now he's traveling with Lena."

Blickensderfer smiled, realizing he was supposed to be rocked by the revelation concerning his former fiancée. "Where are they now?"

"At her home in Bern," the attorney said. "But knowing Lena, they won't be there for long."

"How did he get away from the Russians?"

The lawyer shrugged. "I don't know." He checked his phone for messages, but nothing new had come in. "He's listed as a contractor with Obsidian Optio, the private mercenary company. However, my contact with Obsidian tells me that Shannon never does any actual work for them. This is further evidence that he's CIA. And as for our Russian friends in Malbun, I'm guessing they're dead. This Shannon is a very hard man to kill."

"Not for much longer," said the still-smiling Blickensderfer, lifting the bottle of expensive champagne from a sterling silver ice bucket and pouring himself another glass. "He's traveling with a woman now, and not just any woman. He's traveling with Lena; and Lena is *nothing* if not a distraction." He chortled, savoring the taste of the champagne. "I should probably be thanking Shannon—but I'm not."

The lawyer sipped his coffee and sat back. "I've looked into Pope as well. He's even more dangerous than Shannon. If he *has* marked you for assassination, your chances of survival are not the best. You're going to have to spend a lot more on security."

Blickensderfer shrugged. "It's only money. But do this: send Pope a back-channel communication. State to him plainly that he's made his point. I will immediately cease all dealings with terrorist organizations, however benign. That should appease him. He's going to need me in the future if he's going to fight the growing ISIS threat. He'll need my weapons connections. Make sure he understands that I will be very cooperative when the time comes."

The attorney nodded. "That *might* work."

"It will work," Blickensderfer said. "*If* Pope is what you say he is."

"Then what are you going to do about Shannon?" the attorney asked. "You can't kill him and expect to make friends with Pope."

Blickensderfer considered his options. "Isn't Shannon unpopular with Russian slavers? Hasn't he cost them millions? Haven't Istanbul and other major cities in Eastern Europe been cracking down on illegal prostitution? Well, all we need to do is whisper Shannon's location in the correct places, and I'm sure he'll turn up dead soon enough. But be sure they are careful about Lena."

"That might be difficult to guarantee."

"I'm not asking for a *guarantee*, Gunther. I want Shannon dead and Lena back with me where she belongs. Is that understood?"

"Quite."

"Good," Blickensderfer said. "These temporary little infatuations of hers are not exactly new, but she's a woman of means. She's not about to fall in love with some cowboy who cannot afford to perpetuate her lavish lifestyle."

23

Gil stood in the dark, staring down at the snowy street beneath the window of Lena's bedroom. He was thinking of his wife back in Montana and how much he missed her, but something within him was changing. Or had it changed already? All he knew for sure was that he no longer wanted to go home; no longer wanted the calm ranch life he had once loved. He felt like a shark now—a shark that would drown if it ever dared to stop swimming.

"Come back to bed," Lena said, naked beneath the blanket. "No one is going to come after you here. You're safe with me."

He turned to look at her, his heart breaking, eyes welling with tears. "I can never go back, Lena. The life I had with Marie, it—it slipped through my fingers somehow."

"I'm sorry, Gil, but whatever else the past is . . . it's gone."

He sank into the chair, putting his head into his hands, and began to weep for the first time in many years.

Lena slid from the bed and went to his side, caressing him as she stared out the window, knowing the cry would be good for him; that he would be stronger for it. She understood that men who killed for a living carried demons, and that the only way to exorcise such demons was to let them out. Too many men were not strong enough to let them go, but Gil seemed to possess that strength, and this gave her a certain hope that he might survive.

After a short time, he went into the bathroom and took a shower, returning to lie beside her on the bed, touching her soft blond hair, kissing the nape of her neck. "Sorry about that."

She turned into him. "There's nothing to be sorry for. How do you feel?"

"Better," he said quietly.

"Good."

They hadn't been asleep long when the phone rang. Lena answered. "Hello?"

"You need to let him go, Lena." It was Blickensderfer, and she could tell that he was very drunk. "I understand that he's a fun new toy for you, but you need to let him go."

"Sabastian, it's very late. We can talk tomorrow when you're sober."

"The Russians are going to kill him," Blickensderfer went on, his words slurring slightly. "You know that I can't protect you. You have to let the man go."

"I don't have to do anything. Don't call me late at night anymore, and don't call if you've been drinking." She hung up the phone and laid back on the pillow, staring at the ceiling.

Gil raised up, seeing her clearly by the light of the window. "What did he say?"

"He said I need to let you go—that he can't protect me."

He leaped out of bed. "Get dressed!"

She sat up. "Gil, it's okay. He's just drunk."

He stood looking at her. "We have to go—now!"

"No, Gil. We don't have to go. We're not in Baghdad. Come back to bed. No one will attack my house. This is Switzerland, not Iraq."

He stood on uncertain footing, knowing they should leave but at the same knowing how silly he must have appeared. He glanced warily out the window, his ears tuned for danger—hearing nothing.

"Gil," she said softly. "No one is coming. You're safe."

"I need a gun," he said.

"Tomorrow. Tomorrow we'll find a gun. Tonight come to bed."

He got into bed and pulled up the blanket. "I'm not used to living in the city."

She wrapped herself around him. "What you're not used to is no one trying to kill you."

24

With the moon on the rise, Vaught and Paolina were still stranded on the streets of Mexico City, where they found themselves unable to abandon the dozens of motorists injured in the smashup. The tunnel fire had burned itself out, but only the very worst of the injured had been taken away in a pair of ambulances. The rest were still on the scene, with no professional medical personnel to look after them. The city's emergency services were stretched beyond capacity, and it was easy to imagine that it might be days before the ambulances returned.

Initially, Vaught had insisted that they get back on the move for Toluca, knowing Crosswhite would be worried about his family, but Paolina refused, contending that their help was badly needed there and that Toluca was too far to walk anyway. Very few civilians had remained on the scene after the ambulances had first arrived, most of them fleeing homeward to check on their own families.

Cellular service was knocked out along with electrical power to that part of the city, so without the moonlight, it would have been dangerously dark. Sirens wailed far in the distance where damage to the city had been worse, and flashlights bobbed in the darkness along the street. Many of the burn victims were moaning, and a few children were crying. The cabdriver was in great pain, but he was so thankful to have been saved from the burning taxi that he barely complained at all.

Local shopkeepers had donated a limited supply of food and bottled water early on, so there had at least been something to eat before it got dark.

Valencia had found a Rottweiler puppy to play with, so she was content for the moment, but Vaught had no idea where the animal had come from.

He was well aware that this would be a good time to make a break for the US Embassy, confident that none of Serrano's people would be watching now that the city had been ripped asunder, but the idea was a nonstarter. He couldn't abandon a pregnant woman in the midst of such chaos any more than he could abandon the crash victims, now that he'd taken responsibility for them.

"This is bullshit," he muttered in English, and felt a little better about it.

"Do you have a signal yet?" Paolina asked, standing beside him with a bottle of water.

He checked his phone and shook his head. "It could be weeks before they get service restored."

"I need to find a blanket for Valencia. It's getting cold."

"Stay here with the others," he told her. "I don't want you wandering off in the dark."

He set off across the street, where he saw a light on in

one of the local shops. As he drew closer, he could hear the hum of a generator.

"Hello," he said through the locked gate.

A man in his twenties appeared from the back clutching a pistol. "What do you want?"

"Do you have a blanket I can buy?"

The man went into the back and returned a minute later with a beat-up brown blanket. "Two hundred pesos." Approximately thirteen dollars.

Vaught could see the blanket wasn't worth five bucks, but he was dealing with profiteering now, and he knew it, so he didn't complain. He took the bill from his wallet and handed it over. The second he took possession of the blanket, he could smell that it had been taken from a dog's bed.

He returned to the crash scene and gave it to Paolina. "It's not the best, but it will keep her warm."

"It stinks!" she said.

"Paolina, there's not exactly a lot I can do about it. We have to make do. Give the Red Cross time to show up."

She made a *pffft* sound and knelt to wrap the blanket around Valencia's shoulders.

Valencia said the puppy was hungry and asked if there was any food for him.

"He'll be okay," Vaught said compassionately. "We'll get him some food in the morning."

"Can you go back over there and buy us something to eat?" Paolina said. "I don't think those other people are going to bring us any more."

"I'd rather not go back over there," he said.

"But it's the only shop with a light on."

"I know, but the guy has a gun, and he's not very friendly. Besides, he's gonna charge five times what the food is worth, and we—"

"You're worried about money?"

"No. I'm worried about the gun. It's not a gun he got legally, so he's probably a professional criminal, and we don't need trouble."

She let out a frustrated sigh and sat down beside her daughter.

"Hey, you know what, Paolina? The earthquake isn't my fault."

"No," she said, looking up at him. "It's your fault we're not at home now with my husband where we belong."

"Yeah? How do you know your house didn't cave in? You might have been killed, for all you know."

She pulled Valencia close. "Leave me in peace, Chance."

"Mommy, this blanket smells bad."

"I know, baby, but it's the only one Chance could find. We'll get a clean one tomorrow."

Vaught picked up a jug of water and went to check on the burn victims. One of the women was burned badly on her arms and hands, but there had been no more room in either of the ambulances. She was sitting against a tree in the median, and though she was in a good deal of pain, she was bearing it like a stoic.

"Do you have any aspirin?" she asked. "Anything for pain?"

Vaught remembered seeing boxes of aspirin in the glass case in the shop across the street. "I'll see if I can get some."

He gave the others some water and then went back to Paolina. "I'm going to buy these people some aspirin."

"What about the guy with the gun?"

He dropped the water jug beside her. "I thought you didn't care about him."

"Just be careful," she said quietly.

"How sweet," he muttered, walking off.

Vaught stepped up to the gate again and called inside. This time an older, meaner-looking guy came out of the back.

"What do you need?"

"Two boxes of aspirin," Vaught said. "We've got a lot of injured people across the street there. A lot of them are burned. And three loaves of bread."

The man set the stuff on the shelf attached to the cage door. "Five hundred pesos." This was a little over thirty dollars.

Vaught was tired and annoyed, so he wasn't as accepting of the situation as he should have been. "Do you have to take advantage like that? I told you there's a lot of people hurt over there. The other shopkeepers were very generous."

The guy crossed his arms and stared at Vaught. When he did this, his shirt rode up, exposing another pistol tucked into his belly.

Vaught put the bill on the shelf. The guy took it and shoved the stuff through the opening in the cage.

25

The next morning, Vaught was helping a burn victim to drink water from a bottle, when he looked up to see the mean-looking fellow from the night before coming across the street. It was obvious the guy still had the pistol tucked into the front of his pants and that his mood had not improved. He stalked over to Valencia and said something to her in a harsh tone. The little girl stood staring up at him with the puppy in her arms, and Paolina got between them, telling the man to leave her daughter alone.

Vaught stepped over quickly. "What's the problem, amigo?"

"That's my dog!" the man said, pointing at the Rottweiler pup.

"Well, it showed up here last night," Vaught said. "We didn't know whose it was."

"It's mine!"

"Okay. No problem." Vaught turned to Valencia. "Sweetheart, we have to give the puppy to this man so he can take him to his mama."

Valencia began to cry, and Vaught knelt down. "It's okay, sweetheart. The puppy needs his mama."

Valencia clutched the puppy to her and began to sob into its fur.

Her sadness affecting him, Vaught looked up at the guy. "Can I buy the dog?"

The guy scowled at him. "Six thousand pesos." This was almost five hundred dollars.

"I know that's a fair price, amigo, but I don't have that much cash on me. Can you take three thousand?"

"No."

Vaught turned back to Valencia. "We'll let him take the puppy home, but we'll come back tomorrow to buy him. How's that sound?"

Valencia was not stupid. She knew that to relinquish the dog meant never seeing it again. She continued to weep as Vaught began to gently manipulate the dog from her arms.

At the last second, Valencia redoubled her hold on the animal. Her intention was only to give the puppy a kiss good-bye, but the dog's owner saw this as an attempt to take back the dog, and he lost his patience.

He grabbed Valencia by the arm. "Give me the damn dog!"

Paolina instantly grabbed the collar of the guy's shirt. "Don't touch my daughter!"

The guy shoved Paolina away. She stumbled backward over a tree root and fell to the ground. Valencia screamed.

Vaught stood up, a wild look in his eyes.

The owner of the dog panicked and went for his gun, but before he could get his hand beneath his shirt, Vaught had him by the throat. The two were of equal size and strength, but Vaught knew a lot more about balance and leverage. He took the man down easily, planting him solidly on his back in the median and knocking the air from his lungs.

He snatched the 9 mm Beretta from the guy's pants and quickly hid the pistol in the small of his back, turning to help Paolina to her feet.

The guy lay on his back, gasping for air, struggling to get up.

Vaught knelt beside Valencia and gently took the dog away from her. "We have to give the dog back right now, honey, before someone gets hurt."

He stood up with the dog in one hand and was reaching to help the owner to his feet, when he saw the younger shopkeeper running across the street with his pistol thrust before him.

"Aw, shit!" Vaught hissed, dropping the puppy and grabbing the pistol. "Paolina, get down!"

Paolina leaped on Valencia, covering her with her body as Vaught opened fire on the young man coming at them. He fired twice, aiming low to hit the boy in the legs, and the kid went down, his pistol skidding across the pavement.

Vaught ran into the street and kicked the pistol away before the boy could get his hands on it.

"Fuck you!" the young man sneered as Vaught grabbed him by the shirt to drag him out of the street.

"Shut up!" Vaught said, giving him a kick to the face. "Don't open your mouth again!" He spun around to aim the pistol at the older guy, who was finally getting his feet beneath him. "Sit back down—*now*!"

The man did as he was told, and Vaught gave the kid a kick in the ass to send him crawling. "If you either one of you tries anything stupid, I'll shoot you both!"

A small crowd was gathering, and Vaught was in the process of assessing how much danger he was in, when a pair of Mexican army J8 model Jeeps rolled up, each vehicle loaded with four soldiers and equipped with a turret-mounted, .30 caliber machine gun. Both machine guns were aimed directly at Vaught.

He dropped the pistol and put up his hands. "Where the fuck were you guys last night? The tunnel's burned out, and we have a lot of injured people here!"

A lieutenant climbed out of one of the J8s and walked over, picking up the pistols from the ground. The name tag on his uniform said "Lieutenant R. Felix." He looked over the injured motorists and then gestured with the pistols. "What's happening here?"

Vaught nodded toward the men sitting on the ground. *"Estan abusando de la necesidad de la gente."* These guys are profiteering.

Recognizing Vaught's accented Spanish as coming from the United States, Felix glanced down at the kid bleeding from his knees and stood tapping the pistols against his legs. "For that you shoot them?"

"I shot him because he was going to shoot me"—he nodded at the Rottweiler puppy—"over a dog."

"Whose pistols?" Felix asked.

"Theirs."

"Who are you? Where are you from? Why are you here?"

Fuck it, Vaught thought to himself. "My name is Chance Vaught. I'm a foreign agent working with the Policia Federal Ministerial. Agent Mendoza is my commander here in the city."

The lieutenant glanced around again at the injured people staring back at him. He pointed at the dog's owners with one of the pistols. "Did these men start the trouble?"

Everyone confirmed that Vaught was telling the truth and that he had cared for them during the night. Felix then ordered both dog men taken into custody and walked Vaught out into the street, questioning him vigorously about his connection to the PFM. Eventually he forced the American to come completely clean in order to avoid being arrested himself.

At length, Felix seemed satisfied that Vaught was telling the truth. "Where are you going?"

"Toluca."

"For what?"

"To meet with Chief Juan Guerrero."

"Why?"

"I honestly don't know," Vaught said, deciding to make something up. "That's who my commander in the PFM said to go see."

"I have friends in the Toluca department," Felix said. "Sergeant Cuevas and I grew up together."

Vaught shrugged. "I've never heard of him."

Felix grinned. "You'll be very lucky to survive your mission. Lazaro Serrano is going to be the next president of Mexico."

Vaught smiled back. "Not if the PFM has anything to say about it."

The lieutenant chortled, turning for the J8. *"El león cree que todos son de su condición."* The lion thinks everyone is like him.

"You don't trust the PFM?"

Felix looked back, his eyes shining. "This is Mexico, my friend. All I can tell you for sure is that you are a long way from home. I will call for army ambulances to evacuate these people. Good luck to you."

26

Rhett Hancock and Billy Jessup sat on the balcony of their luxury twentieth-floor hotel room overlooking Tlacopanocha Beach. A Mexican woman in her early forties sat in Jessup's lap, finishing a cigarette while he fondled her breasts through her open blouse. She was a hotel employee and had come to the room earlier in the day to change the bedding and replace the towels. She'd no more begun to strip the sheets before Jessup offered her money to have sex with them.

She took immediate offense and was turning for the door when Jessup flashed four thousand dollars' worth of Ben Franklins. This was more money than the single mother of two earned in a year working for the hotel. So, to her shame, she had returned to the room on her lunch break and allowed the two American men to have their way with her.

She crushed out the cigarette and stood up from Jessup's lap, buttoning her blouse. "My money?" she asked in English.

Jessup led her back into the room and gave her the wad of folded cash from his bag.

She put the money into her pocket and left without another word.

Jessup returned to the balcony chuckling, "It ain't every day you can turn a woman into a whore."

Hancock glanced at him briefly and then back over at the next hotel three hundred yards up the beach. "You mean it ain't every day you can take advantage of a woman with hungry mouths to feed."

Jessup lit a cigarette. "How do you know she's got hungry mouths to feed?"

"She didn't get those stretch marks on her belly making beds, dumb-ass." Hancock smirked and shook his head. "You just paid four grand for a piece of housekeeper pussy. Jesus Christ, you'd fuck anything."

"I didn't see you pass it up."

"Hell, no. You were payin'." Hancock looked back across at the hotel. "Go get the scope. It looks like the party's starting."

Jessup disappeared for a minute and then returned with an M151 spotting scope, setting it up on the table and taking a seat behind it. He glassed the rooftop of the far hotel as people were emerging from a glass-enclosed suite, mingling around a pool with drinks in hand. "I don't see the guest of honor."

"He'll be there." Hancock got up and went inside to the minibar, unscrewing the top from a small bottle of tequila and drinking it down.

"Don't overdo it in there!" Jessup called from the balcony.

Hancock dropped the empty bottle into the trash bin beside the bar. "Just takin' the edge off."

He went to the closet and took out a guitar case, setting it on the bed, and opening it to remove the disassembled Barrett XM500 sniper rifle. He assembled it and set up the bipod, resting the sniper system on the bed, aimed toward the balcony. Then Hancock stepped into the bathroom to take a leak.

When he came back out, Jessup was coming in from the balcony.

"Turn on the movie," Hancock said. "Loud."

Jessup slipped the disc of an old war movie into the DVD player and ran up the volume all the way: machine guns firing, artillery blasting away. Then he returned to the balcony to check the scope a second time, scanning the growing crowd for the mayor of Acapulco. He spotted the dark Mayor Guillermo Cruz dressed obligingly in all white, standing by the glass parapet on the nearside of the pool with two other men, looking out over the ocean. "Target acquired."

Hancock went back into the room, put on his ear protection, and got behind the rifle, finding the mayor in his own scope.

Jessup stood up and closed the curtains and the sliding glass doors to an aperture of twelve inches, to keep the sound of the shot inside the hotel room. Then he sat back down and put his eye back to the scope.

Mayor Cruz was standing broad chested before them at three hundred yards. The shot could not have been more pristine. "Rhett, what the fuck are you waiting for?" Jessup whispered to himself. "Shoot him, goddamnit!"

Hancock studied the mayor's face, the dark eyes beneath thick black eyebrows, and was reminded briefly of an actor from some Mexican beer commercial he'd seen in the US.

Cruz had been the mayor of Acapulco for just six months, but already he was causing the Ruvalcabas a lot of aggravation. The city's tourist industry had fallen off dramatically over the past ten years due to ever-escalating drug violence, and Cruz had based his election campaign on promises to restore the city to its former greatness as an international tourist destination. So far he was working very hard to keep that promise, and not only was he hurting the narcotics trade but also setting the wrong example for other mayors across the country.

So, as they had with Police Chief Juan Guerrero of Toluca, Lazaro Serrano and Hector Ruvalcaba had sent Hancock to make an example of *him*.

The gringo sniper held Cruz dead to rights in the crosshairs. The mayor was doomed no matter what, so Hancock decided to get creative, to wait for the moment to ripen. After fifty long seconds, it appeared that the target was turning to step out of the sight picture, which would have forced Hancock to shoot him before he was ready, but the moment suddenly blossomed as a woman in a yellow dress—along with a man wearing a soccer jersey—stopped to chat directly in line behind the mayor.

Hancock squeezed the trigger. The .50 caliber armor-piercing round blasted from the muzzle of the Barrett with a muffled *boom*, covering the 300 yards to target in just under three seconds to strike Cruz dead-center in the chest at 2,900 feet per second. The mayor virtually exploded from hydrostatic shock, as did the woman directly behind him and the soccer player standing just in front of her. To the naked eyes of the other partygoers, it appeared that all three bodies exploded at the same time.

The party fell into instant pandemonium. People were knocked into the pool as others scrambled to get back inside the suite. Others stood in horrified shock, splattered with blood and viscera. The mayor's three bodyguards took up cover positions, pistols drawn, but there was no way to discern where the shot had come from.

Hancock got to his feet as Jessup came into the room and closed the curtains. "See that shit?" he said with a laugh. "Three-in-one!"

"I saw it." Jessup set the spotting scope down on the table and switched off the movie, secure in the knowledge that the rooms on either side of them were reserved by Ruvalcaba's people. "Look, I think this is my last op."

"Oh, come on," Hancock said. "What the fuck does it matter? The other two were rich assholes like everyone else on that roof."

Jessup shook his head. "It's not that, man. You enjoy this shit too much. You're gonna push it too far one of these days, and I don't wanna be there. I know you don't give a shit about dyin', but I do."

Hancock grabbed a handful of little tequila bottles from the minibar and sat down on the bed. "You gotta do what you gotta do, Billy."

Jessup disassembled the rifle, and a few minutes later, there was a knock at the door. He gave the guitar case to a young man, and the man disappeared.

Jessup closed the door and locked it, turning to Hancock. "What are you gonna do now?" They were beginning to hear sirens down on the street.

Hancock grinned. "First, I'm gonna get fucked up. Then I'm goin' down to the beach and have a swim."

27

TOLUCA, MEXICO
13:00 HOURS

There was still no official body count, but thousands were already known dead in Mexico City. The public transportation system had been devastated by the quake. Key bridges, along with the elevated highway that ran through the center of the city, had collapsed, crippling the public transportation system. This left stranded citizens to the mercy of profiteering cabdrivers, and Crosswhite knew it would take time for Paolina and Vaught to make their way to Toluca.

His Jeep had enabled him to drive a more direct route out of the city than most cars were able to manage, and he now stood facing a group of sixteen Toluca police officers in the empty parking lot behind the police station. There was still no cellular service out of Mexico City, so he was worried about Paolina and Valencia, but he reminded himself that Vaught was with them and tried to put the dilemma out of his mind. There was nothing he could do for the moment anyhow. If he left Toluca to go look for them, his chances of finding them would be almost nil. It was best to stick with the plan and wait for them to show up.

Each Toluca police officer had an M4 carbine slung over his shoulder, but their dark-blue fatigue-type uniforms, like those of many Mexican police forces, were not exactly *uniform*. No four cops were dressed the same, and a few of them wore uniforms a size too big.

"Doesn't matter," Crosswhite muttered in English—but he knew that it did.

He walked up to the youngest cop, a man of about twenty-one years, and offered his hand, introducing himself. He did this with all sixteen men and then stepped back in front of them.

Acting Chief Diego Guerrero came out the back of the station and stood watching.

Crosswhite faced the men. "I can see in your eyes that most of you don't trust me, and I don't blame you. I'm a gringo, so why should you? I could say that Chief Guerrero trusted me, and that should be good enough for you, but Juan is dead, killed by another gringo.

"So instead, I'll tell you a secret: I'm the great-great-grandson of Captain John Cavanaugh. That name doesn't mean anything to any of you, but it should. He was a member of the Saint Patrick's Battalion of the US Army during the Mexican-American War. The San Patricios were two hundred Irish Catholic soldiers who refused to kill Mexican Catholics, and so they deserted to fight for Mexico. They fought with great distinction against the Americans—especially at the Battle of Churubusco—and when Mexico eventually lost that war, every surviving San Patricio was hanged as a traitor by the American army.

"That means one member of my family has already died for this country. That's part of why I'm here, gentlemen. The other reason is that this is what I was trained for: teaching you men how to fight like American soldiers. If you listen to me, if you follow my instructions—and if you trust me—I can train you to outfight the Ruvalcabas on equal terms."

The cops looked at one another, one of them asking, "What about the *francotirador*? It doesn't matter how a good solider you are if a man can shoot you from so far away. We are not an army. There are less than one hundred men in the department now."

"That's plenty," said a voice from Crosswhite's left.

He turned to see Vaught standing there with Paolina and Valencia. Paolina had a bruise on the side of her forehead, and Valencia was holding a Rottweiler puppy.

He grinned at Vaught, weak in the legs with relief. "You came through, champ."

Vaught grabbed briefly at his crotch. "Right here's your *champ*. So what's this bullshit about Irish traitors?"

"Don't blaspheme," Crosswhite said, walking over to Paolina. "That's my heritage you're talkin' about." He put his arms around Paolina and held her tight for a long time, whispering how glad he was to see her and how much he loved her.

The mood among the cops began to change, seeing that Vaught was Mexican American and obviously had respect for Crosswhite. Both men were soldierly and confident, and this became contagious over the next several minutes as Vaught mingled among them, explaining that he'd been up against the gringo sniper in Mexico City, and assuring them at the same time that the man could be outflanked and killed.

"Understand something," he told them. "Any one of

you is as good as either of us. All you need is training. *Believe that.*"

But when he spoke to Crosswhite in private a few minutes later, his attitude wasn't quite so optimistic. "Dude, are you serious about training these people? The Ruvalcabas are gonna roll into this town and mop the floor with these guys."

Crosswhite was watching as Paolina took Valencia into the police station with Chief Diego. "Where'd the dog come from?" he asked.

"Did you hear what I said?"

"I've trained lots worse," Crosswhite said. "They'll do fine."

"I thought we were working for the PFM."

"We were, but the quake changes things, so now we're working for ourselves. I'll make up a story and square it with Pope down the line, but for now, we stay off the grid. We lure the sniper into our kill zone, and we take his ass out. That sound good to you?"

Taking a moment to consider his options, Vaught pulled the can of Copenhagen from his back pocket and tucked a pinch of tobacco into his lip. "Isn't this a little bit above our skill level? I'm not exactly sniper trained, and something tells me you're not either."

"Yeah, well," Crosswhite said with a yawn, "I know a guy, and it so happens he owes me a favor exactly like the one we're gonna need."

28

Mariana Mederos was more than a bit disturbed to answer the door and find Clemson Fields standing in the hallway outside her apartment.

"What are you doing here?"

Fields had always made her nervous, even before she'd learned that he was a black bag guy for Bob Pope.

"Crosswhite has gone off the grid. What do you know about it?"

"Off the grid? Have you seen the news? Mexico City just had a major quake. The whole city's off the grid."

"He has a satellite phone. Protocol dictates that he use it to check in, and he hasn't done that. So he's either dead or he's broken with protocol."

The news was unsettling, but she somehow doubted that Crosswhite would be killed by an earthquake. "Protocol or not, I don't think—"

"What did you meet with him about in Guadalajara?"

She darkened, not liking that Fields knew her personal comings and goings. "It was nothing to do with him going off the grid."

"Are you refusing to tell me what was discussed? Am I hearing you correctly?"

"Listen, Clemson, I don't work for you. I answer directly to Pope. If Pope wanted to know what was discussed, he'd call me. He wouldn't send his little gestapo agent. So what the fuck are you doing here?"

My God, she thought to herself. *I'm starting to talk like Dan.*

There was shadow beneath his smile. "Did he mention the gold he and Shannon hid from Pope?"

She rested her hand on her hip. "Oh, for God's sake. Missing gold now? Really?"

"Crosswhite's a thief. That much is documented. There's no way he'd pass up—"

"Yeah, well, Pope obviously trusts him. So—"

"Pope doesn't trust Crosswhite. He trusts Shannon."

Mariana had never met Gil face-to-face, but she had seen his picture and heard plenty about him from Crosswhite. "And you *don't* trust Shannon?"

"I think Pope might be a little nearsighted where the guy's concerned."

She crossed her arms. "So what do you have on *me*—or rather, what do you *think* you have on me?"

He could see she was no longer quite the naive operative she'd been the year before.

"Have on you?"

"You know I'll report this little visit to Pope, so you must think you have something on me to prevent that."

"I don't have anything on you," he admitted. "But I

know that you have a soft spot for Crosswhite. And I know that Pope considers him expendable."

"So what?" she said, feigning indifference. "Pope considers *me* expendable. Probably you too for that matter— everyone but Shannon. So get to the point."

"Lazaro Serrano is going to be the next president of Mexico."

"Yeah?" She laughed that off as insignificant. "Not if the PFM has anything to say about it. They're building a solid case against him from what I hear, and Pope has assigned Dan to help them."

Fields offered a devilish grin of his own. "Tell me: If Pope is keen to bring down Serrano, why has he been feeding him intelligence for the past six months?"

Mariana saw instantly the myriad dangers in this for Crosswhite, realizing he might be nothing more than a pawn in one of Pope's intricate political chess matches. "What kind of intelligence?"

He cleared his throat. "Let it suffice to say that Serrano is well enough insulated that he has little to fear from the PFM—and least of all from Daniel Crosswhite."

She saw she was being manipulated, but to what end? "You still haven't told me what makes you think I won't report this to Pope."

Fields removed his glasses, cleaning them with a handkerchief. "Pope has plans for restoring the CIA to its former greatness, as you know. I'm one of the men he's chosen to help him make that happen, so if he's forced to choose between you and me—well, you're smart enough to crunch the numbers yourself. You're too new, too young, too inexperienced—and, quite frankly, too female."

"You're a bastard."

Fields was unfazed. "We're members of a very select

group, you and I, and all members have to read from the same page. Crosswhite has gone off that page. I think he's been planning to do so for some time now, and I think this quake has given him the perfect opportunity. Now, tell me what was discussed between the two of you."

She smirked. "He wanted to tell me about the earthquake he was planning."

He stared at her. "Is that supposed to be humorous?"

"Do you see me laughing?" She stepped back into the apartment and closed the door.

Fields smiled on his way back to the car, taking a satellite phone from his jacket and calling Pope. "It's done. If she knows anything, this should set her in motion."

Mariana stood watching him through the drapes of her third-floor apartment, seeing him put away the phone before getting into his car. She realized she would be expected to do something stupid now; something to expose herself or Crosswhite. "Maybe I'll do something different," she muttered to herself. "Maybe I'll do something you'd never expect, just to see the looks on your faces."

She went to the safe in her closet, removing her passport, a satellite phone, and $5,000 in cash. Then she went down to the laundry room—where she was sure there would be no electronic listening devices—and called Crosswhite on the non-CIA-issue satellite phone.

He answered almost immediately. "Okay. How much do they know?"

"Only that you've gone off the reservation," she answered. "Fields was just here. I have intel that I can't share over the phone."

"Then we'd better meet again soon. The clock is running."

Mariana told him where to meet her in Mexico.

"Are you sure about that?" he asked. "There's no turning back if we take that road."

She drew a breath, asking herself if she was sure. "Yes. If what I think is happening is happening, it might be the only road open to us."

"Okay then. I'll meet you there in twenty-four hours. In the meantime, you watch your butt. Hear me?"

"I'll be off the grid within the hour." She switched off the phone and ran back upstairs to her apartment.

29

The ATRU assassin was a former member of German Army Special Forces, Kommando Spezialkräfte. His name was Jarvis Adler. He was thirty-two, blond, and blue-eyed, handsome when you caught him from the right angle. A speed freak and sometime rapist in his spare time, he'd been hired recently as an operator for the CIA out of Bad Tölz. He had no idea why he had been contracted to kill Sabastian Blickensderfer, but he was happy to take the job, glad for the work, and keen to collect fifty thousand dollars—which amounted to only about forty-four thousand euros, but he wasn't complaining. He'd been out of work for almost a year now, fired from his job with a security firm for failing his third random drug test in a row.

"Random," he muttered in disgust, sitting in his car beneath the streetlamp he'd disabled the day before, across the snowy street from Blickensderfer's home. The elec-

tronic dossier he had received on the Swiss banker was the most thorough he'd ever read. Whoever had collated the information had even gone so far as to include the brand of toothpaste that Blickensderfer used.

This attention to detail assured Jarvis that the CIA was quite serious about wanting the banker dead, which in turn gave him to understand that he'd better not botch the operation. It was no secret the CIA had undergone a complete overhaul during the last year, making the agency a great deal more like the World War II–era OSS (Office of Strategic Services) than the floundering CIA of the early twenty-first century, and every counterintelligence agency, from the Russian SVR to the Brazilian SNI, was nervous about it.

The CIA's new director was a man named Pope, who had flown C-130s for Air America during the final year of the Vietnam War, and the word on Pope was that you did not want to end up on his bad side. Unexpected people (two of them women so far) were beginning to turn up dead in unexpected places at unexpected times: people no one wanted to talk about, people with questionable business dealings in the Middle East, wealthy people who were considered untouchable.

People like Sabastian Blickensderfer.

And whoever was ordering the hits wasn't remotely concerned about them looking like accidents. One CEO from a Paris firm had been found dead in a Yemeni parking garage with his head slammed in his car door an estimated twenty-six times. His Arab bodyguards claimed to have been given the day off.

The White House refused to comment on the alleged assassinations, but what could anyone really say? For one thing, there was no proof at all of CIA involvement. For another, the United States had been attacked with two nuclear bombs just eighteen months earlier, bombs that had been manufactured in the old Soviet Union and eventually sold to Chechen terrorists by God knew who. No one liked to say so out loud, of course, but who could have blamed the US if it had retaliated directly against Russia for managing its nuclear arsenal so poorly? Most Europeans were secretly grateful that the crazy Americans had chosen to exercise what was widely regarded as an Olympian display of self-restraint—especially when one considered their wide-reaching response to 9/11.

Mysterious killings in the news were far easier to abide than the US launching another full-scale military invasion in their backyard or provoking Russia into a second arms race. Even the Chinese were satisfied to keep quiet on the issue—smiling to themselves as they obligingly bought up more and more of America's growing debt.

Jarvis had fought terrorists as a German soldier, but he cared little for flags or politics. What he cared about was using his considerable skills to make a living. He was even willing to work for the Islamists if they paid him, though he was pretty sure they were fighting on the losing side.

A light came on in Blickensderfer's house up on the second floor, and Jarvis glanced at his watch to check the hour. Just like the dossier said, Blickensderfer had set his alarm for 04:15.

Before getting out of the car, Jarvis did not check his pistol like they did in the movies. He knew that the suppressed Glock 30 was ready to fire a subsonic .45 caliber round resting in the chamber. He walked casually through the snow toward Blickensderfer's home on the corner and trudged up the steps. Having memorized the security code from the dossier, he punched in the eight digits, and the lock clicked open.

As he stole into the house and closed the door, Jarvis

wondered with admiration how the CIA came by that kind of information. He had intentionally waited for Blickensderfer to wake up before going inside. The idea of killing a man in his sleep looked good on paper, but it could be difficult moving stealthily through a strange house in the dark, and there was no way to be sure if the target was really asleep.

This way there would be no doubt as to whether or not Blickensderfer was awake. The target would be more alert, yes, but there was less uncertainty overall. There would also be light to see by and maybe a little bit of background noise to cover Jarvis's movement through the house.

He moved up the stairs toward the sound of an electric razor, pausing at the landing to listen. When he was sure that Blickensderfer was in the bathroom and not using the noise of the razor as a decoy, he stepped into the master bedroom and crossed to the master bath, aiming the pistol at a naked Sabastian Blickensderfer, who stared back at him from the sink with his blue eyes wide in terror, the razor buzzing in his hand.

"Das ist nicht persönlich," Jarvis told him. This is not personal. He squeezed the trigger.

In that same instant, the frontal lobe of Jarvis's brain exploded, a .45 caliber slug blasting through it from right to left, causing his own shot to miss Blickensderfer's head by a foot and shatter the glass shower stall.

"Mein Gott!" Blickensderfer blurted in horror, dropping the razor to the tile floor and taking a step back. The razor broke apart but continued to buzz.

Jarvis's body lay on the bedroom carpet with what was left of his frontal lobe oozing onto the white shag.

Blickensderfer stood with pebbles of shattered glass beneath his feet, too petrified to move, as a man he had never seen before stepped into the bathroom doorway and crouched to pick up Jarvis's pistol.

The man wore jeans, cowboy boots, and a Carhartt jacket. He stood up and tucked the second pistol into the small of his back, keeping his own .45 gripped in his right hand. "Know who I am?" he asked quietly.

Blickensderfer shook his head.

"I'm Gil Shannon. Know who I am now?"

Blickensderfer swallowed, croaking out "Yes."

"Good." Gil stepped into the bathroom and picked up the noisy razor, switching it off and setting it on the edge of the sink. "I was sent by the CIA to kill you." He gestured over his shoulder at the body. "So was he. Lena gave me the code to your door. I've been in the guest room all night, waiting for him to make his move."

Blickensderfer had never been more frightened or confused in his life. "What—why?"

"Why what?" Gil said.

"Why—why did you stop him?"

Gil shrugged. "I took your woman. I figured I owed you. This makes us even. Now you're on your own. I suggest you hire some very competent bodyguards. Bob Pope wants you dead, and he's never failed yet."

Blickensderfer grew suddenly self-conscious, reaching for a towel to wrap around his waist. "But I sent—I sent word to him that I won't—"

"This isn't about you. Pope doesn't give a shit about you. It's about the message he's sending to everyone else who does business with terrorists. You could take out a full-page ad in the *New York Times*, promising to be a nice guy. It wouldn't matter. You're on the list."

"Forever?"

Gil shrugged again. "That or until he feels like he's wasted enough time on you. The trick is staying alive long enough for him to get bored."

Blickensderfer felt his legs begin to weaken. He

wanted to sit down. The CIA he'd done business with in the past had definitely changed. "Can you—will you help me? I'll pay you."

These were the very words Gil had come to hear. "I don't want your money. I want you to help me with my Russian problem."

Blickensderfer glanced around, dropping the lid to the commode and taking a seat. "I honestly don't know if I can—but I will try."

"Then we'll both try," Gil said, satisfied. "One very important thing: Pope cannot know that I was here—that we had this conversation. No one can. Understood?"

Blickensderfer nodded. "Yes. Yes, of course."

Gil gestured back at the body once more. "Can you arrange for that clown to disappear?"

Blickensderfer glanced uncomfortably at the bloody mess in his bedroom. "Yes." He looked up at Gil. "What about Lena?"

"She's with me now—and that's just the way it is. Can you live with that?"

The banker let out a sigh, hardly able to believe he was still alive. "Yes," he said finally. "I can live with it. But why doesn't Pope protect you from the Russians?"

"Pope isn't a protector. He's an asset manager, and I'm an asset."

Blickensderfer got to his feet, being careful of the pebbled glass. "How does this work?" he asked timidly. "Do we shake hands now?"

Gil chuckled, switching the pistol to his left hand. "It couldn't hurt."

30

Fascinated by all types of world matters, from international trade agreements, to corporate espionage, to the extramarital affairs of the rich and powerful, Bob Pope was the quintessential spy. He spied on all governments, all leaders, no matter how small or seemingly insignificant. He was addicted to the intelligence he gathered and possessed the photographic memory to store almost all of it. His recall capacity was outstanding, and though he had begun to catch himself overlooking minor details in recent months, he was still near the top of his game, close to realizing his vision for the CIA.

Within the next two years, Islamic terrorism would be financially isolated, cut off from the double-dealing tycoons willing to do business with anyone if it meant an extra million or two at the end of the quarter. Already Pope's new CIA was making significant inroads into the Saudi government. Soon even members of the royal family, secretly aiding their Wahhabi friends in Iraq and Pakistan, would begin turning up just as dead as their European counterparts, causing terrorist funding to dry up still faster.

Pope had even found a way to strong-arm the National Security Agency into supplying him with intelligence, taking evidence before Congress to demonstrate that too much of the NSA's time and resources were being wasted in the act of spying on Americans, stressing that the atomic threat, along with 99 percent of all other threats to national security, lie outside the United States, not within.

He was not a politician by any means. He was not delicate in his approach. He was a mathematician, and he knew that wars were won mathematically, believing strongly that the time to worry about politics would come *after* the defeat of fundamentalist Islam.

"Bob," the president of the United States had said to him in private the week before, "I worry it's beginning to get out of hand."

Pope had put on his most innocent face while making his reply. "What is getting out of hand, Mr. President?"

The president looked at him. "This private war of yours."

"Sir, our enemies are finally beginning to run scared. And there's been zero proof of CIA or ATRU involvement in any of our operations."

"Operations?" the president said. "They're *assassinations*, Bob! The world is beginning to see the CIA in the same light it saw the KGB!"

Pope responded in a slightly elevated tone: "Mr. President, with respect, this country was attacked with a pair of atomic bombs—a *pair*, sir. Now is *not* the time for us to worry about the world's perception of the CIA. Our enemies fear the CIA again for the first time since the Cold War—*as they should*—and it's because I've taken the focus off our *own* people and put it back where it's supposed to be: on the enemy."

"You stop right there!" the president said, rocking forward in his chair, his finger pointed across the desk. "*I'm* the one who reined in the NSA."

Pope was undaunted. "And who's keeping them in check, Mr. President? You? Congress? *I'm* the man keeping an eye on them, monitoring their activities. *I'm* the one they fear, sir. Not you—with all respect."

At that, the president sat back, recognizing the truth in what Pope had said. The NSA had long grown out of control, all attempts by Congress to rein it in having failed. "Well, Bob, to be honest, I'm beginning to fear you a little bit myself—and you know I can't allow that paradigm to continue indefinitely."

"You won't need to, Mr. President. You're halfway through your second term. You only need to allow it for two more years. By then, my job will be finished, and we'll leave the next administration a much safer nation to look after than we have right now."

The president doubted it could be that simple, but he paused to allow the tension of the moment to pass.

"The Senate Oversight Committee is asking to see your books. Are they going to find any misappropriated funds?"

"Are they unhappy with our results?" Pope asked, knowing that the Senate loved him.

The president darkened slightly. "Don't answer my questions with questions of your own."

"I apologize," Pope said, adequately chastened. "The Senate Oversight Committee won't find so much as a nickel out of place."

"Which means you've found alternative funding . . . somewhere."

"Are you asking me a direct question, Mr. President?"

The president brought up his pointing finger again. "One slipup, Bob. One shred of credible evidence connecting the CIA to one of your assassins, and I'm pulling the plug. The purpose of the ATRU was to target terrorists, for Christ sake, not shady businessmen."

Pope remained unapologetic, knowing the president still needed him. "I see very little daylight between the two, Mr. President."

"Have I made myself clear, or not?" the president wanted to know.

"You have, sir."

THAT AFTERNOON, POPE punched the security code into the keypad outside one of his private intelligence gathering rooms and entered to find his protégée, Midori Kagawa, sitting at a console with two other young Japanese American women whom he'd hired the year before to help with his ATRU operations. Ever since his time in Southeast Asia during the latter part of the Vietnam War, he'd had a certain affinity for Asian women.

"How are things in Switzerland, ladies?"

"Not good," Midori said.

Pope stopped midstride, his good humor vanishing. "What's happened?"

Midori looked up from the console. "Blickensderfer is still alive, and Jarvis Adler doesn't respond to my communications."

Pope set down his coffee cup. "Ladies, please give us a moment."

The other two young woman got up from their chairs and left the room.

The door closed behind them, and Pope turned to Midori. "Are we exposed?"

She shook her head. "I don't think so, but it's definitely an anomaly. I'm hacked into local traffic surveillance in Bern. Adler's car is parked on the street across from Blickensderfer's house, but Blickensderfer is still alive. I've just confirmed that he's present at a fund-raising dinner where he's scheduled to speak this evening. So either he got lucky and killed Adler himself, or we didn't check back far enough, and he had private security inside the house. Either way, confidence is pretty high that Adler is dead."

Pope pulled on his chin. "And Blickensderfer is acting as though nothing happened?"

"It appears so, yes."

"Interesting. By now he must know that his back-channel message to me has fallen upon deaf ears."

"I'd say that's a safe assumption, but it's only an assumption."

Pope sucked his teeth. "Any word from Gil?"

She hesitated a fraction of a second. "No."

"Then he must still be chasing around with Lena Deiss," he remarked absentmindedly.

"What about Blickensderfer?"

"We'll back off for a moment—give ourselves time to sort out what's happened before risking another attempt. For now, get a message to Gil. Have him contact me direct."

"Priority level?"

"Low."

"So you're not sending him back after Blickensderfer?"

Pope shook his head. "No. Gil has too many principles. In hindsight, it might have been a mistake to send him after Blickensderfer in the first place."

Midori smiled. "You know what they say about the right tool for the right job."

"Well . . ." Pope hesitated a moment. "Adler was the right tool for this job, and look how it's apparently turned out." He picked up his coffee and turned for the door. "Make sure you get that message to Gil."

31

Crosswhite sat beside Mariana on a white leather sofa in the home of Antonio Castañeda, the head of all narcotics trafficking in northern Mexico. His cooperation the year before had been instrumental in preventing Chechen terrorists from using a stolen Russian suitcase nuke to destroy the city of San Diego. In exchange for his cooperation, both the Mexican and US governments had offered Castañeda an informal truce in the "war on drugs." The terms of the truce had been simple: Castañeda agreed to cease all violence against civilians on both sides of the border, and both federal governments agreed to stop hunting him.

Since the truce, violence against civilians in the North had dropped off to almost nil, and Castañeda had consolidated all narcotics power north of Jalisco State. This meant that not a single kilo of drugs crossed the US border without his say-so. The American DEA continued to interdict his drug shipments at will, but Castañeda was no longer targeted for capture or prosecution.

A former GAFE (Grupo Aeromóvil de Fuerzas Especiales) operator for Mexican Special Forces, Castañeda was a bug-eyed man in his late thirties with dark hair and a dark complexion. Enjoying tequila probably far too much for the good of his health, he was a legendary womanizer and took a particular enjoyment in torturing those who betrayed him.

He sat in a white leather chair, smiling at Mariana across the black lacquer coffee table, a glass of straight tequila in his hand. "To what do I owe the pleasure of such an unexpected visit?" he asked her in Spanish.

Mariana had been the CIA's contact and intermediary with Castañeda since the inception of their business dealings, and Castañeda made no secret of the fact that he desired her. Secretly, Mariana feared him a great deal, but she was always careful to keep her fears hidden.

"I'm afraid we have some disturbing news for you," she replied.

He sipped his tequila. "I am listening."

"By all indications," she continued, "Lazaro Serrano will be elected president of Mexico this coming July, and we have good reason to believe that he will not honor the truce after he takes office."

Castañeda continued to smile at her, his eyes almost perpetually glassed over from the tequila. "I understand why Serrano might pose political problems for the gringo government, but I have nothing to fear from him. Serrano is corrupt, yes, but all politicians are corrupt. The truce is good business for everyone. He will respect it."

She girded herself. "Would you feel that way if I told you Lazaro Serrano is the real power behind the Ruvalcaba cartel?"

His smile vanished. "What are you talking about?"

As planned, Crosswhite edged forward on the sofa. "Hector Ruvalcaba doesn't run the Ruvalcabas—Lazaro Serrano does. He organizes their protection and allows them an almost free hand in Mexico City. We also have confirmation that he was behind the assassination of Alice Downly a few days ago. Serrano hates the US. He wants another outbreak of violence on the border so he can eliminate you and consolidate all Mexican drug trafficking under his own tent. That will give him unprecedented power, putting him on par here in Mexico with Carlos Slim." Carlos Slim Helú, a Mexican telecom mogul, was the wealthiest man in the world.

Castañeda sat pondering this alarming revelation. He had long known that the Ruvalcabas enjoyed protection from within the federal government, but there had never been any trouble between the Ruvalcabas and the Castañedas. "How sure is the CIA of this intelligence?"

"Ninety-nine percent," Mariana answered without hesitation.

Castañeda sipped his tequila, displaying a calm he did not feel. "And the CIA has sent you to see me for what reason?"

Crosswhite sat back. "To ask your help in removing Serrano."

The former GAFE operator glanced back and forth between the two of them. "Do you think I am crazy? Assassinating a Mexican president would guarantee my destruction."

"Yes, but Serrano isn't president yet," Crosswhite said carefully. "We've got four months before that happens, so we need to eliminate him soon—before he becomes the de facto president."

An ever-darkening shadow was crossing Castañeda's

brow. "The fact remains you intend to leave *my* mark on his assassination."

"No, we don't," Mariana said.

"If we do it right," Crosswhite pressed, "your name will never be mentioned. And I can guarantee it will be done right—*personally* guarantee it."

"Oh? How can you make such a 'personal' guarantee?"

Crosswhite stared him in the eye. "Because I'm the guy who's gonna pull the trigger." He postured up on the sofa. "Look, the quake down in Mexico City has wiped out the CIA intelligence network for the foreseeable future. Tens of thousands are dead—maybe more—and that mounting body count will hold the world's attention for the next ten days or so. All I need from you is—"

"This is Pope's idea?"

Crosswhite shook his head, knowing that lying to Castañeda could prove deadly. "Pope has me working with the PFM to bring Serrano down legally, but I think it's better to take advantage of the quake: to use the chaos as cover. Serrano is still an unknown politico in the eyes of the outside world. Why not kill an ugly baby in the crib before it starts walking and talking and making a name for itself?"

Castañeda switched his gaze to Mariana. "Why are you willing to act without first getting Pope's consent?"

She saw clearly that Castañeda had grown suspicious. If he realized that she and Crosswhite had gone completely off the CIA reservation, he might have Crosswhite killed and take her for himself. Mariana and Crosswhite had discussed this forbidding possibility ahead of time and decided that, in the event the meeting took a bad turn, Crosswhite would kill her instantly and try to kill Castañeda before his guards could enter the room and shoot him dead.

Dominating the fear rising up in her gut, she gazed calmly back at the man she knew to be a butcher. "Because Pope is hedging his bets," Mariana said easily. "He wants to be in position to call the shots along the border no matter who controls the North. And while I would never say that I completely trust you, Antonio, I do believe you're much more reliable than either Lazaro Serrano or Hector Ruvalcaba."

Castañeda chortled, remarking, *"Más vale malo por conocido que bueno por conocer,"* which translated roughly as, You prefer the bad guy you know to the good guy you don't."

She smiled. *"Más o menos."* More or less.

"It appears, then, I have no real choice," he said, resting his elbows on his knees. "Your man Pope respects the truce but shows me no loyalty. Whereas you, my beautiful Mariana, you understand the value of trust."

"We have always been honest with each other," she said, ignoring his flattery as usual. "And I think such a rapport is worth something, yes?"

He nodded, shifting back to Crosswhite. "Suppose Pope is angry with you for killing Serrano—or the PFM comes after you?"

"That will be my problem," Crosswhite said. "As I've told you already, your name will never be mentioned."

Castañeda sat mulling the circumstances, seeing clearly that foreigners were still using the tactic of divide and conquer to manipulate the destiny of Mexico—and seeing equally that he was in no better a position to alter that paradigm than any of his predecessors. At length, he picked up his glass, finished the tequila, and set the glass back down.

"Very well. How I can help rid my country of the dog Serrano?"

32

Gil and Lena sat across from each other in the back of a prop-driven P-750 XSTOL aircraft, their knees almost touching, flying twenty thousand feet over Hamburg, the second largest city in Germany. Each wore a composite wing suit, sometimes called a "bat suit," which had extra fabric between the legs and under the arms, adding greater surface area to the human form for the purpose of creating lift. This allowed for a human being to glide, or "fly," two and a half meters horizontally for every meter of vertical drop, often at speeds greater than a hundred miles an hour, before finally having to deploy a BASE-jumping parachute in order to land safely on the ground.

Gil's suit was black with red fabric between the legs and arms; Lena's, white with blue fabric.

"Nervous?" she said over the rush of the wind coming in through the open door.

He grinned. "You bet."

She smiled back, liking him very much. "You look like *Die Fledermaus* in that suit with those colors."

"Like who?"

"*Die Fledermaus: The Bat.* It's a German opera—or an operetta, rather."

He laughed self-consciously, having no idea of the difference between the two. "Well, a bat knows a helluva lot more about flying than I do." He tested the zippers on his arms to make sure he would be able to free them easily when the time came to steer his parachute. "You know, doin' this without a formal lesson is really kinda stupid."

"But more fun!"

"For you," he chuckled. "Not for me. I'm a trained paratrooper—not a bat."

"Well, that's about to change." She leaned across and kissed him. "You'll do fine. Just remember to fly the suit like I told you: make your body like a wing. You have to keep rigid; concentrate on strength of muscle."

"Strength of muscle," he muttered, feeling guilty as hell over the fact that Lena excited him much more intensely than his estranged wife, Marie, ever had. They were two entirely different types of women: Marie, loving and gentle; Lena, sexy and adventurous. He reflected briefly on the high divorce rate among Navy SEALs, now understanding it on a visceral level. He told himself that he deserved to die on the jump he was about to make— for many reasons—and with that thought, all nervousness left him.

"Have you done this with Sabastian?" he asked idly.

"With who?"

"Sabastian."

"I don't know anyone by that name." She got to her

feet and grabbed the rail mounted along the fuselage just above the windows, offering her hand. "The light is red. Almost time."

He took her hand and got to his feet.

She put her face very close to his, their noses millimeters apart. "Don't ever mention that name outside of business. We're moving forward—you and me—every second from this day on. Agreed?"

He felt the energy of her personality, their mutual attraction, in the pit of his stomach. "Yes, ma'am."

A few seconds later, the jump light turned green, and they were out the door.

Gil spread his arms and legs, feeling immediately the strong resistance of the air. Lena streaked past him, her white-and-blue suit shimmering in the bright sunlight. He formed his body to match hers and soared after her, bringing his legs up too far behind him and falling forward into a brief tumble before regaining control and leveling off again.

With no hope of catching up to Lena after that, he decided to experiment with the suit, testing its limitations against his free-fall skills, based on his experience as an expert parachutist. The wing suit had long been employed by American Special Forces, but Gil's own focus had been that of a sniper, so wing suit infiltrations had never been incorporated into his training.

He saw at once the potential for such a swift and accurate infiltration system, knowing that the perfection of a chuteless landing technique must still be the ultimate military goal.

Gil soared after Lena's shimmering form, banking left and right, testing the performance capacity of the suit, and found that his extensive free-fall experience very definitely helped to cut the learning curve. As the ground drew within a thousand feet, he deployed the parachute and unzipped the wing sleeves so that he could reach up and grab the steering toggles.

He touched down lightly within a few hundred feet of Lena in a snowy field at the base of a mountain and quickly gathered the chute into his arms. Gil pulled off the helmet and stood looking around at the beauty of the countryside, which was not unlike the Montana of his youth.

She walked up to him with her chute and helmet under one arm, her blond hair blowing in the wind. "So what do you think?"

"I think I like it," he said. "When do we do a BASE jump?" BASE stood for building, antenna, span, earth—*earth* typically being a cliff. "I wanna try it off a mountain—or a bridge."

She vacillated a moment and then replied, "Whenever you like."

He smiled. "You've never BASE jumped, have you?"

She shook her head. "You?"

"A couple times—but with a chute, not a wing suit."

"Have you bungeed?"

His smile turned to a deep frown. "Bungee jumping is for drunken college kids. BASE jumping actually takes balls."

"Good!" she answered. "Then we'll go to Lauterbrunnen. The mountain jumps there are incredible."

"Where's Luaderbooken?"

She laughed. "*Lauterbrunnen.* It's in Switzerland."

He saw their ride, a black Land Rover, coming toward them through the snow. "Don't you ever get tired of Switzerland?"

"No!" she said, not quite offended. "I'm a Swiss. Besides, what's to get tired of?"

He chuckled. "You people are too damn tidy. It makes me nervous. You need to make a mess once in a while."

She laughed. "We made a mess of the hotel room last night."

"Yeah." He gave her a kiss and sauntered off toward the truck. "But that's a *German* hotel room. It doesn't count."

33

The next night, Gil called Pope on his satellite phone. He had intentionally waited to respond to Midori's message regarding the CIA director's desire to talk, wanting Pope to realize that he was no longer at his beck and call.

Pope answered on the second ring. "I was beginning to worry."

"Midori said low priority, and I've been a little busy."

"I imagine you have." Pope chuckled softly. "How are you?"

"I don't know. I've been doing a lot of thinking recently. I might be finished, Bob."

After a slight pause, Pope said, "I guess she must be something."

There was a note to Pope's tone that Gil didn't care for. "She is, and nothing had better fucking happen to her."

Pope's response was immediate and uncharacteristically indignant: "What's that supposed to mean?"

"Just what I said."

"Gil, you're getting paranoid."

"Maybe I am," he admitted. "I've got Russians following me all over Germany. There are two outside in the street right now. Where the hell are they getting their intel?"

"You know damn well they're not getting it from me."

Gil lit a cigarette. He understood that it wasn't fair taking out his frustrations on Pope, but he didn't care. He was too full of guilt, anxiety—and, yes, paranoia. "You dropped the ball in Lichtenstein, Bob. I had no advance warning they were there. If it hadn't been for Lena, they'd have fed me my balls."

"Gil, you can't expect me to keep tabs on every Russian mobster in Europe. You knew they were hunting you—and I do have other operators to look after these days."

"Yeah, I know," Gil said. "I met one of them the other night."

Pope fell silent as a tomb.

Gil sat calmly, smoking, waiting him out.

"So it was you," Pope said at length.

"I need Blickensderfer taken off the list, Bob."

"To keep Lena happy?"

"To help keep my ass alive. I need him as an asset."

Pope sighed. "I think you should come in. Bring Lena back to the US with you. Take all the time off you need, but do it here in the States, where I can look after you correctly."

"I'm going to China."

"*China?*" This obviously threw Pope for a loop. "Gil, China is crawling with Russians. What are you going to do in China?"

"Base jump the Dragon Wall." The Dragon Wall was a mountain in China where people came from all over the world to do extreme BASE jumps. Gil intentionally did not mention the wing suit aspect.

Once again, Pope was left momentarily nonplussed, asking at last, "Is this some kind of phase you're going through?"

"I need an entirely new Canadian passport," Gil added. "A new name. And I need it within forty-eight hours."

"Gil, I don't think—"

"Just make it happen, Bob. I'm asking you for a goddamn favor. And take Blickensderfer off the list so I don't have to kill any more of your sloppy ATRU operators."

"You have to know you'll never make it out of China alive, Gil. Do you have a death wish now? Is that what this is about?"

Gil ignored the question, aware that Pope was back on his heels and wanting to keep him there. "China was supposed to be a one-way trip for me the last time I was there, but here I sit. Are you still looking after Marie for me?"

"You know the answer to that."

"Good. You can have the passport delivered to Lena's place in Bern. We have a couple more jumps to make here in Hamburg before we head back to Switzerland. We leave for China in three days."

"Gil, I don't believe you're going base jumping. Tell me what's in China."

Gil exhaled smoke through his nostrils, crushing out the cigarette in an ashtray beside him on the bed. "Normally your suspicions would be right on target, partner, but not this time. I've decided to jump the Dragon Wall, and that's what I aim to do. I'll send you the GoPro footage."

He was off the phone a few seconds later. Lena stood against the wall with her arms folded. "We're not really going to China, are we?"

"Yes, we are."

"And when did you make that decision?"

"Yesterday—not long after the first jump."

"But the Lauterbrunnen jump is almost as intense as the Dragon Wall. It's also right here in Europe, where there's a lot less danger to you. We can handle the Russians down in the street. They're not going to do anything in broad daylight, and back in Switzerland they can't touch you."

He put out his arms, allowing her to walk into them. "Were you serious yesterday—what you said about us moving forward together?"

She gently took hold of the hair at the back of his head. "You know I was."

"Then we have to go China. It's the only place Pope can't follow me."

34

The next morning, Lena stepped into the bathroom where Gil was catching a shave and told him that his personal satellite phone was ringing. He ducked into the bedroom and grabbed it from his gear bag, seeing Crosswhite's name.

"What's up?" he answered.

"This phone still clean?"

"Yeah."

"You been watchin' the news?"

"I don't watch TV. What happened?"

"Big quake here in Mexico City three days ago. Thousands dead, and the number keeps climbing. Lots of chaos."

"Paolina and the little one okay?"

"They're fine, yeah."

"Good. I just talked to Pope last night. He didn't mention any quake."

"Yeah, well, he's probably waiting to see if I'm alive or dead."

"You haven't checked in? What the hell are you up to now?"

"Me? Midori tells me *you're* headed to China. What the fuck's in China? The Russians will throw your squid ass in the Yangtze."

"I'm counting on it," Gil muttered.

"What?"

"Nothin'. What do you want? I'm in the middle of a shave."

"I need you to cancel your China plans," Crosswhite said. "I'm up to my ass in alligators, and I need you here—without Pope knowing."

"Can't do it."

"What the fuck do you mean, '*can't do it*'? This is no shit, Gil! I'm up against a goddamn Ranger sniper, and he ain't—"

"I told Pope not to send you after him."

"He *didn't* send me after him. I went off the grid. I'm going up against the Ruvalcabas, and I need—"

"Who the hell are the Ruvalcabas? And what do you mean you're off the grid? You got a wife and kid to worry about now. Get your ass *back on* the fucking grid and back under Pope's wing, where you belong."

"Will you shut up and listen to me, goddamnit! You're not my fucking handler, and I've saved your cowboy ass twice. You owe me!"

"I broke your ass outta the brig last year, tough guy."

"*Stockade*, asshole, and you still owe me. You gonna shut the fuck up and listen to what I have to say or not?"

"Goddamnit, Dan, I got too much on my plate already without you adding to it."

Crosswhite laughed. "Hey, this is the life we chose, dude."

Gil grabbed his cigarettes, ignoring the questioning look he was getting from Lena as he sat down on the bed and fired one up. "Go ahead, fuckface. I'm listening."

When Crosswhite finished his story, Gil sat with his elbows on his knees, staring at the floor between his feet, the cigarette burned down to the filter. "I understand your motivation," he said quietly, "but you should walk away. It's not your fight."

"It wasn't my fight in the Panjshir Valley, either, but I jumped in there to save your shot-up ass."

Hating to admit it, Gil knew that Crosswhite was 100 percent justified to call in the favor. "Okay. I'll be there as soon as I can—after mission complete in China."

"Dude, is this China thing really that important?"

"*Dude*, I wouldn't be going back there if it wasn't. Give me five days."

"Christ," Crosswhite muttered. "Okay. Five days, then."

"It's the best I can do, partner. I'm sorry."

"Hey, if it's the best you can do, it's the best you can do. One more thing before I let you go: watch out for a company prick named Clemson Fields. He's Pope's dirty-tricks guy, a real piece of shit—*and he's on to us*."

"Fields," Gil said thoughtfully. "I've heard that name. I'll take it under advisement. You keep your ass down until I get in-country. Hear me?"

"Roger that."

Gil switched off the phone and tossed it aside, turning to Lena. "My life is a mess. Do you know that?"

She smiled. "He must be a good friend."

"He's a reckless asshole." Gil lit another cigarette and

flopped back on the bed. "He's also the most loyal son of a bitch I've ever known."

She got onto the bed, straddling his legs. "You're taking me to Mexico, right?"

He nodded, knowing there was no need to argue with her. "Can Sabastian get his hands on a blank Canadian passport?"

She laid on him with a sigh, not liking to hear the name. "He can get his hands on fifty of them."

"You were right, then," he said, drawing from the cigarette. "He *is* worth more to me alive."

35

Senator Lazaro Serrano shook hands with Clemson Fields outside his office in the Mexican senate building. "Señor Fields," he said happily in English, "how nice to see you again."

"The pleasure is mine," Fields said. "I'm sorry to arrive on short notice."

"Not to worry," Serrano said, opening the door to his office. "Please step in and make yourself comfortable. Did my people arrive on time for you at the airport?"

"They were very punctual," Fields said, passing into the office. "Thank you."

Serrano moved around behind his large, old wooden desk and took a seat. "As you might imagine, things are very, very crazy here in the capital because of the tragic earthquake. I wasn't sure if my people could meet your plane on time."

"I understand." Fields settled into his chair, resting his briefcase on the floor.

Serrano placed his hands flat on the desk. "So what can I do for you, Señor Fields?"

"We have a problem," Fields said, coming straight to the point. "Director Pope thought I should talk to you about it in person."

Serrano appeared stoic. "I am listening."

"Agent Vaught is still alive."

A flicker of uncertainty. "How is that possible? His body was sent back to the United States two days ago."

"The PFM falsified the crime scene," Fields explained. "One of Ruvalcaba's men is a deep-cover agent. He can place you with Rhett Hancock. The PFM is using both Agent Vaught and the deep-cover agent to build a case against you for corruption—possibly even as an accessory to murder."

Serrano was no longer feigning patience. "Why am I only now being told?"

"Well, I couldn't exactly call you on the phone," Fields pointed out, "and the situation has been developing rather quickly."

"You could have come yesterday—even the day before— the very hour you knew that Vaught was still alive!"

Fields remained pacific in the face of Serrano's displeasure. "There was no initial hurry. Vaught was under our control, and it was our intention at CIA to fetter the PFM investigation—thereby protecting you."

"And now?"

"Now Vaught has disappeared, and we need to find him."

Serrano's temper flared. "You should have killed him when he was under your control! Now he's a danger to us all!"

Fields held up a finger. "First, we were not in a position to safely remove him. Second, we didn't have the proper assets in place to do that kind of work. Third, we had to play by the rules.

"And, finally, Agent Vaught poses no danger to the CIA—only to you."

Serrano chortled, rocking back in his chair and reaching for a Cuban cigar. He took his time about clipping the end and lighting it with a stick match, shaking out the match and dropping it into a crystal ashtray. "Hancock is your man, not mine—a gringo sniper trained by the American army. The CIA sent him down here to help remove Alice Downly, and Agent Vaught has seen his face. I am no detective, Mr. Fields, but to me it seems that *both* of these men pose a threat—not only to the CIA but also to your Director Pope."

The naivete of people in high government never ceased to amaze Fields. "I'm no detective either, Senator, but what I can tell you is this: there is no connection between Hancock and the CIA—none—other than your word, which won't carry a great deal of weight with the US State Department. Pope is considered a national hero in my country, as you well know. Hancock was guided to Hector Ruvalcaba through an intermediary, after putting himself on the market as a mercenary for hire. He has no clue that he's working for the CIA because he's *not* working for the CIA. He's working for Hector Ruvalcaba, and Agent Vaught can connect *you* to Hector Ruvalcaba.

"Therefore," he concluded, pointing his index finger at Serrano, "both Agent Vaught and Rhett Hancock are direct threats to *you*."

Had Serrano been in a position to do so in that moment, he would've ordered Fields shot. "You've left me holding the bag, you son of a bitch."

"Not at all, Senator." Now that Fields had broken Serrano's spirit, he would build him back up. "It is still very much our intention to help make you president. That's what we very much want to see happen, and that is why I am here. Mistakes have been made, yes, on both sides. After all, Vaught was in your personal custody following Downly's assassination, was he not? You were in a much better position to deal with the problem than we were, but you failed to do so. However, this isn't about pointing fingers or even about sharing the blame. It's about working together to solve a problem. That's my job, Senator: to *help you solve the problem*. Now, with that understanding, all we have to do is find Agent Vaught, tell Rhett Hancock where he is, and let nature take its course."

Serrano saw immediately that Hancock would want Vaught dead to protect his identity. He watched with veiled trepidation as Fields opened his briefcase, removing a large envelope and placing it on Serrano's desk.

Fields set the briefcase back on the floor. "In that envelope are the names and photos of eleven deep-cover PFM agents, one of whom is Agent Luis Mendoza. Mendoza is the agent who can place you in the same room with Rhett Hancock on the day of Alice Downly's assassination."

Serrano reached forward to lift the envelope, his fingers trembling. He would have gladly paid a million dollars for the names of so many agents, but here Fields was giving it to him for free. "What do you want for this?"

Fields smiled. "Nothing more than your help in controlling the narcotics trade once you become president of this great country."

Serrano held the envelope in his lap, suddenly feeling like a child on Christmas morning. "I thank you for coming to see me, Mr. Fields, and I apologize for my loss of composure."

36

Sixteen infiltrators from the Ruvalcaba cartel had moved into the city early in the day and were now set to assault the Toluca police station with hand grenades and automatic weapons. The assassination of Chief Juan Guerrero days before had been only the first step in Hector Ruvalcaba's plan to move back into the city. As expected, Juan's younger brother, Diego, had taken over as de facto chief of police, and though he was weaker than Juan, city officials were determined to support him. So to finish off the last of the police's determination, Ruvalcaba's men would storm the station and massacre the entire night shift in a shock-and-awe-style attack.

Such a brazen act of violence—not at all uncommon in Mexico—would send a terrifying message to the remainder of the police force, ensuring that Chief Diego Guerrero would be faced with mutiny unless he allowed the Ruvalcabas a free hand in the city. This same terror tactic had been used to great success in many northern border towns, and Hector Ruvalcaba was confident it could work just as well in the South now that Lazaro Serrano was running interference with government officials.

To plan the assault, Ruvalcaba had chosen one of his most ruthless killers, a man in his late thirties whom everyone called *El Rabioso*: the Rabid One. Though his loyalty to the cartel was unquestioned, El Rabioso was picked because of his love for killing policemen. To El Rabioso, *la policia* were nothing more than mangy dogs to be shot dead in the dirt. He had murdered more than thirty of them across southern Mexico over the past ten years, and his name and face were well known.

He sat behind the wheel of his gray Ford Excursion, holding a cell phone, his slow eyes staring balefully up the street at the station where the police were in the midst of shift change.

"How many are inside now?" he asked.

"Twelve or so," answered a paid spy within the police force, the same spy who fingered Chief Juan for Rhett Hancock. "I told you they don't all come in at the same time for shift change."

"Twelve is enough," said El Rabioso. He took a radio from his lap and gave his men the order to move: *"Fuera!"*

Four SUVs converged on the police station. Four men deployed from each vehicle, all of them hurling grenades at the entrance. The nearly simultaneous explosions essentially tore off the front of the building, destroying the security door and causing a breach.

El Rabioso watched with excitement as the raiders, wielding AK-47s, stormed inside. The sight of muzzle flashes and the sound of gunfire were too much for him to sit still. His anxiety got the better of him, and he pulled from the curb, clipping a passing car. The smaller car spun around wildly, and the young female driver was knocked senseless by the force of her air bag.

El Rabioso continued up the street in the big Ford, swearing foully at the stupid bitch for getting in his way.

A bullet came through the windshield, and before he could react, a second bullet took off the rearview mirror. A third round hit El Rabioso in the shoulder, and he cut the wheel hard to the left, crashing into a parked car. He jumped out and took cover behind the engine, gripping a Taurus 9 mm as he tried to figure out who was shooting at him.

Automatic fire tore into the hood of the truck, and he realized he was taking fire from the roof of the police station. The truck sagged on the far side with both tires shot out, and El Rabioso broke cover, running to the small car and yanking the young woman from behind the wheel. Using her as a human shield, he screwed the pistol into her ear and began backing away down the street toward the shadows.

The girl squealed in pain, screaming for help.

"Callate, puta!" sneered El Rabioso. Shut up, bitch!

He saw a muzzle flash on the roof of the station and was struck in his gun arm. The humerus bone shattered, and his arm fell limply to his side, the pistol clattering on the pavement. The girl broke free and ran. The pain from the shattered bone dropped him to his knees, and he vomited in the street.

When he looked up, he saw four heavily armed Mexican cops staring down at him. Chance Vaught was among them, a scoped M4 resting over his shoulder.

"Guess who fucked up!" Vaught said in English.

El Rabioso reached lamely for the Taurus with his left hand, but one of the cops stepped on the pistol.

"*Es El Rabioso,*" said the cop.

"Never heard of him," Vaught said in Spanish, leveling the M4 on El Rabioso. "But there's only one thing to do with a rabid dog. Take your foot off the pistol."

The cop did as Vaught said, and El Rabioso reached again for the weapon.

Vaught shot him through the heart the second his fingers touched the grip.

BACK IN THE police station, Crosswhite stood with his hand on Chief Diego's shoulder, the two of them staring at the bodies of Ruvalcaba's men piled upon themselves in the corridor where they had fallen under the withering fire of the ambush.

"You've won your first battle, Chief. Well done."

"The next one will not be so easy," Diego said, sick to his stomach at the blood congealing on the tile, the smell of raw shit thick in the air. "The gringo sniper will return now."

Crosswhite clapped him on the back. "That's the plan, amigo."

The other cops were busy searching the bodies for money and identification—in that order.

"*Oye!*" Diego barked. Hey!

They looked at him.

"The money goes to the Church! Understood? Every peso!"

His men nodded reluctantly, continuing the bloody search with noticeably less enthusiasm.

Crosswhite turned his back to the men. "May I make a suggestion?"

Diego nodded. "Of course."

"Let them keep the money," Crosswhite said quietly. "You need their loyalty, and they did really, really well tonight. We didn't take a scratch."

"You're probably right."

Diego stepped forward. "You can keep the money," he announced, "but divide it evenly with the men on the roof."

The cops grinned at one another and went back to their grim work with renewed gusto. Ruvalcaba gunmen always carried wads of cash.

Vaught showed up a few minutes later, helping to drag the body of El Rabioso up to the back entrance, where Crosswhite stood smoking. "Turns out this clown was one of Ruvalcaba's top dogs. He's wanted in five states as a cop killer."

Crosswhite nodded. "You and I need to disappear for a couple days, champ. The Federales are gonna be all over this shit looking for an after-action report."

Vaught shook his head. "Not for more than a day. Normally this would be front-page news, but not right now. There's too many people dead in the quake, and the Feds are stretched to the limit. You can go look after Paolina, and I'll stick around here. I look the part."

"Okay, but if the Feds start asking questions, be sure to disappear. Diego knows the drill."

Vaught put a dip of tobacco into his lip and tucked away the can. "How long you think before the sniper shows?"

"Hard to say, but what we did here tonight is gonna piss Ruvalcaba off something terrible, so I don't expect it'll be too long."

"How soon 'til Shannon shows?"

Crosswhite dropped the cigarette and stepped on it. "I got a bad feelin' he might not show at all."

37

Not long after Gil and Lena cleared Chinese customs, Gil spotted a pair of Russians hanging around outside the airport, not exactly attempting to look inconspicuous. "That sure didn't take long," he said, pretending not to notice them as he hailed a taxi.

"What did you expect?" Lena asked. "We were spotted getting on the plane."

A cab pulled to the curb, and Gil opened the backdoor for her to get in. "It couldn't be helped."

"I guess not," she said irritably, climbing into the cab. "Not with you refusing to keep a low profile."

He got in beside her as the driver loaded their bags into the trunk. "If I keep a low profile, they might not know where to find me."

She gave him a look. "Is that supposed to be funny?"

"Relax," he said, kissing her hand. "It would take more

than a baseball hat and a pair of sunglasses to throw these guys off my scent."

"You could at least try." Their flight to Beijing had been marked with similar exchanges.

"Hey," he said, squeezing her hand, "would it help at all if I told you I know what I'm doing?"

"In China," she said dryly. "You know what you're doing in China."

"I do."

"Then tell *me*!"

"I would," he said with a smile, "but then I'd have to kill you."

She pulled her hand away, but he grabbed her face and kissed her. She resisted for a brief second but then slid her hand behind his neck and pulled his lips tighter against hers.

Then she shoved him away. "You're going to get us both killed."

"You knew what you were signing on for. Are we reaching the limit of your courage?"

"Is this a test?"

"As matter of fact, it is." The driver got behind the wheel and closed the door. "So say the word now, and I'll put you back on a plane for neat and tidy Switzerland."

"Now you're just trying to make me angry." She told the driver the name of their hotel, and he pulled from the curb. "It's not the danger that pisses me off, Gil. It's being kept in the dark."

"It's necessary," he said, resting his hand her on knee.

Despite feeling worried, Lena believed that he was telling the truth; she squeezed his hand and looked out the car window. The Russians tailing them in a white sedan were no more careful about being spotted than the two men outside the airport had been. They even went so far as to pull up alongside them at a red light, both men grinning.

"Look how confident they are," she said, feeling true fear for the first time. "They know it's only a matter of time before they get you. We might as well be in Moscow."

Gil chuckled, ignoring them. "I was in Moscow last spring. Had lunch with Putin, as a matter of fact."

She looked at him. "Seriously?"

"Seriously."

Once in their hotel room, they were careful to lock the door and push the minifridge up against it before hurriedly taking a shower and making love.

When they were finished, Lena lay in the crook of his arm, helping him smoke a cigarette.

"This trip has nothing to do jumping the Dragon Wall, does it?"

"We brought the wing suits, didn't we?"

"That doesn't answer my question, Gilbert."

He sat up, flashing back to 1993 when the movie *What's Eating Gilbert Grape* had first come out. He was still pissed at its star, Johnny Depp, for ruining his senior year in high school. "My name is not *Gilbert*—it's *Gil*!"

She laughed, her eyes dancing. "Did I touch a nerve?"

"*Gil*," he said, grinning. "*Gil* Shannon. That's it—no middle name. Got it?"

She gave him a playful salute. "Got it."

"Once we know each other a little better, you *may* call me Gilligan—but not Gilbert, ever."

She laughed again. "Like the TV show?"

"Yes," he said, lying back down beside her, "like the TV show."

She tickled his ear until they fell asleep, awaking eventually to the sound of someone knocking at the door, ignoring the Do Not Disturb sign.

Gil stood to the side of the door in his underwear without looking through the peephole, saying something in a language Lena did not understand. The person in the hall answered, and he opened the door to a small Asian man in his forties.

They spoke briefly, and the man disappeared.

She sat up, holding the sheet over her breasts. "You speak Chinese?"

"Vietnamese," he said. "That was Nahn. I worked with him the last time I was in China. He's says the lobby's crawling with Russians, so he's gonna sneak us outta here. You'd better get dressed."

She got out of bed, reaching for her pants. "How the hell do you speak Vietnamese?"

He pulled a clean shirt from his bag. "My dad was a Green Beret in the Vietnam War. He lived with the mountain tribes—the Montagnards—for six years, training them to fight the Vietcong. I grew up speaking English with my mother and lots of Vietnamese with my dad."

"Wasn't that a little strange?" she asked, buttoning her pants.

He chuckled, a sad look in his eyes. "It was *a lot* strange. But that was my dad."

"Where is he now?"

"Drank himself to death." Gil snatched his pants from the floor and stepped into them. "We need to hurry. Nahn doesn't fuck around."

38

There were always risks involved when Lazaro Serrano and Hector Ruvalcaba met face-to-face, but they had serious matters to discuss, and with the city devastated by the earthquake, Serrano had to abandon his normal security precautions. So the two men met in a brothel run by the Ruvalcabas on the outskirts of the Federal District, where quake damage had been minimal to none.

"Our attack on the Toluca police station was a complete disaster," said Ruvalcaba, a stately looking man in his early sixties, with graying hair and green eyes. He had escaped from a maximum security prison the year before via a tunnel dug from the outside to his prison cell. Serrano had arranged for and funded the tunnel's construction, a service for which he had been handsomely reimbursed. "I still don't know what went wrong, but I lost seventeen of my best people. Apparently the remaining Guerrero brother is not the timid young coward we've been led to believe."

Serrano sat puffing a cigar. "Is this new chief supposed to have killed all seventeen men himself?"

Ruvalcaba made a face. "Of course not. My point is that he apparently possesses the strength of will to hold the police force together even in the face of his brother's very public assassination."

Serrano shrugged. "So the Toluca police have rallied around the memory of their martyred chief. We've seen it before. Juan Guerrero was a brave man—*a man of the people*. It's only natural they would stick together long enough to fight a battle in his name. After all, they are Mexicans, are they not? It's our fault for underestimating them. Now we'll do it right. We'll send Hancock back to Toluca with orders to kill ten or twelve policemen in the street, all in broad daylight. That will put a most definite end to their resolve, I assure you."

Ruvalcaba demurred. "I don't believe it's that simple. But it doesn't matter because Hancock won't go back to the same city twice. I've asked him before, and he has always refused. He considers it too dangerous."

"He works for us," Serrano said. "He goes where he's told."

Ruvalcaba cocked an eyebrow. "*You* tell him that."

Deciding to leave the issue for the moment, Serrano gestured at the large yellow envelope he'd placed on the table when he first arrived. "That is a gift for you. It will take your mind off our *problem* in Toluca."

Eyeing the politician, Ruvalcaba reached out and picked up the envelope. He shook out all eleven files onto the table and sat looking them over. "Are these—these are PFM agents!"

"Straight from the hands of the CIA," Serrano said with a twisted smile.

"Puta madre!" Ruvalcaba pulled one of the photos free from its staple. "This man was one of mine!"

"Luis Mendoza?" Serrano asked.

"You knew already?"

"The CIA told me yesterday afternoon. Mendoza and the American DSS agent are helping the PFM to build a case against us."

"That can't be," Ruvalcaba said. "I've been told they were dead."

"The PFM falsified the crime scene. Both are still very much alive. Vaught has disappeared, but we will get this pig Mendoza to tell us where he is, and Hancock will kill him for us. The gringo sniper has even more to fear from him than we do. You'd better plan on three or four simultaneous abductions. Once word gets out that Mendoza and his family have vanished, the other agents in that file will take extra precautions. And forget the Toluca police for the moment. We'll send Hancock after Mendoza. He'll be more than happy to help once he realizes there are witnesses who can place him behind the rifle that killed Alice Downly."

39

Midori Kagawa had come to work for Pope at the CIA
as an analyst and computer programmer even before
graduating the Massachusetts Institute of Technology,
when Pope was still in charge of Joint Special Operations Command (JSOC). For the past ten years, she had
been blindly loyal to him, deferring to his judgement on
all matters. Recently, however, she had noticed a change
in Pope. There was a coldness to the CIA director now
where before there had been only the distracted genius
concerned with protecting his operators in the field.

Midori believed she knew the cause of the change.
Pope had been shot twice in the chest the year before, in
two separate assassination attempts. He himself had shot
the second attacker to death at point-blank range, and
though Pope had made a full physical recovery, he had
never met once with a psychologist. There were times now

when Midori could see that he was struggling with the emotional trauma of the previous year, and this convinced her that he was suffering from posttraumatic stress.

Since the discovery of Turkish gold in the French storage unit, Pope had become obsessed with expanding the reach and power of the Anti-Terrorist Response Unit. Midori believed that he had set unattainable goals for the new special mission unit—such as reaching into the House of Saud to assassinate members of the Saudi royal family whom Pope had found to be complicit with Al Qaeda in the Arabian Peninsula, the same terrorist network responsible for the now-infamous attack on the US Embassy in Benghazi.

Midori viewed this objective as pure fantasy. Whether an ATRU assassin left evidence or not, the royal family would readily suspect CIA involvement—viewing the *lack* of evidence as evidence in and of itself—and with Saddam Hussein long dead, Saudi Arabia now had much less to fear in the region, and thus much less reason to tolerate the CIA's picking off minor members of its family.

It was true that a lesser member of the House of Saud—a naturalized American citizen—*had* been instrumental in aiding Chechen terrorists to purchase a pair of Russian suitcase nukes eighteen months earlier, but the Saudi royal family had accepted no responsibility for this, instantly disinheriting the man in the wake of the attempted nuclear attacks on US soil.

While Midori remained prepared to assist Pope in his plans for expanding the ATRU to the best of her considerable abilities, she was not prepared to sit idle while he effectively turned his back on the operators who had helped him gain control of the CIA. Without the direct involvement of Gil Shannon, Daniel Crosswhite, and Mariana Mederos, the US Naval Fleet in San Diego

Bay—including two brand-new aircraft carriers—would have been destroyed in a nuclear explosion, and Robert Pope would have been run out of JSOC on a rail. As it turned out, Pope was hailed as a hero before the Senate, and his appointment as director of the CIA had been approved unanimously.

Midori had only briefly considered discussing her concerns with Pope, realizing that to even voice an opinion on the matter would preclude any future assistance she might want to offer Gil, Crosswhite, or Mariana. The way things stood, Pope trusted her implicitly, and she needed to keep it that way in order to remain outside his suspicions. So she didn't view helping Gil save Sabastian Blickensderfer's life as a betrayal of Pope's trust but rather as an act of loyalty to the man who had enabled Pope to ascend to power.

The concern weighing most heavily on Midori's mind at the moment was Pope's willingness to allow Clemson Fields such a free hand in dealing with the Alice Downly assassination. This was another matter she didn't dare offer an opinion on for fear of arousing suspicion. Fields had scheduled a flight to Mexico City via a CIA aircraft without providing any itinerary. The CIA's deputy director, Cletus Webb, had signed off on the flight without asking a single question, fully aware that Fields was Pope's point man in the Mexico crisis.

At first, Midori assumed that Fields had consulted with Pope before scheduling the flight, but that assumption proved false, after she'd asked Pope in passing, "Any idea what Clemson Fields is doing in Mexico City?"

Pope had merely shrugged. "I told him to fix the Alice Downly problem. He's probably using the earthquake as cover to get into the capital unnoticed. Agent Vaught made a real mess of things down there, and we'll have to smooth Mexico's ruffled feathers at some point, so it might as well be now. Don't concern yourself with Fields. He's been around a long time."

Something else worrying Midori was that Pope had expressed no concern for Dan Crosswhite's well-being since the quake, nor had he directed her to attempt contact. So she decided to make contact on her own, using Dan's private number and catching him in the middle of training the Tolucan police officers.

She told him about Fields's flight to Mexico City.

"So Doctor Doom is here in Mexico." Crosswhite did not sound overly impressed. "He gave Mariana the gestapo treatment up in Texas a couple days ago. I don't know what he and Pope are up to, but I've gone off the grid for now. I've got some personal shit to handle down here, and the PFM has its hands full with the earthquake."

"What about the case against Serrano?" Midori asked. "They're letting him go?"

"Ya know what?" Crosswhite said. "Why don't you ask Pope what's going on with Serrano? He's the one who's been feeding intel to that fat drug-dealing bastard."

Midori had no knowledge of any communications between Pope and Lazaro Serrano. "Are you sure? What kind of intel?"

"I have no idea," Crosswhite said. "Hold on a second . . ." In the background she heard him giving lengthy instructions to a Tolucan police officer in Spanish before coming back on the phone. "Yeah, so anyway," he continued, "Fields let that slip while he was playing 'operation mind crime' with Mariana. So whatever he's cooked up with Pope, it sounds like we've *all* been left out of it. All I can tell you for sure is that I'm done steppin' and fetchin' for that son of a bitch. He's playing both ends against the middle, and I won't tolerate it."

"How sure are you Fields wasn't making it up?"

"It doesn't matter if he was," Crosswhite said. "Pope put the fucker on the case. He broke the faith, and I will not work for a man who uses me like a pawn."

Midori needed a friend to confide in, and she knew she could trust Crosswhite. "He's sick, Dan. I think he's messed up in the head from being shot last year. He's not the same man."

"I'll bet he is fucked up," Crosswhite said. "Hell, he's probably got PTSD, but that's not my problem. He's playing games with my life and the lives of my family."

"Well, I don't know what to do," she said. "I'm afraid if I say anything, he'll stop trusting me."

"Is he getting paranoid?"

"No. Why?"

"Because if he's really got PTSD, he could easily become paranoid. So, yeah, don't ask him any questions unless you want him getting suspicious."

"Shit."

"*Shit* just about covers it. Hey, have you heard from Gil?"

"He's in China," she said. "He's in touch with our asset in Beijing. He'll be out of contact the entire time he's inside the border. Chinese electronic surveillance is too dangerous."

"Does Pope know Gil asked you to arrange the asset?"

"He asked me not to say anything." Midori didn't mention that she'd been communicating with Gil behind Pope's back for some weeks now, since the discovery of the Turkish gold.

"Good boy," Crosswhite muttered to himself. "We're finally on the same page."

"What does that mean?"

"It means Gil's not drinkin' the Kool-Aid anymore—which is good to know."

"I'm worried about him. What's he really doing in China?"

Crosswhite laughed. "You tell me, baby, and we'll *both* know!"

40

In the dark of night, the first two Ruvalcaba men stole silently, albeit somewhat awkwardly, into the bedroom of PFM Agent Luis Mendoza's twelve-year-old daughter, clumsily clamping a chloroform-soaked cloth over her mouth and nose. Not until the girl was secured with nylon cable ties and removed from the house did the other men move on Mendoza and his wife.

Agent Mendoza was smacked awake to the sight of his wife sitting on the edge of the bed with the barrel of a nickel-plated revolver stuck into her mouth.

The blood in his veins ran cold with horror. "Take me," he said calmly to the four men in black ski masks. "There's no need to involve my family."

Mendoza and his wife were thrown onto their bellies, secured with cable ties, and put to sleep with chloroform before they, too, were removed from the house.

A half hour later, Mendoza was brought back to con-
sciousness with a bucket of water. He was strapped naked
to a metal office chair in a dingy auto repair garage. His
wife and daughter were tied naked, also soaking wet, to a
support beam in front of him, their arms stretched above
their heads, wrists bound with wire. There were eight
masked men standing around, two of whom were in the
midst of sexually molesting Mendoza's wife and daughter.

The wife and daughter were sobbing with fear and re-
vulsion, and the sight of the abject terror in the eyes of his
daughter—the light of Mendoza's life—was more than
he could endure. Tears spilled down his cheeks, and he
began to plead.

The largest man, the apparent leader, came forward
and sat down backward on an old wooden folding chair,
resting his arms along the chair back. "You are going to
give me the names of the agents you work with, amigo.
Also, the names of your superiors. You will tell me where
they are working and where their families live. And for
every lie you tell me . . . every question you refuse to
answer . . . your wife and daughter will suffer."

Mendoza had broken out in a cold sweat. "I'll tell you
all that I can. Just make them stop."

But the men did not stop, and the hysterical sobs of his
wife and daughter continued.

Mendoza tried in vain to block out the plaintive cries
of his little girl as she begged him to help her. He tore
his eyes away from her molester's bloody fingers, gnashing his teeth in anguish. His scrotum contracted, and his
penis shriveled. His heart raced with excruciating anxiety, and for one frightening moment, he was so tightly
gripped by despair that he was unable to breathe. "Make
them stop!" he gasped. "I'll tell you all that I can! Just
make them stop—*for the love of God!*"

"They will stop when you tell me what I want to know," the masked man replied. "Now, who do you—"

Mendoza's daughter squealed in pain as her tormentor's probing became more invasive, sending Mendoza into a mindless a rage. *"Make them stop!"* he shrieked, his vocal cords nearly tearing in his throat. *"Make them stop! Make them stop! Make them stop!"* He continued to shriek his demand over and over like a man coming unhinged, veins bulging as he strained against the leather straps binding him to the chair.

Fearing that Mendoza's mind might be on the verge of snapping, the leader—who had never personally interrogated anyone—signaled for the tormentors to back away from their victims.

The men did as they were told, and Mendoza fell to weeping, unable to meet the shattered gaze of his wife. His head drooped forward, swaying from side to side as he muttered prayers for God to intervene.

The leader produced a tape recorder from his jacket pocket and switched it on. "Now give me the names, amigo. Give me the names, and this will end."

Mendoza's mind reeled with dread. Of course he was willing to give up every deep-cover agent working for the PFM, but there was a major problem: he didn't know any of them. Deep-cover agents were kept isolated from one another, and on the rare occasions they did meet face-to-face, their real names were never used. He knew only the real names of three direct superiors, and he was horrified because he knew the man in the mask would never be satisfied with just three names.

"I am a deep-cover agent," he croaked, his voice raw from the force of his shrieking. His daughter was still crying, but his wife had managed to calm herself, and she was attempting to soothe the child in her own trembling voice. "We're kept separate from one another," Mendoza went on, "but I can give you the names of three of my superiors."

The masked man held the recorder to Mendoza's mouth. "Say their names."

Mendoza spoke the names of each man as clearly as he could, providing all of the personal information that he remembered.

"Very good," said the man in the mask. "Now, I need more names, amigo. Give me more names."

Mendoza did not bother repeating the truth. He made up a name, claiming the man was a deep-cover agent working in Tijuana.

The man in the mask switched off the recorder and sat with his hands drooped over the chair back. "You just told me you are kept separate from one another. But now you suddenly have another name for me?" He shook his head with a heavy sigh. "Either you were lying to me before, amigo, or you are lying to me now. Which is it?"

Mendoza understood there was no escape from the impossible paradox in which he was trapped. "That might not be his real name," he explained, trying his best to speak directly, to keep the fear from his voice. "We don't use our real names—*none* of us do—and *this* is why. Surely, you must understand that."

The man in the ski mask scratched his head. "Why do you lie to me, amigo? Why do you want to make me hurt your family? Can't you hear your beautiful daughter crying? Do you think I would go to all of this trouble for three little names? *Eh?* No! I would not!" He turned to a man standing near a red metal cabinet. *"Usa el soplete."* Use the blowtorch.

"No!" Mendoza shouted. "No! Please!"

The man near the cabinet turned up the hissing blue

flame of a propane torch and stepped over to Mendoza's wife.

"Noooo!" Mendoza shrieked as the man grabbed one of the woman's ample breasts and put the flame to her nipple.

Mendoza's wife let out a screech of agony, writhing violently as her daughter's screams of terror were added to the horrifying chorale.

Mendoza lost all control himself, going completely berserk, screaming vile names at the man in the mask, spitting and snarling, straining against the leather straps with such impotent fury that his bowels let loose in a gush, and the stench of hot feces filled the air.

"Te seguiré al infierno!" he screamed with such ferocity that his voice broke in a painful rasp. I'll follow you to hell!

A door burst open on the far side of the garage, and a man shouted in English: "That's enough! *Bastante!*"

Everyone, including Mendoza, jerked their heads in the direction of the voice as the gringo sniper came stalking across the bay, grabbing the torch from the man's hand and hurling it across the garage.

"What the fuck is wrong with you?" he bawled, glaring at the masked leader sitting backward in the chair. "Are you fucking animals? You're worse than the fucking Taliban!"

The masked man got to his feet.

Hancock snatched a glass jar of bearing grease from a workbench and used two fingers to scoop out a glob of it, tossing the jar aside. "Get the fuck outta my way!" he growled at the torch man, smearing the grease over the woman's charred nipple. "Sadistic fucking animals!"

"This is not your business!" the big leader said in accented English. He was a head taller than Hancock and stood looking down on him, broad chested and imposing.

"You wanna bet?" Hancock stepped into the bigger man's space, his eyes blazing fire. "Get on the fucking phone and call Ruvalcaba! You dumb fucks were told to bring these people here and wait for the interrogator. *I'm* the fucking interrogator! Now back your ass the fuck up before I gouge out your eyes and skull-fuck you!"

The bigger man took a very reluctant step backward, knowing that Hector Ruvalcaba valued the gringo sniper's life over all of theirs.

Mendoza's wife and daughter stood sobbing while Mendoza sat naked in his own shit, looking pleadingly toward the gringo. "Please!" he begged, weeping pitifully. "I've given them every name that I know."

Hancock stepped past the leader, spinning the wooden chair around to take a seat in front of Mendoza. "Listen," he said easily. "These jackasses don't even know why you're here. I'm sorry about what they did to your wife, I am, but if you can tell me what I need to know, I promise they won't touch her again. All I need to know is where to find the Americans. Tell me where I can find Chance Vaught and Dan Crosswhite."

Mendoza's eyes grew big around, his heart breaking with the crushing realization that, by saving Vaught's life—against his better judgement—he had brought this nightmare to his wife and daughter. "I deserve to burn in hell," he whispered.

"We all do," Hancock said sympathetically. "Tell me where they are, amigo. Tell me, and all of this goes away. I promise."

"Toluca," Mendoza croaked, having now lost all desire to live. "You will find them in Toluca."

Hancock patted him on the head. "Good man."

He got to his feet and took a Sig Sauer .357 from the small of his back, blowing Mrs. Mendoza's brains all over the man standing beside her. Then he shot the little girl. Mendoza's chin was drooped against his chest when Hancock shot him through the top of the head.

His work done, the gringo turned to leave, but that's when he noticed a curious trickle of blood on the inside of the child's thigh. Glancing at the man nearest her, he saw the fellow's fingers were red with dried blood. "You sick fuck!" He shot him through the liver.

The child molester went down in a heap, crying out in agony.

Hancock could not have known it, but this fellow was the leader's younger brother.

When the leader grabbed for the gun beneath his jacket, Hancock heard the sibilance of leather and whipped around with unbelievable speed, shooting the leader through the face. The big man pitched over backward into a pile of old radiators with a crash, and his nickel-plated revolver went clattering across the grimy concrete.

Hancock gestured with the Sig at the younger brother, who now lay writhing in the grime. "Let him bleed to death. The rest of you assholes get this mess cleaned up! Now!"

At least a couple of the remaining six men must have spoken English, because they moved quickly to begin untying the bodies.

Hancock went out the back exit, slamming the steel door after him. "Fucking amateur night!"

41

"I don't understand why we didn't take a plane to Zhangji-ajie," Lena said from the passenger seat of a stolen Land Rover as they rode north along the scenic S10 highway in Hunan Province. They had just crossed the eighth-highest suspension bridge in the world, spanning 1,080 feet above the Lishui River. Of the world's one hundred highest bridges, forty-two of them were located in China.

"I wanted to see some of the country," Gil said with a glance at the rearview mirror. "Look at those mountain ranges. They make Montana look like West Virginia."

Lena, who had never been to the United States and thus could not appreciate the comparison, sat staring at the side-view mirror, watching the black Mercedes-Benz directly behind them. Three Russians had followed them from Chongqing, despite Nahn's supposed efforts to throw them off the scent.

"A plane would have been a thousand times safer," she said. "How long have you known we were being followed?"

"Since we left the hotel."

"And you said nothing?"

"I didn't want to worry you." He put his foot on the brake pedal, slowing abruptly to agitate the Russian driver behind him as he'd done a half dozen times since leaving Chongqing three hours earlier. "I like knowing exactly where they are. I also like knowing they're probably racking their brains trying to figure out what the hell we're doing in China."

"*Pffft! I'm* still trying to figure out what the hell we're doing in China."

"We're jumping the Dragon Wall."

"Mmm-hmm," she said. "You know that Victor Kovats was killed jumping the Wall, right?"

"Who's Victor Kovatch?"

"*Kovats*. He was the Hungarian wing suit champion."

"Oh, the *Hungarian* champion!" Gil chuckled sarcastically. "I'll bet he had to be pretty good to be the Hungarian champ."

She suppressed a smile, both amused and offended by his American air of superiority. "You should know the best wing suit fliers in the world are from Europe."

He laughed. "And they're apparently splattered all over China."

She laughed too in spite of herself, slapping him on the shoulder. "You Americans think you're so great!"

For reasons Gil could not quite pin down—competitive reasons, perhaps?—Lena brought out the conceit in him. "Well," he said, "how many Europeans have HALO'd into Iran from the back of a Turkish 727?"

An experienced parachutist, Lena knew that a HALO

jump was a High-Altitude, Low-Opening parachute jump employed by Special Forces to infiltrate enemy territory. Her jaw hung open. "You did that?"

He did not answer the question directly. "So who's got bigger balls now? Me or Kovatch?"

"Ko*vats*," she said quietly, her ardor beginning to smolder. She slid her hand along the inside of his thigh. "Why were you in Iran?"

He thought briefly about his plans for the future—should there be a future, considering the insanity factor of the jump he planned to make—and decided to share a classified secret: "I was sent in to assassinate a bomb maker and his pregnant wife."

She sat back with a gasp. "You murdered a pregnant woman?"

He shook his head. "I shot her, but I didn't kill her. I killed her husband and her father, though. Then I kidnapped her back to Afghanistan, and she gave birth to a baby boy that same night. The kid'll probably grow up to become a damn terrorist, thanks to me. Last year, I killed the CIA man who ordered me to shoot her without telling me she was pregnant." He took his eyes off the road just long enough to meet her gaze. "How do you like me now?"

She put her hand on his knee. "No wonder you can't go back to your old life."

"How could anyone go back?" he muttered, thinking of Marie. "The things I've done . . ."

Her voice felt thick to her as she spoke. "You and I were destined to meet, Gil."

"Dunno about that." He was eyeing the mirror again, wishing he could kill the Russians now instead of having to wait, but it was necessary to the plan. "Maybe we were—if you believe that kinda crap."

An hour later, they were approaching Zhangjiajie, the city nearest to Tianmen Mountain National Park in northwestern Hunan Province. Tianmen Mountain was often called the Dragon Wall because of the winding, serpentine road that led up to the almost five-thousand-foot-high summit from which wing-suit fliers from all over the world launched themselves into the sky like Wile E. Coyote.

Victor Kovats had died there on October 8, 2013, during the World Wingsuit League Championships. His parachute had failed to deploy just shy of the landing pad, and he impacted the trees at nearly a hundred miles an hour.

When they arrived at their hotel, Gil parked in front and got out, smiling at the Russians as they drove slowly past and signaling for the driver to roll down his window.

The blond Russian stopped the car, staring with his dead blue eyes as he put down the window, waiting to hear what Gil had to say.

Gil saw the Bratva tattoos on the Russian's neck. "You can park right over there and just bring our bags up to the room," he wisecracked.

Without giving any indication that he'd understood, the Russian put up the window and pulled past the hotel.

Lena was afraid of the Russians outside of Switzerland. "Why do you antagonize them?"

"It was necessary," he said, opening the back of the black Land Rover Defender to remove their bags.

An Asian man on a bicycle emerged from around the corner of the building and pedaled past in the same direction as the Russians. Lena recognized him at once as Nahn. "Hey, that's—" She turned to Gil. "He got here ahead of us! You wanted him to see which car they were in!"

Gil gave her a wink. "Never fuck with the United States Navy."

She laughed and shook her head. "My God, you're arrogant."

"Only around you, baby." He pulled her carry-on from the back of the truck and handed it to her. "Here. It won't kill you to carry one up yourself."

She laughed again, taking the bag. "Fuck you, Gil."

42

Mariana Mederos had rented a small apartment outside of Puerto Vallarta in order to remain close to Antonio Castañeda, pending completion of Crosswhite's mission in Toluca. After Serrano and the gringo sniper were dead, she would have to make some decisions regarding her future with the CIA. For now, though, she had a purpose, and that was to arrange for any logistical support that Crosswhite might need from Castañeda's people in the South. Under normal circumstances, she would have been afraid to remain in the same city as Castañeda, alone and unprotected, but she was beginning to see that, despite his ruthless nature, the former GAFE operator did adhere to a certain moral code. There was no way of divining the limits of that code, but it did provide a small degree of predictability.

She was walking north along the beach with her feet

in the surf when her cellular began to ring in her bag. She did not recognize the number, but it was from the DC area code: 202.

"Hello?" she said, convinced that it would be Pope.

"I'm surprised you answered," said Clemson Fields.

His voice had a nerve-grating nasal overtone that Mariana recognized at once. "What do you want?"

"I see you're down in Vallarta," he said. "Do you have time to meet me in Tijuana?"

Mariana's desire to meet Fields in Tijuana—or anywhere else—ranked right up there with her desire to be eaten by a shark. "For what?"

"By now, I'm sure you've heard that Alice Downly was killed by an ex-Ranger sniper working for the Ruvalcabas. I've tracked his spotter, Billy Jessup, to Tijuana, and I need you to get close to him so you can learn the sniper's location."

"And how do you suggest I do that?"

"That will be up to you," Fields said, "but Jessup has a fondness for Mexican women."

"In other words, you expect me to sleep with him."

"I expect you to do whatever you can to help end this crisis. I won't waste time sparring with you, Mariana. You know the gringo sniper is hunting Agent Vaught and is therefore hunting Crosswhite as well. Even if you no longer care about the future of the CIA, I believe you do care about Dan Crosswhite. Or am I wrong?"

She realized that both Fields and Pope were under the impression that she and Crosswhite had slept together, and this annoyed her, but they were right to assume she cared about him. This annoyed her as well. They had discovered a weakness, and Fields was exploiting it.

Very well. If men were going to exploit her weaknesses, she would fly to Tijuana to exploit one of theirs, but sleeping with anyone was out of the question; she'd sooner resort to using a pair of scissors to get the information she wanted. "The spotter's name is Jessup?"

"Correct," Fields said. "I'll fill you in on the gory details when you arrive. You can call me at this number with your itinerary. How soon should I expect you?"

"Maybe tomorrow afternoon. But all future meetings between you and me will be in a public place."

He chuckled. "You've nothing to fear from me, Mariana. I'm not an assassin."

"I'd never accuse you of possessing the courage, Clemson. I just don't trust you as far as I can pick you up and throw you."

There was a tense moment of silence at Fields's end before he said, "I'll wait to hear from you."

With the call ended, she dug the satellite phone from her bag and called Crosswhite to tell him about the conversation.

"What do you think?" he asked her.

"It *sounds* legit," she said, "but if Pope has been working with Serrano, how can they not already know how to find the sniper?"

"Consider this possibility: Suppose the sniper actually works for Pope. Suppose he's part of a cell within the ATRU? If that's the case, Fields might be in the dark. I don't know how much he knows."

"But if the sniper was part of the ATRU, Midori would know."

"Not necessarily," Crosswhite replied. "Midori said Pope has become more secretive lately—maybe even paranoid— and if *Pope* had Alice Downly assassinated, he's got every reason to keep her in the dark."

The idea chilled Mariana to the bone. Could Pope have gone that far? "But why would he want Downly dead?"

"Who the fuck knows?" Crosswhite said with disdain. "I've never understood how he thinks. Hell, he stabbed a dude in the face with an ice pick last year during the hunt for the loose nuke. He didn't even give Gil a proper chance to interrogate the guy—just buried an ice pick in his face and started asking questions."

Hearing this told Mariana that Pope was capable of anything. "Speaking of Gil, can you reach him by sat phone?"

"No. As long as he's in China, he's completely blacked out, and you can bet that's exactly why he picked China too. Whatever the fuck he's up to, he doesn't want Pope poking his nose in it."

"What if he doesn't make it back? Can you and Vaught handle the sniper without him?"

Crosswhite snorted. "Will we have a choice?"

That made up her mind. "I'll leave for Tijuana in the morning."

"Listen, I don't want you taking any unnecessary risks for me."

"Would you say that to me if I was a man?"

"You being a woman doesn't have shit to do with it. The difference is that I care about you, and I don't trust Fields any farther than I can throw his skinny ass."

She laughed without sharing why. "This is the business we chose, remember?"

"That it is," he admitted, knowing she had to go to Tijuana—regardless of the danger.

43

Dressed in a black SWAT uniform, Crosswhite tucked the phone into his leg pocket. "Fields is on the move."

Vaught stood leaning against the outside wall of the police station, a dip in his lower lip, an M4 slung over his shoulder. "What's he up to now?"

"He's drawing Mariana north to Tijuana, away from Castañeda; says he's got a line on the sniper's spotter. Sounds like it might be a legit lead, but it's too soon to tell."

Chief Diego Guerrero was there too, equally armed, but he understood almost none of what was being said. "What's happening?" he asked in Spanish.

"Our enemy in the CIA is making his move."

Diego carried an ugly cut over his right eye from where he had collided with the barrel of another officer's carbine the day before during a house-clearing exercise.

He had begun to move much more like a soldier over the past couple days of drilling. Crosswhite and Vaught were both satisfied with his progress, and they never passed on an opportunity to build him up in front of his men, who were catching on faster than he was.

All of the officers had taken to wearing black balaclavas over their faces whenever they patrolled in public now, as did Crosswhite and Vaught. This was not an uncommon sight in Mexico, and it solved the problem of Crosswhite's drawing unwanted attention because he looked like a gringo. As expected, the Mexican Federal Police had spent less than a day investigating the ill-fated assault, rushing back to Mexico City as soon as possible, where they were still badly needed to maintain order in the wake of the earthquake.

"Does that mean the sniper will return?" Diego asked.

"It means that from this day forward," Crosswhite said, "we should assume he's already here. I suggest that everyone—you included, Chief—continue wearing their balaclavas when patrolling the city. That will make it impossible for him to single any of us out. He might decide to shoot some men at random to scare us off the streets. If he does, we'll zero his position and outflank him."

"How difficult will that be?" Diego's fear of the sniper was evident.

Crosswhite put a hand on the young police chief's shoulder. "A sniper always has the first shot. There's nothing we can do about that, so we have to accept it. The trick is in knowing which direction to move after he pulls the trigger. Your men need to be vigilant at all times."

A lieutenant stepped out the back door of the building, gesturing urgently with a sheaf of papers. Diego excused himself.

"What's that about?" Vaught wondered.

"Looks serious, whatever it is."

Diego returned, offering the papers to Crosswhite. "My men found these bodies on a road outside of town. We haven't seen this type of civilian execution since before my brother was appointed chief."

Crosswhite sorted through print-offs of a half dozen cell phone pictures. Three naked bodies had been found dumped on a dirt road: a man, a woman, and a girl, all of them obviously shot in the head. The printer quality was not the best, but there was no mistaking Agent Luis Mendoza's protruding Adam's apple in the profile pic of his blood-smeared face. Mrs. Mendoza's charred breast was equally evident.

"Like I said," he muttered, passing the pictures to Vaught and walking off. "He's already here."

Vaught opened the file. "Oh my God," he whispered, seeing the little girl's exploded head.

Diego saw the blood drain from his face. "Do you know those people?"

"It's Agent Mendoza and his family." Vaught turned away and vomited his lunch onto the ground between the wall and a parked police cruiser.

44

Strolling casually into Pope's office, Fields took a chair across the table near the window. The CIA director did not acknowledge him, sitting with his eyes focused on a laptop screen, his fingers moving slowly over the keys in gentle taps. Fields didn't know it, but Pope was hacked into the Chinese Guojia Anquan Bu mainframe (Chinese Ministry of State Security), and he was searching to see if the Chinese had discovered an ex–Navy SEAL operating in their country. So far there was no such indication.

He closed the laptop and looked across at Fields. "How are things in Mexico?"

Fields took off his glasses and began cleaning them with a handkerchief. "Crosswhite and Mederos have met with Castañeda," he said. "I don't know what was discussed, but I doubt it was in the interest of the agency."

Pope set aside the computer with a sigh. "I'm sure they mean well."

"I'm not." Fields put the glasses back on.

Pope stared with his powder-blue eyes. "Is this in reference to missing gold again?"

"Gold or no gold," Fields said. "You need to accept that all three of your most trusted children are up to something."

While Pope did believe that Gil and Crosswhite were up to something, he didn't believe they were up to the *same* thing. And he knew for a certified fact that, whatever they were up to, it had nothing to do with any missing gold. He knew this because every ounce of bullion stolen from the *Palinouros*—a yacht owned by a corrupt Turkish banker in the Mediterranean—the year before, had been accounted for behind door number nine of the French storage unit.

How silly, he thought, his mind drifting. *People are so prone to conspiracy theories. As if Gil and Crosswhite could ever sell gold bullion on the black market without me catching them.* But this was the lens through which Fields viewed the world, and the reason that Pope had put him in charge of the Mexico crisis in the first place. Fields was predictable.

"They didn't steal any gold," he said, dismissing the notion. "What's happening with Serrano?"

Fields let the question of gold pass for the moment. "He's cooperating, but if things go bad for him, he'll attempt to throw you under the bus—he as much as said it."

"There's no record of our dealings with Hancock," Pope said. "It would be my word against Serrano's. No one paid attention when Manuel Noriega accused Bush I of colluding with him as director of the CIA in the mid-seventies. Everyone believed it was probably true, but nobody paid attention."

"Still, we might have backed the wrong horse," Fields went on. "There's some low-level buzz in the Mexican media. They're accusing Serrano of arranging Ruvalcaba's 'escape' from prison last year. Few journalists have been brave enough to write about it, but if the story picks up momentum, it could put Serrano out of the race for president. Meanwhile, Castañeda continues to honor the truce."

"Castañeda's intelligent," Pope conceded, "but he has no political tics; no one to run interference for him with the Mexican government. That makes him problematic in the long term. It's true that Ruvalcaba is less intelligent, but he's easier to control. Our most immediate problem is Vaught. How do we stand?"

Fields sat up in the chair. "I've told Serrano to send Hancock after him. It's the most expedient solution."

Pope nodded. "In that case, Hancock will have to go too—eventually."

"I already thought of that, so I've tracked Billy Jessup to Tijuana. Once I have him, I should be able to learn quite a bit concerning Hancock's movements."

"I trust you have the necessary assets in Tijuana?"

"I'm leaving tonight." Fields was satisfied that Pope was not asking for details because he wasn't sure how he would have reacted to him manipulating Mariana. "I'll have things in order within a few days. Jessup isn't going anywhere soon. He's too busy living the Tijuana nightlife."

"Hancock won't be easy to remove," Pope warned. "I misjudged his mental stability, but his skill set is sound. Has he figured out the CIA put him in touch with the Ruvalcabas?"

"Not that I know of."

Pope's mind began to drift again, but he came back

on tangent. "Midori asked me what you were doing in Mexico City. Did you meet with anyone other than Serrano while you were there?"

"I did. I made it a point to drop in on the head of the PFM. He thanked us for our cooperation in allowing them to use Agent Vaught—though the quake seems to have derailed their investigation for the time being."

"Good," Pope said. "That will make it easier to explain why you took a company jet to Mexico, if anyone ever comes asking. Continue to be careful, Clem; there's no way to know who's watching what anymore."

45

There was a knock in code at the hotel room door, and Gil let Nahn into the room. The Asian man gave him a small brown paper bag, and they spoke in Vietnamese while Lena applied her makeup in front of the mirror. Nahn finally left as she was finishing her lipstick.

"He doesn't speak English?" she asked, capping the tube and turning around.

Gil took a bottle of lighter fluid from the paper sack and set it on the table. "I've never asked."

"He speaks Chinese, I assume?"

"His Cantonese is perfect. That's what they speak down south, closer to Vietnam. Up here they speak a lot of Mandarin dialect. His Mandarin is passable but not perfect."

"Can the people here tell he's not Chinese?"

"Probably, but he doesn't try to pass himself off as Chinese, so it doesn't matter. There are a lot of Vietnamese living in China. What's important is that our Russian friends across the street can't tell the difference." He took the Zippo lighter from his pocket, pulled off the bottom and began soaking the cotton wadding inside with lighter fluid. "I have to go out for a while—be back in an hour or so."

"Out to do what?"

"Nahn needs to show me something."

"Show you what?"

"Where the Russians parked their car. I'll disable it so they can't follow us to the Dragon Wall. There are too many places in the park where they could pull some shit."

"Can't Nahn disable the car?"

He put the lighter back together, tucking it into his pocket. "The man isn't being paid to risk his life." He shrugged into his Carhartt jacket and gave her a kiss. "Back in an hour or so."

"It's the *so* part that concerns me. Aren't they watching our hotel?"

"No. Nahn says they paid the concierge downstairs to call them if we leave."

He gave her another kiss and slipped out the door.

Nahn was waiting for him in the back hall, where he gave him a small rucksack, and they took the stairs down to the first floor, leaving out the back. They skirted behind the restaurant next door and crossed the street a block down, making their way back behind a row of lesser buildings to arrive eventually at the rear entrance of the Russians' older hotel.

"Are they still in their room?"

Nahn checked his cellular to see if he'd received a text from the cleaning woman he had paid to keep an eye out. "All clear," he said in perfect English.

They went inside and took the stairs to the top floor. Nahn showed Gil how to access the elevator shaft through a maintenance panel in the janitor's closet.

"Okay," Gil said, removing the access panel. "If all goes as planned, I'll meet you by the river."

"Good luck, my friend." Nahn closed the closet door and disappeared back down the stairs.

Gil took a small headlamp from the rucksack and slipped it over his head, switching on the red light and easing himself into the elevator shaft through the maintenance hatch. Using the ladder mounted on the wall of the shaft, he descended three floors to the top of the elevator car and gently stepped aboard, locating a small electrical box that Nahn had wired directly into the elevator's control panel. The elevator doors opened and passengers stepped aboard. Gil took hold of the cable attached to the top of the car and steadied himself for the ride.

The old car descended seven floors to the lobby, and the passengers disembarked. Someone else stepped aboard, and a few seconds later, the elevator was going back up. Nahn had assured him there was plenty of headroom even if the car went all the way up to the tenth floor, but in the almost pitch dark, Gil could not resist the instinct to keep low.

The car stopped on the ninth floor, and he took his cellular from his pocket, texting Lena to meet him in the lobby of their hotel as quickly as possible with only her carry-on. Then he used a screwdriver to pry open the trapdoor in the roof of the elevator, wedging it in place to keep the door open just enough for him to peer down into the car. Two Chinese passengers stepped aboard, and the elevator descended to the lobby.

Five minutes later, the elevator was called to the third floor, and Gil sat watching like a spider as all three Russians walked aboard, pressing the button for the lobby. He flicked the kill switch on the electrical box, and the Russians were trapped.

The blond driver Gil had spoken to the day before jabbed the button with his thumb, but the elevator didn't move. He pressed the button to open the doors, and again nothing happened. They began talking in hushed tones as the blond continued to jab the lobby button.

Gil eased two gallon-size plastic zipper bags from the rucksack, resting them at the edge of the trapdoor. Each was filled with two parts gasoline and one part dishwashing soap. He took the Zippo from his pocket and opened the trapdoor all the way.

"Top o' the mornin' to ya, boys."

The Russians looked up with their eyes wide, completely stunned to see the American looking down at them, a red light shining from his forehead. They touched impotently at their jackets for pistols they didn't have, stealing wary glances at one another.

Gil nudged the plastic bags over the edge. The bags broke open upon impact with the floor, splashing the homemade napalm all over the Russians, and they began shouting for help, hammering on the doors.

Gil flicked the Zippo alight. "*Dasvidanya,*" he muttered, dropping the lighter into the car and flipping the trapdoor shut.

The elevator car was engulfed instantly in flames. The trapped men screamed horribly as Gil climbed onto the ladder with flames licking out around the edge of the trapdoor.

The screams died out after only a few seconds, the Russians' lungs scorched by the intense heat, and Gil climbed quickly up to the tenth. The hotel fire alarm was ringing by then, and he mixed in among the guests as they left their rooms calmly, most of them complaining about the inconvenience. By the time they arrived at the landing to the eighth floor, however, the stench of burning gasoline was evident, and they began to hurry. Arriving at the fifth floor, they smelled burned flesh and began to scurry downward in controlled panic.

Arriving at the lobby, Gil walked calmly out the front door and crossed the street to his hotel, stepping inside, where Lena and a half dozen other guests were watching the commotion across the street. The fire had quickly burned itself out due to the lack of oxygen in the elevator car, so there was no smoke or flame to be seen from the street.

"What happened?" she asked.

Ignoring her, Gil locked eyes with the concierge, pointing at him with his thumb and index finger and pretending to take a shot. The concierge instinctively took a step back, and Gil glanced up at the security camera with a sneer, turning for the door and taking Lena by the arm. "Time to fly, baby. Let's go."

46

Thirty-year-old Captain Fa Chao of the Chinese Ministry of State Security stood looking at the partially charred bodies of the dead Russian Bratva lying crumpled on the floor of the elevator, their clothes burned away almost completely. The stench made his stomach turn, but important people would be watching him very carefully to see how he handled this, so it was imperative that he dominate his nausea and look the part of an experienced and capable leader.

"Who are they?" he asked peremptorily.

The head police investigator offered him a paper sack containing three scorched Russian passports. "The fire burned itself out quickly. The passports are still legible."

Chao examined the passport photos, noting the Bratva tattoos about the men's necks. "They're Mafia?"

"It's possible," the investigator said. "We think they were killed by an American staying at the hotel across the street. The concierge over there said these men were asking about him yesterday morning. The propellant was gasoline, but what we still don't understand is how he managed to trap these men inside the elevator."

Chao leaned into the elevator, looking up at the trapdoor. "Has anyone checked the roof of the car?"

The investigator turned to one of his men, barking orders to get a ladder.

A stepladder was produced within minutes, and one of the Chinese officers pushed open the trapdoor, climbing onto the roof of the car with a flashlight in his teeth. A minute later, he stuck his head down through the hole. "Someone has wired an electrical switch into the control panel." He handed down Gil's rucksack. "He left a screwdriver and this empty backpack."

The investigator took the rucksack and gave it to Chao.

Chao looked inside and handed it back. "I want to talk to that concierge."

Again the investigator barked his orders, and two officers went to bring the concierge.

They returned five minutes later with the nervous-looking young man standing between them.

Chao gazed at him, his eyes menacing. "I want to know everything. Lie to me, and you will be very sorry."

The concierge told him all that he knew, admitting that the Russians had offered him a week's pay to call them the second the American or his woman showed up in the lobby.

One of the police officers produced the hotel ledger, pointing out Gil's alias: Conner MacLoughlin.

Chao looked at the concierge. "The ledger says he's Canadian."

"Yes, I know," the concierge said. "But the Russians said he was American."

Chao took the investigator aside, talking in a low

voice. "Go across the street and take custody of the security video. If these Russians believed their killer was American, he could be CIA. I want him caught before sunset—alive. Is that understood?"

"Yes." The investigator disappeared down the stairs.

Chao returned his attention to the concierge, gesturing at the bodies with the charred passports. "You admit to calling these men when the Swiss woman came down to the lobby?"

"Yes," answered the concierge, a bead of sweat trickling down his temple.

"Place this man under arrest," Chao said to the officers. "He's an accomplice to murder."

"That's not true!" the concierge blurted, pointing at the bodies. "I was helping *them*, not the American!"

Chao, recognizing his blunder at once, was embarrassed to have it pointed out to him by a simpleminded concierge. "So you say!" he snapped. "But if you had not called them, they would not have been trapped in this elevator to be burned alive!"

The concierge lowered his eyes, unable to refute the fact placed before him.

Chao smirked in satisfaction. "Take him away."

The investigator called Chao to meet him across the street in the hotel security office, where they reviewed the security video together. They saw very clearly the American pantomiming shooting the concierge with his finger before grabbing the Swiss woman by the arm and practically dragging her out the door.

"It appears the woman might be in danger as well," Chao said. "Send the suspect's photo to the Ministry of State in Beijing immediately. They can scan it with facial recognition software to learn if he's in the database."

The investigator snapped his fingers, signaling for one of his men to take care of it at once.

Two more police officers appeared. "These tourism brochures were found in their hotel room."

Chao looked the brochures over. "They were planning to visit the Zhangjiajie Forest."

Another officer stepped into the doorway appearing slightly winded, as if he had been running. "The suspect was just spotted fleeing south in a black Land Rover. One of our men is in pursuit."

Chao and the investigator shouldered past him out the door and ran across the lobby toward the exit.

"Be sure he's taken alive!" Chao repeated as they jumped into a waiting police car in front of the hotel. "I don't care how many of your men he kills—*I want him alive!*"

"We'll do our best," promised the investigator.

Chao knew that catching an American CIA agent alive in the middle of Hunan Province would be a lot like catching a unicorn, only better, because it would guarantee him a promotion to the Beijing office.

The investigator got on the radio, making it clear to his men that the suspect was not to be killed under any circumstances.

Chao sat in the backseat as they raced through the streets of Zhangjiajie in a wild attempt to join the chase. Excited reports were now coming over the radio saying the suspect in the Land Rover was driving like a lunatic, and that so far he had already taken out three police cars by ramming them off the street.

"Drive faster!" Chao shouted. "I want to be there when he's caught!"

THE LAND ROVER was battered, but it was built like a tank compared with the Chinese-made Chery QQ patrol cars chasing after it.

"Break it in the way you're gonna drive it!" Gil snarled,

ramming the tiny police car out of his way as it tried to get alongside him. The police car jumped the curb and crashed into the corner of a building. "Three down, half a million to go."

He was disoriented now because of the chase, listening in frustration as the GPS system tried bringing him back on course for the city of Chongqing. He and Lena had never made it to the Dragon Wall. The local police had responded far more quickly than he'd planned for, giving him serious doubts about his escape plan.

Maybe burning three men alive in an elevator had been a little overkill.

"Well, go big or go home," he muttered, cutting the wheel and gunning it around a corner to bring himself back onto the proper heading. He didn't think it would be much longer before the police started shooting at him. Their fuel-efficient little cars couldn't keep up with the Land Rover, and they were just no match in a ramming contest.

He felt sorry for the person Nahn had stolen the Rover from, because the truck wouldn't be fit to use for a garbage can by the time he was finished with it.

CHAO WAS ON the phone calling for a roadblock to be set up on the far side of the Lishui River. "If he's stupid enough to try for Chongqing, we'll trap him on the bridge!" he said excitedly, tossing aside the phone. "Do your men understand he's to be taken alive?"

The investigator was getting tired of the government man's incessant hounding. "They understand very well. There's no need to continue pestering me about it."

Chao took immediate umbrage as they flew past a disabled police car that had crashed into the back of a city bus. "Do you realize how important this is? If this man is CIA—"

"I understand very well!" the investigator barked over the back of the seat. "And he'll be taken alive. So relax and let us do our jobs!"

The driver cut the wheel so sharply that Chao had to grab the handhold over the door to keep from being thrown across the seat. The radio was alive with a cacophony of excited calls requesting additional units. They were trying to box in the suspect, but there were never enough cars because the American was picking them off one at a time.

Someone called out asking for permission to open fire on the tires.

"No shooting!" Chao shouted. "Tell them no shooting!"

The investigator grabbed the radio, ordering no shooting under any circumstance.

"He's definitely headed for Chongqing," the driver remarked. "There's no other place for him to go from here. It's the bridge or nowhere."

Chao sneered. "We have him. He'll never make it off the bridge."

GIL ANSWERED HIS phone, knowing it would be Nahn. "Whattaya got?"

"You'd better hurry!" Nahn said. "They're blocking the far side of the bridge."

"They sure got their shit together in a hurry!" Gil checked the mirror to see that he'd picked up another cop car. There was steam coming from beneath his hood now, and there was a bad shimmy in the front right. "Have your people gotten Lena to the airport?"

"She'll be on the ground in Taiwan in six hours."

"Excellent." Gil jerked the wheel to ram the lone police car out of the way. "How's the fog on the bridge?"

"Thick but passable."

Gil saw the pillars of the Lishui River Bridge drawing into view over the hill. "See you in a bit."

He tossed the phone out the window and jammed the pedal to floor, speeding up the grade to the bridge approach. As the suspension bridge came fully into view, he glanced up at the mirror to see five police cars in hot pursuit, finally enough of them to box him in. He saw brake lights in the fog on the bridge and realized traffic was coming to a stop because of the roadblock at the far end.

"Not a good sign," he muttered, cutting onto the safety median and racing past the slowing cars. The police cut onto the median right behind him, lining up to follow in echelon along the four-foot-high guardrail.

Out of the fog appeared a flatbed tow truck with its ramp down, its yellow lights flashing atop the cab. "This is gonna taste like shit!" Gil locked up the brakes, skidding out of control up the ramp.

CHAO LEANED FORWARD in the backseat of the fourth police car in the line, watching in triumph as the battered black Land Rover slid cockeyed up the tow truck's ramp to slam into the back of the cab. He let out with a cheer, but sucked it back in as the Land Rover caromed off the cab and careened over the guardrail.

"No!" he shouted, watching the Land Rover tumble off the bridge and disappear into the fog. "No, no, no!" He banged his fists on the seat like a child throwing a tantrum, all hopes of securing a Beijing post lost forever.

The investigator smiled in the front seat, Chao's livid outburst music to his ears.

47

Forty-eight hours after the Land Rover impacted the surface of the Lishui River, Director of the CIA Robert Pope discovered that the Chinese Ministry of State had learned Gil's true identity through facial recognition and was in the process of searching the river for his body. Deep river currents had washed the Rover more than a half mile downstream before it was located, and by the time Chinese authorities fished it from the drink, all of the windows had long been broken out of it.

Pope sat before his computer, staring at the screen for a long time. At length, he took off his glasses and then sat looking out the window. It would be his responsibility to break the news to Marie Shannon. The poor woman had been through so much already, and now her ultimate nightmare had become a reality.

He rocked back in the chair, lacing his fingers behind his head.

So far the Chinese were not telling the outside world that they had identified an American CIA agent operating within their borders, and Pope doubted very seriously they ever would. There were too many reasons to keep it secret, and almost nothing to gain by making it public. This meant he could take his time about telling the White House. Had Gil been captured alive, the political situation would have been much different, so the colder, more calculating part of Pope's persona took solace in the fact Gil had not been captured, and he hoped that his body would not be found, though he was certain the Chinese would make every effort.

There had been some initial confusion in Beijing as to what had happened to Lena Deiss, but the Ministry of State quickly tracked her to Taiwan, where she was now outside its reach. Pope briefly considered sending an agent to intercept her there, but something told him to let the sleeping dog lie for now. If Gil's body was found, and the Chinese decided to make a public stink about it, there would be time enough for looking into Lena Deiss.

Pope's most immediate responsibility was to Gil's widow.

He got up from the chair and went to find Midori in her office, where she sat collating intelligence files on their developing Saudi operations.

"Gil's dead," he said quietly. "I'm going to Montana to tell his wife. I'll be back in twelve hours."

Midori stared at him.

"He crashed off a bridge in Hunan Province," he went on. "They're still searching the river for his body."

"My God," she croaked. "What happened? I mean . . . how?"

He shrugged. "It looks like he set some Russians on fire in a hotel. I don't know what he was thinking. Anyhow, the police caught up to him before he could get away this time."

"Fire? What about Lena Deiss?"

"She made it to Taiwan."

"Are we going after her?" Midori paid close attention to the drift of his gaze as he pondered his response.

After a few moments, Pope answered, "No. We've got enough to focus on."

"What about Blickensderfer? If Gil's dead, are we going to resume the operation?"

"Keep him under surveillance for now. I'll decide about him later." He returned to his office and called the airfield.

48

Marie Shannon was in the stable with her horses when she heard the rotors of the incoming helicopter echoing off the frozen foothills surrounding the ranch. The winter air was cold and crisp, so there was a sharpness to the sound that caused the hair to rise on the back of her neck. Her 120-pound Chesapeake Bay retriever, Oso Cazador (Bear Hunter), came trotting into the stable to stand protectively at her side, growling low in his throat. Helicopters had come to the ranch before, and they had always been harbingers of trouble.

Marie went to the door, her heart hammering in her chest as she watched across the ranch. A US Air Force Black Hawk helicopter was coming in low out of the east, a giant sky-blue dragonfly sweeping up contrails of snow along its approach. It set down a hundred yards from the stable, and as its door slid open, Marie prayed against heaven and earth for Gil to appear.

When a tall man with white hair stepped out of the aircraft, her eyes flooded with tears, and she sank into a crouch, hugging the dog tightly to her. "Daddy's dead," she whispered hoarsely.

Marie forced herself back to her feet, wiping away the tears as she stood in her maroon Carhartt and watched the man trudging toward her through the knee-deep snow, holding up the wide collars of his overcoat against the blowing cold.

By the time he arrived at the stable, he looked chilled to the bone. "Mrs. Shannon, how do you do? I'm—"

"Bob Pope," she said, her brown eyes penetrating. "There's no one else you could be."

He nodded sadly. "Yes. Yes, I am. I apologize for arriving unannounced like this. I'm afraid I bring bad news that I couldn't imagine sharing with you over the telephone."

She steeled herself. "Where was he killed—or can't you tell me?"

"China," he said quietly. "I don't have all of the details, but I'm willing to share what little I know."

She swallowed the egg-size lump that had formed in her throat. "What was he doing in China?"

"The truth is, I'm not sure. I didn't send him." Pope had not yet worked out whether to mention Lena Deiss. "He said something about BASE jumping from a popular mountain in Hunan Province."

She crossed her arms, her eyes remaining steady. "Mr. Pope, please don't expect me to believe that my husband was killed in a BASE jump."

"No," he said. "That's not what happened. I'm not sure he ever made it to the mountain, to be honest."

Marie had lived on the ranch all her life, and she was accustomed to the harsh Montana winters, but she felt suddenly cold. "We'll go inside," she said softly. "I can see you're freezing."

"Yes," he said with a kind smile, his boyish blue eyes grateful. "I am."

Pope followed behind her and the dog as they crossed the ranch to the new house, rebuilt the year before, after Muslim terrorists had burned it to the ground.

Inside, the house was quite warm. A fire blazed in the fireplace, and the smell of an apple pie baking in the oven pervaded. Marie's mother, her long gray hair in a thick horsewoman's braid like her daughter's, stood in the kitchen doorway wiping her hands on a towel. She met Marie's forlorn gaze and realized that her son-in-law was dead. Lowering her eyes, she turned back into the kitchen.

"Make yourself comfortable," Marie said, taking off her coat.

Oso trotted into the kitchen to see what kind of food he could score from Grandma, who spoiled him rotten.

"Thank you," he said, taking a chair near the fire.

"Does your flight crew need some coffee brought out?"

What a fine woman this is, Pope thought to himself. *What was Gil thinking, running off with the likes of Lena Deiss?* "No," he said. "They're fine. The helo is warm enough, and I believe they brought a thermos, actually."

"Okay." She settled into the rocking chair opposite the CIA director. "I'd like to know what happened, please. Every detail."

Again, Pope felt the stab of Lena Deiss. "I'm afraid I'm very short on details. I don't know how much Gil might have told you, but during his last mission for me, he took it upon himself to rescue a dozen or so young Russian women who'd been sold into prostitution. He killed quite a few members of the Russian mob in the process, and they put a price on his head. Judging from the intelligence I've gathered so far, it appears he ran afoul of three Russians during his trip to China and ended up killing them. There was a police chase, and Gil's truck crashed off a very high bridge into a deep river. I've been keeping tabs on the situation, and it appears his body was found just a few hours ago."

Tears spilled down her cheeks. "Will they send him home?"

"I can almost guarantee they will not," he said. "I don't expect China to admit that Gil was in the country. He was traveling on a Canadian passport under another name, and for this reason, they have assumed, incorrectly, that he was there to carry out a mission for the CIA. For the Chinese to admit the CIA is carrying out operations so deep inside of their country would be embarrassing to Beijing. It could also complicate the trade negotiations now taking place between China and the US. As you probably know, China is accustomed to getting the better end of most trade deals, and they're not likely to risk the status quo over an incident such as this. Had Gil been captured alive, things would be very different, but that's not the case."

"Luckily for the CIA," Marie said, not kindly.

"For the CIA, yes," Pope admitted. "For me personally, much less so. Gil was my friend, as was his father, and I hold myself partially responsible for what's happened. I've kept him extremely busy these past couple of years. I pushed him too hard, and I think he lost himself—lost track of what was most important to him. My apology doesn't even begin to make up for that."

Marie ignored the apology. It was useless to her. "So that's it. No funeral at Arlington. No recognition. Nothing. He's just gone."

"I'll tell the president when the moment is right. After that, I'm sure there will be a private ceremony at Arlington if you'd like to have one."

"For what? To bury an empty box? To be given a goddamn flag in exchange for my husband?"

"Only if you desire it," he said quietly.

"I certainly don't desire it!"

"I misunderstood. I'm sorry."

Her tone turned accusatory. "I sometimes see drones over my ranch," she said sharply. "I assume that's to keep an eye on my mother and me?"

"That's been done at Gil's personal request, yes."

"Well, he's dead. So will the spying continue?"

"I think once his death is made public—perhaps in a few months—any danger to you will pass."

"Then I should expect to see your drones until then?"

"I can order them to fly higher, if you like. You won't see them."

"I would appreciate that."

"Consider it done."

She drew a breath, unsure if she truly wanted to ask the question that had been haunting her for months. "Can you tell me if he was seeing anyone?"

Pope did not hesitate. "To my knowledge, Gil was still very much in love with you. I have *no* knowledge of him spending time with any other women."

She nodded, wiping her nose with a tissue. "Is there anything else I need to know?"

"I don't believe so, but I'd like to leave you my card. I'll remain at your service for as long as I'm with the CIA."

She felt her anger spike but conquered the urge to tell Pope just how much she despised him and the CIA. "That's very kind of you," she said carefully. "Thank you."

He stood to leave. "Is there anything else you would like to ask before I go?"

She looked up at him, heartbroken. "Those women you say he rescued—they're home now? They're safe?"

He smiled. "Yes."

"That's all, then. Thank you for coming."

"It was my responsibility to come."

"Yes," she said. "It was. Have a safe trip back."

A few minutes later, she stood beside her mother in front of the big bay window at the back of the house, watching the helicopter lift off. It flew away to the east, and only when it was gone from sight did she sink to her knees to weep.

Short and stout, her mother stood with her hand resting on her Marie's head, her own eyes full of tears as she stared off across the snowy linen landscape.

Oso whined to go outside.

49

With training over for the day, Crosswhite was drinking a beer with Vaught and three other policemen at the firing range when his satellite phone rang in his jacket pocket. Seeing that it was Midori, he ducked into the concrete building where they conducted their urban warfare training.

"Go ahead," he answered. "It's me."

"Brace yourself," Midori said. "I have bad news."

"Shit," he said, fearing that Mariana had gotten into trouble. "What is it?"

"Gil was killed two days ago in China."

Crosswhite's stomach hit the floor. "What the fuck are you talking about?"

"He set some Russians on fire in Hunan—on an elevator. The police chased after him, and he crashed off a bridge into the Lishui River. We are hearing that they claim to have found his body a couple of hours ago."

Crosswhite sat down on a concrete stoop, resting his forehead in his hand. "An elevator? Midori, what happened? That doesn't tell me anything."

"That's all I know," she said helplessly. "The Chinese are keeping a tight lid on it. Nothing has been released to the public, and I'm not the one who hacked into their system. Pope is the only one with access, but for what it's worth, I really don't think he's hiding anything on this. He's in Montana now breaking the news to Gil's wife."

"Christ," Crosswhite said. "After all the shit he's been through . . . to get run off a bridge in Jumbuck, China. How high?"

"Eighth highest in the world."

"So pretty fuckin' high."

"Yeah," she said quietly. "Pretty high."

"That's it, then," he said, running a hand through his hair. "Gil's gone. *Fuck*, I can't believe it!"

"I'm sorry, Dan. I know you were close."

"It's worse than that," he muttered, lighting a cigarette. "He was my only friend." *That's not true*, he thought. *Mariana's my friend*. "Well, it doesn't sound like they'll be shipping him back to the States, does it?"

"I'm sorry. I forgot to mention: the intel stream says he's already been taken to a crematorium."

"Bastards!" he hissed. "So was he over there working for Pope?"

"No. We have no clue what he was really doing over there. Pope doesn't think we ever will."

"What about the woman—the Swede?"

"She's Swiss."

"Whatever!"

"She's back in Switzerland."

Crosswhite spit in the dust. "Well, I just might have to pay her a visit myself one fine day."

"If you do, be sure to keep me in the loop. I'd like to know what really happened. I won't tell the boss."

"Okay," he said quietly. "Thanks for calling. I appreciate it."

Crosswhite put away the phone and looked up to see Vaught standing in the door with a beer in his hand.

"What happened?"

"Gil's dead. The goddamn Chinese ran him off a bridge. Can you fuckin' believe that?"

"Shit, man. I'm sorry."

"Yeah," Crosswhite said. "Everybody's sorry. You might as well cut out of here. Head for our embassy in DF and get yourself home."

"What are you talking about?" Vaught said.

"There's no reason for you stay involved in this. Mendoza's dead, these cops are almost ready, and that sniper's out there gunning for you. You've seen his face."

Vaught tossed the beer half-finished into a corner. "Yeah, and what happens to your family when he blows you in half like he has everyone else?"

"My family's taken care of no matter what happens to me—never mind how."

"Good, but you're not getting rid of me. I owe that son of a bitch."

Crosswhite smiled. "Don't you think you owe Serrano too?"

Vaught waited to hear the rest of what was on his mind.

"If this caper's gonna work," Crosswhite said, "three key people have to be taken out: the sniper, Serrano, and Ruvalcaba."

"What caper?"

"Mariana and I are putting Castañeda in charge of the southern cartels. That'll give him exclusive rights to the narcotics trade."

Vaught's eyes widened. "On whose authority?"

"Our own."

"Why Castañeda?"

"He's honoring the truce. And he's willing to continue."

"You bet your ass he is!" Vaught hated Antonio Castañeda. "Who wouldn't be with a monopoly on the drug trade?"

"Look," Crosswhite said. "It's our only chance to salvage anything out of this entire fucking mess. If Serrano takes over the north, border violence will resume. He hates the US. But with Castañeda in control, the CIA holds the reigns, and civilians don't get butchered. It's that simple."

Vaught could see no other way. "So what's your plan?"

"You stay here and deal with the sniper; I'll go handle Serrano. Whichever one of us survives goes after Ruvalcaba. How's that sound?"

"Honestly? It sounds like Pope belongs on that list too."

"I agree, but Pope's a bridge too far. So we'll go after Mexico's chief of station instead: Mike Ortega. We'll take his family and force him to set something up."

"No way!" Vaught said. "Absolutely not. I draw the line at kidnapping."

"We're not gonna hurt 'em, champ."

"I don't care. Ortega might be a dumb-ass, but he's on our side. You're just pissed at him because he insulted your wife."

Crosswhite smirked. "Okay. You come up with a better idea. I'll sit here and wait."

Vaught was out of his depth, and he knew it. "You can't be serious. You can't really be willing to kidnap a man's family."

"You have no idea the shit I've done for far less worthy causes. And I'll tell you like I tell everybody else at this same crossroads: this is the business we're in. You're either willing to do what needs to be done, or you're not."

Vaught dug the Copenhagen from the cargo pocket of his trousers, putting a pinch of tobacco in his lower lip. "Your man Shannon: He did this same kinda shit?"

Crosswhite shook his head. "Gil had principles. He was a better man than me—by a lot—but I have to play to my strength."

"Which is what?"

Taking a last drag from the cigarette, Crosswhite flicked it out the door. "I don't give a fuck about consequences. I never have."

50

"I have to meet with Fields in Tijuana," Mariana said to Antonio Castañeda, seated by his pool. The last time she'd seen the pool, she'd watched Crosswhite drown a man in it. To be back there gave her the creeps. "Can you supply me with two men I can trust to watch my back?"

Castañeda sipped from his glass of tequila, his beady eyes glossy—the only outward effect that excessive amounts of alcohol seemed to have on him.

"I'm not sure that's a good idea."

"You don't have any men you can trust around me?"

"*Pffft!* I have dozens of men I can trust."

"Then what's the problem?"

"The problem, my beautiful Mariana, is that if Fields or his men see two of *my* men following you around, they'll know exactly who they are and take steps to neutralize them."

Sometimes Mariana allowed herself to forget that Castañeda was an ex–Special Forces operative. Making it a point never to forget again, she said, "So do you have any suggestions? I can't go up there alone. Fields is too dangerous." She explained about Fields wanting to use her to get to Jessup.

"I see," Castañeda said. "He wants you to sleep with him."

She cocked a dark eyebrow. "He's knows better."

The drug lord set aside his drink, leaning forward to rest his elbows on his knees. "Do you honestly believe that? Tell me how else do you think you will get this man Jessup to talk to you about the gringo sniper? Military men disclose that kind of information only under the most *intimate* of circumstances."

She immediately thought of Anna Chapman, the Russian spy arrested by the US Justice Department in 2010 and deported back to Russia. Married to a British national, Chapman was purported to have slept with a number of rich and powerful American men during her intelligence gathering operations in the US. Even the thought of being used in that manner was enough to make Mariana bilious.

"I'll think of something."

Castañeda reached for the glass, resting back in his chair. *"Suerte."* Good luck.

"About my support?"

He drew a breath, taking time to think it over. Had Mariana been anyone else, he would have left her on her own, but she had earned his admiration somehow. When they'd first met two years earlier, he'd given very serious consideration to abducting her and leashing her to his bedroom wall, but his inclinations had changed over the past eighteen months.

He whistled across the pool to a beautiful young woman in her early twenties who lay naked on a chaise lounge. "Tanya!"

Tanya sat up, her brown skin glistening with oil. "*Sí, papi?*"

"Go get your sister, my love."

Tanya got up, slipped into a silken red robe, and strode into the house. She had long raven hair to the small of her back, and a perfect physique.

"My God, I love her." Castañeda chortled happily and took a drink. "Why won't you agree to stay with me for a while?" he asked Mariana. "Give me six months of romance, and you'll never have to work again. You can leave the CIA and live wherever you like in the whole world."

Though Mariana knew she was pretty, she also knew she did not possess Tanya's stunning beauty or that of her older sister, Lorena. "You only want me because you can't have me," she said, now accustomed to his gallant overtures.

"You make me burn with desire," Castañeda said, his throat feeling tight. "And it agitates me very much—because taking you against your will would only spoil it."

"Then use that," she said, maneuvering him. "Let me be the one woman you actually respect."

He smiled. "I must think about this."

Lorena came from the house wearing skintight jeans and a red-and-white soccer jersey tied in a knot just above her navel. She was so similar in appearance to her younger sister that most people who saw them together believed they were twins. "*Sí, Papi?*"

"*Mi amor,*" he said, his voice liquid and sweet. "Mariana needs someone to look after her in Tijuana. There is a CIA man up there who might wish to do her harm. I want you and Tanya to go with her and keep her safe for me."

Lorena glanced at Mariana. *"Sí, papi."*

"You will leave within the hour. Go and tell your sister."

Lorena went back inside.

Mariana looked at Castañeda. "Are they . . . reliable?"

"If you ever see either of them use a straight razor, there will be no need to ask."

She felt a chill. Both young women were truly beautiful, but there was an undeniable lifelessness behind their obsidian-colored eyes. "It's smart," Mariana admitted. "No one will ever see them coming."

"No one ever does," he said, taking a drink. "I choose my women very carefully."

"Like you've chosen me?" she asked, continuing to maneuver him.

"One kiss," he said, leaning toward her with his beady eyes so unattractive. "Please."

"I'm a terrible actress, Tony. I promise you'd be disappointed."

He sat back with a frustrated smile. "I suppose you're right." He thumped his fist lightly on the arm of his chair. *"Me has embrujado."* You have bewitched me.

51

Rhett Hancock had arrived in Toluca early in the day to begin his reconnaissance of the town, riding in the backseat of a Dodge Charger with darkly tinted windows and two of Ruvalcaba's men riding up front. All three were heavily armed, determined not to be taken alive.

Now it was night, and Hancock sat alone in his room on the north side watching pornography on television with the sound turned down. He was tired of living in motels and hotels, tired of being bored all the time. Nothing pleased him anymore, not even sex. The only thing that excited him was having a target in the crosshairs, and there weren't enough of those to sustain him.

He fumbled with an empty tequila bottle beside him on the bed, tossing it onto the floor without thinking. The bottle shattered against the tile.

"Fuck," he muttered, making a mental note not to climb out on that side of the bed in his bare feet.

The blond actress on the TV screen was having sex with two men at the same time. She reminded Hancock of his second girlfriend. Her name was Jennifer, the only girl he had ever loved, and he had accidently killed her on his seventeenth birthday.

They'd been driving home on a Saturday night in young Rhett's restored 1977 Pontiac Firebird, having spent the night drinking around a bonfire at a buddy's farm in Kansas. Racing along on a black moon night, they sang aloud to a lonesome Lynyrd Skynyrd tune with the T-top open, the wind blowing through Jennifer's long blond hair. The song began to increase in tempo, and she cranked up the volume as Rhett downshifted into third, gunning it through a wide curve and out onto his favorite stretch of open road.

"Lord, I can't change!" they sang. "Won't you fly . . . high . . . free bird, yeah!"

From the pitch-black, a ten-point buck leaped in front of the car.

Rhett hit the brakes, cut the wheel, and promptly lost control. There was only one tree along that stretch of road, a hundred-year-old red oak, and they hit it head-on doing better than seventy-five miles per hour.

He came to in a ditch the next morning, sitting up in the mud with a splitting headache, dried blood caked to his face. The first sight he saw was the Pontiac smashed against the tree. The second sight was Jennifer's mangled body wrapped around the pillar post of the windshield, most of her face sheared off by the glass.

Rhett was put on juvenile probation for a year, working manual labor jobs after school and drinking in secret. He withdrew from his family and hardly ever spoke.

At the age of eighteen, he was put on adult probation, where he remained until his twenty-first birthday. At the age of twenty-three, after a brief legal battle to seal his juvenile record, he was able to enlist in the United States Army.

The rest, as they say, was history.

Hancock sat staring at the porn star in his drunken stupor, allowing himself to think of Jennifer for the first time since the morning of the crash. The pain of thinking back on her smile, her voice, even the smell of her became more than he could stand. He snatched the Sig Sauer from beside him on the bed, thrust it under his chin, and squeezed the trigger.

The hammer dropped with a click, but the gun did not fire.

"What the fuck?" he said in shock, breaking out in a cold sweat and jacking the slide to eject the bullet.

He examined the round to see a perfect pin strike in the center of the silver primer.

"No fuckin' way," he whispered. Sick to his stomach, he got out of bed and stepped on a shard of the broken tequila bottle. "Motherfucker!" he swore in pain, falling back on the mattress and grabbing his foot to pull out the jagged piece of glass. "Motherfuckin' son of a bitch!"

The cut was not big, but it was deep in the sole of his foot, just forward of the heel. It hurt badly and bled profusely. Hancock glanced at the television. The girl was up on all fours now, her two comrades really going to town on her.

He grabbed the pistol and hurled it at the old television. To his amazement, the weapon bounced off the glass picture tube and clattered across the tile. He sat staring after the gun for a long moment, feeling more hopeless and lost than ever before. Hancock's eyes welled with tears, and he began to sob. He fell over on the mattress and cried himself to sleep.

In the morning, he awoke hung over with a foul taste in his mouth. His foot was throbbing, but the bleeding had stopped. He got out of bed on the safe side and limped over to his rucksack on a chair near the window, digging out a military first aid kit and taking it back to the bed. He filled a syringe with lidocaine and injected the foot near the wound, wincing as he depressed the plunger. Then he injected himself at the ankle. When the entire foot was numb, he pressed his thumbs down hard on either side of the wound to get it bleeding again, squeezing out a pea-size globule of pus. Wiping away the pus with a wad of cotton, he injected five hundred milligrams of amikacin directly into the wound to kill off any remaining infection.

Next, he took a foil packet of sutures from the aid kit and closed the wound with three stitches. Hancock slapped a patch of sticky black adhesive tape over it and went to take a shower, standing beneath the water for a long time.

By the time he emerged from the bathroom, he'd made an important decision: he would follow Billy Jessup's example and attempt to live a normal life. Maybe he'd move to Thailand. Or maybe he'd stay in Mexico; buy a fishing charter up in Baja. That seemed a relaxing way to live. One thing was sure: he didn't dare go back to the States.

Hancock grabbed his ruck from the chair and pulled out two unopened bottles of tequila, which he took into the bathroom and poured down the toilet. He dropped the caps into the trash and set the empty bottles on the back of the commode.

He was finished drinking, but he wasn't finished killing. Chance Vaught was still loose in Toluca, and Vaught could finger him for the Downly hit. If he was going to have any shot at all of leading a normal life, he'd need a clean slate. Otherwise the stress of watching over his shoulder for the FBI would drive him back to the bottle, and he'd eventually end up right back where he'd been the night before: with a gun stuck up under his chin.

52

Lena Deiss sat across from Sabastian Blickensderfer at his personal table in Bellevue Palace, the most exclusive restaurant-hotel in the city. Still unable to understand what had happened in China, she had drunk nearly three glasses of wine and barely touched her plate.

After rushing her out of the Zhangjiajie hotel, Gil had almost dragged her around back to the parking lot, where he'd delivered her into the arms of three waiting Chinese men, saying only, "Go with them! I'll meet you in Chongqing." The men had hidden her in a small van and raced off for the airport. A small plane flew her on to Chongqing, where Nahn had met her to break the news that Gil had crashed off the bridge and was killed.

"He spoke English," she muttered in the same language.

Blickensderfer looked up from his plate of *rippli*, a

smoked pork loin. *"Was hast du gesagt?"* What did you say?

"The Vietnamese guide," she replied in German. "He spoke English. But Gil always spoke to him in Vietnamese."

"Well, he didn't want you to know what they were talking about." He sat chewing. "It's obvious they were using you as cover for a mission of the CIA. I told you, Lena, Americans cannot be trusted."

She looked at him. "He saved your life."

The Swiss banker forked more food into his mouth and kept chewing. "To win your confidence, my love. Are you so blind? And now that he's dead, we'll see how long before *Herr* Pope sends another assassin to my door."

She didn't want to believe she'd been used, but what Sabastian was saying made perfect sense.

He sipped his wine. "Are you coming back to me, or was I simply your easiest way out of Thailand?"

She demurred for a moment. "I need time, Sabastian."

He reached across to touch her hand. "The American gave you an adventure—an adventure I admit I could never have given you—but such adventure could not have lasted. You know that, my love. The man was a runaway train, and a runaway train will always jump the track sooner or later. I'm just grateful he was decent enough to have you spirited out of China before getting himself killed. It might have taken me months to win your release."

"Not to mention a great deal of money."

He put down his fork and looked at her. "When have I ever complained about spending money on you?"

"Never," she said quietly, averting her eyes. "I shouldn't have said that."

"I would have spent whatever it took to get you back." He picked up his fork and began to eat again. "You've embarrassed me, but for me to forgive you is the easiest thing I know how to do." He paused for a drink of wine, setting down the glass. "By the way, I never got around to canceling our wedding, so . . . well, the plans are still set."

"If I agree," she said, "no more dealings with terrorists. I insist."

"There is no need to insist. The surest way for me to end up dead at the hands of the CIA would be to resume with those affairs. I've already been to death's door once. I have no intention of going back anytime soon."

They ate in silence over the next couple of minutes.

"There's something we've never spoken of." He wiped his mouth. "During our time apart, I realized I would like for us to have a child. How do you feel about that?"

She swallowed, the notion slightly appealing. "I'll consider it."

During the limousine ride back to his house, he put his hand on her thigh and nuzzled her ear.

Though Lena realized she would never be truly in love with him, Sabastian had always treated her with affection, and she was a woman with needs like anyone else. She put her hand over his and rested her head against his. "Don't cancel the reservations."

He kissed her hand. "I've missed you."

I'm sure you have, she thought to herself, heartbroken with the realization that her only chance for true happiness had crashed off a bridge in Hunan, China.

53

The neighborhood around Agent Mike Ortega's house was mostly untouched by the earthquake, but the damage to the shopping plaza just a few blocks away had been considerable, and electrical power still hadn't been restored to the area. Even cellular service remained spotty at best.

"You gotta be smooth," Crosswhite warned Vaught, the two of them sitting in a car just across the street. "This woman won't be a pushover. I'm sure Ortega's told her how to keep an eye out for kidnappers."

"I'll be smooth enough." Vaught got out of the car and shut the door, hating why he was there.

A few seconds later, he rang the bell to the Ortega house.

Nancy Ortega came out and stood inside the locked gate. She was tall, a Mexican American with short dark hair. "Can I help you?" she asked in Spanish.

Vaught offered his badge and identification to show he worked for the Diplomatic Security Service. "Mrs. Ortega," he said in perfect English, "I'm agent Vaught with the DSS. I'm afraid there's been an emergency involving your husband, Mike."

She stepped forward and took his identification, examining it carefully. "What kind of emergency?"

"He's been abducted. We're not sure by who yet, but I and another agent are here to bring you to a safe location."

She handed his credentials back to him and took her phone from her back pocket.

"Mrs. Ortega, before you do that—"

She looked up, her gaze fearful.

"It's not likely you'll get through to Mike, but if you do, keep in mind we don't know who might answer his phone. The abduction hasn't been made public, so you *could* jeopardize our chances of getting him back. Please take that into consideration."

Nancy Ortega was in a quandary, holding a wrist to her forehead as she tried to decide the best course of action. "We're not supposed to leave the house if there's an emergency. We have security measures built in."

"I'm aware of that," he said easily. "But so are the police—and they'll find a way in. Believe me."

"The police?" She glanced around warily. "Are you saying he was taken by the police?"

"Nancy," he said, deciding to make the conversation personal, "Mike was working with us to catch Alice Downly's killer. We've discovered that corrupt police officials were involved—and, yes, that's who we *think* took him, but we don't know for sure. That's why it's imperative we get you and your children out of here as soon as possible."

"But . . ." She glanced at her phone. There was no signal. "But we're not supposed to leave if anything happens. We're supposed to lock down the house, and . . ."

"And what?" he asked patiently.

"Wait for help from—from the government," she said lamely.

"Nancy"—he pointed across the street to Crosswhite and then back to himself—"that's who we are. I'm sorry we're not the US Marines, but that kind of rescue would probably cause an international incident."

She stood biting the inside of her cheek. "I can trust you?"

"Of course," he said, feeling like shit. He and Crosswhite were taking on a huge responsibility using Ortega's wife and children as pawns.

"Where will we go?"

"To a safe house in Toluca. It's nothing fancy, but it's out of the way. We're working *very* closely with the police there."

"And you trust them?"

"Ninety-nine percent."

She allowed a thin smile. "I didn't know any police in this country could be trusted to that degree of certainty."

Vaught felt even more like shit. "We've been working with these men to fight the cartels. They're very brave and very dedicated."

"I need some time to get my children ready."

"Ten minutes," he said. "No more than that—please."

"Okay." She went inside.

Vaught went back over to the car. "She's getting the kids ready."

Crosswhite glanced at the rearview mirror. "So she bought it?"

"For now, but if she gets a signal on that phone, she's gonna call Ortega. I saw it in her eyes."

"Even after you told her it might get him killed?"

Vaught nodded. "She's already breaking protocol by leaving with us, and she knows it."

"Well, this way is better than going in there and taking them against their will."

"Nothing happens to them," Vaught said, pointing his finger. "You got that? *Nothing!*"

"Relax," Crosswhite said. "They can stay with Paolina and Valencia. I'll give Pao the same cover story you just gave Ortega's old lady, and they'll get along like peas in a pod. The kids can eat pizza and chase around after the puppy."

"Shit!" Vaught hissed, having second thoughts. "After this, I'm a goddamn kidnapper; for the rest of my life I'm a goddamn kidnapper."

"Hey, champ! Do you wanna let Serrano get away with having Downly and your whole fuckin' team blown away? Get in the fuckin' car, and let's go."

Vaught remembered seeing his men rocketed and shot apart before his eyes, and the anger of that day came back in a rush. True, the gringo sniper, the Ruvalcabas, and the crooked cops had all played their part—but the operation itself had been Serrano's call.

"We're gonna have to disable her phone," he said quietly. "We've got cellular service in Toluca."

"I'll take care of her phone," Crosswhite said. "Just get 'em in the car, so we can get back. The last thing we need is to run into a *narcobloqueo* after sundown." A *narcobloqueo* was a common type of roadblock set up by narcotics traffickers to create civil panic and disrupt emergency services.

54

Mariana decided to meet with Clemson Fields in a public gymnasium, where a girls' volleyball tournament was taking place on two separate courts. Lorena and Tanya, whom she had come to think of as "the twins," were seated three rows behind her, wearing gaudy, sequin-studded LA ball caps pulled low over their eyes.

Fields came up the stairs to the second tier and took a seat beside her. "I didn't know you were a sports fan," he said dryly.

"Really? I'm surprised you didn't see it in my file. I only played volleyball all through high school and college."

Noting her self-assured tone, he took a casual glance around to see if they were being watched. There were a few other Americans in the crowd, but they were obviously caught up in the games being played simultaneously down on the floor.

He handed her a slip of paper. "Jessup has been staying at that motel. He sleeps most of the day and goes out around nine. Those are the clubs and bars he likes to hit."

She folded the paper away into her pocket without looking at it, waiting to hear what else he had to say.

Fields attempted briefly to wait her out but then realized she was intentionally keeping her counsel. "It will take a little time for him to open up to you, but—"

"Oh, do you think so?" she said, taking her eyes off the game. "You mean he won't just blurt out the sniper's name and location the second I let him buy me a drink?"

"Do you understand how important this is?" Fields asked, restraining the impulse to raise his voice.

Mariana was beyond tired of being spoken to in the peremptory tone that CIA men took with her. "What I understand is that you think I'm going to fuck this guy for information!"

He turned his head toward the game. "Lower your voice."

"Or what?"

He looked at her, seeing the defiance. "Do I need to remind you I'm the only one looking out for your interests at the moment—as well as those of your friend Crosswhite?"

"No, you don't, but how many other operatives do you have lined up to take my place?"

She had him on that point. There was no one else in-country he could use for what he had in mind. If all he was looking for was a woman to fuck Jessup for information, Tijuana was full of hookers who were far better qualified than Mariana. "I'm not a man to trifle with, Mariana. I warn you."

"I'll call you when I have something." She got up to leave.

He took her by the wrist. "I want daily reports."

She jerked free of his grasp. "I *said*, I'll call you when I have something!" With that, she walked to the end of the aisle and disappeared down the stairs.

Watching her leave, Fields pondered her smart mouth, realizing that she must be in contact with Crosswhite, but he couldn't think of how that accounted for the sass he was getting. She'd been more intimidated by him back in Texas. Something had changed, and he needed to find out what before that something bit him in the ass.

Feeling uneasy, he got up and trudged down the stairs. The twins followed after him at a safe distance.

They trailed him to a rented car. Catching a taxi, they told the driver to follow the blue sedan. They stopped at a motel a couple of miles from the gymnasium, watching from the backseat as Fields got out and knocked at the door to room 11. A handsome Mexican man answered, and the two stood talking.

"I WASN'T ABLE to find out where she's staying," Fields said. "I couldn't work it into the conversation."

"I probably should have followed you and tailed her," the Mexican replied in perfect American English. His name was Villalobos. He was a pipe hitter out of Phoenix, a former marine with three tours in Iraq. "Why couldn't you work it in?"

"She's different now." Fields scanned around for anyone watching. The cab at the curb with two nattering young women in it didn't register as much more than a blip on his radar. "She's grown a spine somehow."

"She'll be easy enough to reacquire," Villalobos said. "I'll keep an eye on Jessup every night. Then tail her back to her hotel after she establishes first contact. Don't worry. This prissy bitch isn't gonna fuck him on the first run."

"She isn't gonna fuck him at all."

There was a hint of concern in Villalobos's eyes. "You're sure about that?"

Fields nodded. "Initially, I thought I could intimidate her into taking one for the team—Jessup's not a bad-looking guy—but like I said, she's different now."

"This means I'll have to be creative when the time comes. And I might not have a chance to call you before I make my move."

"I trust in your powers of improvisation," Fields said. "That's why you're here and not those two clowns from Baja."

THE TWINS WATCHED as the men finished talking. The Mexican stepped back into his room, and Fields returned to his car. Twenty seconds later, he was pulling into the street.

"Do you want me to follow?" the cabby asked. A wolfish-looking fellow in his early thirties, he was staring at them in the rearview mirror.

"We're getting out here." Lorena locked eyes with him as she crushed $500 worth of pesos into his hand, easily a month's salary. "Don Antonio Castañeda is grateful for your service. He always remembers those who help him—and he *never* forgets those who *fuck* him!" She gave the drug lord's name a few moments to sink in before releasing his hand.

The cabby felt his urine turning to ice water as he attempted to push the money back into her hands. "Please, I don't need your money!"

"Keep it," she told him, getting out after Tanya. "And remember: you've never seen us!"

55

With a quarter of Mexico City's streets still blocked, it was tough to make good time, especially at night. The city was a huge, sprawling metropolis, and neither Crosswhite nor Vaught made the best navigators.

"Is it just me," Crosswhite said, "or does every part of town look the same in the dark?"

"Are you lost?" Nancy asked from the backseat, with her children seated on either side of her: a boy of six and a girl of eight.

"More like disoriented," Crosswhite answered.

"You can get off at the next exit," she said. "Then cross through Colonia El Mirador."

Vaught looked over the back of the seat, seeing that Nancy was keeping an eye on her phone, watching for a signal. "How well do you know the city?"

"Pretty well," she said, thumbing the touch screen. "I take it you're both new in town?"

"Me more than him," Vaught said. "He at least lives here."

"Only a year," Crosswhite said, exiting the freeway and driving down the avenue into a blacked-out section of the city. "Shit. No power here either."

"Make a left up ahead," she said. "Go south toward Colonia San Luis Tlatilco. I assume you're headed for Highway 134?"

"Yeah," he said, following her instructions.

"Damn," she muttered. "Only three percent battery."

Vaught turned around to face the front, a smile coming to his face.

The daughter began to cry, and Nancy hugged her close. "It's okay, baby. The charger's in the trunk."

His smile disappeared.

They turned another corner, and there was a city bus on fire in the middle of the street, blocking passage.

Crosswhite hit the brakes. "*Narcobloqueo!*" He shifted into reverse.

Men with guns and masks appeared from the shadows, ordering everyone out of the car. Crosswhite shifted into park and dropped his phone onto the floor, where he hoped it wouldn't be seen.

Vaught stuffed his DSS badge deep into the seat. "Everyone keep calm," he said to the kids. "It's gonna be okay."

The doors were jerked open, and both men were pulled out. Nancy and the children were allowed to get out on their own, but one of the men took her phone and stuck it in his jacket pocket, telling her and the children to stand over by the building and keep quiet.

Crosswhite and Vaught were pushed against the car and searched.

"Why are you here, gringo?" one of the men asked.

"I'm a permanent resident," Crosswhite said. "My identification is in my wallet."

The man took his wallet and tossed it to another guy. Crosswhite turned around, his hands up. "You can have the money," he said easily, "but can I keep my permanent resident card? Getting a new one from immigration is a pain in the ass."

The guy with the wallet took out Crosswhite's ID, examined the green card with a flashlight and gave it back to him. "How many years do you have here?"

"Five," Crosswhite lied. "I live with my wife and daughter in Toluca. That's where we're going now."

They questioned Vaught, who told similar lies, saying he was originally from Monterrey, up near the border, to cover his accent. "These are my wife and children," he said, gesturing at Nancy and the kids.

"Where is your wallet?" asked the man with the gun.

"In the trunk with our bags."

Someone took the keys and opened the trunk, rifling through Nancy's suitcases. He tossed the phone charger to the man who'd taken her phone. "I don't see any wallet."

"It's in the red gym bag."

The man tossed the trunk a second time. "There is no red gym bag."

Vaught looked at Nancy. "You didn't put my bag in the car? Everything I need is in that bag!"

"I didn't see it," she said. "You told me all the bags were in the carport."

Vaught swore foully, shaking his head. "Everything I need for work is in that goddamn bag! My computer . . . everything! Now we have to go all the way back!"

"It's not my fault!"

"Shut up," the man told them. "Argue later."

Another man searched the glove box and found nothing of value. "Do we want the car?"

"Let them go," said the man who'd taken Crosswhite's wallet. "They have children, and the car is nothing special."

A minute later, everyone was back in the car, and the burning bus was growing smaller in the rearview mirror.

Vaught looked at Nancy. "Your passports are in your pocket?"

"Of course," she said, grateful to be alive.

"Smart thinking," he said with a smile. "Thanks for going along with the program back there."

"What choice did I have?"

"Well, you were quick on your feet. That was a big help."

"Where's your wallet?" Crosswhite asked.

Vaught pulled it from the seat. "Stashed it first thing. If they'd seen my badge, we'd be screwed."

"We're gonna need money for the tolls on the highway," Crosswhite said. He looked at Nancy in the mirror. "Do you have any money?"

"A few hundred," she lied, wearing five thousand dollars in US fifties around her waist in a money belt. "You can have if you need it."

"We should be fine," Vaught said, "but thank you."

"Where was *your* badge?" she asked Crosswhite.

"I'm not DSS. I'm CIA like—like your husband."

"Do you know him?"

"We've met only once, actually."

"So you're not attached to Mexico station?"

"Not directly."

"Then you're an operator. That's why Washington sent you for me?"

She's sharp, Crosswhite thought. *We'll definitely have to be careful with her.* "Yes, ma'am."

"You're both ex-military?"

"Yes, ma'am."

"That makes me a little feel better." Before the *narcobloqueo*, she'd been worried to death about her husband. Now she couldn't help being terrified for her children as well. "I thought we were in real trouble back there."

"The narcos don't usually make war on civilians," Crosswhite said. "It happens, but it's not their policy. If you give them what they want, they usually let you go. *Usually*."

"But the Ruvalcabas have been worse recently."

"That's true," he admitted. "Which is why I say *usually*. But we're working to put a stop to Hector Ruvalcaba."

"You do know that Ruvalcaba is supported by the politician Lazaro Serrano."

Crosswhite stole glances with Vaught. "Yes, ma'am. And we're working to stop him too."

"Mike mentioned something about the government here building a case against him."

"Well, the earthquake has changed all that. Now the plan is to remove him altogether."

"Which is why they've brought you in?"

Definitely fast on her feet, he thought. "Yes, ma'am. That's why they brought me in."

"So why a DSS agent?" she asked Vaught. "Are you the one who was assigned to my husband after chasing the sniper that killed Alice Downly?"

Vaught glanced over the seat. "That's me."

Nancy turned back to Crosswhite. "Is your wife Cuban, by any chance?"

Again, Crosswhite glanced at her in the mirror, a thin smile pursing his lips. "Yes, ma'am. My wife is Cuban. Mike seems to share a lot with you—more than he should, it sounds like."

"You're the one who punched him, aren't you? The ca-brón who sent him home with that goose egg on his head."

He couldn't help chuckling. "Yes, ma'am, I'm the cabrón."

"You hit my daddy!" accused the little boy.

"I did," Crosswhite confessed. "And I apologize."

The little boy lurched forward and hit Crosswhite on the back of the head before Nancy could grab his arm. "I hate you!"

"You don't hit people, Alejandro!"

Crosswhite chuckled again. "It's okay. He's entirely justified in this instance. I'm sorry for hitting your dad, Alejandro. You're a good man to defend him. I respect that."

The rest of the ride to Toluca was uneventful. They pulled around behind Crosswhite's apartment, and Paolina came out the back door. He got out fast and hugged her, whispering something into her ear before asking her aloud to show the kids to their room. Vaught helped Nancy repack their rifled bags in the trunk.

After a few seconds, Crosswhite's phone rang beneath his seat in the car, and he ran to get it.

"Crosswhite," he answered. "Yeah, we're just arriving at the safe house." He pretended to listen for almost a minute. "And all that's confirmed? Roger that. We'll stand by here."

He stuck the phone into his pocket and turned to Nancy. "We've confirmed Mike was taken by some cor-rupt cops working for Serrano. For the moment, it doesn't look like they plan to hurt him. More likely, they plan to hold on to him until after the election. Once Serrano is president, he knows he'll be untouchable. I'm guessing he probably intends to free Mike as a gesture of good faith to the CIA."

"But the election is three months away!"

"Don't worry," Crosswhite said gently. "We know where he's being held. It's not far from here, so Agent Vaught and I will put together a plan to get him back. In the meantime, you need to stay here and out of sight with Paolina, because it's also been confirmed that Mexico City PD is looking for you and the kids. They raided your house about an hour after we got you out." He looked at Vaught. "We weren't cutting it quite as close as I thought, but it was close enough."

Vaught grunted.

Nancy gave Crosswhite a brief hug. "Thank you."

"It's okay," he said. "Better get inside now. We'll bring the bags in."

When she was gone, Vaught looked at Crosswhite and shook his head. "You believed every word of bullshit you just told her."

Crosswhite shrugged. "If I don't believe it, how the hell can I expect her to?"

56

Crosswhite had returned to Mexico City early in the morning, leaving Vaught to keep an eye on Ortega's family. Nancy and Paolina were getting along well, and the children were having fun playing with the puppy, which Valencia had named Chance at Crosswhite's urging. Paolina remained unaware that Nancy and the kids were there under false pretenses.

Vaught didn't like being cooped up in the house. He wanted to be at the police station with the men. Things were too quiet around town for his comfort, and he was already bored playing babysitter. Not to mention he still felt like a shitheel using a woman and two children as pawns in a war that was partially of his making. Mendoza and his family were already dead. How many more innocent lives would it take to bring down Serrano and the gringo sniper? There had to be a limit. But then again, that was what men like Serrano counted on: people being afraid to risk innocent lives.

"Breakfast?" Paolina asked from the kitchen doorway, much nicer to him now.

"Yes, please."

Ortega's son brought over the puppy and placed it in Vaught's lap, saying in English, "You have the same name, so you have a *dog's* name!"

Vaught chuckled, scratching the pup's ears. "Sounds that way, doesn't it?"

Nancy brought him a plate of eggs and refried beans. "How soon will you hear from Dan?"

"I'm not sure." He handed the puppy back to the boy and accepted the plate, noting the worry on her face. "I've got a good feeling though, Nancy. I think he'll have good news when he calls."

She looked away, blinking her eyes to prevent them from tearing up. "I hope so. Corrupt police scare me more than anything. They're twice as dangerous as regular criminals."

"That's true, but they're also twice as vulnerable."

She returned to the kitchen.

Paolina brought her own plate into the living room and sat down in the chair beside Vaught, checking to make sure Nancy wasn't paying attention. "Daniel took his pistol with him. He doesn't usually do that. What's going on?"

"Mexico City is a dangerous place to be right now. There's a lot of civil unrest, and he's a gringo."

Paolina moved her food around on her plate with her fork. "Is there any chance she'll get her husband back?"

He glanced toward the kitchen. "Normally, I'd say probably not, but under the circumstances, I think the chances are pretty good."

"What's different about these circumstances?"

"Dan is different. He's on top of it."

She looked at him, her pretty young face appearing more adult than usual. "Is he in danger this morning? I want the truth."

"Aside from the chaos in Mexico City, he shouldn't be in any danger."

He was pushing a piece of tortilla around his plate to mop up the last of the egg yolk when he heard what sounded like a distant clap of thunder. He jerked his head toward the door. "That was a fifty!"

57

Chief of Station Mike Ortega was frantic over his missing family.

"I'm telling you, nothing's even been touched!" he shouted at Clemson Fields over a secure satellite phone. "The car's still here! No forced entry—nothing! They just vanished!"

"I can't help you if you're going to shout," Fields said. "Have you called anyone besides me?"

With effort, Ortega forced himself to lower his voice. "Not yet."

"Well, don't."

"I'm terrified! I called her phone, and a man answered. I asked to talk to Nancy, and he hung up! What if she was taken by the Ruvalcabas?" Ortega started to tremble. "How in hell could they know who I am?"

Up in Tijuana, Fields was beginning to wonder if

giving Serrano the list of deep-cover PFM agents had been such a good idea. Now even Ortega had been compromised, which made him a liability. "From what I understand, there's been a leak inside the PFM. Agent Mendoza and his family are missing."

"*Oh my God!*" Ortega began to feel dizzy. "Mendoza knows who I am! He gave me up!"

"You have to calm yourself," Fields insisted. "I'm sending some men, but you need to stay in the house and listen for the phone until they arrive. If your family was taken, someone will certainly call. Whatever you do, do *not* involve local law enforcement. Is that understood? You have to be patient and give me time to get assets in place."

"This is all because of that goddamn Vaught!" Ortega moaned. "He got me into this!"

"Am I wasting my time with you?" Fields was losing patience. "Are you going belly-up before I have a chance to fix this?"

Ortega stood in his kitchen trying to get a grip on himself. "No," he finally croaked.

"Good. My men will be there late this afternoon. In the meantime, your job is to wait for the phone to ring and gather whatever intelligence comes your way. Read me?"

"I read you," Ortega mumbled, starting to cry.

"We'll get this sorted out. Just keep calm." Fields broke the connection.

Ortega sat down at the kitchen table, resting his head in his hands. He was sure great violence had already been done to his wife, and probably his children. His greatest fear was that the phone would never ring.

After a minute, he sat up and wiped his eyes, nearly jumping out of his skin at the sight of Dan Crosswhite standing in the kitchen doorway. "How the fuck did you get in here?"

Crosswhite tossed Nancy's key chain onto the kitchen table.

Ortega saw the keys and sprang to his feet.

Crosswhite took a Glock 22 from behind his back and aimed it at his face. "Sit your ass back down."

Ortega did as he was told. "Where's my wife?!"

"She's fine. So are the kids."

Ortega swallowed the lump in his throat, afraid to believe what Crosswhite had just said. "How do I know you're not lying?"

"You were talking to Fields?"

Ortega nodded.

"He's working with Serrano—but you knew that already, didn't you?"

Ortega's eyes floated. "What are you talking about?"

"I don't have it all worked out yet." Crosswhite pulled out a chair and sat down across from him. "Tell me who ordered the hit on Alice Downly."

Ortega shrugged. "Serrano and Ruvalcaba. Who else?"

"And who's the gringo sniper?"

"How should I know? What does this have to do with my family? Tell me where they are!"

"Is Fields sending men?" Crosswhite asked.

"Of course. Now tell—"

"What's he sending them for?"

"To help me find Nancy and the kids! Why else?"

Crosswhite frowned. "Are you that fucking stupid? You're compromised, Mike. Your house is compromised. Your family is compromised. Your whole goddamn reason for being in Mexico is compromised. Do you really think Fields is sending men to *help* you? That's not what he does."

Ortega's face twisted with confusion. "What the hell are you . . ." His voice trailed off.

"He's is sending men to make you disappear, dumb-ass."

"You're crazy! Where's Nancy?"

"With my wife."

Ortega didn't know whether to be relieved or furious. "*You* took them!"

"I didn't *take* anyone. I invited her to come along, and she accepted."

"She'd never do that! She's been trained."

"Trained? That's funny. All I had to do was tell her you'd been abducted by the same people who killed Alice Downly. The second she heard that, she packed her bags, grabbed the kids, and jumped right in the car. Why would she do that, Mike? Do you share state secrets with your wife?"

Ortega looked down at the table top. "You son of a bitch."

"That's damn stupid, putting your old lady at risk. Where do you think we are, Disneyland?"

"Why did you take my family?"

"I know somebody within the CIA had Downly killed," Crosswhite said. "Or at the very least, they turned their heads while Serrano had her killed. She wanted US Special Forces to operate south of the border, like they did in Colombia. She wouldn't go along with CIA plans to put Serrano into power, so somebody had her whacked—that, or they set her up for Serrano to do it.

"And it would have worked, except Vaught fucked it up by chasing the sniper and placing Serrano at the scene. That's when Fields was sent down here to clean up the mess. But then there was a major quake, and everything went to shit. How am I doing so far?"

Ortega simply stared.

Crosswhite sat back, keeping the pistol ready. "The look on your face tells me I'm pretty goddamn close. I took your wife, Mikey, because I need you to fill in the blanks."

Ortega bared his teeth. "You didn't have to drag my family into this, you bastard!"

"Your ambition dragged your family into this. What else do you think put them in my path? You used them for cover after accepting this post because you thought it would get you a cushy assignment up in DC. So don't pawn this shit off on me. Admit it: you were complicit to the Downly hit."

Ortega's eyes drifted again, and this time Crosswhite caught it. "You piece of shit!" he snarled, getting to his feet.

"I wasn't complicit!" Ortega blurted. "I wasn't! I didn't know a goddamn thing about it until afterward. I swear to God! It was my job to help Fields clean up the mess that Vaught made—that's all!"

Crosswhite put the muzzle of the pistol to Ortega's head. "Who sent that fucking sniper down here? Tell me now, or I'll blow your brains all over the wall!"

"Pope! Okay? Are you happy? It was Pope!"

"Gimme the sniper's name!"

"Rhett Hancock! His name's Rhett Hancock!"

The name meant nothing to Crosswhite. "Tell me more."

"Pope hired him through a back channel. The crazy bastard doesn't even know he's working for the CIA. He thinks he's working for Serrano. Now Fields has orders to kill him—after Hancock kills Vaught. That's all I know!"

Crosswhite began to pace the kitchen slowly, realizing that the ATRU had become even more dangerous than he'd previously thought. "Here's what you're gonna do, asshole: you're gonna arrange a meeting with Serrano and draw him into the open for me."

Ortega was aghast. "Me?! I don't have that kind of influence. Are you crazy?"

"You'll contact Serrano," Crosswhite went on. "You'll tell him Fields has gone rogue; that Pope can't control him. You tell him Fields is moving to take him out and that you have to meet with him as soon as possible to put together a plan."

Ortega thought it over. "I want to talk to my wife before I do anything."

"No. You don't talk to your wife until after you've done what I need you to do."

"Why? What harm can it do?"

"It can do a lot of harm," Crosswhite said. "Right now, your wife has no idea she's a prisoner. She thinks Serrano's people are hunting her and the kids. If I let you talk to her, you'll ruin everything with that big mouth of yours, and I'll be forced to treat her like a prisoner. I'll have to lock her and the kids in a concrete room until this is over. Is that what you want, dumb fuck?"

Ortega slouched back, brooding over his predicament. "Swear to me they're okay."

"What good would that do?" Crosswhite was disgusted by the sight of the man sitting before him. "Sit up in the chair like a man. Have some self-respect and stop feeling sorry for yourself. It's no wonder Fields is sending somebody to kill you."

Ortega sneered. "I've read your file, asshole. The only reason you're not rotting in prison for murder is because Pope saved your hide. Now here you are judging him and me both. You're a fucking hypocrite."

Crosswhite stared at him, wanting to slug him with the

pistol, but there was a measure of truth to what Ortega had said. "Yeah, well, *no soy una moneda de oro para caerle bien a todo el mundo.*" This was a Mexican phrase meaning, I'm not a gold coin to be liked by everyone.

Ortega chortled scornfully. "Speaking of gold, Fields knows about that too. You and your thieving buddy Shannon are—"

Crosswhite kicked him over in the chair. "Not only is Shannon dead, you piece of shit, he's worth fifty of you!" He kicked Ortega in the rump. "Get your ass off the floor! You got a phone call to make before Fields's people show up and put a bullet in your head."

58

Sid Dupree was smoking pot and watching television in the back room of Señor Sid's Jet Ski Rental when he heard the door open and a customer enter the shop. He set aside the pipe and stepped out to see a fellow gringo flipping the Closed sign around. "What the hell you think you're doin', fella?"

The gringo turned to face him, a small backpack over one shoulder, his chiseled visage set. "I heard once that an American can buy things here he can't get anywhere else in Mexico. That still true?"

Dupree stepped out from behind the counter. "Depends who you heard it from." He was very tan with a shaved head, in his early sixties, and in good shape.

"A man named Steelyard."

Dupree's face split into a grin. "How is the old bastard?"

"He's dead," the gringo said.

The grin disappeared. "What happened?"

The gringo told the story, and when he was finished, Dupree stood looking sad. "Well, if a man's gotta go, I suppose that's the way to go, goddamnit."

"I agree," the gringo said. "Can you help me or not? I ain't here to waste your time or mine."

"What do you need?"

"Somethin' to shoot and somethin' to drive."

"That ain't gonna be cheap."

"Important things never are."

"This way." Dupree led the gringo out back to an open yard cluttered with old Jet Skis, broken sailboards, and a couple of beat-up Winnebago campers. Five or six dogs lounged about in the sand, and there were at least ten cats sunning themselves.

"Sorry about the smell," Dupree said, referring to the heavy odor of dog and cat feces. "Keeps people from nosin' around."

He led the gringo behind one of the Winnebagos to where an old sky-blue VW Beetle sat rusting away on four flat tires. "It's gonna take a little bit of work," he said, ducking into the camper. An air compressor kicked on a few seconds later, and Dupree remerged with an air hose. "We gotta roll this piece of shit outta the way."

It took a few minutes to inflate the tires, and then both men rolled the VW forward. Dupree grabbed a rusty shovel and dug down through about two feet of sand until the shovel hit something made of metal. After some more digging, he uncovered a steel footlocker. He pried off the lid to reveal a cache of weapons: AK-47s, M4s, MP5s, an M40A5 sniper rifle, and assorted pistols.

"What exactly are ya lookin' for?"

The gringo crouched down and took out an old Government Model 1911 pistol, checking the action to make sure it would cycle the rounds properly. "This'll do."

"You're kiddin' me. I thought you wanted somethin' to shoot."

The gringo stood up, hiding the pistol in the small of his back. "I'm lookin' to protect myself. Not start a revolution."

"Hell, I got one-a those under my mattress I coulda sold ya."

"How much ya want for it?"

"A thousand," Dupree said. "And that's at a Steelyard discount. I take a lotta risk keepin' this shit around."

"It's a fair price," the gringo said. "Got anything to drive?"

"Well, if ya want somethin' clean, it's gonna take a couple of days and run you at least ten grand. I don't deal in cars, and the Mexicans I do business with are gonna charge at least that when they realize you're in a hurry."

The gringo pointed to a battered green 1971 Dodge pickup parked near the building. "That run?"

"Yeah, it runs good, but it's mine, and I don't really wanna sell it."

"I'll give you nine grand, cash, for the pistol, the truck, and two boxes of cartridges."

The doubt in Dupree's eyes was plain to see. "When?"

"Right now."

"You on the run from the law?"

"I'm on the run from a lot more than that. We got a deal or not?"

Dupree crouched down, taking two boxes of GI ball ammo from the locker and handing them to the gringo. He slammed the lid shut and stood up. "Remember, amigo, you get caught with so much as a bullet in this country, and you're goin' to jail."

"Got it."

They covered the locker over with sand and rolled the VW back into place, scattering the tire tracks with their feet. Then the gringo set his pack on the hood and unzipped it, counting out nine thousand dollars in used $100 bills.

If Dupree was shocked to see so much ready cash, he didn't let on.

"We gonna deflate the tires?" the gringo asked, handing over the money.

Dupree took the cash and turned for the shop. "They'll be flat again in half an hour. I'll get your keys."

The gringo reached in the open window of the car to snatch an old tan ball cap from the passenger seat. "Canyonlands, Utah" was stitched to the front of it in brown lettering. "How much for this?"

Dupree turned around. "Smell like cat piss?"

The gringo took a sniff. "Nope."

"In that case, it's free."

The gringo pulled on the cap and followed him into the shop.

59

A frustrated Clemson Fields arrived at Villalobos's motel and knocked sharply at the door to room 11. Villalobos was not answering his phone, and there were pressing problems in Mexico City. He needed a man he could depend on to neutralize Ortega before the guy realized his wife and kids had probably been chopped into little pieces and showed up at the US Embassy in hysterics, blabbing everything he knew about the Alice Downly affair.

"Come on, Villalobos, open up." He stood, looking around. Villalobos's car was parked right in front of the room.

Putting his ear to the door, he could hear music inside. "Hey!" He thumped the door with the heel of his fist. "Late night or what? Open up. We've got trouble down in DF."

There was a small restaurant across the street, so he

crossed to the road to check if Villalobos might be eating breakfast. The man was not there, so Fields went back to the room. He thought briefly to involve the motel manager, but an old instinct left over from the Cold War told him he'd better not. He went to his car and took a lockpick set from his briefcase.

"I haven't picked a lock in ten years," he muttered, glancing around before fitting the needles into the lock. Luckily, the lock was old, so he was able to get the door open in under three minutes.

Fields slipped into the dark motel room and switched on the light. What he saw made him catch his breath. Propped on a pillow, Villalobos was tied naked to the bed with strips of torn sheet, his arms and legs outstretched, a blue condom over his shriveled penis, and his chest covered in blood that had spurted from his severed jugular vein. His empty wallet lay on the table near the door, and a blanket was thrown over the television which was on, playing Mexican music.

For the first time in his thirty-year career, Fields felt the impulse to run, but he ordered himself to remain calm. He'd been in a similar situation in East Berlin in 1980. "This is no worse than that," he told himself. "And I'm not being hunted by the KGB."

He peeked through the curtains to be sure no one was watching the motel and stepped into the bathroom. A bloody white hand towel lay on the floor. He found five or six strands of long, dark hair on the shower stall floor, but this was an almost useless clue. Eight out of ten women in Mexico had long dark hair.

"Murdering whore," he mumbled, moving back into the room.

Realizing he had no way to safely dispose of the body, he unplugged the television and stood with hands on his hips, looking at the corpse. Villalobos's dark eyes stared down at his shriveled genitalia. "Thank God this is Tijuana," Fields said to himself. "In any other city, this would draw a lot of attention."

He searched Villalobos's bags and discovered that the murderer had stolen his silenced H&K pistol. At least he didn't have to worry about the police finding the weapon in the room.

Five minutes later, Fields was sitting at a red light, wondering what to do about Ortega. "Damn it." Now he had no choice but to call the clowns from Baja.

60

Midori walked into Pope's office unannounced and shut the door. "We need to talk about Fields."

Pope looked up from his computer, rocking back in his chair. "Have a seat."

She took the chair before his desk. "He's run amuck. He just called the boys from Baja."

"I'm aware of that."

"They're maniacs."

The CIA director took off his glasses, rubbing the bridge of his nose. "Fields has a tough job down there right now. As you know, my primary Mexico assets have gone off the grid. So he's doing the best he can with what he's got to work with."

"You mean he's doing the best he can to cover up the fact you had Alice Downly assassinated."

Pope let out a sigh. "It would appear that I've trained you too well."

"Tell me why you did it, Robert."

"I'm trying to stabilize the border. Downly wanted to escalate hostilities. The president was in support of sending Special Forces troops into Mexico, and I couldn't talk him out of it. Such an escalation would get out of hand, and many, many innocent people would die."

"So it's mathematics?"

"*Life* is mathematics."

"No. Life is breathing human beings. And you've lost sight of that."

"You're wrong," he said quietly. "I'm the only person in this town who *hasn't* lost sight of it. What is one life weighed against thousands? Or hundreds? Or even just dozens? We kill based on numbers, and numbers never lie. You know that as well as I do. Are you upset because I weighed the life of an American woman against the lives of hundreds of Mexicans and found her wanting?"

"You broke the law."

"We break the law every day. That's our job."

Aware she was losing the battle of logic, Midori changed her tack. "Do you know that Fields is using Mariana to get to Jessup?" She noted the hint of surprise in his eyes. "You didn't, did you?"

"Mariana left the reservation," he said obdurately.

"She left because Fields scared her off of it!"

"She left because she worries more about Crosswhite than she should." He was showing irritation for the first time. "She's throwing away her career over a man who belongs in prison."

"My God, what a hypocrite you've become."

"There is no hypocrisy. Crosswhite murdered in Chicago for personal profit. The people we kill from this building are killed to serve the greater good. That's a mathematical fact."

"And suppose Fields orders the Baja boys to kill Mariana?"

"If she isn't smart enough to avoid that trap, she doesn't have what it takes. I shouldn't have to remind you that I didn't order her to Mexico. She went down there of her own volition, and she met with Castañeda *without* consulting me."

"I see. That's why you don't care what happens to her." Midori got up from her chair. "What about me, Robert? Am I expendable?"

He looked up at her, his expression suddenly soft and calm. "You're my most loyal protégée, and I value your life above all others."

She walked out of the office, and he sat staring at his computer, wondering if Mariana would do as he'd planned. *I'm not so sure now*, he thought to himself. *She's become less predictable.*

61

Serrano's assistant, Oscar, found him trimming rose bushes in the garden on the south side of the estate, where a large marble water fountain had recently been installed. The senator was dressed all in white and wore a wide-brimmed gardening hat against the sun.

"That man from the CIA is on the phone."

Serrano looked up from his work. "Fields?"

"No, the other one. The *pocho*: Ortega." *Pocho* was a pejorative term used to refer to Mexicans born in the US. *Chicano* would have been more politically correct.

Serrano had met Ortega only once and had not been overly impressed with him. "What does he want?"

"I don't know," Oscar said. "He won't tell me, but he insists it's extremely important."

Serrano took off his sun hat and gloves, and Oscar gave him the house phone. "This is Lazaro Serrano. I'm very busy today. How might I help you, Señor Ortega?"

"We need to meet," Ortega said. "You're in danger. Clemson Fields is planning to move against you."

Serrano wasn't sure if the feeling that began to rise up in his gut was fear or anger, but it certainly threatened to spoil his afternoon. "What's happened? Fields and I have an agreement."

"I don't know about your agreement," Ortega said, "but I have received an Operational Immediate from Director Pope warning me to protect you. We have to meet. I have classified information that you need to hear at once."

"What kind of classified information?"

"I can't be specific over the telephone."

"Very well," Serrano said with an impatient groan. "Come here to the estate, and we'll talk it over."

"I'll be arriving with a gringo," Ortega said. "Pope has sent him from the US to neutralize Fields, and he wants the two of you to meet."

"Fine, fine," Serrano said. "How soon will you be here?"

"Within the hour."

Serrano broke the connection and tossed the phone to Oscar. "The CIA is becoming a very large annoyance to me, Oscar. This man Pope up in Washington believes I work for him." He wagged his finger. "I do *not* work for him. And to prove it, I should send the heads of these two men back to him in a FedEx box."

Oscar smiled dryly. "I think it might be too soon for such a flamboyant gesture. You have an election to win."

"Which is the only reason I will not have these men killed—yet." He drew a white sleeve across his perspiring forehead. "Apparently Fields has decided to double-cross me. I don't suppose I should be surprised."

"Why would he cross you? You have an agreement."

Serrano chuckled. "Perhaps he's realized I have no

intention to honor the agreement." He put his hat and gloves back on and picked up the rose snips. "Be sure the guards are alert. Ortega is bringing another one of Pope's assassins with him. I tell you, Oscar, once I am president, it will be a pleasure to run these interfering gringos out of our country for good. They're like a plague of rats."

Ortega and Crosswhite arrived fifty minutes later, and Oscar showed them out back to the pool, where Serrano's mistress had been told to sunbathe naked on a raft as a distraction. Her Chihuahua floated nearby on a separate raft. Crosswhite recognized the purpose of the woman's presence at once, but this didn't prevent him from staring.

"Nice view," he remarked, taking a seat at the table in the shade.

"If Serrano's seen your file," Ortega replied, "it'll be our last."

"Don't get cranked up. Let me do the talking and keep your mouth shut."

Serrano came out of the house flanked by a pair of capable-looking bodyguards, crossing the patio and offering his hand to Ortega. "Good to see you again," he said in Spanish. "Who is your associate?"

Crosswhite offered his hand, saying in Spanish, "Good to meet you, Senator Serrano. I'm David Pendleton."

Serrano motioned for them to be seated. "So, gentlemen, do I understand that Clemson Fields wishes to see me dead?"

"We believe that to be the case," Crosswhite replied.

Serrano eyed him for a moment. "I'm sorry, who I am talking to? To you or to Señor Ortega?"

"You're talking to me, sir. Without offense to Agent Ortega, he's only an intermediary in this instance. Director Pope wishes for you and me to establish a rapport so that we might work together to neutralize Agent Fields."

"What has happened with Fields?" Serrano wanted to know. "We have an arrangement that should be very agreeable to him."

"If you don't mind my asking," Crosswhite said, "what is the nature of that agreement?"

Serrano was hesitant but decided to disclose the information. "He has asked me to secure a villa for him on the coast where he might retire when this operation is over."

Crosswhite looked at Ortega, conjuring his story on the fly. "See?" he said in English. "It's the same every time. He doesn't even change his MO."

Ortega didn't have to pretend to be uptight. He shrugged. "Fields is old school."

Serrano was not fluent in English, but he understood more than he spoke. "What does *MO* mean?"

"*Modus operandi*: method of operation." Crosswhite sat in closer to the table, as if taking Serrano into his trust. "Fields is a confidence man—an actor. He often strikes these little agreements in order to give a false sense of security. The idea is to convince you that he needs something from you on a personal level, which makes you trust him more. He already has a house on the coast up in San Diego, so I doubt seriously he needs one down here. You're being manipulated, Senator."

Serrano began to simmer. "Why would Pope send such a man to me?"

"In Pope's defense," Crosswhite continued, "this is the first time Fields has acted contrary to his directives. The truth is that we don't know his exact intentions, but he's contacted a couple of assets in Baja and ordered them here to Mexico City. At first, we believed he was sending them after Chance Vaught and Dan Crosswhite"—he watched Serrano closely here for any hint of recognition—"but a text message was intercepted naming you as the target, and Pope contacted me immediately. As luck would have it, I was vacationing up in Guadalajara, which enabled me to get here quickly. My personal guess—and this is only a guess—is that Fields has cut a better deal with Antonio Castañeda regarding the narcotics trade. I'm guessing this because we know he was recently in Vallarta."

Serrano lost his temper at the mention of Castañeda's name. "Castañeda should have been killed months ago! The CIA should never have arranged that stinking truce with him! What right do you gringos have meddling in Mexican affairs? The fool we have for a president now should have told you to put that truce in your ass, but no! He rolled over like the dog that he is and put his feet up!" He pointed his finger in Crosswhite's face. "I will tell you this, my American friend: when I am president, there will be no truce with Antonio Castañeda. That dog will be hunted down!"

Crosswhite sat back. "I'm glad to hear you say that. I'm sure Director Pope will be equally pleased."

"I do not care about Director Pope!" Serrano grated. "I do not work for Americans. Is that clear? *Yo trabajo para el pueblo mexicano!*" I work for the Mexican people!

Crosswhite wanted to laugh at the outrageous lie but remained passive. "Director Pope is not under the impression that you work for him. It is his understanding the two of you are working together to consolidate the narcotics trade and stabilize the region. He apologizes for Fields's exceeding his mission parameters, and I assure you he's acting in good faith to put the situation right."

Realizing he needed the CIA on his side until after the election, Serrano allowed himself to be mollified. "It can be hard to find reliable men. I see why Director Pope chose you. You are very direct, and you say what you mean. He should have sent you to begin with."

Mike Ortega stole a glance at Crosswhite, hating him and wishing he could expose him to Serrano then and there, renouncing him for the liar he was. Instead, he went along with the ruse, interjecting, "Fields and Pope share a lot of history. No one is more disappointed by Fields's lack of discretion than Director Pope, I promise you."

Serrano nodded, satisfied for the moment. "As for the other two dogs, Vaught and Crosswhite, they'll be dead shortly. Your man Hancock has moved into Toluca, and the city will soon be back in my hands."

Crosswhite's hackles went up. "Back in your hands?"

"Yes. Hancock is coordinating the attack. Ruvalcaba's men will soon be moving into the city to subvert the police there. Toluca is very important to business traffic coming up from Chiapas in the south, and the Guerrero brothers have been a thorn in my side for too long."

"You know for a fact that Vaught and Crosswhite are there?"

"Yes. My spy on the Toluca police force has confirmed this. The Americans have been training the officers that remain, but it won't do them any good. Most of the police force quit when Juan Guerrero was killed last week, and his younger brother is not the same caliber of leader. He has only seventy-five men left, and Toluca is too big a city to hold with seventy-five men."

"Won't this new chief call the state police for reinforcements?"

"Oh, I'm sure he will," Serrano answered. "But the state police commander belongs to me, so I regret to say there won't be any reinforcements to send to Toluca. The earthquake here in Distrito Federal has caused far too much devastation to risk weakening the city's peacekeeping forces. A nation's capital must be protected above all else." He smiled. "Would you not agree?"

Crosswhite forced himself to return the smile. "Yes, I would."

"So, how exactly do you suggest we deal with Fields?"

"This is an initial contact," Crosswhite said, sounding very professional. "To give you and me a chance to establish a rapport. I'll spend the rest of the day here in the city, making arrangements with my people over at the embassy. Then tomorrow, or the next day at the latest, I'd like to meet back here with you and Captain Espinosa of the Policia Federal to discuss what I've put together."

Serrano was thrown off balance. "How do you know Captain Espinosa?"

"I don't know him," Crosswhite said, "but I understand he's the officer who took initial custody of Agent Vaught after he exceeded his authority in pursuing the sniper. If that's the case, it seems to me Espinosa might be a man we can count on when the time comes to deal with Fields."

"You're rather well informed," Serrano remarked.

"I have to be, Senator. We're not dealing with a fool. Agent Fields is a veteran of the Cold War. He knows his craft and is a dangerous man with dangerous assets at his disposal. Your life is important to Director Pope, and I haven't come here to disappoint him."

Though Mike Ortega was impressed by how sincerely Crosswhite was laying it on, he didn't understand why they should risk involving the most corrupt and dangerous cop in the city. He opened his mouth to speak, but Crosswhite kicked him in the leg to shut him up before he could utter a sound.

"I will contact Captain Espinosa," Serrano said, deciding he liked the idea. "I'm sure he will be interested to meet you."

"I'm grateful you've taken the time to meet with me

today. It makes my job much easier." Crosswhite got to his feet. "I know you're a busy man, Senator, so we'll be going."

They shook hands all around, and when Crosswhite and Ortega were gone, Oscar came out of the house holding a drink in each hand. "How did it go?"

Serrano ignored the drink that was offered him, pointing in the direction Crosswhite had left. "*That's* a gringo I can work with!"

62

Vaught stood in the back lot of the police department looking at the blood-soaked interior of an armored police truck. The sniper's .50 caliber round had pierced the armored driver's door of the Ford pickup truck and killed both officers in the front seat as they'd sat at a red light. This meant the sniper had been firing on a flat trajectory from street level—a bolder approach than either Vaught or Crosswhite had anticipated.

He turned to Chief Diego and his lieutenant. "How are the men taking it?"

Diego shrugged. "They're angry—and scared."

"More angry or more scared?"

"Angry."

"Did they respond the way they were trained?"

"They tried to," the lieutenant said. "There were no men riding in the bed of the truck, and the two in the backseat were unable to hear the shot because of the armored windows. By the time another unit responded, the sniper had stopped firing, and there was no way to triangulate his position."

"Right," Vaught said. "All four men were riding inside the cab because they wanted to avoid being shot." He shut the door and put his finger into the hole made by the gringo sniper's armor-piercing round. "This proves they're no safer inside than out. In fact, they're safer in the back because they have a chance to hear the shot, see what's going on, and return fire. Inside, they're sitting ducks."

Diego turned to the lieutenant. "Make sure every man coming on shift sees the hole in the door before going on patrol. Give orders that only the drivers are to be inside. Impress upon them that they have a better chance to dismount and fight if they are riding in back."

The lieutenant said, *"Sí, señor,"* and disappeared inside the station to begin roll call.

Vaught made sure they were alone and walked Diego around the far side of the truck. "I've heard from Crosswhite up in DF. There's a traitor among your men. Serrano has someone on the inside, and he's been feeding the Ruvalcaba's information about our training exercises."

Diego nodded. "I've suspected this. The day Juan was killed, the sniper's position and timing were too perfect. Unfortunately, there's no way to know who it is. I cannot openly accuse any of my men without proof."

Vaught bumped him on the shoulder. "Come with me."

He led Diego inside the motor pool, where the men kept their equipment. The officers' body armor and ballistic helmets sat on shelves in open wooden lockers along the garage wall, much the way firemen keep their turnout gear ready in a fire station. Each locker had the officer's name stenciled above it in white lettering.

"How long has officer Robles been on the department?"

Diego glanced around, making sure they were still alone. "About six months. He's a good man. You've seen him in training."

"Yeah, he catches on pretty fast," Vaught agreed. "Didn't your brother take over as chief about six months ago? Was Robles hired before that or after?"

"Juan hired him personally—a couple weeks after he became chief."

"Did either of you know Robles before he applied?"

"No. He was recommended by a city councilman."

"Well, that's a strike against him right there," Vaught muttered, reaching for Robles's ballistic helmet and handing it to Diego. "See anything wrong with that?"

Diego examined the helmet, finding it sound. "No."

"We all wear balaclavas over our faces when we're on the street, so we're impossible to distinguish from one another in uniform." He pointed at the helmet. "Look again."

Diego turned the helmet in his hands. There was a nondescript scuff of white paint on either side of it, one directly above the right ear, the other a little higher and closer to the back of the helmet.

Diego looked at Vaught. "These marks are no more than a few days old."

"I've checked all the other helmets," Vaught said. "Officer Robles seems to be the only one of your men who wants the sniper to know who he is."

63

The boys from Baja were cousins, Fito and Memo Soto, both age thirty, contracted by the old guard of the CIA the year before Pope was appointed director. They were contract killers who specialized in making a mess of things. No one would ever mistake their work for that of professionals, but sometimes it was a good idea for a hit to look like the work of a jealous girlfriend or a tweeker jacked up on methamphetamines.

They rang the door bell of Ortega's house.

Fito was the taller of the two, with dark hair and a beard. "I thought this cabrón was supposed to be waiting for us."

Memo was bald, with blue catlike eyes. He shrugged and rang the bell again. "That's what Fields said."

"Obviously, there's nobody here," Fito remarked. "Call the man and see what he wants us to do."

Memo made the call, and Fields answered on the second ring. "Yes?"

"Hey, your man isn't here," Memo said. "What do you want us to do?"

"Are you inside the house?"

"No, we can't get inside. This place is built like a prison."

"You need to get inside and verify that he isn't there."

Memo rolled his eyes, handing the phone to Fito. "He says we have to get inside."

Fito took the phone. "Listen, we can't get inside. Everything is barred up."

"It's imperative you make confirmation," Fields insisted. "The target has to be neutralized. I thought I made that clear."

"What do you want us to do?" Fito asked. "Use our heat vision to cut the fucking door open?"

"I don't care if you have to ram the house with your car," Fields said. "But get inside and make confirmation."

"And suppose he's not here? Then what?"

There was a long pause at Fields's end. "I don't know. He should be there."

"You keep saying that."

"I don't care what you have to do," Fields repeated. "Get inside and make confirmation. If he's not there, abort the mission and come to Tijuana. I have more work waiting for you."

"What kind?"

"The same. Call me when you've got confirmation."

Fito gave the phone back to Memo. "He says we have to get inside no matter what."

"Fuck him, I'm hungry." Memo was rubbing his ample belly. "Let's go get something to eat. After that, we'll call him back, say we got inside, and the dude wasn't here. How's he gonna know the difference?"

Fito smiled. "I like it. He wants us up in Tijuana right away. Somebody else to kill."

"Same money?"

"He didn't say, but we didn't come all this way for free. He's paying us for this wasted trip."

They crossed the street and were about to get into the car when Memo spotted a gringo walking up the sidewalk wearing blue jeans, a black T-shirt, and a tan ball cap. He stopped in front of Ortega's house and rang the bell.

"Who the hell is that?"

"Let's find out." Fito shut the car door, and the two of them went back across the street, stepping onto the sidewalk on either side of the gringo.

"You live here?" Fito asked in English.

The gringo looked at him, his chiseled visage set. "You a cop?"

"Maybe. What's your interest in this house?"

"Friend of mine lives here."

"What's your friend's name?" Memo asked.

The gringo ignored him, staying focused on Fito.

"He asked you a question," Fito said.

"I heard 'im."

Fito became uncomfortable beneath the gringo's gaze. "What are you doing here?"

"Right now I'm waitin' for you to do somethin' stupid."

Fito sniggered. "We have a tough guy here, Memo."

"That's good," Memo said. "I like tough guys."

The gringo whipped around like a blur, delivering a vicious overhand right to Memo's chin. Memo went down like he'd been hit by a sniper, and the gringo spun back around, bashing the lunging Fito in the face with his left elbow.

Fito saw stars, crashing to his knees with one of his front teeth broken off at the gum line.

The gringo grabbed him by the hair and bashed him again with his fist, busting his nose and shoving him over against the gate to the carport. A quick search, and he found Fito's silenced .22 Ruger pistol.

He stuck the muzzle down the front of Fito's pants and squeezed the trigger. The pistol went off with a hiss, and Fito felt the hot .22 caliber round ricochet off the sidewalk into his buttock.

He shouted in pain, grabbing his ass.

"Looks like I missed!" the gringo sneered, adjusting the muzzle.

"Don't!" Fito gasped, grabbing the gringo's wrist in fear for his testicles.

"What the fuck are you doin' here?" the gringo growled.

Fito began to blab, telling all that he knew.

"Where's Fields now?"

"Tijuana."

"Who does he want you to kill in Tijuana?"

"I don't know. He hasn't told us yet."

Knowing it would be dangerous to leave a pair of dead men on the sidewalk, the gringo stood up, delivering Fito a brutal knee to the face. Fito slouched over, unconscious. The gringo wiped his fingerprints from the pistol with the tail of his shirt, tossed the weapon over the carport wall, and disappeared down the street.

64

Officer Robles appeared in the doorway to Chief Diego's office. He was in his late twenties, a clean-cut-looking kid. "Sergeant Cuevas said you wanted to see me, Chief?"

"Go see Agent Vaught out back," Diego said, seemingly preoccupied with paperwork. "He requested you ride with him tonight."

"*Sí, señor.*"

A few minutes later, Robles found Vaught waiting for him in the back of an armored black-and-white pickup truck. The truck bed was enclosed with a roll cage, which allowed officers to stand up during patrol and to rail-mount a light machine gun. He climbed up into the back dressed in his SWAT gear and shook Vaught's hand. "Thank you for requesting me."

"Sure," Vaught said, pulling the black balaclava up over his face. "We're expecting trouble tonight, and I want a good man with me." He reached out and took the helmet from Robles's head. "Better let me trade with you. Your helmet's marked up."

"No, it's okay," Robles said, reaching for his helmet back. "It fits my head."

"It's cool," Vaught said, strapping the helmet on. "We wear the same size."

Sergeant Cuevas climbed into the back of the truck, donned his helmet, and pulled up his balaclava. "Better put that helmet on," he said to Robles. "We're patrolling the north side."

The north side of town was the worst, the area where they suspected the gringo sniper to be hiding among Ruvalcaba's people.

"We're going to draw the sniper's fire," Vaught said with a grin. "Try to flush him out."

"I'd like to have my helmet back," Robles said, his good humor beginning to fade. "I don't like wearing other people's helmets."

Vaught laughed. "Don't worry about it. I don't have lice."

"I'm serious," Robles said, putting his hand out. "Give me my helmet."

The driver of the truck got out of the cab and stood watching.

"Sorry," Vaught said. "I'm keeping the helmet."

Robles looked at Sergeant Cuevas. "Tell him to give me my helmet."

"Why?" Cuevas asked. "What's so special about it?"

"It's mine. I have the right to wear my own equipment."

"It belongs to the department," Cuevas said. "I've reassigned it to Agent Vaught." He took the other helmet from Vaught's hand and thrust it toward Robles. "I've reassigned this one to you. Now put it on. We're patrolling the north side."

Robles stood looking between the two men, realizing he'd been discovered. "I quit." He turned to dismount the truck, but Sergeant Cuevas whacked him over the head with the Kevlar helmet, and he went down.

The driver jumped into the back, and the three men wrestled Robles into a pair of handcuffs. Then Sergeant Cuevas produced a roll of duct tape and taped Robles's mouth shut. They pulled the balaclava over his face and stood him up, shackling his hands to the roll bar behind the machine gun, making him look like the gunner—the first man the sniper would likely shoot. Vaught put the helmet on Robles's head and pulled the chin strap good and tight.

"It's you and me tonight, baby!" He turned to Sergeant Cuevas, switching back to Spanish. "You'd better dismount, Sergeant. There's no sense giving the sniper more than one target to choose from. We'll let our man Robles here take all the risks."

Robles shook his head furiously, protesting as best he could with his mouth taped shut.

Vaught drew a razor-sharp folding knife from his harness and pressed the point to Robles's throat. "You'd better stand up and face this like a man."

Robles began to cry, shaking his hands, begging to be set free.

Revolted by the traitor's cowardice, Sergeant Cuevas stepped into him, kneeing him in the groin. Robles sagged against the back of the cab with a groan and threw up in his mouth. They had to peel the tape off fast to prevent him from aspirating: sucking vomit into his lungs.

He retched once more, and they allowed him to cough himself out before applying a new strip of tape. This time Robles made no attempt to protest his fate.

"You earned this," Vaught said, pulling the balaclava up to hide the younger man's face. "So accept what you have coming. If you fuck this up, I will stab you, I swear to God."

Sergeant Cuevas got into a black-and-white Dodge Charger with three other officers, and both vehicles rolled out, with the pickup in the lead.

65

Mariana hadn't had too much trouble getting Billy Jessup to notice her in the nightclub. The trouble was getting him to *un*-notice the twins sitting three tables over, where they pretended to be interested in the half dozen inebriated young men vying heavily for their attention.

"Those two seem to be distracting you," she said, drinking from a bottle of Tecate beer.

"I'm sorry," Jessup said with a laugh, embarrassed to be called on the carpet for gawking. "I just don't see that every day."

His Spanish had turned out to be too poor to carry on a conversation, forcing Mariana to talk to him in accented English, which required a conscious effort on her part to keep from breaking character. "You don't see what every day?"

He laughed again. "They're just really hot."

"And I'm not?"

"Yeah," he said. "You're beautiful. It's just . . ." He laughed again, sounding more stupid each time. "There's just different kinds of pretty, that's all."

"So you prefer women who look like *putas*?" Sluts.

Again the annoying laugh. "I don't know if that's what I said."

"Well, go over and talk to them. That's obviously where you want to be."

He turned his back to the far table. "No, this is where I want to be. Your English is very good. Where did you learn?"

"I've lived on the border all my life. My whole family speaks English."

"Do you like the US?"

She nodded. "What are you doing in Mexico?"

"I've been doing some consulting."

"Consulting?" She put on her most interested face. "My brother's a consultant in DF. What kind of consulting do you do?"

"Well, it's not . . ." He hadn't counted on her knowing a damn thing about consulting. "It's more like security work—security consulting."

"For banks and things like that?"

"No, no." He took a drink from his beer. "More like, um . . . more like bodyguard-type work."

"For politicians?"

He chuckled. "Sort of."

"What do you mean, 'Sort of'?"

"Well, I don't know . . . just *sort of*." He laughed again.

She gave his sizeable biceps a squeeze, noting the bottom part of a military tattoo sticking out beneath the sleeve. "You're a mercenary, aren't you?"

Jessup knew women well enough to know they didn't

start squeezing on you unless they were at least *contem-plating* taking off their clothes. "Suppose I am?"

She shrugged, offering a flirtatious smile. "Suppose you are?"

"Would that bother you?"

"I guess it depends."

"On what?"

She sat forward into the table, making the moment more intimate. "If I decide to fuck you at some point in the future, and I find out you're down here working for the DEA . . . or the ATF . . ."—she took a drink, and her expression turned almost vicious—"I'll cut your fucking balls off in your fucking sleep."

Jessup felt himself stiffen inside his jeans. "Believe me, the last people on earth I work for is the ATF or the fucking DEA."

"Because the people *I* work for," she went on, "they don't fucking play. Do you understand?"

He took a drink and set down the bottle. "And just who do you work for?"

"Way too soon." She sat back. "But he's the kind of man who'd feed us *both* to the fucking sharks if I hooked up with you and you turned out to be a fucking narc. I got rules I have to follow."

He pushed the beer aside. "You wanna get outta here?"

She smiled. "Again, *corazón*, way too soon. There's no way I'm fucking you tonight, so relax. I don't even know your real name."

"Yes, you do." He dug his California driver's license from his wallet and put it on the table. "See, Billy Jessup."

Mariana looked at it. "Your name is actually *Billy*. Not William?"

"I was named after my daddy. His name was William, but everybody called him Billy."

"I like that," she said thoughtfully. "I think you should name a kid what you're gonna call him."

Realizing he wasn't going to get laid, Jessup pushed aside his disappointment and settled in for conversation. "So do you want kids?"

"Sometimes. You?"

He shrugged. "I'd like to have a son. But a daughter would be okay."

She could see he was telling her the truth. "It doesn't sound to me like you're in a position to start a family right now."

"I can quit whenever I want. Nobody owns me."

"Must be nice." She put on her sad face and took a drink from her beer.

"What, you can't quit?"

She pretended to force a smile. "We don't know each other well enough, Billy. You don't know the kind of people I work for."

"I'm not stupid," he said. "You work for the cartels, and we're in the North—which means you work for Castañeda."

She looked suddenly angry. "Liar! You *are* with the DEA!" She stole a look around the club. "You're gonna get me killed!" She grabbed her purse and began to get up.

The second he grabbed her arm to stop her, she knew she had him.

"I don't work for the DEA, okay? I work for Ruvalcaba."

Mariana stole another quick glance around, lowering herself back into the chair. "That's even worse!" she hissed. "What are you doing up here? Trying to get yourself killed?"

"Well, I don't exactly work for him anymore. I quit a few days ago."

"Just like that? And you're not scared to be walking around Mexico?"

"They don't really care about me. They care about my partner; he's the one who's important."

She pushed up the sleeve of his T-shirt to get a good look at his Airborne Ranger tattoo. "Are you the one I've heard rumors about?"

He shook his head. "No, that's not me; that's my partner."

"So it's true," she said quietly. "There *is* a gringo sniper."

He drank from his beer. "It's true, all right. And he's not really anybody you'd wanna meet."

66

Fields couldn't believe his eyes.

"I send you two jamokes to do a job that should have taken you two minutes, and this is how you come back looking? What did you do, pick a fight with Manny Pacquiao?"

Fito was humiliated and angry, his broken tooth hurting him, but he resisted the urge to smart off, knowing they'd fucked up big-time. "A gringo showed up."

"What gringo?"

"I don't know. We've never seen him before."

Fields sat looking back and forth between them. "One man did this to you? Why didn't you shoot him?"

Fito looked at the floor. "He took my gun."

"Took your gun."

"He was a professional."

"I'm sure he was," Fields remarked. He described Crosswhite, but the cousins looked at each other, shaking their heads.

"No, he didn't look anything like that," Fito said. "This man had light-brown hair and light-colored eyes—almost gray."

Fields had no clue who else it could have been. He looked at Memo. "What about you? You don't talk anymore?"

Memo looked at the floor.

"His jaw's broken," Fito said. "We just came from the hospital. They wired it shut."

"This is fabulous." Fields got up from the edge of the bed in his hotel room. "One looks like he was hit by a truck, and the other one's a mute." He let out a sigh, longing for the days of the Cold War, when professional assets were plentiful and Congress never asked any hard questions.

"Listen," he said, turning around. "There's a woman in town; she's getting some information from a contact. Once I've got the intel, you're going to dispose of her. Is that clear?"

"How soon?"

"Within the next couple of days, but I'm having doubts as to whether or not you can even handle a girl."

"We can handle her!" Fito insisted. "We just got surprised by this guy. You didn't tell us there might be some crazy gringo running around down there."

"Well, you'd better be able to handle her," Fields said. "Because I'm not paying a dime for the ass kicking you two clowns received today. Did you even get into the house?"

"Yes!" Memo said through clenched teeth.

"I got in through an unlocked door on the roof," Fito lied. "The house was empty."

"This was before or after your spanking?"

Fito averted his eyes. "Before."

Fields opened a file on his laptop, showing them photos of both Mariana and Jessup. "Here is a list of bars and clubs. That's the motel he's staying at. I don't know where she's staying yet, but she's stalking him, so go find her and stay on her! Do nothing—and I mean *nothing*—until you're given the word. Is that clear?"

"Yes."

"About this gringo you ran into . . ." Fields stood thinking. "Did he say why he was there? Did you tell him anything—anything at all?"

Fito shook his head. "We just asked him what he was doing there, and he sucker punched Memo. I went for my gun, but he was too fast."

When the boys from Baja were gone, Fields called Pope on the secure satellite phone.

"We've got a new player," Fields said. "The Baja boys ran into a gringo outside Ortega's place. He literally beat them up on the sidewalk in front of the house and left them lying there."

"Sounds like something Crosswhite would do," Pope remarked.

"That's what I thought, but I described him, and they say no. This guy had light-brown hair and light-colored eyes."

"You just described half the men in America."

Fields chuckled. "You should see these two clowns. Whoever it was really worked them over. One has a busted nose; the other's jaw is wired shut."

"Has Mariana made contact with Jessup?"

Fields was startled. *Goddamn that Midori!* But he recovered quickly enough. "I don't know yet. I'm expecting first contact tonight."

"I don't want anything happening to her," Pope said. "She has a great deal of potential."

Which is exactly why she has to go, Fields thought to himself. "That's understood. You have no idea who this new player might be?"

"No. He must be working for Ortega. You still have no intel on who took his wife and kids?"

"Nothing factual, but it almost has to be Serrano. Or maybe that Federale captain—Espinosa, I think his name is—the crooked cop who turned Vaught over to Ruvalcaba's people."

"What about the leak at the PFM?"

Fields was not accustomed to Pope asking so many pointed questions. It meant that he was beginning to lose confidence. "I don't know where that stands."

"Three of their deep-cover agents have turned up dead," Pope said. "You weren't supposed to give them anyone but Mendoza."

"I felt we needed to increase our odds."

"How many names did you give him?"

"All of them."

There was a short pause at the other end of the line. "I realize you have a tough job down there, Clem, and I realize you're working with the junior varsity, but you have to do better."

Coming from Pope, "you have to do better" was tantamount to an ass chewing. "I understand," Fields said. "Do you have anyone you can send me?"

"I gave you Crosswhite, Vaught, Ortega, and Villalobos. Those four men were all you should have needed.

Now you've pulled Mariana into the lineup. I want this operation wrapped in three days, Clem. That's all I can give you. After that, I'll have to call in a whole different team."

Pope broke the connection without another word, and Fields threw the phone at the wall. Then he grabbed his jacket and headed out into the night for the first time in years.

67

TOLUCA, MEXICO
02:00 HOURS

The moment Hancock had gotten word that a lone police truck was patrolling the northern part of town, he'd gone straight into action. Northern patrols were not rare, but the Toluca police force was less than half its normal size now, so the northern sector was generally overlooked after dark. The report was that the truck carried a machine gunner, which probably made the patrol feel safe operating alone. Machine gunners were prime targets in any war, and Hancock was ready to give the police an education.

He lay prone on the rooftop of a single-story house overlooking a well-lit four-lane avenue. After a half hour of waiting, the truck finally drew into view at two hundred yards, coming toward him at an oblique angle up the street. He scanned the men in the back of the truck, spotting the white marks on the helmet of Ruvalcaba's informant. The gunner was making a futile attempt to appear small behind the machine gun.

Hancock smiled, centering the crosshairs on the front of the gunner's helmet and squeezing the trigger. The Barrett .50 caliber bucked against his shoulder, and the machine gunner's head exploded inside the helmet.

To Hancock's surprise, the truck suddenly accelerated up the avenue at high speed in his direction. A second later, he heard the rumble of a Dodge Hellcat V8 engine screaming up from behind.

"What the—" He looked over his shoulder to see the black-and-white Charger screeching to a stop on the far side of the avenue. Four heavily armed cops dismounted and dashed across the street.

He turned for a shot at the driver of the pickup, but he was too late. The truck had already veered up onto the sidewalk.

Having just gone from predator to prey, Hancock sprang to his feet. The cops crossing the avenue called out to one another, shouldering their weapons and opening fire.

"Goddamn Ranger tactics!" he snarled, running for the stairs with a hail of bullets flying past his head.

He scrambled down the concrete stairwell, dragging the rifle behind him as he wriggled out a back window. His only secondary weapon was the Sig Sauer .357. This was the reason most snipers did not work alone. If he'd had Jessup to back him up with an M4, his situation would have been much less urgent.

An explosion blasted open the steel door to the front of the building, and that's when Hancock really felt the devil bite him in the ass. The last thing he wanted was be to run down from behind and wind up in a Mexican prison. He turned and thrust the barrel of the Barrett back through the window, firing at the first figure to come into view. The policeman's chest exploded inside his body armor, and the other officers dove for cover.

"Keep moving!" someone shouted in English, repeating it immediately in Spanish.

"Vaught!" Hancock hissed acidly, retreating out the back of the house.

Automatic fire tore through the door behind him as he slammed it shut and kicked over a pile of construction timber to block it.

Another burst of fire, and a round tore through his shoulder. The sniper lost his balance and pitched over into a table. Scrabbling back to his feet, he dashed across a courtyard and hurled the Barrett over a seven-foot brick wall, the top of which was lined with shards of broken beer bottles set in cement to discourage people from scaling it. Hancock leaped up and grabbed the top of the wall, feeling the glass cutting into his fingers. He threw a leg over, and the glass bit into the inside of his thigh, ripping open the crotch of his trousers and slicing his penis.

He dropped down on the far side of the wall and grabbed up the rifle. The scope didn't appear to be broken, but that didn't matter. He was out of the fight, wounded, and in need of immediate extraction.

Running through the night, Hancock called for his two bodyguards to pick him up at a prearranged emergency extraction point two hundred yards up the street. They were waiting for him when he got there, and he dove into the backseat, pulling the door closed. "Go!"

The driver sped off.

"What happened?" asked the man in the passenger seat.

"The sons of bitches laid a trap!" He grabbed his medical bag from the floor on the backseat and rifled through it. "They even sacrificed a man to draw me out!" Wriggling his bloody trousers down to his knees, he examined his torn penis and was relieved to find that the cut was less severe than he'd thought. The bloody member would need only a couple of stitches, but he wouldn't be laying any pipe for the next few weeks. The bullet wound to his shoulder was a through-and-through, and the wounds to his legs and hands were nothing—just more superficial combat damage that no veteran soldier would let himself worry too much about.

"But I need a shitload of stitches," he grumbled, unscrewing the lid from a bottle of alcohol. "Get me to the medico."

"Was it the Americans?"

Hancock's veins were burning with anger. "Who the fuck else?" He poured the alcohol over his penis and swore viciously at the pain, slapping a patch of gauze over and binding it tight with tape. "They want a war," he muttered, tearing off the tape with bloody fingers and jamming the roll back into the bag, "I'll give 'em a goddamn war! I'll give 'em a war they'll wish they never fuckin' had." He looked at the passenger, who was staring aghast over the back of the seat at his bloody genitalia. "Call Ruvalcaba! Tell him to send me at least a hundred men. No more fuckin' around! We're gonna kill every last cop in this fucking city!"

68

Mariana arrived at her motel having drunk more than she'd planned. Paying the cab driver and keying into her room, she did not notice the blue sedan that followed her from the nightclub. She dropped her purse on the bed and went into the bathroom to brush her teeth. Just as she was stepping into the shower, there was a knock at the door.

Thinking it must be one of the twins checking up on her, Mariana wrapped herself in a towel and went to have a look through the peephole. It was Fields.

"Shit!" she whispered, realizing he must have tailed her.

She got dressed and answered the door. "What are you doing here? I told you I'd call when I had something."

He stepped pugnaciously into the room, invading her space and forcing her to take a step back.

"What have you learned?" he asked, moving toward a chair.

"I'm making good progress . . . and I didn't say you could sit down."

"I didn't ask your goddamn permission!" His eyes were flinty and cruel. "Now close the door and tell me what was said! In case you haven't noticed, I'm done putting up with your shit—and so is Pope!"

There was a cold, predatory nature about him tonight, and his right hand was hidden inside the deep pocket of his overcoat. From the bulk of the weapon, she thought it must be a silenced pistol. She closed the door and took a chair near the wall, now more paranoid than ever.

"Start talking," he said, not kindly.

She told him about her evening with Jessup in detail, omitting his obsession with the twins, who were due back any time.

"You've got him on the ropes, for Christ sake. Why didn't you invite him back here? One smooth fuck, and you'd have had the whole enchilada tonight!"

"I already told you that's not going to happen!"

He glared at her. "If you can't get Jessup to give up Hancock, you're useless. Do you understand what *useless* means in our business?"

"*Hancock?* You already know his name?"

In his entire career, Fields had never let an asset's name slip. There was no better proof that this upstart little bitch was getting under his skin.

"I also know where to find Crosswhite's family." He let that hang in the air a moment. "I know exactly how to hurt him. So if you don't give me the sniper's location by this time tomorrow night, I make a phone call—just one—and your *friend* will be sorry he was ever born. Have you forgotten he has a baby on the way? I haven't. You're a slick little cunt, but you are not as slick as you might think." He got up from the chair and dumped her purse onto the table.

She jumped up from the chair. "Get your fucking hands off my things!"

He snatched her satellite and cellular phones, along with her passport, and jammed them into his pocket.

"You son of a bitch! Give those back!"

He gestured with the bulky weapon hidden in his pocket. "Step away."

She did as he said, and Fields went to the door. "If I were you"—he pointed at her crotch—"I'd put that thing to good use and get this operation wrapped up."

He stepped out and drew the door shut behind him.

Mariana stood staring at the door. What was she going to do now? There was no way Jessup would give up the gringo sniper over lunch the next day—not unless she seduced him—and she was sure that Fields would follow through on his threat to have Paolina and the baby murdered. Hell, now that he'd stolen her passport, she couldn't even return to the US without going to the American consulate and suffering through days of bureaucratic red tape.

FIELDS WAS ABOUT to pull out of the parking lot when he saw the twins arrive in a cab, instantly recalling having seen them at the curb in front of Villalobos's motel two days before.

"You clever bitch," he muttered, now wanting to strangle Mariana with his bare hands. Fields backed into the shadows and sat watching the girls pay the driver. By the way they walked to their motel room, just three doors over from Mariana's, it was easy to see they'd been drinking.

He got out of the car and walked across the parking lot to the twins' room, listening at the door. They talked for a couple of minutes, and the television came on. He went around back and listened at the bathroom window for the shower, then he walked back around to the front, drawing a ball-peen hammer from his coat pocket and standing off to the side as he knocked on the door.

"*Quién es?*" Tanya asked. Who is it?

"*La pizza.*"

Tanya opened the door a crack, keeping the security chain in place. "We didn't order—"

Fields rammed the door open with his shoulder and bashed Tanya in the head with the ball of the hammer. She dropped to the floor without a sound, and he kicked the door closed with his heel, stalking directly into the bathroom and ripping back the shower curtain. Lorena spun around, eyes wide, and he bashed in her skull. She fell to the bottom of the stall, and he beat her over the head a second time for good measure, wiping the hammer clean with a towel and dropping it into the toilet. Blood poured from Lorena's head, mixing with the shower water and running down the drain.

Before leaving, Fields ripped Tanya's clothes from her body to give the appearance of sexual assault and dumped both purses onto the bed, stuffing their money into his pocket. He found Villalobos's suppressed pistol and jammed it into his coat. Tanya was still breathing when he left.

As he walked to his car, it occurred to Fields that he hadn't killed anyone in more than twenty years. He'd almost forgotten how invigorating it could be.

69

After losing the gringo sniper the night before, Vaught had gone back to Crosswhite's place to check on Paolina and Ortega's family. He caught a few hours' sleep and then returned to the police station shortly after sunrise to find it bustling with seventy-five agitated policemen. He found Sergeant Cuevas in the motor pool talking with four trusted men.

Cuevas and the other four officers were each armed with the Mexican FX-05 Xiuhcoatl "Fire Snake" assault rifle. The FX-05, an indigenous weapon manufactured by the Dirección General de Industria Militar del Ejército (General Directorate of Military Industry of the Army), was reserved for the Grupo Aeromóvil de Fuerzas Especiales (GAFE) Special Forces Airmobile Group. The rifle fired the NATO 5.56 mm round, and instead of the barrel being rifled with traditional lands and grooves, it was rifled with polygonal grooves like the Glock pistol. A sleek, deadly looking weapon, it boasted a higher rate of fire than the American M4, with a slightly lower muzzle velocity.

Sergeant Cuevas's rifle sported a Heckler & Koch AG36 40 mm grenade launcher. Vaught had seen photographs of the still top secret rifle, which had first entered GAFE service in 2008, but this was the first time he was seeing one in real life.

"Where the hell did you find those?"

Sergeant Cuevas grinned. *"Clasificada,* amigo." He cleared the weapon and handed it over.

Vaught examined the rifle. "I hate to admit it, but I'm jealous."

One of the men immediately unshouldered his rifle, offering to trade Vaught for his M4, but the American smiled and shook his head. "Thanks, but I haven't trained with it." He gave Cuevas's weapon back to him. "You guys have been training in secret?"

Sergeant Cuevas gave him a wink.

Vaught thumbed toward the building. "I know we lost a man last night, but what's the entire force doing here at eight o'clock in the morning?"

"Ruvalcaba's men have been spotted entering town from the south," Sergeant Cuevas said. "An hour ago they hit one of our patrols and wiped it out. Chief Diego called the state police for reinforcements, but the pig Serrano is influencing the state police commander. They're using the earthquake in the capital as an excuse to not send help."

"Cocksuckers!" Vaught muttered in English. "How many are we going up against?"

Sergeant Cuevas shrugged. "We don't have much of an idea, but you can believe it's more than seventy-five."

"Are the men going to defend the city?"

"Yes. They know we wounded the sniper last night, and they're eager for a fight."

Vaught was glad the sniper had left a blood trail; otherwise the men might not have been quite so high-spirited. "You know that son of a bitch is still combat effective, right?"

Another wink from Sergeant Cuevas.

"How's Diego holding up?"

"He's scared, but the men respect him for hiding his fear. They're ready to follow his orders."

"Good," Vaught said. "I wish Crosswhite was here. We could use him."

"Have you talked to him? Will he be able to stop Serrano?"

Vaught had his doubts. "I honestly don't know. He's done a reconnaissance of Serrano's estate, and he has another meeting with the fat bastard today. But even if he's successful, it won't be in time to help us—not if Ruvalcaba's men are already here."

Sergeant Cuevas was concerned for Crosswhite's safety. "How can he kill Serrano on his own property and hope to escape alive?"

"I asked him the same thing."

"And?"

"He said he'll have to see how the situation develops."

Cuevas shook his head. "Crazy gringo."

"Well, you know how they are."

"Yes, I do," Cuevas said, "and you're *half* gringo, so how crazy are you?"

Vaught grinned. "I'm not crazy, Sergeant. I'm just too stupid to know when to run the other way."

70

Upon arriving at Serrano's estate, Crosswhite and Mike Ortega were searched by two of Serrano's security men before entering the house. Oscar Martinez then showed them to a small sitting room and asked them to make themselves comfortable. "Señor Serrano and Captain Espinosa are discussing some business matters. I'm sure they won't be long."

"Thank you," Crosswhite said, sensing that Oscar was paying him closer attention than most men normally did and wondering idly if Serrano knew that his personal assistant was gay.

He'd spoken with Vaught the night before, directly after the failed attempt to bag the sniper, but he did not have his satellite phone with him this morning, so he was completely unaware of the situation developing in Toluca. Mariana had not called to check in the night before, nor had she answered her phone, and this concerned him, but there was nothing he could do about it at the moment.

Ortega, meanwhile, was a nervous wreck. He'd spent a mostly sleepless night handcuffed to Crosswhite's left wrist a cheap mattress in a crappy motel, and he had no clue what the crazy ex–Green Beret had planned.

"You have to tell me *something*," he whispered. "How am I supposed to play along if I don't know why we're here?"

"No one's expecting you to know anything," Crosswhite said in English. "You're a dumb-ass, and they know it, so just be yourself, and you'll do fine."

Ortega scowled. "You'd better know what you're doing."

"Or?"

"Or we'll never get out of here alive."

Crosswhite patted him on the back. "We'd be lucky if all they did was kill us, Mikey."

"That doesn't make me feel any better."

"It's not supposed to."

Oscar returned a short time later and showed them outside. Today Serrano's mistress lay beneath a sunshade reading a magazine. She wore a green robe made of silk, and her Chihuahua sat beside her, chewing on a piece of rawhide.

She glanced at Crosswhite, who smiled at her, and went back to reading her magazine.

Lazaro Serrano and Captain Espinosa of the Federal Police were seated at the stone table beneath a tree. Captain Espinosa wore a formal-type uniform but was not armed.

Two bodyguards stood off to the side near the garden wall, much the same as they had the day before, pistols bulging beneath their jackets in shoulder holsters.

"Agent Pendleton," Serrano said happily, almost arrogantly, getting up from the table to offer his hand to Crosswhite while ignoring Ortega altogether. "It's good to see you again. I apologize for the wait, but I haven't had time to speak in much detail with Captain Espinosa before this morning. I was just telling him I believe you're the kind of man we can work with in the coming months—should Director Pope wish to continue our relationship."

"That will be entirely up to the director," Crosswhite said, offering his hand to the black-eyed, mustachioed Captain Espinosa. "Dave Pendleton, Captain. Good to meet you."

Espinosa's grip was firm and confident, unlike Serrano's, which was limp and clammy. "Good to meet you," he echoed.

"So," Serrano said as they settled around the table, "what are your plans concerning Clemson Fields? Have you spoken to your embassy?"

"I have," Crosswhite said, aware that Espinosa was scrutinizing him. "We think he's in Tijuana right now. If that's the case, it might be necessary for me to acquire him there." He looked at Captain Espinosa. "That might be something you can assist us with, Captain."

Espinosa stared coldly. "Are you under the impression that I work for the CIA?"

"Not at all, sir," Crosswhite replied coolly. "As I mentioned to Senator Serrano yesterday, our primary goal is to remove the immediate threat to his safety. After that, we hope to see him elected to the office of the president, and from there to assist him in the removal of Antonio Castañeda in the North."

Espinosa brushed a fly from his nose. "The CIA wants to be very deeply involved in Mexican affairs these days."

Crosswhite glanced at Serrano and then back to Espinosa, deciding that the pleasantries were over. "Well, if I may speak openly, Captain, Alice Downly was an American diplomat killed on Mexican soil with your assistance. Am I correct?"

Espinosa stiffened in the chair, glancing askance at Serrano. "I have no idea where you get your information."

"For the sake of argument," Crosswhite said, "I'll accept that as a yes. Now, please understand that my superiors in the CIA aren't losing any sleep over Downly's death. Quite to the contrary, Director Pope is relieved to have her out of the way. *However*, the US State Department is an entirely different matter. They've been holding off because Mexico City has suffered such a terrible disaster this week, but trust me: the US Secretary of State is gearing up to make real trouble over this Downly business. The best way for us to avoid any danger to both you and Senator Serrano is to see the senator elected president. That will put him in control of the political arena here and mitigate any threat to you. It's *my* job to help make that happen, and that's the service I'm here to offer. Now, if that's not agreeable to the senator, he just has to say the word, and I'll get on a plane today—leaving you gentlemen to deal with Fields and his band of assassins on your own."

Crosswhite sat back, noting that Serrano's cocky air had suddenly dissipated. *Something just changed*, he told himself. *What is it?*

Ortega cleared his throat, as if he were about to speak. Crosswhite gave him a look. "I remind you, Mike, that you're here as a courtesy to your station and nothing more."

Ortega was instantly cowed, and this caused Serrano

to appear even more confused. "Will you clarify something for me?"

"If I can, Senator."

"Are you here as Director Pope's direct representative? Or some other faction of the CIA?"

"As I told you yesterday, I am here at Director Pope's personal direction. Why do you ask?"

Serrano nodded, glancing at Captain Espinosa. "Because it might interest you to know, *Agent Pendleton,* that Clemson Fields called me shortly after you left yesterday. We had quite a long conversation about you."

Crosswhite showed no change in his expression. "I assume he had many glowing things to say?"

Serrano shook his head. "None at all. In fact, he says you are a liar. I described you to him, and he said that your real name is Daniel Crosswhite—that you and Agent Vaught are working with the PFM to have me thrown into prison."

"And?" Crosswhite said.

"And?" Serrano glanced again at Captain Espinosa. "And *what?*"

"I don't know, Senator. You spoke with Fields, not me. What else did he say? Whatever it was, you seem to be very impressed by it." He locked eyes with Captain Espinosa. "Or is this the moment where you order us both shot?"

Ortega felt his anus pucker up tighter than an Italian tenor's trousers.

Serrano and Espinosa had both expected Crosswhite to be shitting himself at this point, but he obviously wasn't remotely concerned, and this left them both in a genuine quandary.

"Do you have some identification?" Espinosa asked.

Crosswhite took a blue passport from his back pocket and tossed it onto the table.

Espinosa checked it over. "This says you are Canadian."

"I *am* Canadian."

"Then what are you doing working for the CIA?" Serrano blurted.

"At the moment, I'm trying to help save your life. Did you really expect Fields to admit to what he was up to?" Crosswhite returned his focus to Captain Espinosa, recognizing the glowering lawman as the most immediate threat. "You should have advised the senator much better than that, Captain."

If Espinosa had sat up any straighter in that moment, his spine would have snapped.

"What are you talking about?"

"What am I talking about? Why would you allow the senator to speak with Fields at all? What were you thinking? I thought you were supposed to be looking out for this man. Now Fields knows I'm in Mexico. He knows everything that *you* two know. He even knows that I've taken Agent Ortega and his family under my protection."

He saw Serrano and Espinosa exchange more dazed glances. Realizing he'd guessed correctly, he dug in his heels. "That's right. Fields told you that Ortega and his family have disappeared. Did he ask where they were? Did he happen to mention he wants them dead? I'll bet he left that part out." Crosswhite took a pack of cigarettes from inside his sport jacket and lit one.

"I don't mean to be rude, gentlemen. I understand this is Mexico, and I respect your sovereignty—I do—but we're playing on the *world* stage here. That's why it doesn't matter if I'm from Canada or Ireland or fucking Norway." He pointed at Serrano with the cigarette between his fingers. "What matters is keeping you alive, Senator. And without me—without Pope's blessing—your road to the presidency will be *long* and *narrow*. Now, do you want my help or not? Because my services happen to be in great demand."

For a fleeting second, even Ortega thought Crosswhite was telling the truth.

"I do," Serrano said quietly. "You must understand that—"

"What I understand is that you need to tell me what else Fields had to say and what else you said to him. That way I can assess the damage that's been done and come up with a way to fix it." Crosswhite crushed out the cigarette on the table top, glancing at Ortega. "What are *you* looking at?" he said in English. "Did you think I was making all this shit up?"

Ortega shrugged and shook his head, obviously more confused than anyone else at the table. "I—I don't—"

"Shut up." Crosswhite turned back to Captain Espinosa, keeping the initiative. "Was I incorrect? Are you not the senator's advisor?"

Espinosa glanced at Serrano.

"He's a trusted advisor, yes," Serrano said. "But he didn't—I didn't speak with him before I spoke with Fields. It was my decision to speak with Fields. My error."

Crosswhite feigned incredulousness. "I'm sorry, Senator, but am I to understand that you *have* no political advisor?"

Serrano stiffened, his embarrassment beginning to show as he realized that Crosswhite was accustomed to dealing with much more sophisticated power brokers.

Crosswhite let him off the hook, turning back to Espinosa. "My apologies, Captain. I was under the impression you were an actual advisor."

Now Espinosa was also embarrassed—not to mention annoyed with Serrano—exactly as Crosswhite had planned. Crosswhite saw too that even the bodyguards were off balance, which meant they'd been briefed to expect an entirely different kind of meeting with an entirely different outcome.

Now that everyone was sufficiently agitated, he said, "Excuse me, but can one of these two gentlemen show me to the restroom?"

"Um, yes," Serrano said. "Of course." Grateful for an opportunity to gather his thoughts, he gestured for one of the bodyguards to show him the way.

Crosswhite stood up and moved toward the house, pausing for the bodyguard to catch up.

Captain Espinosa glanced at Serrano, his face an open display of displeasure at having been made to look foolish in front of the CIA.

As the bodyguard approached, Crosswhite spun into him, striking the vagus nerve in the side of the man's neck with the inside ridge of his hand. The bodyguard's entire body went ramrod stiff, and he toppled over backward, landing on the ground without making any attempt to break his fall. Crosswhite launched himself at the second bodyguard, pouncing like a mountain lion to jam his thumb deep into the man's eye socket and stealing the Glock pistol from beneath his jacket.

He turned and shot Espinosa in the throat as he was rising from his chair. The police captain pitched over into Serrano's lap, and Serrano stared in wide-eyed disbelief as Crosswhite shot him in the forehead. The fat man fell over against the table and flopped to the ground. Two more headshots finished the bodyguards, and Crosswhite stalked over to where Serrano's girlfriend sat, too petrified to move or make a sound.

The Chihuahua barked at him twice as he pointed the

pistol into her face, speaking calmly in Spanish. "I'm with the CIA. Do you know what that is?"

She nodded, the magazine still in her hands.

"If you give anyone an accurate physical description of me, I will find you, and I will kill you. Do you understand?"

"Yes," she croaked in English.

"You got a helluva set of tits, honey." With that, he turned and walked back to the table, where Ortega sat in his own piss, trembling like a dog shitting a peach pit, blood from both men spattered on his face.

"I told you all you had to do was be yourself," Crosswhite said.

Expecting to see Crosswhite and Ortega lying dead on the ground, Oscar Martinez came out the back door carrying a pair of black rubber body bags and stopped dead in his tracks.

Crosswhite aimed the pistol at him. "Those other two assholes still out front?" he asked in English.

Oscar nodded.

"What was supposed to happen?"

"I was to . . . I was to . . ." Oscar's jaw began to tremble.

"It's okay," Crosswhite said. "You can tell me."

"I was to put your bodies into these bags and to . . . to call Ruvalcaba's people to come take you away."

"Go out front and call those other two assholes back here. Double-cross me, and I'll feed you to that goddamn Chihuahua."

Oscar ducked back inside, and Crosswhite followed a few steps behind.

Ortega was still sitting in the chair staring at the bodies on the ground when he heard two more shots inside the house. A few seconds later, Crosswhite walked up and smacked him in the back of the head. "Get your ass up, Mikey. We're done here."

Ortega got unsteadily to his feet. "Will you take me to my wife and kids now?"

Crosswhite took him by the arm, setting off toward the house. "What I *should* do is drown you in the goddamn pool, you piece of shit."

71

Mariana stood outside the door to her motel room, watching as the twins' sheet-covered bodies were loaded into an ambulance. She didn't know who had discovered them, and she didn't ask, but she knew from overhearing the police that they believed the girls to be prostitutes, robbed and murdered by a client wielding a hammer. The forensics people had taken the sisters' fingerprints, expecting them to match up with those from another grisly murder scene a few miles away.

Mariana doubted there would be a match, as the twins had never mentioned killing Villalobos.

The police questioned her briefly, and she denied knowing anything, but she knew it had to have been Fields.

Her cab ride to meet Jessup for lunch was not a pleasant one. She glanced out the back window to see Fields following in his blue sedan. There were two Mexican men in the car with him, and now that he'd taken both of her phones, she had no way of calling Crosswhite or Midori or even Castañeda for support. She decided to keep a hard-copy list of every phone number in the future, but now that Fields had let slip the name Hancock, she didn't think he had any intention of allowing her to live.

Her urge to run to the US Consulate was strong, but there would be no real protection for her there. Consulates were not embassies. They were not in place to serve US citizens abroad. Their primary function was to provide visa services to foreign nationals. Any services they provided to American nationals were treated as courtesies rather than as any sort of US citizens' rights. And once Mariana was finally admitted into the secure facility—which would probably take at least a couple of hours due to her lack of identification—there would be no leaving again until and unless they allowed her to leave. Pope would know within an hour of her arrival at the facility, and there was no way to predict how he might react. She now believed he had ordered Downly's assassination, and for all she knew, he would advise the consulate general of Tijuana to treat her as a fugitive—or, worse, a potential terrorist.

Realizing that the US Consulate building could all too easily become a prison, she decided she was safer on the street, where she could at least move around.

She arrived at the restaurant to find Billy Jessup waiting for her at the bar.

"What's the matter?" he said. "You look worried."

Survival instinct kicked in. "I'm in trouble." After all, Jessup was a man and, in a bizarre way, the closest thing to a friend she had at the moment.

"What kind of trouble?"

"I'm being followed. I think they're looking to kill us both."

He glanced at the entrance. "Out front?"

"Yeah. Blue car."

He took her hand. "Let's get the fuck outta here."

Jessup led her into the back through the kitchen.

"Hey, you can't pass through here!" said a kitchen worker, attempting to block their way.

"Go fuck yourself," Jessup muttered, shoving him aside and leading Mariana out the back door. Ducking into the alley, they didn't make it three steps before they were caught in a cross fire: Fito and Memo firing Taser guns from behind adjacent Dumpsters.

Mariana was hit in the neck with close to 40,000 volts at 25 watts; Jessup, in the shoulder. They went down convulsing as Fields pulled up in the car. They were both zapped again and dumped into the trunk.

Twenty minutes later, they were unloaded at gunpoint behind a dilapidated office building in a deserted section of town. Fields shot Mariana in the leg with a freshly loaded Taser, and she went down again, convulsing on the concrete.

"That's an attention getter," he said with a twisted smile.

Jessup stood watching with his hands behind his head, wanting to help, but Fito and Memo were covering him front and back with pistols.

When she recovered well enough to speak, Fields stood over her. "What did Crosswhite and Shannon do with the gold they found in Paris?"

She glared up at him, now sure that he intended to kill her. "I don't know anything about any gold, you fuck!"

He zapped her again, and she screamed, her bladder finally letting go.

"That's enough!" Jessup shouted.

Fields glanced at him. "If he says another word, shoot him in the head."

Fito aimed Villalobos's silenced pistol at Jessup's face, and Fields returned his attention to Mariana.

"Crosswhite would not have gone so far off the reservation unless he had money and a plan—not with a wife and a baby on the way. So you'd better tell me what he's up to, or it's going to be a very long afternoon for you."

Mariana was too badly convulsed in that moment to speak, so he stood waiting patiently.

Jessup began to wonder if he was caught up in something to do with the CIA.

Fields knelt down beside her, looking into her wild eyes. "Just breathe," he said calmly. "We've got all day." He stood back up, taking her satellite phone from the pocket of his overcoat. "I tell you what we'll try. We'll give your boyfriend a call and see what he has to say about your little predicament."

She drew a deep breath, forcing out the words. "He won't tell you anything. He'll know it won't do any good."

"I think you're right. I think he'll let you die. But this way, he'll know it's his fault." Fields stepped on her throat with his shoe to prevent her calling out before he was ready, and she began to strangle.

Crosswhite answered. "Where the hell have you been? Are you okay?"

"I'm a little annoyed at the moment, actually," Fields said. "How are you?" There was a pregnant pause at Crosswhite's end. "What, no smart-ass remark? I'm disappointed in you, Daniel."

"Where is she?"

"I literally have my foot on her throat. Would you like me to send you a photo?"

"What do you want?"

"First, I want Chance Vaught eliminated. Then you can do me the service of eliminating Rhett Hancock. By now, I'm guessing Ortega has given you that name, so you can go ahead and eliminate Ortega as well."

The second that Jessup heard Hancock's name, his mind caught on fire with the flames of betrayal, and he knew that Mariana had set him up. *Bitch!* he thought to himself.

"I'll take care of Hancock soon enough," Crosswhite said. "Mariana's got nothing to do with any of this, so—"

"Lie!" Fields said. "I know all about your arrangements with Castañeda. She's every bit as involved in this as you are. So dispense with the bullshit. Is Vaught there with you? Kill him now, or I'll kill your little sweetheart here."

"Vaught's not with me," Crosswhite said. "The Ruvalcabas have declared war on Toluca PD. They're moving to take over the city, and Hancock is with them. Before it's over, I'll kill him, or he'll kill me. That's all I can guarantee. Now, let Mariana go."

Fields covered the receiver with his hand, saying to Fito, "Kill him."

Jessup made a break for it, but Fito shot him down before he'd gone ten feet.

Field's put the phone back to his ear. "Tell me what happened to the gold you and Shannon hid in Paris?"

There came a tired sigh from Crosswhite's end of the line. "Fields, I know it won't do any good to tell you this, but every ounce of that gold went to Pope. Now he's using it to fund the ATRU. By the way: I do have Ortega. If you hurt Marina, I promise you he'll testify before the Senate subcommittee."

Fields chortled, grinding his foot against Mariana's throat to the point that her eyes began to bulge. "You'll have to bluff harder than that, Daniel. Ortega will never testify truthfully. He's got way too much to lose, and it would be his word against Pope's. Who do you think the Senate will believe?"

"Let her go," Crosswhite said. "That's the only way we can make a deal."

Fields put the phone down close to Mariana's mouth and released the pressure. "Say hello."

"Dan!" she rasped. "Don't—!"

He crushed her throat shut again, choking off her warning. "Now, tell me: Does it sound to you like you're in a position to give me ultimatums?"

"Fields, I'm only gonna warn you once."

"Warn me what?"

A green 1971 Dodge pickup came skidding around the corner of the building and slid to stop in the gravel. A gringo wearing a tan ball cap jumped out with a 1911 pistol and began firing at the run.

"It's him!" Fito shouted, returning fire as he dove for cover behind Fields's car, but Memo was already down and bleeding out.

Fields hauled Mariana to her feet by the hair, using her as a shield as he backed quickly into the building through a broken-out window. She kicked to get free, but she was too weak from electrical shock and strangulation.

The gringo ran low along the wall while Fito's bullets ricocheted off the concrete above his head. When he heard Fito's empty magazine clatter to the cement, he charged at the car and dove across the hood, grabbing Fito's gun and landing on top of him. He jammed the muzzle of the .45 into Fito's belly and squeezed the trigger.

Fito squealed like a child, instantly relinquishing his grip on the weapon.

The gringo got to his feet and threw the pistol over a fence, walking around the car and into the building. With the broken glass crunching beneath the heels of his worn cowboy boots, he found Fields hiding in an empty office, holding one of the twin's straight razors to Mariana's throat.

The moment Fields saw him, his eyebrows soared in disbelief. "You're dead!"

Gil Shannon pointed the 1911 into his face, his chiseled visage set. "Not hardly. Drop the razor and let go of her."

Fields did as he said, and Mariana stumbled away, sliding down the wall, rasping for air.

Gil shot Fields in both knees.

Fields collapsed, wrapping his arms around his legs and gnashing his teeth in pain.

Gil reloaded the weapon and crouched beside him, saying in a calm voice: "Operation One-Way Trip. China Mission, September 2005. You ordered three Vietnamese agents murdered after my extraction. Why?"

"Go fuck yourself!" Fields grunted, in more pain than he'd ever known.

Gil shot him in the foot, and Fields writhed around in even more agony, calling him filthy names. After giving him a minute to shout himself calm, Gil repeated the question.

"Just kill me!" Fields sneered. "Kill me, you fucking bastard!"

"I will when I'm ready," Gil said quietly, aiming at the other foot. "Tell me why."

"It was a closed operation, you motherfucker! You know what that means: *no fucking witnesses!*"

"Who gave the order?"

"It was Pope's operation! He gave the orders, and I saw to it they were carried out! Now *fuck you!*"

"You slipped up," Gil said. "One of the agents survived, and he gave me your fucking name." He stood up and shot Fields dead. "Now reap the whirlwind."

He went to Mariana, who lay against the wall, crouching down to help her sit up and using a finger to gently push the hair from her face. "You okay?"

She nodded, gripping her shoulders against the ache left over from the violent muscle contractions. "How are you alive?" she asked. "Even Pope thinks you're dead."

"I learned to fly recently." He lifted her from the floor. "Still workin' on my landings, though."

She slid an arm around his neck, resting her head against his shoulder as he carried her out to the truck. "How did you know where to find me?"

"Midori hijacked one of Pope's surveillance drones last night when Crosswhite couldn't reach you. She's been watching you ever since. I was arriving at the airport when she saw you being stuffed into a trunk. She vectored me in by phone."

She looked at him. "Does Dan know you're alive?"

"Only you and Midori. And that's how it has to stay."

"For how long?"

He opened the squeaky door of the truck and set her down on the passenger side. "Forever."

"My passport," she said, pointing at Fields's car. "He has my phones and my passport."

Gil retrieved her belongings and then ducked through a hole in the fence, finding the silenced pistol and wiping off his fingerprints before tossing it into a pile of garbage.

A couple of miles into their trip to Puerto Vallarta, Mariana felt well enough to carry on a conversation. "Can I ask you something?"

He glanced at her, one hand dipped over the wheel as they rattled along. "Shoot."

"How much gold did you two hide from Pope?"

"Is that what Dan told you—We took gold?"

"No, he denies it, but nothing else explains the way you two are acting."

Gil seemed to give it some thought before deciding how to answer. "Can you see me and Crosswhite fencing gold bullion on the black market without Pope catching us?"

"I guess not," she admitted. "Not if you put it that way. But tell me what's going on. Why was Fields so convinced?"

"Hold the wheel a minute." She held the wheel while he lit a cigarette with a match. "Lost my lighter in China." He tossed the match, still smoking, onto the dust-covered dashboard. "We found six million in Swedish bearer bonds in the same storage container and walked out with them under our jackets."

A smile spread across her face. "The perfect crime; totally untraceable."

He exhaled smoke. "Pope was so busy brokering the gold over next few weeks, he never even noticed our trip to the Caymans."

"When did you first start to lose faith?"

"Crosswhite lost his after Earnest Endeavor. I didn't lose mine until Pope left me hanging in Lichtenstein. The Russian mob moved right into the same hotel I was staying at. He missed it, and I damn near bought it. That's when I realized his mind was on much bigger things than me. The old Pope would never have made that mistake."

"So what now?"

"Now . . ." He took a drag from the cigarette. "Now we get Pope to appoint you Mexico chief of station."

She gaped at him. "Are you high?"

"What's wrong? You don't want the job?"

She sat up in the seat. "Want the job? How are we going to get him to give it to me?"

"We won't leave him any choice."

"What about Dan?"

Gil shrugged. "What about him?"

"He was counting on your help with the sniper."

"Dan can handle Rhett Hancock."

"You know him?"

"I know *about* him. He's a good shot, but he's nothing special. Besides, if I stick my nose into that fight down in Toluca, Pope will recognize my kill patterns and figure out I'm still alive. I can't risk that. I went through too god-damn much trouble getting myself killed."

"Well, if I have to keep your secret, I at least want to know how you did it—and why."

He stopped for a red light and looked at her, the merest hint of a grin on his face. "I can see what he sees in you."

Her face flushed, and she looked out the window. "You don't know what you're talking about."

Gil chuckled and pulled through the intersection. "*Why* is my secret, but *how* is easy enough to tell . . ."

72

Gil's battered black Land Rover caromed off the back of the flatbed tow truck's cab and careened over the guard-rail to disappear into the fog.

The exploding air bag was a problem for the first half second—the hot gas and powder stinging Gil's eyes as he released the seat belt. But the vehicle rolled over to the right as planned, and he opened the door, allowing the centrifugal force to throw him clear. After that it was simply a matter of spreading his arms and legs, soaring away though the fog in the black wing suit.

Unable to see the surface of the river, he kept an eye on the altimeter Velcroed to his wrist, conscious of the fact he was picking up a good deal of speed as he descended. Thirty feet from the surface, the mist cleared well enough to see, and he braced himself for impact, skidding into the water at an angle of 20 degrees doing better than sixty miles per hour. The impact bloodied his nose, knocked the wind out of him, and dislocated his shoulder, but he rolled onto his back and kept himself afloat until Nahn came motoring out of the morning fog to haul him into a small boat.

They were ashore within three minutes, where Nahn reset his shoulder by sitting on the ground, putting his foot into Gil's armpit and giving his wrist a stiff pull. The joint popped back into the socket, and Gil sat up with a groan, working the shoulder.

"How was your flight?" Nahn asked with a grin.

Gil got to his feet, unzipping the soaking wing suit. "The service was a little slow."

They were in a van headed for Chongqing ten minutes later. Upon their arrival at a secluded airfield, the two were flown in a private plane to within a few miles of the Vietnamese border, where both men parachuted out of the aircraft at low altitude, gliding over the border to land safely in northern Vietnam, where Nahn's nephews were waiting to take them to Hanoi.

From Hanoi, Gil was able to access his bank account in the Cayman Islands and make all the necessary arrangements for his trip to Mexico.

At the airport, Gil and Nahn shook hands.

"Thanks, old friend. I owe you more than I can repay. And don't worry. The man who betrayed you will pay for what he did. You have my word."

Nahn smiled, saying, *"Ai làm nấy chịu."* Roughly translated: whoever sows wind shall harvest storm.

73

Midori appeared in the doorway to Pope's office. "You wanted to see me?"

He looked up and closed his laptop. "Come in and shut the door."

She did as she was told, taking the seat before his desk and crossing her legs.

The vein in his head was pulsing, though his face showed no outward emotion. "You've been a very bad girl."

"Oh?" she said innocently. "How so?"

"Lazaro Serrano is dead."

She shrugged. "I don't know what that's got to do with me. I've never even been to Mexico."

"Fields isn't answering his phone."

She shrugged again. "It isn't my day to watch him."

"Yet it appears you've been doing exactly that. What's

more, last night you took personal control of a UAV"—an unmanned aerial vehicle—"and more than twelve hours of surveillance footage have been illegally purged from all three databases."

"Again," she said, "I don't know what that has to do with me. The CIA doesn't have stealth drones in the skies over Mexico. The president himself said so last week on national television."

He sat staring at her.

"You can't have me prosecuted, Robert. We both know that. So you can either get over it, fire me, or have me killed. Which is it going to be?"

Pope ignored what he considered hyperbole. "Is Fields dead?"

She laced her fingers in her lap. "Extremely."

He reddened. "Ortega?"

"No, but Crosswhite has him on ice. I don't expect he'll kill him unless Ortega does something stupid."

Pope took off his glasses and tossed them onto the desk. "So who's running the goddamn show down there?"

"Mariana Mederos—and she appears to have all of her ducks in a row."

"Does she, indeed? What are her intentions?"

"I don't know. I suppose we'll both have to wait and see."

"This is entirely unacceptable!"

Midori grabbed the arms of the chair and sat forward. "Do you ever listen to yourself? *Unacceptable*, Robert? You assassinated an American diplomat!"

He darkened. "I'm not the first director to do so."

"And you might not be the last, but Alice Downly was *your* last—at least as long as I'm working for you. I won't be party to it. I've gathered enough intelligence to demonstrate that you were complicit in her death. If I turn up dead, that intelligence goes public. And I'm not just talking about WikiLeaks. You can fire me, and I'll go away quietly—I'm not a vindictive person—but I have no control over what happens after I'm dead. My protector is beyond your reach."

"Your *protector*?" He opened the middle desk drawer, taking the top from a prescription bottle and swallowing an anxiety pill, chasing it with a drink of water. Then Pope tossed the pills back into the drawer and slammed it shut. "Damn you!"

"Damn *you*," she said quietly.

"I trusted you!"

"I trusted *you*."

Pope stood up from the desk and went to the window, looking out over the campus with his arms folded. "What about Hancock?" he said finally.

"Crosswhite and Vaught are organizing the defense of Toluca. They plan to kill him during the battle. That's as much as I know."

He turned around. "Battle? What the hell's going on down there?"

"Crosswhite couldn't get to Serrano in time to stop the Ruvalcabas from moving to take over the city. The fighting began about an hour ago. The Mexican government has its hands full in Mexico City, where the Ruvalcabas are causing chaos, which means they're not sending any reinforcements."

"So it's civil war."

She shook her head. "Not really. Just another battle for a Mexican town while the federal government keeps its back turned. More like business as usual, I'd say."

"I want to talk to Crosswhite. I assume you're in contact?"

"He won't talk to you. He's made it clear you have no say in what's going on down there right now."

"He and Mariana are working together?"

She nodded. "Vaught is with them."

Pope stood stroking his chin. "They're setting themselves up to take over Mexico station."

"Robert, with Fields dead and Ortega fully compromised, they *are* Mexico station."

The die was cast, and the CIA director saw there was nothing he could do about it. "What do they need from me?"

"They haven't asked for anything. They don't trust you anymore; not after you turned them over to Fields. He tried to have them both killed. I'll take it on faith you knew nothing about that—and if you did, I don't ever want to know."

"Who killed Fields?"

Not entirely convinced it was the correct move, Midori stuck to the plan and followed Gil's advice. "Mariana projected his movement; she acted first."

Pope's eyes widened. "You're telling me she preempted him?"

"That's correct."

"She did it herself?"

"Of course not. She maneuvered him into position for Castañeda's people."

"She's learning," he muttered, retaking his chair. "Her plan must be to consolidate the drug trade under Castañeda. Bad choice. But with Serrano dead, Ruvalcaba becomes a nonstarter."

"She can work with Castañeda. He respects her—at least for now—and he's content to honor the truce."

"Time will tell the truth of that. Where is she now?"

"She's safe. That's all she'd say."

He elected not to waste time trying to get Midori to betray Mariana. "How much do your assistants know about this?"

"I've protected you completely, Robert—like I always do. The only difference is that I've taken steps to protect myself as well."

He sat thinking. "Who's she sending after Ruvalcaba? She must have someone in mind."

Midori kept her poker face. "All she would say is that she's sending someone who knows what they're doing."

"Then we'll just have to trust her," Pope decided. "With Hector Ruvalcaba out of the way, Castañeda becomes the last major player. The southern cartels will fall in line under his leadership to avoid a war, but we'll have to keep an eye on things down there. If another upstart shows his face . . ."

"Mariana will already have a professional team in-country to take him out."

He chuckled, in spite of his annoyance at having been outmaneuvered. "Yes, I suppose she will, provided that their little coup is successful."

Midori watched him closely as he spent the next couple of minutes pondering the mathematical probabilities, muttering at last to himself, "Something doesn't quite add up, though. There's an unknown variable left over at the end of this equation."

Seeing genuine puzzlement in his eyes, Midori smiled inwardly, delighted that Pope had no idea Gil Shannon might still be alive.

74

TOLUCA, MEXICO
14:30 HOURS

The first firefight between the Toluca police and the Ruvalcabas took place near the center of town. Entirely by chance, two patrol trucks spotted a car with four of Ruvalcaba's men sitting at a traffic light. The police attempted a traffic stop, and the cartel members opened fire.

One police officer was wounded in the hand, but all four Ruvalcabas were killed by automatic weapons fire. After that, word spread through town, and within a half hour, the civilian population was in lockdown mode; they were not strangers to drug violence in their streets.

Crosswhite and Vaught stood inside an Oxxo carryout store near the scene of the shooting, talking with Chief Diego and Sergeant Cuevas. Crosswhite had reached town only fifteen minutes earlier, but Vaught had briefed him fully by phone prior to his arrival.

"I understand your desire to hold the center of town,"

Crosswhite told Diego, "but this isn't that kind of fight. There's nothing of value here, either to us or the enemy. The center of town is a symbol—nothing more. We have to hunt these people down and kill them."

"But if we give up the center of town," Diego said, "the people will think we've abandoned them and go over to the enemy."

Crosswhite began to argue, but Vaught caught him by the arm. "He's right. We have to hold the center of town. Symbolism is important here."

"Goddamnit, we don't have enough men for that!"

"If I may?" said Sergeant Cuevas.

Crosswhite nodded.

"Twenty-five men can hold the center of town if the rest maintain a close orbit, crisscrossing at regular intervals to give the appearance of a greater presence. In the meantime, the patrols can sweep the streets and engage when necessary."

Crosswhite liked the idea in principle. "That will work until nightfall. After that, they'll block many of the streets with *narcobloqueos*, and we'll have to modify the tactic. But I like the plan. It should get us through the day and keep the people from thinking we've run out on them."

"But after dark, we'll pull the patrols much closer to the center," Diego insisted. This was a tactic similar to that used in the north along the border before the truce with Castañeda had been struck. By day, the police had patrolled freely, whereas by night, many towns had been forced to suspend police services altogether to avoid their officers being killed in ambushes.

Crosswhite wanted to employ much more aggressive tactics, but it wasn't his police department, and the men weren't trained well enough for night action. Still, he wasn't satisfied to fight a holding action. He took Vaught by the shoulder and walked him aside as three other officers came into the store to talk with the chief.

"With everyone bunched up together around the center of town tonight, Hancock's gonna have a target-rich environment to work with."

"I was thinking the same thing," Vaught said. "We should detach from the main body and be ready to move on him the second he fires."

"He'll have skirmishers. We won't be able to run right up on him the way you did last night."

"I'll talk Cuevas into giving me that grenade launcher of his. We'll hit 'em hard and fast. Hell, we might even get Hancock in the barrage."

"If we could be so lucky," Crosswhite said, snatching a pack of cigarettes from the rack behind the counter.

Vaught grinned. "Gonna pay for those?"

"I'm defending the city. If that's not payment enough, they can root through my pockets when I'm dead."

Sergeant Cuevas stepped up and tossed a fifty-peso note onto the counter. "I have Diego's permission to detach my team after sundown to work with you. There will be seven of us to move on the sniper when he fires. One of us should get through to him." He offered Vaught his FX-05 with the AG36 40 mm grenade launcher.

Vaught took a dip from his can of Copenhagen. "I won't need it if you're coming along, Sergeant."

"I've fired the grenade launcher only twice," Cuevas said. "I'm sure you have a better eye for it."

Crosswhite tore the cellophane from the pack of smokes. "Vaught's not trained on the weapon system. That makes you the grenadier, Sergeant." He turned for the door. "Thanks for the cigarettes, by the way."

When he was gone outside, Cuevas looked at Vaught. "Did he really kill Serrano?"

Tucking away the tobacco can in his pocket, Vaught nodded. "Are you conflicted by that . . . believe you should arrest him?"

Cuevas smirked and started for the door. "I'd sooner arrest him for stealing the cigarettes."

75

Hector Ruvalcaba moved through his fortified home like
an angry tiger. With Lazaro Serrano dead, he was entirely vulnerable and without protection from the federal
government. Within ten days, his detractors would discern this vulnerability, and he would once again become
a fugitive from justice. Even Captain Espinosa was dead.
There were other police officials he could bribe, as well
as those in government, but with earthquake relief occu-
pying everyone's efforts, there was no time to meet with
them; no way to arrange for protection.

The Policia Federal Ministerial would soon begin for-
mulating plans to take him back into custody and return
him to that pigsty of a prison. Were it not for his great
wealth hidden in bank accounts offshore, his own people
would be abandoning him already. Now he would be

forced to live on the move, fighting a running drug war with that dog Antonio Castañeda in the North.

Life, business, and freedom were about to become a great deal more expensive.

Ruvalcaba's wife found him in the study, gathering documents into a briefcase. She was twenty years younger than he was, with short-cropped dark hair. Although pretty at a distance, upon close examination, it was easy to see that at forty-five she had already undergone a good deal of plastic surgery. Her breasts, ass, lips, and nose were not exactly original equipment.

"Is it really necessary for us to leave today, Hector? We're supposed to have dinner with the—"

"Dinner?!" He looked at her dismay. "There are no more dinners, Victoria. We're fugitives. Our protection is gone."

"Well . . ." She stood with her hands on her hips, refusing to accept that the high-society life to which she had grown accustomed over the past thirteen months was finished. "There's still plenty of money. Just pay someone else."

He shut the briefcase and stared at her. "Pay who?"

"I don't know . . . somebody!"

"I have to cultivate contacts, arrange for negotiations. Those things take time, and right now there is no time. Once I'm in custody, that's it."

"You worked it out last time. They even dug you a tunnel."

He came from around the desk, taking her by the arms. "Serrano was one of the most powerful men in Mexico. Do you think anyone can arrange for a tunnel?" He shook his head and grabbed a computer from another table. "You should pack a couple of bags. We're leaving soon."

She started at him. "I'm not going. I'm staying here."

"You *can't* stay here."

"Why not? I haven't broken any laws."

"That doesn't matter. Castañeda's people will hurt you to get to me."

She shrugged. "So leave some men here to protect me. Leave Adrian and his team."

He'd suspected that she and Adrian, the head of household security, had been messing around behind his back, but he'd overlooked it because of his own frequent indiscretions.

"Like anyone else, Victoria, Adrian can be bought."

She crossed her arms. "I'm not living on the run. My friends are here in the city."

"How long do you think they will remain your friends after my face is back in the papers?"

She knew already which of their friends secretly despised her husband. "I'm staying."

"Fine," he said at length. "I won't force you—but you're putting yourself in great danger."

"I knew I was putting myself in danger when I married you, but this is the life I wanted, and I won't give it up."

Ruvalcaba took the briefcase from his desk and kissed her on the cheek on his way out of the study. "I'll call when I can."

He got into the backseat of his black Escalade and called Hancock on the phone. When the American answered, Ruvalcaba asked if he'd heard the news about Serrano.

"I just got word," Hancock said. "We don't need Serrano."

"How are you progressing?" Hector wanted to know.

"We got a slow start this morning, but we killed four cops in an ambush half an hour ago, and that caused them to pull back closer to the center of town. We hold most of the outlying areas now. They're doing what I expected them to do. By nightfall, we'll have all the police in one place, more or less, and after that, it's just a battle of attrition."

"I need this victory," Ruvalcaba said. "I have to bolster my reputation."

"Don't worry, Mr. Ruvalcaba. You'll own the city of Toluca by sunrise tomorrow. Then you can order the town council to appoint whoever you want as chief."

"If you deliver the town as you say, I will deposit a bonus of one million dollars directly into your account."

"That's very generous."

"And there will be another two million waiting for you after you have removed Antonio Castañeda."

"Castañeda will be difficult," Hancock said. "He's had Special Forces training, and his security is very—"

"Five million," Ruvalcaba said, knowing that he needed to spend whatever it took to remove Castañeda.

"I'm not bargaining, Mr. Ruvalcaba. I'm telling you that he'll be very difficult to remove."

"Difficult," Ruvalcaba said. "Not impossible."

"No, sir. Not impossible."

"Very good. Finish your work in Toluca, then meet me down in Chiapas. We have much work to do, you and I."

Ruvalcaba finished the call and looked at his driver. "Take me to the airfield."

76

Within ten minutes of meeting Gil Shannon, Antonio Castañeda knew he was speaking with a man of action. Obviously an accomplished professional, there was no bravado about him, no sense of ego, nothing cocky or challenging in his manner. It was plain to see that Gil's deeds spoke for themselves and that he had nothing to prove to anyone.

Castañeda was sad and angry to have lost Lorena and Tanya. They'd been the most reliable and loyal of his people—not to mention the finest of his lovers. But he knew that if he hadn't sent them to Tijuana, Fields's man Villalobos would have killed Mariana, thus destroying his chances of consolidating the narcotics trade under his power. Later he would weep for the girls in private, but for now, there was business to take care of.

"I thank you for avenging their deaths," he said to Gil

in English. "That is a valuable personal service to me. How may I repay you?"

Gil thought for a second. "You can build a school down in . . ." He looked at Mariana. "What state did you say was the poorest?"

"Chiapas."

"Chiapas," he said. "You can build a school down in Chiapas."

Castañeda chortled. "Chiapas is not part of my territory at the moment."

"But it soon will be. That *is* the plan, correct?"

Castañeda smiled pleasantly at Mariana, not in his normally flirtatious way, and then looked back to Gil. "That is the plan, yes."

"Then if you're serious," Gil said, "build a school, and we'll call it even."

"Consider it done. Now, what assistance can I provide you in removing Ruvalcaba—provided *you're* serious about wanting to do the job yourself?"

Mariana had already explained to Gil that Hector Ruvalcaba had been reported dead twice in the past eight years, and that only last year he had successfully escaped a maximum security prison to resume control of the southern cartels. Gil wasn't interested in taking anyone else's word for it that Ruvalcaba was dead. "I want the job done correctly. I don't speak the lingo, and I stick out like a sore thumb down here, so I don't wanna have to come back and correct anyone else's mistakes."

Castañeda nodded, appreciating being in the presence of a professional. "You're sure I cannot interest you in something to drink, my friend?"

"Thanks. I never drink when I'm working. It's nothing personal, I promise."

This left Castañeda feeling a little disappointed, but

it was that kind of a day. "He died badly, this dog Fields who murdered my girls?"

"Very," Gil said.

"What assistance will you need?"

"I need a quality weapon and a guide who speaks good English—a tough son of a bitch . . . but not somebody who's gonna get carried away."

Castañeda gestured at Mariana. "Look no further, señor."

Gil shook his head. "No more fieldwork for her. She'll be taking over Mexico station pretty soon, and I don't want in her harm's way."

This was the first Castañeda had heard that, and it gave him a burst of adrenaline. "Is this true?" he asked her. "Pope is appointing you chief of station?"

She glanced at Gil. "It's not official, but . . . *Mr. Cochran* is convinced it will happen if we're successful in removing Ruvalcaba."

Castañeda understood that Cochran was not Gil's actual name. "Then you are a man of genuine influence."

"I happen to be in a very unique position," Gil replied. "And I intend to make the most of it, to the mutual benefit of all parties—excluding Hector Ruvalcaba."

"But Pope does not want me taking over the narcotics trade. Won't that pose a problem?"

"Pope wants to tell the president he's stabilized the border for the long term. With Ruvalcaba dead, you'll be the only man left who can make that happen. No one else has the power or influence to prevent another drug war. Pope will have no choice but to accept that reality and appoint Mariana as chief of station."

Seeing the logic, Castañeda winked at Mariana. "It would appear we are at last true partners."

She smiled in spite of herself, recognizing that, yes,

she now needed Castañeda as badly as he needed her. "It would appear."

"And you, Mr. Cochran, what is your interest in Mexico? Since you are obviously not here as a representative of Mr. Pope."

Gil shrugged. "Some people are inclined to pull an injured man outta the street; others stand and watch. I've never just stood by. And I've never had any fucking use for those who do."

"I thank you for that," Castañeda said. "My country has a bloody history. Too many good men—those who would not stand by to watch—have been gunned down like dogs in that very same street you speak of. This unfortunate aspect of our culture has allowed men like me to thrive for the last hundred years, since the revolution."

Gil was surprised by Castañeda's self-deprecating remark. "Men like you?"

"I was once a soldier like yourself. I used to believe in the cause of my country. But the infection of corruption is too deep for any one man to cure. The people must demand the cure from our government. Until they do, men like me will continue to prosper. It is much the same in your country, no?"

"It's getting worse," Gil conceded, avoiding a political discussion.

"But you *will* continue to honor the truce," Mariana said to Castañeda. "You will not take action against civilians on either side of the border, and you will make public examples of the men who do. Otherwise I will have to withdraw the support of the CIA—along with its protection."

He cocked an eyebrow, glancing at Gil. "I used to believe she was so soft and delicate."

"Blood hardens everybody," Gil said. "Can you supply me with a good man?"

"I can do better than that," Castañeda said confidently. "I can supply you with a man who has trained at Fort Bragg with your Green Berets."

"Okay," Gil said chuckling.

Castañeda smiled curiously. "That is funny?"

Gil smiled. "A Green Beret will do in a pinch."

Castañeda laughed, getting the joke. "His name is Poncho, and you will be able to trust him with your life."

77

Night was falling as Hancock briefed his security team on the west side of town. His wounds from the night before were stitched and dressed, but the deep gash on his inner thigh was still suppurating, and the sutures threatened to tear if he lowered into a crouch.

"Remember," he said, "we don't have to kill them all. We just have to break their spirit. They'll try to isolate me like they did last night, so it won't be possible for me to take more than one shot from any position. Your job is to keep them off me long enough for me to displace. Once we've got them confused and disorganized, that's when the rest of our people will attack from the east."

"What do we do about Serrano being dead?" someone asked.

"Fuck Serrano!" Hancock stepped into the fellow's face. "Ruvalcaba has plans to kill Castañeda and take over business in the whole damn country. *That's* who we work for! Understood?"

The man nodded and took a step back, glancing at his compatriots, who looked at him askance.

For Hancock, the issue had become even more personal since the night before. Not only could Vaught still identify him, but in the process of almost killing him, he'd damn near forced the sniper to castrate himself on a broken beer bottle. That was too close for comfort, and Hancock planned to even the score.

There was no way to penetrate the center of town—yet. Police presence was too heavy, so he selected a pharmacy on a corner four blocks from *el centro* and set up on the roof. Putting his eye to the scope, he watched from three hundred yards as police trucks crisscrossed the intersection at irregular intervals.

"No one's on foot," he mumbled. The police were either hiding inside the buildings or maintaining a cruising speed high enough to make themselves hard to hit at a distance. With the city on lockdown, there was no civilian traffic, so it was safe for them to ignore the traffic lights.

The sound of a distant gun battle erupted to the south. The shots trailed off after a few seconds, and Hancock wondered dully who'd gotten the better part of the exchange.

Light from a streetlamp glinted off a glass door as a police officer stepped from a coffee shop. Hancock squeezed the trigger on instinct. The door shattered a third of a second later, and the officer was blown in half at the waist.

"Time to move!" he hissed to the two men lying prone just behind him, getting up as quickly as he could without tearing his stitches.

SERGEANT CUEVAS SPRANG from a table inside the coffee shop and ran to the door where the lieutenant lay blasted open on the sidewalk. The glass was blown toward the lieutenant, which meant the shot had come from the west.

Crosswhite and Vaught were already up and priming their weapons, moving past him out the door.

"He's displacing!" Crosswhite shouted. "Let's move!"

Vaught, Sergeant Cuevas, and two other officers loaded into an armored truck. Crosswhite took three more in another, and both trucks sped off down the street in the direction of the shot.

Chief Diego remained in the coffee shop, now their command post, alerting all patrol units by radio that the sniper's attack had begun.

Sergeant Cuevas floored the accelerator. "He must have fired from the roof of the pharmacy."

Vaught sat beside him on the passenger side, while the two officers in back aimed their rifles over the top of the cab.

Four narcos darted in front of the pharmacy, blazing away with AK-47s, but the bullets ricocheted harmlessly off the windshield. The men fumbled to reload, and the cops in the back opened up with their FX-05s, killing one narco and wounding another in the leg.

Cuevas braked hard and cut the wheel left, tromping the accelerator to pursue the fleeing men around the corner, running over the wounded narco and killing him.

Vaught let out with a guttural "*Hooah!*"

Crosswhite, in the truck right behind them, cut the wheel right to circle around the pharmacy in the opposite direction. A car sped out of the alley just in front of him, and he rammed it aside with the heavily armored truck. The officers in back fired directly down into the car, killing everyone inside. A second car sped out of the alley and slipped around behind them. Crosswhite caught a glimpse of the gringo sniper's face in the backseat and shifted into reverse, jamming the pedal to the floor and throwing his arm over the back of the seat to see where he was going.

The car sped away around a corner, and he cut the wheel to spin the truck back around. He grabbed the radio and barked out a description of the car—a midnight-blue Dodge Charger—and that it was headed in Vaught's direction.

Vaught answered that they'd already spotted the car and were in pursuit.

Crosswhite shifted into drive, and a flaming Molotov cocktail impacted the windshield, engulfing the front of the truck and obscuring his vision. He turned on the wipers and pressed the washer fluid button, but the reservoir was empty. The wiper blades quickly melted from the heat of the flaming gasoline and smeared the glass with melting rubber.

"Fuck!" He dismounted and grabbed a fire extinguisher from the behind the seat.

Before he had a chance to use it, they were engaged by automatic fire to the right. One of the officers in back was hit and dove out on Crosswhite's side of the truck, holding his shattered forearm. The other two men returned fire and drove the gunners back around the corner, but yet another narco jumped out and fired an RPG.

Crosswhite and the wounded officer threw themselves flat as the rocket impacted the cab of the truck and exploded, killing both cops in back.

Crosswhite fired through the flames, knowing from experience that the enemy would use the fire as cover to press its attack. Three narcos went down, and he grabbed the wounded officer by the harness, helping him up. They fell back behind a line of three parked cars to fight a holding action.

"Drove right into an ambush!" he said, changing magazines.

The wounded officer fired his pistol over the hood of a car. "It's a thing that happens."

SERGEANT CUEVAS DROVE as fast as he could but couldn't catch the gringo sniper's car. More units were converging on the area, but the west side of town had been left out of the patrol box because there were too many crooked streets and tight turns.

"We should have anticipated." Cuevas shook his head in aggravation. "He's leading us into a trap!"

"I think you're right," Vaught said. "Break off! Let 'im go."

"Chinga su madre!" Cuevas hit the brakes and watched the Charger disappear around a corner.

"It's okay." Vaught glanced up at the rooftops to check for enemy rocketeers. "He's saying the same thing right now."

78

Hancock sat watching out the back window of the car. "Shit. They're not following!"

The driver pulled to a stop in front of an alley where ten narcos lay in ambush, three of them holding RPGs. "Should I go back?"

"No. Fuck it, they're onto us," Hancock answered. "They'll pull back to the center of town now and circle the wagons. We're gonna have to dig them out of the square."

The guy in the passenger seat, busy talking on the phone, looked back at Hancock. "Our people destroyed the other truck four blocks over. They have two cops pinned down, and it sounds like more are on the way. What do you want our people to do?"

"Let's go!" Hancock banged his fist urgently on the back of the seat. "If we can draw these assholes into a stand-up fight, we can wipe them out!"

The driver shouted for the men in the alley to load into their cars and follow.

Hancock ejected the magazine from the Barrett, topping it off with a single .50 caliber cartridge and slapping it back in. "Call our people on the east side and tell 'em to begin their attack."

CROSSWHITE AND THE wounded cop huddled behind the wheel hub of a shot-up SUV, using the engine compartment as cover. The enemy was not moving to take them out, but nor would it allow them to retreat.

"Why haven't they fired another rocket?" wondered the cop. "We should be dead by now."

"Because they're using us as bait." Crosswhite searched desperately up and down the street for an avenue of escape, but there just wasn't any cover. "They want to draw us into battle and smash us."

"Can they do that?"

"If they have the numbers, they can. We don't even have a radio to warn our men away."

As if to emphasize the point, a police truck rounded the corner and came roaring down the street, siren wailing. A rocket streaked out of the alley and blew off the tail end, throwing wounded cops into the street and sending the truck careening out of control into a building.

Crosswhite fired on the alley and ran out to recover the wounded policemen. Dragging them to cover behind the wrecked and burning truck, he shouted for the driver to warn the other units away—but the man didn't hear him because he was already on the radio calling for more help.

Vaught and Sergeant Cuevas arrived from the opposite direction with two more trucks right behind them.

"We gotta get the fuck outta here!" Crosswhite said. "A pitched battle is exactly what we don't want!"

"Roger that!" Vaught slung his weapon and reached to help a wounded man to his feet.

Another RPG, fired from a rooftop this time, hit the last police truck in line and set it ablaze, effectively blocking their southern avenue of escape.

Crosswhite took a shot at the rocketeer. "Who's selling these cocksuckers all the goddamn rockets? It's like fuckin' Fallujah out here!"

Sergeant Cuevas fired a 40 mm grenade at a caged storefront and blew open the door. "Put the wounded inside the shoe store! This is our command post."

"It's more like the Alamo," Crosswhite growled, heaving a wounded man over his shoulder. "But it'll have to do."

They moved the wounded men inside, and Crosswhite helped the cop with the shattered forearm lash the wounded appendage to his harness, giving him his spare pistol ammo. "Remember your training," he told him. "Hold the pistol in the crook of your leg to reload, and jack it against the heel of your boot to release the slide. Got it?"

The cop nodded.

"Good man!" Crosswhite bashed him on the shoulder and went to the door.

The police had positioned the remaining two trucks in front of the building to provide more cover, mounting a light machine gun to the roll bar.

"We've got more men on the way," Cuevas said. "We'll be okay."

"Until Hancock sets up at the north end of the street," Crosswhite said. "These are your men, Sergeant, but I'd get that gunner down out of the truck. He's a prime target."

Cuevas stepped over and ordered the gunner to set up

beneath the truck with the bipod, covering the north end of the street. Then he reached into the cab for the radio to brief Chief Diego on their situation.

Having done what little he could for the wounded, Vaught came over, wiping his bloody hands on his trousers. "Whattaya think?"

Crosswhite swiped at his bleeding forehead, where a piece of spall from a ricochet had cut him open. "Hate to say it, but Diego should pull the rest of his people back and let us die on the vine; stick to his plan and hold the center of town. But he won't do that. He'll send every man he's got to save our asses."

"And so would you," Vaught said.

"I dunno . . . maybe." Crosswhite was pissed at himself for letting things get so badly muddled so early in the battle. "Those RPGs change the entire ball game. I didn't expect they'd have so many. And once Hancock shows up with that fuckin' fifty of his, we'll be like ducks at a carnival." He lit a cigarette, sucking the smoke deep into his lungs. "God*damn* him!"

"We'll get it sorted out," Vaught said confidently.

Crosswhite counted two walking wounded and three critical. "We don't even have stretchers. They got rockets, and we don't even have fucking stretchers to evacuate these men."

"Hey, let's focus on what we *do* have."

"Which is what?" Crosswhite asked him. "What've we got, dude? We got ten men with rifles and two walking wounded! We're barricaded in a goddamn shoe store, and every truck that rolls in here to relieve us is gonna get blown up. I'm telling you, I've seen enough combat to know when you're fucked. And, buddy, we're *fucked*."

"Unless we make a break for it right now and leave the wounded behind."

Crosswhite took a drag. "Is that what you're suggesting?"

Vaught shook his head, knowing that wasn't an option.

"Exactly. So we're back to being fucked."

Sergeant Cuevas came into the shop. "Bad news. I've explained the situation about the rockets to Diego, and he says Ruvalcaba's men have begun attacking from the east. He doesn't like it, but he's agreed to pull the rest of our forces back to the center of town. There's no more help coming."

Crosswhite exchanged grim glances with Vaught.

"Maybe we can hold out until daylight," Vaught ventured. "The government can't ignore this battle indefinitely—not with Serrano being dead."

Crosswhite exhaled smoke. "Don't kid yourself." He dropped the cigarette and stepped on it. "I didn't kill that asshole in time to make any difference here. Let's hope Mariana has better luck killing Ruvalcaba. At least that way things won't be a total loss."

Mariana had called him earlier in the day, telling him that Fields was dead and that she had a plan to remove Hector Ruvalcaba—a plan she didn't dare share with him over the phone.

79

Gil knocked on the door to Mariana's expensive though rustic hotel room in the town of San Cristobal de las Casas, the same city where the Zapatista Revolt had taken place more than twenty years earlier. She answered the door and let him in. A fire burned in the fireplace to ward off the damp chill in the air.

"Build the fire yourself?" he asked, reminded of his hearth back home in Montana—a hearth he would never see again.

"The bellboy built it for me. I don't know anything about building fires."

He tossed his rucksack onto the bed. "That's for you— in case things go bad."

She opened the ruck and saw that it was stuffed with banded American cash. "Gil, this is an awful lot of money."

"And you'll need it if Crosswhite and I get killed. There's a little black book in the side pouch there with the names and numbers of people who can help you disappear. They already think I'm dead, but if you tell them you got their names from me, they'll help you. They're reliable men: retired Navy SEALS living outside the US—soldier of fortune types, but rock-solid people."

"Thank you," she said.

"Don't mention it. It's something Crosswhite should have done for you already, but he doesn't think ahead. It's just not how he is."

"He's definitely an *in-the-moment* kind of guy," she agreed. "What do you think of Poncho?" They hadn't yet had a chance to talk about the ex-GAFE operator that Castañeda had sent along to assist Gil.

He nodded. "My gut tells me he's reliable. We've talked, and there's nothing sloppy about him. I get the feeling he's not really a personal fan of Castañeda, but it's too soon to tell."

"And if you guys are successful? Will I see you again?"

"Probably not, but I'll give you a call to let you know when Ruvalcaba's dead. After that, it's up to you to handle Pope."

"I'm afraid of him."

"You're smart to be afraid, but don't ever let him see it. When this is over, wait a week—maybe ten days—then call him and tell him to meet you down here in Mexico. Do *not* go to him. Buy him dinner in a ritzy restaurant and break the situation down for him in black and white. Don't *ask* him for a goddamn thing. *Tell* him how things are: that *you're* the new chief of station. He's smart, so he'll already be leaning in that direction. It'll be your job to erase any doubts he might have."

She was less convinced. "How do you know that?"

Gil shrugged. "I know him. I know how his mind works . . . what he values. You'll be the one to give him a stable border, and that will make you valuable."

"But I haven't done anything."

He arched an eyebrow. "You took a helluva risk acting on your own initiative to put Castañeda in charge. *You* did that. Pope respects boldness of action. Now, the key is to succeed and take credit for the operation. He'll know Crosswhite helped, but that won't matter. He'll also know you had help from other assets here in Mexico, and that's what being chief of station is: managing assets. Hell, that's all Pope is, an asset manager, and he's damn good at it."

She smiled. "Except he let his most valuable asset get away."

Gil wondered if that was true. "Well, it's not a mistake he'll make again, so bear that in mind."

"He won't be pissed about Fields?"

"What's to be pissed about? You've demonstrated Fields was the wrong man for the job. Pope has no ego. He's the most practical man alive—*too* practical, in fact. That's his weakness: he forgets how *im*practical everyone else is."

"Will I have a way of getting in touch with you?"

"You can get a message to Midori if there's an emergency, but don't worry. You won't need me. You'll have Crosswhite—unless he finally figures out how to get himself killed. And be sure to keep Vaught on your ledger too. Don't let DSS have him back. He's a renegade, and that's a good card to have in your deck. His career in DSS is probably shot anyhow."

She edged closer to the fire, feeling the warmth on the

backs of her legs. "I should be writing this down. I can't believe you're going to abandon me after tonight."

That made him chuckle. "Well, you've got Crosswhite."

She looked concerned suddenly. "What am I gonna do about him, Gil? He's such a . . ."

"Such a what?"

"I don't know," she said, her cheeks reddening, "but Pope won't want to let him go. He's too goddamn good at what he does."

"I just told you: *you're* chief of station. Crosswhite's workin' for *you. I'm* workin' for you. You're cleaning up Pope's mess in Mexico—covering up the Downly assassination; doin' what Fields and that idiot Ortega *couldn't* do—and that's exactly what you remind Pope of when this is over. Can you do that?"

She crossed her arms, drawing a breath as she remembered the electrocution she'd received from Fields, being raped in Havana the year before, and witnessing more than a half dozen killings, all while working for Pope. She had more than earned the position of station chief.

"Yeah," she said, feeling pissed. "I can do it. *Fuckin' A* I can do it."

He gave her a wink. "I gotta go."

She offered her hand. "Thank you for saving my life. I owe you and Dan both now."

He took her hand and gave her a peck on the cheek. "Don't ever put your life on the line for Crosswhite again. Understand? He's too goddamn reckless; he doesn't consider the consequences."

"But—" The look in her eyes was almost mournful.

"If he gets in a jam, I'll be around, but for now, we gotta hope he and Vaught can take Hancock down on their own, because you'll need a clean sweep to impress

Pope." He picked up the rucksack, zipped it closed, and dropped it back on the bed. "Keep the cash in a safe place. If Dan or I fail, Pope might send assassins from the ATRU to clean house. If he does, don't worry about anyone but yourself. Get the hell out of Dodge—and remember the black book."

80

Hancock had slithered into position behind a large tree, which had been growing out of the sidewalk for so many years that the concrete had been pushed up. He was a hundred yards from where the police had taken cover behind their protective barrier of armored trucks in front of the shoe store. Putting his eye to the scope, he placed the crosshairs on the face of the cop manning the machine gun beneath the truck.

Smiling, he squeezed the trigger. The shot echoed like thunder, and the machine gunner's head evaporated.

Hancock didn't roll behind the tree against the chance that someone had seen his muzzle flash. Instead, he kept his eye to the scope waiting to see if anyone would have the balls to return his fire. To his surprise, the police made no attempt to return fire; instead, they were rushing into the shop.

He shifted aim and fired into the clutch of men, hitting two cops with one shot and splattering their bodies. He squeezed the trigger again, and blew off another man's shoulder. A fourth round took off an officer's leg, and after that there were no more live targets within view—save for the now one-legged officer writhing on the sidewalk four feet from the doorway.

"That's right," Hancock whispered. "Call your buddies to come get you."

Someone threw a length of rope out the door, and the wounded officer grabbed hold of it. Hancock blew off his arm at the elbow. A smoke grenade was tossed out onto the sidewalk, and he began to lose visual contact, so he squeezed the trigger again, hitting the wounded cop in the belly and blowing him apart.

As the gray smoke billowed up around the trucks, Hancock put an armor-piercing round through the engine block of each one. Then he put a round through the transformer up on the telephone pole. Sparks exploded from the old steel box, and the street fell into darkness. Satisfied that the police inside the shoe store weren't going anywhere, he pulled back and trotted up to the corner, where his bodyguards stood waiting by the car. Twenty other men, some with RPGs, were fanning out to cover the street.

Fighting could now be heard on the east side of town: automatic weapons fire and the occasional *boom* of an explosion.

"How's the attack going?" Hancock asked the man with the phone.

"It goes well," the man said. "The police have fallen back to the center of town. They have prepared positions . . . sandbags . . . machine gun emplacements. It will be hard to dig them out, but you can pick them off easily. We should go."

"My work is here." Hancock was loading rounds into the Barrett's magazine. "At least one of the gringos who can identify me is in that building down there—probably both. Tell our people in the east to take their RPGs to roof level and fire down into the machine gun nests. The police don't have the men or equipment to hold the center of town against rockets. If our people move aggressively, we'll own the city by midnight. Once we've proven ourselves, Serrano's friends will support Ruvalcaba, but we have to demonstrate our strength right here, right now, so tell them to get on it!"

The man got back on the phone, and the driver stood looking at Hancock. "I've heard that Ruvalcaba is on the run," he remarked.

"Sure he is," Hancock said, smacking the magazine back into the rifle. "Wouldn't you be? With Serrano dead, Mexico City's not safe for him. He'll stay in Chiapas until he can negotiate with the government for a safe return. Look, it all hinges on what we do here tonight. By morning, there will be a new chief of police, half of your people will be cops, and it'll be like this never happened. That will give Ruvalcaba a lot of breathing room."

The driver nodded. "Okay," he said, "but it's good the rest of the men don't know he's running away."

"The rest of the men are idiots." Hancock slung the great weapon. "Shit, half of them can't even fucking read."

The driver took offense. "My mother can't read. Is she an idiot?"

Hancock grinned. "Not unless she's lugging an AK-47 for Ruvalcaba."

The driver was hard-pressed to hide his irritation. "How much time are we going to waste here? Those cops down there aren't a threat."

"Yes, they are," Hancock insisted. "They've got two

Green Berets with them, and Green Berets are too dangerous to let live in a battle like this—and they're dangerous to me personally. So we stay and kill them."

SERGEANT CUEVAS'S BODY lay on the sidewalk just outside the door to the shoe store, his left shoulder having been blown off and part of his lung hanging out the top of his exploded rib cage.

Much of the smoke from the grenade had blown back into the building, making it even tougher to see in the dark, and no one dared use a flashlight for fear of the sniper.

Purely on impulse, Vaught dashed out the door, grabbed Cuevas's FX-05 with the 40 mm grenade launcher, and leaped back inside without drawing any fire.

Crosswhite jumped to his feet. "That was a goddamn stupid thing to do!"

"Tell me about it." Vaught slung the weapon. "I'm going after him."

"The fuck are you talkin' about?"

Vaught pointed up. "Along the rooftops. He shot out the lights, and now it's dark as shit out there. He won't expect me to come after him—not any more than he did the first time."

Crosswhite drew from a cigarette, the cherry glowing bright red. "And the first time worked out so well for ya."

"If it hadn't been for crooked cops, I'd have bagged his fuckin' ass."

Crosswhite wanted to go with Vaught, to carry the fight to the enemy, as had always been his nature. But tonight he had to admit the truth: he wanted to see Paolina again, he wanted to see his baby girl born, and his best chance of that was staying inside the shoe store and waiting for the fight to come to him. "Fuck you," he muttered, flicking away the cigarette with a shower of tiny sparks.

"For what?" Vaught asked indignantly.

"For being like I *used* to be."

Vaught put a hand on his shoulder. "You're just old and scared, dude. It's nothing to be ashamed of."

Crosswhite smirked and knocked the arm away. "Kiss my ass."

The conversation had been in English, so the other five combat-effective officers hadn't understood what was being said. When Vaught went to the back of the shop, mounting the stairs to the roof, they asked Crosswhite where he was going.

Crosswhite answered, *"Él va a cazar al francotirador gringo."* He goes to hunt the gringo sniper.

81

Vaught closed the hatch, moving across the roof in a combat crouch, relieved to be free of the death trap below. Was he abandoning the others? Possibly, but not out of cowardice. He had a score to settle with Rhett Hancock, and if he made a mistake, the sniper would make him pay with 42 grams of lead moving at 3,000 feet per second. The FX-05 was fixed with a red dot scope, giving him a small measure of "night vision" when it came to aiming, but until he could close the distance, Hancock would hold every advantage—not the least of which being that Vaught had no idea where the hell he was.

He crossed to the next rooftop and went to the edge, stealing a glance at the street below and pulling quickly back. Men were converging on the shoe store with rifles and RPGs. He could shoot some of them and buy Crosswhite some time, but if Hancock was watching, they'd be his last shots. Still, his instincts were telling him the sniper was not set yet, so he swung the rifle over the parapet and fired a grenade at the lead RPG man.

The grenade hit the wall next to the rocketeer, blowing a hole in the brick wall and killing the man instantly.

Vaught immediately opened up with the FX-05, cutting down six more men as they scrambled to find cover where there was none. The weapon ran through ammo a little faster than he was accustomed to, but he hit everyone he meant to before pulling back to reload. He would not go back to the well a second time, no matter how tempting.

Hancock, meanwhile, had been moving along a rooftop on the opposite side of the street when Vaught opened up. He heard the grenade explode and saw the flashes of Vaught firing on full automatic. But by the time he got the Barrett unslung, Vaught had disappeared behind a large plastic water tank called a *tinaco*. So he set the bipod of the giant rifle on a ventilation duct and waited for Vaught to reemerge on the opposite side. When he didn't reappear, he began to suspect he'd been spotted.

VAUGHT STOOD WITH his back against the tinaco, indeed having spotted a shadowy figure on the far roof. Confident he'd come within a breath of having his guts blown out, he tapped on the tinaco with his knuckle to make sure it was full of water, which would stop even an armor piercing round from coming all the way through.

The cannon across the street went off a few seconds later, and he felt the impact of the round reverberate through the tank. Water began leaking out onto the roof—and not from one hole but two. Hancock had shot the side of the tinaco near the bottom, leaving entrance and exit holes no more than six inches apart.

A second shot boomed out, and water began running out from two more holes.

"How much water you got over there?" the sniper shouted.

Vaught wasn't sure, but he doubted the tank held more than three hundred gallons. The great gun went off again, and two more holes appeared on the opposite side.

After a fourth shot, water was literally gushing from the tank.

"*Goddamn*, that's gotta be scary!" Hancock taunted, his laughter carrying over the distant echo of the battle being fought on the east side of town. "Two minutes from now, you'll be dead!"

Vaught sank into a deep crouch against the side of the tinaco, measuring the distance to the next rooftop, where a three-foot-high parapet encircled the edge. But the truth was that even if he made it to the next roof, Hancock's armor piercing rounds would easily defeat the simple clay-brick and mortar parapet, which had not been built with the intention of stopping antiaircraft bullets.

"The bastard's right," he muttered, thumping the muzzle of the rifle against his forehead in frustration. He double-checked the distance to the south, back the way he'd come, where the parapet was thicker, but the distance was twice as far.

Then he remembered the smoke grenade in his trouser pocket. "Dumb-ass!" he hissed at himself, pulling the grenade and popping smoke on the north side of the tinaco.

"You'll still never make it!" Hancock shouted. "Too far!"

Vaught jumped out on the south side of the tank where there was no smoke, firing the grenade launcher and pulling back.

The grenade detonated, and he took off north through

the smoke, sprinting across the roof and vaulting the thin parapet to run clean across to the next building and into a concrete cupola encasing a stairwell.

Hancock, covered in mortar dust, sat up behind the air duct and rested back on his hands, a loud ringing in is ears.

"Clever prick," he muttered, spitting out bits of grit.

He got back behind the Barrett and saw the smoke dissipating over the far rooftop. His prey had escaped—but only for the moment. He used his phone to call the men below, ordering them to hunt Vaught at street level.

The narcos in the street fired an RPG through the door of the building into which Vaught had escaped and stormed inside.

Vaught heard the explosion and started back up the stairs. Hiding inside the cupola, he waited and fired on the first shadows to appear below, killing three men and forcing back the rest.

Vicious threats were called up to him, but he ignored them. He did not step out onto the roof, believing that Hancock would burn him down the second he showed himself.

Knowing he had the angle on the men below and plenty of ammo to keep them at bay for the time being, he was content with a standoff.

"We'll let the situation develop," he said quietly, crouching down and tucking a pinch of tobacco into his lip. "Good shape here . . . good shape."

82

Chief Diego Guerrero had the makings of a disaster on his hands, and he didn't need Special Forces training to see it. His force was outgunned and outnumbered at least two to one. He'd tried calling again for federal assistance, but the phone lines were down, and the enemy had managed to knock out cellular service as well. He supposed they had destroyed the cell towers, a common tactic.

Wounded men were being brought into the coffee shop by twos and threes now, leaving blood all over the place. One machine gun emplacement had already been hit by an RPG from the roof of the bank, and the enemy was moving in and out of their perimeter almost at will. There were no more motorized patrols. The trucks that weren't burning were being used to move or provide cover for the wounded.

"There's no more word from Sergeant Cuevas," said

another sergeant, tossing aside the radio. "They must be dead."

"It doesn't matter," Diego said. "We're going to lose the city. There are too many of them. And with the rockets . . ." He shook his head. "I've failed. It's time to consider surrender."

"Surrender?" the sergeant blurted. "Are you crazy? They'll line us up and shoot us!"

Diego shook his head. "No. Only me. I will offer my life in exchange for yours. Ruvalcaba is smart enough to see the sense in sparing the men. A slaughter will only make it more difficult for him to buy friends in the government."

The sergeant, a man named José, pointed out the window. "Ruvalcaba's not out there! He's probably hundreds of miles from here! Do you think you can negotiate with wild animals?"

Diego was calm. "What choice do I have but to try, José? The men will certainly be killed otherwise—all of them."

"Then let them die fighting," José insisted. "Not stood up against a wall!"

Diego looked around at the almost twenty bleeding men crowding the coffee shop, many of them barely conscious. "What do you men think?"

"We fight on," one of them said. He gestured with a pistol. "Or we kill ourselves."

"No surrender," said another.

"Never surrender!"

"Never!"

The others nodded in stubborn agreement.

"Very well," Diego said. "Then we will fight." He accepted a carbine from an officer too badly wounded to walk and collected his spare magazines. "Let's go, Sergeant. Our Calvary awaits."

They ducked outside and darted across the square to the nearest machine gun emplacement.

Diego took a knee beside the gunner as bullets flew through the trees over their heads. "How much ammunition do you have?"

"After this belt, one box," the officer said. "We're going to lose the square, *Jefe*. You should take a truck and try to get through to the capital. Someone has to tell what happened here."

Diego patted him on the back. "That will be a story for someone else to tell. I will never abandon you men."

The officer squeezed the trigger, putting a burst into a parked car where a couple of narcos had just taken cover. One of the narcos sprawled out dead, and the other scurried back around the corner of the bank.

"There!" José exclaimed, pointing above the courthouse. "I saw a man with an RPG."

Diego looked around. His men were pulled into a protective perimeter in the town square, using their trucks, as well as park benches, statues, and trees, for cover. He estimated that half his force was dead or wounded. "Let's go," he said to José. "We have to kill the man with the rocket."

"*Jefe*, no!" the gunner said. "It's too dangerous. We you need you here."

"He's right," José said, grabbing Diego's arm. "I'll take someone else. You stay and lead the men."

Diego watched him pick a man, and the two officers ran off toward the courthouse. "I wish my brother were here," he said plaintively.

"You're the *jefe*," the gunner said. "We stayed to fight with *you*."

Diego nodded and said a silent prayer, asking for help—not from the Virgin, as he normally might have done, but from his brother: *Juan, if you are watching, and*

if there is any help to send these men, now would be very a
good time.

Then he made a separate pact with God.

JOSÉ USED HIS key, and both officers slipped unseen
into the courthouse, dashing to the back of the building and up the staircase. José noticed the officer wheezing
during the climb.

"What's wrong?"

"I was hit crossing the park."

José saw him holding his side in the dim light. "Can
you continue? You can wait for me here."

"There are many men on the roof," the officer said.
"I've seen them taking shots at us. You're going to need
me, but we'd better hurry. I'm losing a lot of blood."

Putting from his mind the fact that the officer would
be dead soon whether or not they were successful, José
continued the climb to the third floor. There he found
the door to the roof locked, as it should have been. He
grabbed his key ring. "They must be using ladders," he
observed.

"I'm sure they're accessing the annex roof in back—
climbing up from there."

"I hadn't thought of that." José put the key into the
lock. "Are you ready?"

"Yes, but what's the plan?"

"Open the door and shoot everyone."

The wounded officer couldn't help laughing. José
laughed with him. "Okay? Let's go!"

He turned the key, pushing open the door, and they
scrambled out onto the rooftop, where better than twenty
narcotraficantes were crouched behind the parapet overlooking the park—four of them armed with RPGs for
delivering a coup de grâce to the police forces below.

"Puta madre!" José hissed, having expected to find five or six men.

Both cops opened up on full automatic, moving low and fast, as the Americans had trained them. They mowed down six men apiece before the narcos even knew they were under attack, killing all four rocketeers, and ducking behind an air-conditioning unit to reload.

One of the narcos grabbed up an RPG and fired just as the wounded officer was raising up for another shot. The rocket hit him in the face and took off his head without detonating, exploding somewhere behind the courthouse as José raked his weapon along the parapet, knocking over a half dozen more narcos on the first pass. The remaining six men scattered, firing on José from all directions as he ejected the spent magazine and slapped in a new one.

He was hit multiple times as he rose up from behind the unit, determined to live long enough to clear the roof. Placing controlled bursts in what felt like slow motion, pivoting left to right in a tight corkscrew that carried him through an arc of better than 180 degrees, the sergeant killed or wounded the last of the narcos.

The carbine ran dry, and he landed on his tailbone with bone-jarring force, biting his tongue and falling over onto his back. In the moments before his death, José lay looking up at the stars and remembering—strangely he thought—that his worthless brother-in-law still owed him twenty-six hundred pesos.

83

An RPG tore through the steel security curtain of the shoe store display window, blasting fragments of molten steel and glass through the shop like a giant shotgun blast. One officer was killed outright, and Crosswhite was thrown across the floor. Shoes and wounded men caught fire, and Crosswhite jumped back up, running to the door and shooting at the shadows in the street.

The carbine shattered in his hands, followed by the instant *boom!* of Hancock's .50 caliber.

He threw himself flat as the great rifle *boomed* again. The big bullet ricocheted off the concrete, sending hot pieces of spall into the wounded. The men screamed and tried to crawl deeper into the shop.

"We have to surrender!" one of the officers shouted.

Crosswhite grabbed his carbine away from him. "Surrender then, goddamnit. Let 'em cut your balls off! See to the wounded!" he ordered another, not knowing what else to say.

He could feel his lacerated hands bleeding as he mounted the staircase to the roof, finding it hard to keep a good grip on the weapon. "Motherfuckin' sonofabitch!" he snarled. "Goddamn cocksucker, I'll blow your fuckin' brains out!"

He threw open the hatch and crawled out onto the roof, knowing exactly how naked he was but too pissed to care. Paolina and the baby were in the back of his mind, but he knew now that he would never see his young wife again—that some other man would raise his daughter.

"Fuckin' Pope! Cocksucker!" he sneered, belly-crawling toward the parapet. "I'm gonna die on a goddamn shoe store, you motherfucker!" He glanced up at the sky on the off chance one of the CIA director's stealth drones might be up there and gave it the finger.

Hancock's rifle went off again, and he sprang into a crouch, firing at a pair of shadows on the far rooftop. Both shadows went down, and he dropped flat, rolling to the south side of the roof without taking any return fire.

The rocketeer beside Hancock was hit in the face and killed instantly. Hancock was hit in the shoulder. He swore a blue streak as he crawled closer to the parapet, pulling the Barrett after him by the strap, not knowing if the smart-ass on the far roof would have any grenades to pitch across.

"Shit just got real," he told himself, knowing the bullet was still in him, possibly embedded in the bone, and feeling that the stitches in his leg were torn open.

"Hey!" he shouted, stuffing gauze into the shoulder wound. "Who the fuck are you?"

"Fuck you care?" Crosswhite called back.

"Got me pretty good, asshole!"

"Stand the fuck by! I'm about to do better!"

Hancock laughed, crawling south along the roof in the direction of the voice.

Crosswhite crawled quickly toward the north, keeping low behind the parapet. A few seconds later, Hancock's rifle went off, and an armor-piercing round blasted a hole in the brick-and-mortar parapet, very close to where Crosswhite had been.

He sprang up and fired at Hancock's silhouette just as the sniper was squeezing the trigger a second time, the carbine slippery in his bleeding hands.

Hancock fell over.

"How'd I do that time?" Crosswhite shouted across. When Hancock didn't answer, he smiled. Crosswhite knew he hadn't killed him—his aim had been off—but he'd hurt him.

"I'll wait for him to come back up for air," he said to himself, opening fire on the narcos below and shouting to his cops that the sniper was down.

The police downstairs began firing into the street, and Ruvalcaba's men fell back.

Hancock's shadow appeared once again over the parapet, but Crosswhite fired on him before he could raise the heavy rifle, driving the sniper back undercover.

"Come on, show me some more!" Crosswhite taunted. "Lemme air that shit out for ya!"

Hancock's sluggish movement had told Crosswhite that the gringo sniper was badly hurt.

"Don't you die on me over there! You suck that shit up and fight me!"

Hancock sprang up unexpectedly, firing a round through the parapet one foot from where Crosswhite was crouched.

"Fuck me!" Crosswhite murmured, displacing fast and firing at the sniper's silhouette before he could track him.

84

Pope sat staring with bloodshot eyes at a television monitor, watching an aerial view of the battle for Toluca in
infrared. Midori stood behind him, her arms crossed in
bitter disapproval. After Crosswhite had thrust his finger
toward the sky, there had been no doubt that it was him.

"I hope he kills that son of a bitch and comes for you,"
she said, ashamed to have been even a small part of what
was happening.

"Perhaps he will," Pope said quietly. "The UAV's at
bingo fuel. I have to bring it back to American airspace."

"Do something!" she implored. "Help them!"

He turned to look at her, a slightly incredulous look on
his face. "What do you suggest I do?"

She pointed at the screen. "Call somebody down
there!"

"There's no one to call. It's quite out of my hands."

"Is the drone armed?"

"Of course not."

She smirked, her emotions getting the better of her. "You say that like it's an impossibility."

He gave her a frown. "I don't send armed UAVs over allied countries; you know that very well." Returning his attention to the monitor, Pope gripped the joystick and banked the aircraft northward. "I shouldn't have invited you to watch."

"Why did you?"

"I don't know. I thought . . . I thought we might re-establish a trust. I see now that all I've managed to do is make things worse between us."

Midori had worked for Pope for over ten years, and she knew him well enough to understand how sincere a gesture this had been. Because of that, she was unable to help feeling compassion for him. "You really don't understand what you've done, do you?" she said. "You've started a war down there. Those men are dying, Robert."

He put the UAV on autopilot and turned in the chair, gently taking hold of her hands. "We've watched thousands of people die on these monitors. Tonight is nothing different. Don't forget that two nuclear weapons came across that border—*two*. I cannot allow that to happen again. Not if it's within my power to prevent it."

She pulled her hands free. "Do you still think that's what this is about? Tonight has nothing to do with the border—nothing."

"I've already admitted to you this operation got out of hand. But it got out of hand only because Vaught exceeded his mission parameters—an accident of fate—an unknown variable that I could not have accounted for ahead of time. What's happening down there now is fate playing itself out, nothing more."

"And when the smoke clears?"

"I have no idea. We have to see who's left standing."

Midori stared at him, her slow eyes dark and sad—a sadness brought on by the irrevocable truth that the Pope she had respected and admired for so many years no longer existed. He had evolved into a man who could reduce a human life to nothing more than a blip on a screen. And he could do so with little more care than it took to brush his teeth.

"I'm going home now," she said quietly.

"Good night," he said in his gentle voice.

She put her hand on the doorknob. "By the way, it's official: Lena Deiss and Sabastian Blickensderfer are getting married in eight days. Do you still want me to continue surveillance?"

"No," Pope replied, turning back to the monitor and placing his hand on the stick. "Discontinue all surveillance. We've wasted enough time on Blickensderfer."

85

Vaught waited for his moment and then fired a 40 mm high-explosive grenade into the doorway at the bottom of the stairs. He charged down and machine-gunned the survivors, stomping a crawling man's neck on the way out the door.

"Jackasses," he sneered contemptuously.

Stepping into the street, Vaught could hear the fighting on the east side of town reaching a gut-wrenching crescendo—sustained bursts of automatic fire and multiple explosions—and he was hit with the dreadful realization that Diego and his men were being slaughtered.

Down the block, he heard Crosswhite and Hancock harangue each other a last time. Vaught immediately zeroed the sniper's position and dashed across. "Got you now, motherfucker!"

HANCOCK HAD BEEN hit straight across the back by one of Vaught's NATO rounds. Both shoulder blades were grazed, and his infraspinatus muscles spasmed painfully every time he attempted to lift and aim the rifle. His fingers were tingling, and he was going into shock.

"Time to go," he groaned, dragging himself and the Barrett into the stairwell. Hancock trotted down to the ground floor, ducking into the street, where the narcos were gunning it out at almost point-blank range with the policemen in the shoe store.

He knew from the ferocity of fighting on the east side that the city was about to fall. "My work here is done!" He ran off up the sidewalk through the dark until he made it to the corner where his bodyguards stood waiting impatiently beside the midnight-blue Dodge Charger.

"Let's get the hell out of here. I need a medic."

The other two men gladly loaded up, and the car sped off.

CROSSWHITE VERY NEARLY shot Vaught when he appeared on the rooftop across the street. But Vaught gave him a wave and fired an HE grenade into the narcos below, killing four men and opening up on full automatic.

With apparently no sniper to worry about, Crosswhite stood up and opened fire as well.

The narcos were now caught in a murderous cross fire with nowhere to run. Within ten seconds, fifteen men lay dead in the street.

"Is the son of a bitch dead?" Crosswhite shouted over.

Vaught took a small flashlight from his harness, flashing it around. "I don't see him!"

"He's gotta be there! Look for a blood trail—he's hit!"

Vaught found the trail of blood and followed it down to ground level, where Crosswhite and five other police officers met him in the middle of the street, all of them looking at one another in dismay.

"He can't have disappeared!" Crosswhite said. "He's hit—I hit him!" He turned toward the bodies. "Check these assholes!"

Everyone took out a flashlight and checked the corpses for the face of a gringo, but Hancock was not among the dead.

"Goddamnit!" Vaught shouted. "How did you lose him?"

"What the fuck are you talkin' about?" Crosswhite retorted. "He was on your side of the fucking street!"

"Fuck!" Vaught kicked a body. "We had him, Dan! *We fucking had him!*"

The fighting on the east side suddenly fell off to nothing, and everyone knew the city had fallen.

"Well, shit!" Crosswhite said in disgust. "There's no time to worry about it now. We gotta get the wounded outta here. We'll escape across the west side."

A pair of trucks came roaring around the corner, and everyone brought their weapons to bear.

"Hold fire!" Vaught shouted, seeing that the trucks were loaded with federal troops.

Chief Diego jumped down from the running board of the lead truck, his left arm in a sling and blood dripping from his fingers. "Thank God some of you are still alive!"

Lieutenant R. Felix got out on the driver's side, his troops already dismounting to form a defensive perimeter around the shoe store, spreading out up the street. The officers led the medics inside, shining their lights on the wounded men who were covered with the dust and debris of battle.

Vaught recognized Lieutenant Felix from the morning after the quake. "We didn't lose the city?"

Felix shook his head. "Toluca still belongs to the people. Where is Sergeant Cuevas?"

"He's over there." Vaught gestured at the body. "The sniper got him. I'm sorry. He was a damn good man."

"Yes, he was," Felix said, going to the body and making the sign of the cross upon seeing the face of his dead friend.

Crosswhite led Diego into the shoe store so that he could see his wounded men. "How many did we lose?"

"Half, I think," Diego said, kneeling down to take the hand of a young officer who was obviously dying. "Yes, I think half."

"Who sent the army?"

Diego had already begun to say the last rights over the young officer. When he finished, he kissed the man's forehead and rose to his feet, thumbing the tears from his eyes. "I'm sorry. What did you ask me?"

Confused, Crosswhite looked down at the dead young man and then back at Diego. "You're a priest?"

"No. I am not ordained, but I hope that God will accept this man into His Holy Kingdom long enough for me to become so."

"I don't understand. We just won! You're going back to the seminary?"

"I promised God that if He saved the city, I would return to the priesthood. He sent the soldiers, and the city was saved. I will keep my promise."

Crosswhite opened his mouth, but seeing the look in Diego's eyes, he knew there would be no point in trying to dissuade him. "Well . . . well, good job, then!" He bumped Diego briskly on the shoulder with a bloody hand. "You're a brave man, Diego. You kept your men together, and you saved the city. Juan would be proud of you."

"The Holy Father saved the city, and my brother sits at His right hand. Thank you for shedding your blood with us. I am forever in your debt." Diego shook Crosswhite's hand, turning for the door and stepping out just as Vaught was striding in.

"Who sent the army?" Crosswhite asked him quietly.

Vaught glanced outside. "That lieutenant out there, Felix, he was good friends with Cuevas. Cuevas got through to him just before the attack, and Felix talked a battalion of men into acting without orders. The federal government doesn't even know they're here yet."

"Well, you can bet your ass they'll be taking credit for the victory by sunrise. Come on, let's get these men loaded up. I wanna get home to my wife."

"Hey, ya know," Vaught said, following his lead, "I've been meaning to ask you something."

"What?" Crosswhite positioned himself to lift one of the wounded men by the shoulders.

Vaught took the man's ankles. "Does Paolina have a sister?"

"Yeah, she does," Crosswhite said, grunting as they lifted the man from the floor. "She's about four years old. Want her number?"

Vaught laughed, backing out the door. "You're such an asshole."

"PULL OVER," HANCOCK said, seeing an army truck flash through an intersection up ahead. "Stop the car!"

The driver stopped in the center of the road. "What's wrong? We have to go. The army is here!"

"I can see that. Put the car in park."

The driver shifted into park. "What are we doing, cabrón? We don't have time for this!"

"That's no shit." Hancock raised his .357 Sig and shot him through the face. Then he quickly shot the passenger in the back of the head, blowing out his teeth.

He took off his US Army dog tags and slipped them

around the passenger's neck before getting out of the car and jamming the Barrett into the front seat butt-first, leaving the barrel sticking out the window. Stripping his battle gear and extra magazines, Hancock dumped it all in the passenger's lap and pulled the pin from a grenade, tossing it into the backseat and ducking away down an alley. The grenade exploded, engulfing the car quickly in flames.

86

STATE OF CHIAPAS, MEXICO
18:00 HOURS

Gil and Poncho sat smoking Delicados cigarettes in the undergrowth near a winding jungle road just after a rain, ten miles south of the pueblo Frontera Comalapa near the border with Guatemala. Their faces streaked with charcoal, each wore the digital-camouflage battle dress uniforms of the Mexican army, and each was armed with an FN SCAR Mk 17 CQC rifle with a thirteen-inch barrel, chambered in 7.62×51 mm NATO.

Poncho was a dark-skinned Mexican with distinct Aztec features, handsome and somewhat short of stature at five foot six. His English was nearly perfect, with only a slight accent. A former GAFE operator like Antonio Castañeda, he had trained with the Green Berets in Fort Bragg, North Carolina, in the early 2000s.

Gil took a deep drag from the Delicado. "Shit," he

muttered, suddenly light-headed. "There's nothin' delicate about this fucker. It's like smokin' a tire."

Poncho chuckled. "Delicados aren't for little girls."

Gil snickered. "I wish you'd'a warned me. I feel like I oughta put on a dress."

Poncho smiled. He'd been paying Gil close attention for the past ten hours. "What the hell are you doing down here sweating your balls off in the jungle? I can tell from talking to you that you don't have an interest in our problems—our politics."

Gil took another drag and shrugged. "This is where the fight is right now."

Poncho felt he understood. "I know who you are, you know. I don't remember your name, but I recognize your face from a magazine. You're the SEAL sniper who won the Medal of Honor."

Silence hung in the still jungle air, the sun beginning to shine down through the trees in smoky rays. "Partner, you got me confused with some whole other body."

"No, I don't."

Gil scratched his unshaven neck where the sweat was beginning to irritate his skin. "Then I'll ask you to keep it a secret, soldier to soldier. The world thinks I'm dead, and I want it to stay that way."

"Why?"

"I got taxes I don't wanna pay."

Poncho snorted, deciding the real answer must be none of his business.

"Let me ask *you* something," Gil said. "What are you doing working for a butcher like Castañeda? You're a soldier through and through. It's obvious."

Poncho crushed the cigarette against the trunk of a giant fig tree, tucking the butt into a pocket. "I didn't come to work for him until after the truce with the government. I accept only special operations like this one. He pays very well, but I won't make war on civilians. He knows that."

"You helped him kill off the *Zetas*?" Pronounced "*seta*," for the letter *z*, the Zeta cartel had terrorized Mexico for decades until Castañeda had crushed it with military-style tactics.

"Yeah," Poncho said. "Those we didn't kill either went into hiding or came to work for us."

"So where does your loyalty lie? With Mexico? Or the money?"

Poncho looked at him. "If it was with Mexico, I wouldn't be working for Castañeda. I'd be a bricklayer like my father." He hesitated. "I'll tell you a secret, though: solder to soldier."

Gil waited to hear.

"If he ever breaks the truce and starts warring on civilians again, I'll kill him myself. That, he *doesn't* know."

"Sounds like maybe your loyalty lies with Mexico."

"I'll let you say it." Poncho averted his eyes. "I'd feel like a hypocrite."

"All war is hypocrisy." Gil took a drag. "It's a thing we gotta live with."

Poncho's radio crackled in his earpiece, and he touched the throat mike, acknowledging the transmission. "We're on," he said, getting to his feet.

Gil snuffed the cigarette and got up, shrugging to adjust his harness. Seconds later they were moving fast at port arms toward the dirt road. With each footfall, Gil felt the bite of the titanium implant in his right foot, the result of a gunshot wound eighteen months earlier. He was used to the pain by now, knowing the implant wouldn't fail him in combat.

Poncho dashed across the road to take up position behind a giant fig tree. Gil remained on the opposite side, skirting east of Poncho's position to conceal himself behind a boulder that had been pushed there during the road's construction decades earlier.

A small convoy of three shiny black four-wheel-drive vehicles came through the curve at forty-five miles per hour. The first truck passed Poncho's position, and he tossed a spike strip across the road just before the second truck in line went by.

All four tires on the second truck deflated, and the truck slewed around on the road, skidding to a controlled stop.

As the lead truck approached his position, Gil stood up and machine-gunned the driver, killing him with a burst of .308 caliber fire through the neck and head. The truck crashed off the road into a ditch. He biffed a fragmentation grenade after it and then darted toward the other vehicles. The grenade exploded as the men in the truck were dismounting with their weapons. The explosion tore apart the truck and hurled their mangled bodies into the bush.

Poncho was firing on the third vehicle, which had swerved off the road to avoid crashing into the second. He killed the five men before anyone had the chance to open a door.

All four doors of the second truck, however, were flying open, and armed men were jumping out shooting. Gil shot two of them dead and rolled for cover to reload.

The gunners fired on Poncho, driving him back to cover behind his fig tree, and then quickly jumped back into the truck. The driver gunned the Vortec engine, throwing dirt with the flattened tires and pulling away.

Slapping a fresh magazine into the rifle, Gil sprang back up and shot the driver. The truck swerved sharply, and the remaining gunman dove out with the vehicle still in motion, taking a wild shot at Gil as he bounced on the road. Gil raked him once with automatic fire, and he lay still.

Poncho opened the back door of the truck and found Hector Ruvalcaba cowering on the floor of the backseat. He grabbed the old man by the collar and yanked him out, dragging him into the road. "Welcome home, cabrón."

Ruvalcaba shielded his eyes from the now-blazing sun. "Wait!" he said in Spanish. "I'll pay you whatever you want—millions!"

Poncho looked at Gil, who stood in the road calmly reloading his rifle. "He says he'll pay us whatever we want."

Gil drew his 1911. "You wanna do it, or you want me to?"

Poncho pointed south. "Garrucha isn't too far from here, half an hour through the jungle by Jeep."

"So? What's in Garrucha?"

"This asshole was born there."

Gil took a second to light a cigarette. "I'm not from around here," he said carefully, "and sometimes I can be a little slow on the uptake. But why the hell do we wanna take him home?"

"Because they hate him in Garrucha, worse than the devil."

"I'll pay you!" Ruvalcaba blurted in heavily accented English. "Whatever you want!"

Gil stood looking at the man, the cigarette poised at his lips as he harkened back to Afghanistan, where village justice was swift and final.

"You don't wanna go home?"

Ruvalcaba shook his head. "Please. You are American, no? I'll pay you a hundred times more than the FBI!"

"I don't work for the FBI." Gil looked at Poncho. "You thinkin' there'll be less hypocrisy this way?"

Poncho shrugged. "Something like that."

Gil pointed the pistol into Ruvalcaba's face. "Take off your clothes. If I have to tell you twice, I'll plant this Fort Lewis boot so far up your ass you'll have to untie the laces to take a shit."

Poncho laughed. "What the hell does that mean?"

Gil gave him a wink. "It sounds tough; that's all that matters."

A HALF HOUR later, Poncho drove a battered white Jeep Renegade into the small village of Garrucha and stopped near a large pen full of goats. Chickens ran to and fro, and human faces began poking out of shabby brick homes. Having heard the firefight up on the mountain, the villagers had run for cover the second they heard the Jeep come splashing down the jungle trail.

Poncho took Ruvalcaba by the arm and pulled him from the Jeep, shoving him down in the mud naked, with his hands bound behind his back.

"Please!" Ruvalcaba begged Gil in English. "I am a very rich man!"

Recognizing Ruvalcaba, the villagers could scarcely believe their eyes, and figures began darting from house to house, spreading the news of his unbelievable return.

Three men came around a corner and walked out into the trail holding machetes over their shoulders. The machetes were not weapons, but the tools they used to make their living.

Poncho pointed at the naked man sitting in the mud. "If you want justice for your children, here he is."

Shocked to see the man who had tortured and abused their region for the past ten years, the men stood looking at one another. More villagers appeared, and soon twenty men stood talking in a quiet group.

"What's to talk about?" Gil wondered aloud. "Just hack the fucker and be done."

"This isn't the Middle East," Poncho said. "These are superstitious people. They believe in the Virgin, and they have to reach a consensus on how to deal with this."

"Catholic?"

Poncho shrugged. "Mostly."

Gil was increasingly impatient when it came to religion. He'd seen too many people maimed and murdered over it. "What's *mostly* mean?"

"They're Catholic with Mayan superstitions. It's hard to explain because every village down here is different. But, yeah, they consider themselves Catholic."

"Learn somethin' new every day, I suppose." Gil looked down at Ruvalcaba, who sat trembling at his feet. "Whatever you did to these people, I'm pretty goddamn sure you're gonna regret it."

Ruvalcaba lurched forward, shamelessly attempting to embrace Gil's leg between his neck and shoulder, like a cat fawning its owner. "Shoot me—please!"

Gil stepped away. "This is between you and your people."

"They're not my people!" Ruvalcaba attempted to stand.

Poncho knocked him over with the rifle butt. "His men come here a couple times a year: steal the boys to work in their meth labs; steal the daughters to use as whores. Most of them are never seen again."

Three of the older men came forward, leaving their machetes behind near a wall. They asked to talk with Poncho in private.

"Please!" Ruvalcaba hissed. "Shoot me!"

"One more word," Gil told him, "and I'll kick your face in."

A couple of minutes later, Poncho returned, hauling Ruvalcaba to his feet and shoving him toward the villagers.

A group of men held him while another group made preparations to tie him to a tree. The women began gathering stones into a pile. The teenagers were told to round up the children and take them down the trail to the church. The kids held hands and sang a happy religious-sounding song as they walked away through the trees.

Gil watched the pile of stones grow. "I expected machetes."

Poncho shook his head. "No machetes in the Bible."

Shaking a cigarette from the pack, Gil proffered it, and Poncho plucked it out, lighting it off of Gil's.

"We can leave. Ruvalcaba's in good hands here."

Gil drew from the cigarette, watching in dull amusement as Ruvalcaba attempted to reason with the villagers, his mournful overtures falling upon deaf ears as they tightly bound his wrists and ankles to the tree. "I wanna stay and make sure. This asshole's cheated death too many times."

Poncho took a drag. "He won't cheat it today."

"All the same."

The first stone was the size of a baseball, cast by a woman whose son had been kidnapped the year before. It struck Ruvalcaba in the sternum with a heavy thud, and the old man let out a deep groan. Another stone was thrown. And another. Soon it became a free-for-all that lasted nearly ninety seconds. Many stones missed, but just as many hit the mark, and by the time the last one was hurled, Ruvalcaba was drenched in blood, his face unrecognizable, and his chin lolled against his chest.

As the villagers walked away down the trail toward the church, Gil stepped up and found a pulse in Ruvalcaba's neck. "You'd better tell 'em he's still alive."

Poncho glanced after them. "They know."

"So where the hell they goin'?"

"He'll be dead soon."

"Not soon enough. Don't they understand that's how this bastard keeps surviving to fight another day—because people underestimate him?"

"What can I tell you?" Poncho said. "If he survives, they'll say it's God's will."

"God's will, my ass." Gil flicked away the cigarette and drew the 1911.

"Por favor?" someone said from behind. Please?

He turned to see an old cane farmer of at least eighty standing there with his hand out. *"La cuarenta y cinco . . . por favor?"* The forty-five . . . please?

Poncho spoke with the farmer and translated for Gil. "The Ruvalcabas kidnapped his granddaughter four years ago. Some of the kids found her dead along the road a few weeks later. He's got bad arthritis in both shoulders, so he couldn't throw any stones, but he says he carried a forty-five like yours in the army when he was a young man."

Gil offered the pistol to the farmer butt-first. "Tell 'im there's a round in the chamber."

As smoothly as if he'd been handling the pistol all of his life, the old man thumbed down the slide lock and put the muzzle up against Ruvalcaba's head, squeezing the trigger and blowing the drug lord's brains out the other side of his skull. Then he wiped the gore from the muzzle with the tail of his shirt and offered the weapon back to Gil butt-first.

Gil shook his head. "You keep it, partner. One soldier to another."

Poncho translated, and the farmer nodded, tucking away the pistol as he strolled off in the opposite direction of the church.

Poncho stood watching him. "And now?"

Gil let out a tired sigh. "Now I gotta go see about a girl."

They mounted up, and Poncho gunned the Jeep back up the trail toward the jungle road, throwing mud and slimy jungle muck in all directions. By the time they reached the road, both men were completely splattered.

Poncho stopped to disengage the four-wheel drive.

Gil jerked his thumb back toward the village, his face smeared with black muck. "Sure you don't wanna head back down?"

Poncho glanced over his shoulder. "Why?"

Gil wiped the muck from his eyes. "You missed a fucking mud hole back there. I thought you might wanna go back and hit it."

Poncho gave him a wink. "We didn't get stuck. That's all that matters."

87

Eight days later, Mariana met with Pope in a fine Italian restaurant in one of the city's wealthiest districts. With a stomach full of butterflies, she stood as he approached the table, offering her hand.

His grip was warm and firm. "Hello, Mariana. You're looking well."

"Thank you, Bob. I appreciate you making the trip."

He smiled dryly. "Did I have a choice?"

"Of course. You're the director."

They made themselves comfortable, and she signaled the waiter. "The driver I sent—his English was sufficient?"

"I'm sure you know that already," he replied, not unkindly.

Their orders were taken, and Mariana spread a linen napkin in her lap, looking at him and smiling. "I'll come right to the point: Rhett Hancock, Hector Ruvalcaba,

Lazaro Serrano, Captain Espinosa, and Clemson Fields are dead."

"All the heads of the five families," he said quietly.

Never having seen the film *The Godfather*, the macabre witticism was lost on her. "The southern syndicates have decided to come in under Castañeda in order to avoid a war that would cost everyone a lot of unnecessary blood and treasure. There is one lone holdout: a trafficker down in Tabasco State who hates Castañeda too badly to accept the conditions, but his people are already walking away from him. He won't last the month."

Pope studied her, his gentle blue eyes calm and focused behind his glasses. "And if Castañeda breaks the truce . . . renews violence along the border?"

"He won't do that. He has everything he could possibly want now. He understands that the DEA will continue to interdict his shipments north of the border whenever they can. And he's even agreed to tip them off from time to time to keep them looking good in the news."

Pope sipped his water. "Things change."

"True. Nothing is forever, but if he decides to break the truce, I have someone in place to remove him: someone very close, whose loyalty is more with Mexico than with Castañeda."

"Interesting." Pope spread the napkin in his lap, secretly satisfied with the way the situation had developed. "You've been very hard at work."

"I've had a lot of help."

"And I'd like to know who from. Not even Crosswhite can be in multiple places at the same time."

She smiled. "Like you said, I've been very hard at work."

"And in exchange for this hard work, you expect to be appointed chief of station?"

Mariana hardened her gaze, conveying a confidence she'd actually begun to feel over the past few days. "Your Mexico network is smashed. I've already sent Mike Ortega and his family home with orders never to return. You no longer have any contacts in-country, you don't speak the language, and you have no one to replace me with—not with my qualifications."

Pope opened his mouth to speak, but she pressed her assault. "I've presented you with a stable border that you can present to the president—taking full credit, of course. I'm the only agent who can guarantee that stability for any foreseeable length of time. Castañeda knows you plotted to have him killed. He respects the power of the CIA, but he no longer has *any* respect for you. Fortunately, he *does* respect me, and he knows that he and I can help each other.

"In short, my network is already in place. It's stable, well connected, and growing more influential by the day. For all intents and purposes, I *am* chief of station. Now, you can fire me, strip me of my affiliation with the agency—even have me killed—but you'd be stupid to consider it, and we both know it."

"Would I?" he asked, realizing she had the sight now.

"You always have a plan B. I admit it took me awhile to realize that it was me, but once I saw it, the rest was easy."

Befuddled by the rapid expansion of her acumen, he toiled to perceive its breadth. "Crosswhite's not sharp enough to have discerned that. Who's been counseling you?"

She ignored the question. "Are you going to make my appointment official? Or am I to be recalled?"

"Did Fields try to kill you?"

A dark shadow creased her. "The son of a bitch is dead, isn't he?"

He rested back in the chair. "Then he acted against my instructions. I want that clear between us."

"Are you going to make my appointment official?"

He nodded. "Yes. Congratulations, Mariana. You're chief of station."

She breathed a hidden sigh of relief. "Thank you."

Their salads arrived, and the wine was poured by a waiter with a linen napkin draped over one arm. When he was gone, she took a sip and set down the glass.

"Crosswhite has asked to be retired from service, and I've granted his request. He's no longer available to you."

This didn't surprise Pope at all. "Should I take it he remains available to you?"

"A trust like ours is rare."

He sucked his teeth. "Does he know you're in love with him?"

"*I* don't know that I'm in love with him—nor does it matter. He's married with a baby on the way, and I'm not his type. You shouldn't expect to disarm me with these adolescent jibes, Bob. I'm not the same person I was the last time we spoke."

"It's a damn good thing," he murmured, half to himself. "What about Chance Vaught?"

"I'm glad you bring him up. His career with DSS is over. That much is clear. And the agency needs to cauterize the Downly bleed as soon as possible"—she locked eyes—"for the good of all.

"Not only does Chance know Mexico, he looks the part, has family in-country, and speaks the language like a Mexican; not to mention he's a damn good operator. I've offered to make him my principal operative in-country, and he's accepted. I assume you can handle the paperwork to start getting him paid—retroactive to last week?"

Pope chuckled, liking what he was hearing. "What makes you so sure this wasn't my plan A?"

In no humor for playful banter, she didn't so much as blink before replying, "Too much has happened down here you know absolutely nothing about." His smile disappeared. "Mexico is mine. If you want things to run smoothly, you'll stay out of it. What's more, if I catch any of your ATRU people—men *or* women—operating in my province without my knowledge, I'll send them back to wherever they came from in rubber body bags marked 'Return to Sender.'"

Pope's smile returned, satisfied fully that Mexico station was in the right hands. He reached for the glass and took a sip of wine. "It's too bad you had to lose your innocence. Personally, I liked you better the other way, but you were too soft, too trusting. That's obviously changed."

Seeing an opening, she decided to take it. "From what Crosswhite tells me, Gil Shannon trusted you with his life—and apparently that's exactly what it cost him."

Believing that Mariana had never met Gil in person, Pope took the barb as it was intended, unable to mitigate the off-putting effect of it. "No one from the ATRU will set foot in Mexico without advance notice from me and close coordination between you and Midori. You have my guarantee. If I should happen to change my mind on this point, I'll let you know. Fair enough?"

Having just gotten everything she'd hoped for—as Gil had assured her she would—Mariana lifted her glass. "To Mexico?"

He touched the rim of his glass to hers. "To a stable border. I don't care a tinker's damn about Mexico."

88

Lena Deiss looked resplendent in her wedding gown. Her heart thudded in her chest as she walked up the aisle toward a smiling Sabastian Blickensderfer, a bouquet of white roses clutched to her breast. Both sides of the towering cathedral were filled to capacity with admiring friends and adoring family. There was a genuine buzz in the atmosphere—a buzz akin to that of a royal occasion—and Lena was content with her decision to marry.

Sabastian had matured since their reconciliation, and he had begun to pay her more attention. Lena had matured as well in the short term, forcing herself to admit that chasing a life of adventure was childish and fanciful. Not even the men who lived that life lived it for very long. They died young, and they died tragically, and they left heartbreak in their wake.

Now she was focused on being a wife and eventually

a mother. There would always be plenty of money, and Sabastian had promised to build her the house she had dreamed of. Well, to be honest, it would be more of a modern castle than a house, but wasn't that a rich husband's job, to treat his wife like a queen? Besides, if she would be expected to tolerate his occasional indiscretions, a castle wasn't too much to ask.

Halfway up the aisle, however, all of her contentment and focus went out the window.

At the far end of a pew on Sabastian's side of the aisle, she glanced at the set and chiseled visage of a man she had believed dead, his piercing gray eyes staring back at her.

Certain that her own eyes were playing tricks, she blinked and shook her head. In that space of time, the ghost had disappeared.

My God! she thought to herself, stealing a backward glance down the wall to make sure she hadn't seen whom she thought she'd seen, flashing a smile to some friends to cover her awkward lapse.

Her friends smiled back excitedly, giving her a collective thumbs-up of encouragement. The rest of her trip up the aisle was spent in the panicked realization that she could never be content as a wife and mother. She suddenly saw herself taking lovers behind Sabastian's back, as he would take lovers behind hers, both of them living the same mutual lie their respective parents had lived, raising a son or a daughter who would in turn grow up to perpetuate that same lie.

She took her first step at the base of the altar and, for an alarming moment, thought she was going to be sick. Sabastian saw it on her face and stepped down to offer his hand.

"Thank you," she whispered, stepping up to his side and taking his arm.

"Are you okay?" the priest asked for their ears alone.

She nodded, her breath coming in shallow drafts.

"Very well," he said, switching on his tiny microphone and lifting his gaze to the congregation.

"Dearly beloved," he began in a gentle voice, "we are gathered here today in the presence of witnesses to join Lena and Sabastian in the bonds of holy matrimony. Commended to be honorable among all, this is not a union to be entered into lightly, but reverently, passionately, and lovingly. These two persons—"

Lena cleared her throat, and for a fraction of a second, the priest's attention faltered.

"—present now to be joined—"

She cleared her throat again, and this time he looked directly at her, switching off the microphone. "Are you sure you're okay?" he asked quietly.

She shook her head, breaking out in a sweat and pulling Sabastian's arm to bring him closer. "I can't," she whispered. "I'm sorry, but I can't do this!"

Sabastian closed his hand over hers, looking into her eyes and smiling. "You might have said something a little sooner, my love."

Tears spilled down her cheeks. "I'm sorry . . . I truly thought I could, but I can't."

The cathedral could not have been quieter in that moment had it been completely empty.

He kissed her lips and caressed her face.

"I'm so sorry," she croaked, the tears flowing.

"For what?" he asked softly, brushing away the tears. "For being the smarter of us?"

She put her arms around him, and they held each tightly for a long moment. Finally, he whispered into her ear, "Don't be afraid. I'll take care of everything."

They separated, and he asked the priest for the microphone. The perplexed young priest took the slender wire from around his neck and handed it to him.

Sabastian switched on the microphone, put his arm around Lena's waist, and turned to face the congregation, confident and composed.

"Dear friends," he said, seeking out faces on both sides of the aisle that he knew he could count on. "Dear family." He kissed Lena's hair. "Lena and I thank you from the bottoms of our hearts for the love you have shown us both by coming here today. We apologize for this last-minute change in plans, and we beg your forgiveness. We are all imperfect human beings—I more imperfect than most— and we have all made mistakes in our lives." He paused to smile compassionately over the crowd. "Lena and I have decided *against* making a mistake here today . . . but will you please—*if you love us*—will you *please* join us at the reception hall? There is a fine meal and some very expensive champagne awaiting us all, with an orchestra and dancing that will last the entire night. So please, *please* honor us by joining us in a celebration of this life which we are all so *privileged* to live."

With that, he handed the microphone back to the priest, and to Lena's astonishment, the congregation began to applaud as Sabastian took her by the hand and led her down the aisle. They arrived at the entrance, and he turned them both to face back toward the altar, waving airily as everyone began standing.

"How was that for poise?" he said into her ear.

Her eyes flooded again. "You'll be a legend."

"No," he said, laughing, "but nor will I look the fool."

89

Lena arrived home by limousine the next morning, a little drunk, utterly exhausted, and entirely relieved not to be married. The reception had been a truly gala affair, with many friends congratulating her and Sabastian for having had the courage and the wisdom to change their minds even at the risk of disappointing so many people. A number of opportunistic men had even had the bad taste to invite themselves into her life now that she had chosen not to wed, and she was sure that more than one or two women had made similar overtures to Sabastian, who was once again one of the most eligible bachelors in Bern.

She slipped off her heels in the foyer and mounted the staircase in her bare feet, holding the train of her wedding gown in one hand and leaning on the railing as she ascended the stairs. Her brother Joaquin, who now lived in Germany, was in town for the wedding, and she heard him showering in the master bath as she entered her bedroom, crossing to the walk-in closet.

She put her heels on the shelf and stepped back into the bedroom to see Gil standing in the bathroom doorway with a white towel wrapped around his waist.

She was immediately overcome. At first her shock was so complete that she couldn't cry or even breathe. Then her face contorted, and she sank to her knees, weeping into her hands.

Gil was nearly as stunned to see her as she was to see him, having expected her to be long gone on her honeymoon. He went to her, and she smacked him away, but then she grabbed on to him, erupting in a torrent of heavy sobs.

She eventually fell asleep in his arms.

He lifted her from the floor and was laying her down on the bed when her brother appeared in the bedroom doorway, his tie undone, hair a mess, and a half empty bottle of champagne gripped in his right hand.

Joaquin remembered Gil from when Lena had brought him to Germany ten days before, and knowing his sister as well as he knew her, he was no more surprised to find Gil in her bedroom than he'd been when she'd changed her mind at the altar.

He grinned, pulling the door closed as he left.

Gil stretched out beside Lena on the bed and watched her sleep. She slept for two hours, and when she awoke, she was still unable to speak to him, still not entirely convinced he was real. She opened her arms, and he lay down against her.

He awoke with her running her long fingers through his hair.

"I still had the key," he said quietly. "I needed a shower, and I thought you'd be in Paris by now."

"Why?" she whispered.

"Isn't that where the honeymoon was supposed to be?"

She gripped his hair. "*Why*, Gil?"

"Oh." He caressed her belly over the tight-fitting gown. "You said you wanted us to move forward—and there was no other way."

"You could have told me."

"No. You had to believe I was dead. *Everyone* had to believe it. Otherwise Pope would have known I wasn't."

"Is he that smart?"

"Yeah, he is. He might figure it out yet."

"You were at the wedding—you saw me see you?"

"I got there too late. If I'd shown myself . . ."

"You disappeared so fast," she said with a sigh. "I thought it was my imagination."

"Are you married?"

She pulled his head back to look into his eyes. "What do you think?"

He raised up onto an elbow. "Jesus Christ, you were beautiful. It was almost more than I could take." He held his fingers a millimeter apart. "I was this close to exposing myself."

She knew there must be some other reason he'd faked his death. If he had truly gone to all that trouble just for the two of them, he would have done whatever was necessary to stop the wedding.

"Do you love me?"

He kissed her. "I love you."

"Is the real reason you faked your death anything I have to worry about?"

He smiled, loving that she was so intuitive. "Nothing at all."

"Will you tell me why someday? When you're ready?"

"Yes."

She wrapped her arms around him. "I told you we were destined to be together, Gil. Not even death could stop it."

He chuckled, burying his face in her hair. "That's not at all wildly exaggerated."

She laughed, twisting free and rolling to her belly. "Undo me. This fucking thing fits me like a suit of armor, and I want to consummate our relationship."

He flipped her onto her back again, gathering up the train of the gown to expose her thighs. "Suit of armor or not, it stays on you—at least for the first run."

Her laughter filled the room. She'd never been so happy.

EPILOGUE

Five months after the Battle of Toluca, Rhett Hancock was fully recovered from his wounds. He now owned a fishing charter called the *Beetle*, and he was giving serious thought to taking it down the coast to Panama or Colombia, where he could go into business for himself without drawing attention. He didn't need the money, but he was bored most of the time now, and he thought it would be good to have people to talk to once in a while.

He still drank tequila, though not as much, and he was less haunted by the car accident that had taken his girlfriend's life years before. One problem remained, however: the nagging urge to shoot people. Not just anybody, but somebody.

With a casual wave to another fishing charter anchored a hundred yards away, he stretched out on the deck and pulled the stock of a suppressed M40A5 sniper rifle into his shoulder. He put his eye to the scope and scanned the shore where a naked Antonio Castañeda was partying on a private beach with seven equally naked young women. There was a bonfire and five bodyguards standing around. One of the guards had some kind of sniper rifle slung over his shoulder.

"Amateur hour," Hancock muttered. "I'll pop your boss and put one between your eyes before you can scratch your nuts."

"That'll be a piece a shootin'," said a voice from behind.

Hancock jumped to his knees, grabbing the rifle and spinning around. He wasn't fast enough to bring the weapon up before a man in a black wet suit shot him three times in the torso with a silenced Glock 23. The .40 caliber hollow-points knocked him over backward, and the M40 fell from his hands as he sprawled against the gunwale.

Gil Shannon pulled back the hood of the wet suit.

A longtime admirer, Hancock recognized his face at once. "What the fuck? You're supposed to be dead."

"I know it." Gil took a seat on an empty fish cooler, keeping the pistol trained.

Hancock felt the life quickly running out of him. "How did you—How did you know?"

Gil looked out to sea. "You bought your rifle from the wrong man."

"Fuck me," Hancock mumbled, feeling incredibly sorry for himself. "I knew there was somethin' about that guy I didn't trust. He's an ex-SEAL, isn't he?"

Gil nodded. "Want me to finish the job? Or you wanna ride it out?"

"I'll ride it out," Hancock groaned. "Won't be long." He sat staring at the deck where his blood pooled beside him, strangely numb. "Didja ever . . . didja ever just *need* to pull the trigger?"

Gil frowned. "No. I do it because I'm pissed."

"Pissed?" Hancock gave him a queer look. "What at?"

"Dunno." Gil was still staring out to sea. "Sometimes I think I was born pissed."

"That's gotta suck." Hancock began to swoon a little, blinking to keep awake. "What's with the Glock? I thought you swore by the 1911—least that's what everybody said."

Gil looked glumly at the pistol in his hands. "I have to worry about covering my kill patterns these days."

"I know what you mean." Hancock chortled sardonically. "That's why I gave up the fifty."

"You shoulda gave it all up, considerin' the fix you're in. No one had any idea you were still alive until you bought that rifle."

"I guess I was stupid; the need just got to be too strong."

"Well, you ain't gotta worry about it much longer."

Hancock wiped at the blood leaking from the bullet holes in his torso. "You're right about that." A warm feeling washed over him. "I think I'm about ready to give it up here . . . Why'd you do it—fake your death?"

"Robbed a stagecoach."

Hancock's eyes glassed over. "Well, brother . . . your secret's safe with me." His head sagged to the side, and he was gone.

Gil sat staring at him without seeing him, thinking of all that had come to pass. He hated to admit it, but he was glad to be dead, confident that he could trust Midori, Mariana, and Lena to guard his secret. Midori, because she needed him to protect her from Pope. Mariana, because she would need him to help look after Crosswhite. And Lena, because she and Gil were destined to be together—whether he believed that kind of crap or not.

He wondered idly if Mariana and Crosswhite had

slept together. Crosswhite had said no, but Gil thought they must have. To his mind, nothing else accounted for the bond they seemed to share. But then, he hadn't known that many women, so maybe he wasn't the best person to judge.

In fact, he'd only ever shared a genuine bond with one woman in his life: his wife, Marie. And when that bond had inexplicably begun to dissolve, he'd found himself rudderless on what seemed to be an endless ocean, with only Pope to guide him through a starless night.

Then he met Lena, and he knew, just as sure as God made little green crocodiles, that he could never go home to Marie—to his wife, who would have waited for him until doomsday.

Why did I die? he asked the sea. *It's simple. I died for Marie, and only for Marie. Now she can mourn me and start a new life—a life with a man who hasn't seen the things I've seen; who hasn't done the things I've done. A man who can sit in front of the fire at night and hold her hand without feeling like he has to claw his way through the fucking wall for a breath of air.*

He was still lost in the daydream when Sid Dupree brought his fishing charter up alongside the *Beetle*, smoking a joint and idling the motor. A few seconds later, he tossed Gil a line. "We good here?"

"We're good." Gil got up to tie off the line and handed the rifle across. "Put that where she won't see it."

Dupree stowed the rifle in a locker beneath a bench and tossed him a small charge of C4 with a timer. Gil took the charge below. Then he came back up and dragged Hancock's body into the cabin, shutting the door and stepping aboard Dupree's boat. He untied the line, and they motored away toward the setting sun.

Three minutes later, there was a muffled explosion, a

flash of light beneath the greenish surface, and the *Beetle* went straight to the bottom in seventy-five feet of water, taking the gringo sniper with her.

Gil tossed the pistol overboard and glanced back toward the beach, shaking his head. "That ugly bastard has no idea how close he came to gettin' his head blown off."

"If anyone deserves it," Dupree said, "it's him. Is he that important?"

"At least for now, yeah."

Dupree offered him a hit off the joint. "The fucker sells good weed, I'll give him that."

Gil laughed and pushed the joint away, stripping out of his wet suit and jamming it into the locker with the rifle. "She'll be wakin' up anytime now, so cut the chatter."

The old Navy SEAL smiled. "You better hope she never finds out you drugged her."

Gil waved him off. "I didn't *drug* her. It was just a little diazepam to make her sleepy. How soon 'til we're back in Baja? We gotta catch a plane."

"Be there by mornin'. Where you guys off to, anyhow?"

"Ho Chi Minh City. I wanna lay low awhile longer, and I got some people to see."

"Ho Chi Minh City?" Dupree took a deep toke from the joint and held it in. "Shit, ain't that where Saigon used to be?"

"Yeah, that's where it used to be." Gil edged him aside and took the wheel. "Let me have the con, ya damn hippie. I don't wanna end up in Australia or some goddamn place."

Dupree took a seat. "Shit, I was navigatin' the ocean in minisubs when you were still shittin' your drawers."

"I hear ya," Gil said, checking the compass and steering three points to starboard. "That's why you had us headed for Midway Island."

"Eat me," Dupree mumbled. "At least I've *been* to Midway."

A short time later, Lena came up from below, looking well rested. "Sorry I fell asleep, guys." She hugged Gil from behind. "The beer and the sun made me sleepy."

He gave her a kiss. "It wasn't the beer. I drugged you so I could swim over to another boat and kill a guy."

She chuckled, nipping playfully at his ear. "It wouldn't surprise me."

What the hell? he thought. *She can't say I didn't tell her the truth.*

ABOUT THE AUTHORS

SCOTT McEWEN is the coauthor of the *New York Times* number one bestseller *American Sniper*, made into a 2014 feature film starring Bradley Cooper as Chris Kyle, Navy SEAL, CPO, deceased, and directed by Clint Eastwood. Scott also coauthored *Eyes on Target: Inside Stories from the Brotherhood of the US Navy Seals*. He grew up in the mountains of eastern Oregon, where he became an Eagle Scout, hiking, fishing, and hunting at every opportunity. He obtained his graduate degree at Oregon State University and thereafter studied and worked extensively in London, England. Scott practiced law in Southern California before he began writing. Scott works with and provides support for several military charitable organizations, including the Navy SEAL Foundation.

THOMAS KOLONIAR is the author of the post-apocalyptic novel *Cannibal Reign* and the coauthor of the national bestseller *Sniper Elite: One-Way Trip*, *Target America*, and *The Sniper and the Wolf*. He holds a bachelor of arts degree in English literature from the University of Akron. A retired police officer from Akron, Ohio, he currently lives in Mexico.